DISCARD

Also by Ayelet Waldman

FICTION

Red Hook Road
Love and Other Impossible Pursuits
Daughter's Keeper

NONFICTION

Bad Mother: A Chronicle of Maternal Crimes,
Minor Calamities, and Occasional Moments of Grace

LOVE AND TREASURE

LOVE AND TREASURE

Ayelet Waldman

ALFRED A. KNOPF

New York 2014

THIS IS A BORZOI BOOK
PUBLISHED BY ALFRED A. KNOPF

Copyright © 2014 by Ayelet Waldman

All rights reserved. Published in the United States by Alfred A. Knopf,
a division of Random House LLC, New York, and in Canada by
Random House of Canada Limited, Toronto,
Penguin Random House Companies.

www.aaknopf.com

Knopf, Borzoi Books, and the colophon are registered trademarks
of Random House LLC.

Library of Congress Cataloging-in-Publication Data
Waldman, Ayelet.
Love and treasure : a novel / Ayelet Waldman.—First edition.
pages   cm
"This is a Borzoi book"—T.p. verso.
ISBN 978-0-385-53354-6 (hardcover)—ISBN 978-0-385-53355-3 (ebook)
1. Reminiscing in old age—Fiction.   2. World War, 1939–1945—
Confiscations and contributions—Hungary—Fiction.   3. Holocaust,
Jewish (1939–1945)—Hungary—Fiction.   4. Jewish property—
Hungary—Fiction.   5. Domestic fiction.   I. Title.
PS3573.A42124L695 2014   813'.6—dc23   2012049781

Jacket image: *A Still Life of a Tazza with Flowers*
by Jan Brueghel the Younger (details). Private Collection/Johnny
Van Haeften Ltd., London/The Bridgeman Art Library
Jacket design by Kelly Blair

Manufactured in the United States of America
First Edition

To Michael, only and always.

LOVE AND TREASURE

Prologue

MAINE

2013

JACK WISEMAN, IMMERSED AS EVER in the pages of a book, did not notice the arrival of the bus until alerted by the stir among the other people waiting in the overheated station lounge. The pugnacious chin he aimed at the coach's windows had a bit of Kleenex clinging to it, printed with a comma of blood, and his starched and ironed shirt gaped at the collar, revealing pleats in the drapery of his neck and a thick white thatch of fur on his chest. He squinted, caught a glimpse of the glory of his granddaughter's hair, and pulled himself to his feet. He tore a corner from the back page of somebody's discarded *Ellsworth American* and tucked it between the pages of his old Loeb edition of Herodotus, measuring with a rueful snort the remaining unread inches. He had never been a man to leave a job unfinished, a fact on which he supposed he must have been relying, perhaps unconsciously, in undertaking to reread, for what must be the eighth or ninth time, this most garrulous of classical historians.

As the bus disgorged its first passengers, Jack got momentarily lost in contemplation of the disembarking soldiers, home on leave from the very ancient battlefields as in the book he was reading, from Babylon and Bactria, their camouflage fatigues the color of ashes and dust, the pattern jagged, like the pixels of a computer screen. Then Natalie's hair kindled in the bus's doorway, and he held up the little green-backed volume to catch her attention. He could tell from the look of shock that crossed her face in the instant before she smiled that pancreatic cancer had taken even worse a toll on him than he'd imagined. Her lips moved.

He lifted a finger, motioning her to wait. He pressed a button on his hearing aid and said, "Sweetheart! You made it."

"Hey, Grandpa." Her eyes were bleary, the red dent in her cheek from whatever she had been leaning against reminding him of how she used to look as a child, waking from an afternoon nap. Or perhaps it was her mother he was remembering, an image coming from farther away and longer ago. He took note of her pallor, the bruised look of the skin under her green eyes, and thought that she had likely come to Maine as much to flee her own troubles as to lose herself in the alleviation of his. Indeed the possibility of her finding consolation in worry over him was one of the reasons—not that you needed a reason to want to see your only granddaughter—he had agreed so quickly when she first called to say that she wanted to make the trip.

"Are you hungry?" he said. "There's not much in Bangor, but if you can wait, the Grill's open. I could take you there."

"You could take me? You drove?" she said.

He just blinked at her, tempted to employ one of her own favorite childhood expressions: *Duh*. He had been expecting this line of inquiry.

"How else would I pick you up?" he said.

"I figured you'd call a taxi!"

"Dave had a fare. Round-trip to Portland. I couldn't very well ask him to turn it down, not in the off-season. Business is slow."

"Oh, is it?" She shook her head with disapproval that was affectionate but sincere. "So this isn't about you being stubborn and proud?"

"They make a great pumpkin pie at the Grill," he said. "How's that sound?"

She reached for his chin, and with a mixture of tenderness and reproof picked the bit of Kleenex from his shaving cut.

"Why didn't you call a Bangor cab?" she said, having inherited the full genetic complement of Wiseman stubbornness, if not pride.

"A Bangor cab!" he said, sincerely horrified by the notion. "Those guys only take Route One! We'd be stuck in mill traffic for hours, this time of day."

By now they had reached the car, a Volvo DL wagon that for twenty-three years, in the summertime, over breaks and sabbaticals, had ferried first Jack and his wife, then Jack alone, from New York City to Maine and back again. He wondered if it was worth leaving the blue behemoth to Natalie. Like all his possessions—like everything that chance or fate had ever entrusted to his care—he had kept the car in impeccable order. Properly maintained, it might run for years to come. But Natalie might not care to pay the steep New York parking fees. She might, once he was gone, never again care to make the long drive to Red Hook, Maine. And though she was, and would always be, his *tzatzkeleh,* his little treasure, his love for her was as free of illusion as it was of reservation. There was little evidence in the way that she had recently conducted her life to suggest that she knew how to maintain anything at all.

"Do you think you'll want the car?" he said as he opened the driver's-side door for her. He walked around, opened his own door, got in, and handed her the key. "Or should I put an ad in the paper?"

"Don't sell it right now. We'll need it while I'm up here. Unless you're planning on coming down to New York?"

"There's hospice here, same as there. Except here I'm in my own home, and in New York I'd be forced into some misbegotten nursing home. Thanks to the grateful generosity of Columbia University."

"Grandpa, you weren't really living in that apartment. You were there like, what? Three months a year?"

"More like four."

"They have so many full-time faculty members to house. You can't blame them—"

"Forty-six years, Natalie. It wouldn't have killed them to make it forty-six and a half."

She started the engine and then let it idle, warming it up the way his regimen required. They sat listening to the engine in the chill of the car's interior, giving him ample time to regret his bitter words. Having faced or lived through some of the choicest calamities, both personal and world historical, that the twentieth century had to offer, Jack Wiseman had rarely given way to bitterness until now. He supposed it must be a symptom of the disease that was killing him.

"You could stay with me," Natalie said at last. "There's plenty of room now that Daniel's moved out."

"I'm here," Jack said. "And you're here now, too."

"Yes."

"Might I ask how long you plan to stay?"

"As long as you need me."

"It shouldn't be too long."

"Grandpa."

"Anyway. Good of the firm to let you go."

"I had vacation saved up." She put the car into reverse with a show, again for his benefit, of checking the rearview and both side mirrors. Then she sighed and put the car back into park. "Actually, that's not true."

"What's not true?"

"I'm not taking my vacation time. I quit."

"You quit?" He thumped his hand on the dashboard. "To take care of me? That's absolutely unacceptable, Natalie. I won't allow it."

"It wasn't because of you. They would have given me leave." She eased out into the street, speeding up slowly so as not to risk a skid on the icy road or, more likely, his reprimand for taking it too fast.

"Why then?" he said.

"Why." She sounded exasperated, with his question, with herself, maybe just with having to tell the story again. "Well, I was in a coworker's office, and she was responding to a set of interrogatories. Those are, like, questions from opposing counsel in a lawsuit."

He waited.

"They were from Daniel's firm."

"He wrote the questions?"

"No. He's in the corporate department. This was a litigation document."

"And?" He noticed that she had put her blinker on. "Not Route One," he said sharply. "Keep going until you hit Forty-Six."

"Okay."

. "Seeing a document from Daniel's firm made you quit your job?" he asked, wondering if his brain was slowing, if there was some obvious connection here that anyone but a dying old fool could see.

"It made me realize how entangled our lives are. He could end up at my office for a closing. Or I could end up at his for a settlement conference. I just don't want that to happen."

"You quit a job making twice as much money as I made in my last year as a tenured professor because you were afraid you might bump into your ex-husband in a conference room?"

"It sounds ridiculous."

"It *is* ridiculous."

"I just want a fresh start."

"Doing what?"

"I don't know. I don't want to talk about this anymore. Is that okay?"

He nodded. Not talking about things was always, in the view of Jack Wiseman, a viable if not preferable option. In this case, in particular, because all that he could think of that he wanted to say to his granddaughter boiled down, in the end, to: *What the hell happened to you?* She had always been so sensible, resilient, purposeful, even single-minded. But ever since her divorce—no, from the moment she had unaccountably decided on her hasty and ill-advised marriage to Daniel Friedman—the kid had been a fucking mess.

"Turn right at the blinking yellow," he said, but her turn signal was already on. In this regard, at least, she still knew her way.

The Red Hook Grill, an arrangement of vinyl-sided boxes stacked like lobster traps alongside Caldecott Falls, was the only restaurant in town that stayed open all through the off-season. In the gathering gray twilight of a frozen afternoon it blazed like a gaudy promise of warmth and comfort, and though the bar was topped with Formica and the pie with Cool Whip, the locals depended on it—Jack depended on it, too—to cheer the endless dark tunnel of a Down East winter. Jack placed his usual order—fish-and-chips, with onion rings swapped for the fries—though he knew he wouldn't be able to eat more than a bite or two. He hadn't been able to tolerate much of anything for a while now, despite what the doctors had promised when they'd convinced him to have the stent put in to relieve his jaundice. He was dropping weight so fast he thought he might vanish before the cancer killed him.

Natalie's usual was a hamburger and a Diet Coke, but today she ordered a milk shake, a black and white, and, when Louise brought the food, dropped a straw into the frosty metal blender cup that the Grill always served alongside its shakes and slid it across the table toward Jack.

"It might be easier to get that down."

He patted her hand and out of gratitude and good manners took a sip, with a show of relish, of the thick and saccharine confection. He loathed milk shakes.

At the end of the meal, Louise came over with a piece of pie, on the house, baked that morning from blueberries frozen at the end of last summer.

"Tide you over till next summer," she said.

She and Natalie exchanged a look. Louise put her hand on Jack's shoulder.

"How are you, Jack?"

"Fine, Louise," he said.

And then he felt obliged to take a bite of pie. It tasted to his dysfunctional palate like vinegar and salt.

"Very tasty," he said.

"Thank you, Louise," Natalie said.

As they watched Louise make her way back to the kitchen Natalie said, "Ever since Daniel left, everyone's always asking me, 'Natalie, how are you?' like they expect me to break down crying or tear out my hair or something. I never know what to say."

"It's for just such moments that the word 'fine' was invented."

"I guess. Daddy calls me every morning and says, 'How bad is it today, Sugarbear?' and I give him a number from one to ten. For the first month or two, I was pretty steadily in the ones and twos, but eventually I worked my way up to around a five."

"Your father does the same with me. Every morning." Jack was fond of Neil Stein, his son-in-law, closer to him than he'd been to his daughter. Close enough, in fact, that this daily ritual of checking in comforted rather than annoyed him.

"What number do you give him?" Natalie asked.

"I try to stay above a six."

"Pancreatic cancer and you're a six. My dumbfuck husband cheats on me, and I'm a one. Okay, that makes me the most selfish person in the world."

That made Jack smile.

"I'm glad you're here, darling," he said. "Now come on." He pushed back in his chair. "Let's go out and look at the falls before it's too dark to see anything."

"It's probably really slippery. And it's still snowing."

Jack shrugged on his coat and pulled on his gloves. He handed her his scarf. "Put this on. I don't know what you were thinking, bringing a coat like that to Maine in January."

"I wanted to look nice for you."

"You always look nice to me."

"I wanted to look nice for me, then. It, you know, it helps."

Because, she meant, she felt ugly and unwanted on the inside.

"I understand," he said. "Come on, gorgeous."

He took her arm as they walked through the snow to the edge of the water, whether to steady her or himself he wasn't sure. They reached the falls, a mysterious tidal churn of seawater that reversed direction with each turn of the tide. It must have been slack tide; the water milled in the narrows between the near and far shores as if uncertain which way to turn. Natalie threw a stick into the water, and they watched it drift irresolute on the swell.

"Your life is not over, Natalie. You will meet someone new."

"Will I? I want what you had with Grandma. That kind of great romance. The first time you saw her, you knew."

"Did I? How interesting. Tell me, what did I know?"

He could see that he had shocked her.

"That, you know. That she was the one."

"The 'one.'" He shook his head.

"Grandma wasn't the one?"

"Your grandmother was a beautiful woman with a good heart, and I loved her very much. Was she 'the one'? That I don't know. That strikes me as awfully simplistic."

"What happened with Daniel wasn't too complicated, Grandpa. He loved me. Then he didn't. Or maybe he just loved her more."

"Perhaps. Or maybe he is just a little shit."

"Whoa!"

"Is that simple enough for you?"

She laughed so hard that she was obliged to take a Kleenex out of her pocket and blow her nose.

"Look," he said, pointing to the water where a seal's slick head had popped up. "That's how seals sleep. With their bodies below and their heads like snorkels just above the surface."

"Oh, my God," she said. "You never liked Daniel."

"I never liked Daniel."

"Why didn't you say something before we got married?"

"I didn't think you were very likely to listen."

Though she had been going out with Daniel Friedman for years with marriage a frequently discussed, oft-deferred possibility, in the end they had married on an impulse, without advance notice or, as far as Jack could tell, any discussion at all. Daniel's parents were on their way to a vacation in Nova Scotia; Jack had offered them his guest room and a chance to break the long trip from New York before they headed up to catch the ferry in St. John. Natalie and Daniel were already scheduled to spend the week with Jack, along with Neil. It was on realizing that what remained of their respective families was going imminently to assemble in the same house for a day and a night that Natalie had abruptly decided to get married. Jack thought it was a rotten idea, but he held his tongue, figuring that the young man would find a way to weasel out of it. But Daniel, true to his weasel soul, had allowed the ship to sail knowing that its hull was ruptured, and so Jack had found himself hosting a pretty little ceremony by the seaside, at which Natalie's and Daniel's immediate families were joined by a haphazard collection of acquaintances who happened to be in the vicinity of Red Hook, Maine, on the afternoon of June 20. When, a mere three months later, Daniel had stunned poor Natalie by confessing to having been, for the last two years, sleeping with a junior associate, Jack had not been surprised.

"You're right," Natalie said now. "I wouldn't have listened, because I'm an ass." She kept her gaze fixed on the seal, and Jack saw a worried look come into her eyes, familiar to him from the time she was a toddler. "If a shark comes up while he's sleeping, does he wake up?"

The chills began a few miles from home, and by the time they reached the pair of whitewashed posts that marked the entrance to his long gravel drive, Jack's whole body was shaking, legs shuddering, teeth clacking together. He grasped one hand with the other to keep them from flopping around in his lap like fish on a line. The car crunched through a blue-white canyon of banked snow up the drive. As Natalie pulled all the way to the front steps of the house, Jack closed his eyes. He did not have the strength even to open his door, let alone to get out of the car. He waited, listening to the creak and slam of the trunk lid, the banging of her bags against the steps of the porch.

"Grandpa?" Natalie said. She had opened his door and was hovering over him, a note of panic in her voice. "Are you okay?"

"Just tired," he said.

"You're sweating."

He could feel sweat pouring down his forehead, pooling in his armpits and between his legs.

"I could use a nap," he said.

He allowed her to hoist him out of the car and help him into the house, but when she tried to follow him into his bedroom, he drew the line. He closed the door and, after a feeble attempt at the buttons of his shirt, crawled under the comforter and let the fever overtake him. He slept for twelve hours and woke at six feeling better than he had in weeks, well enough even to load and light the woodstove. Well enough to put a pot of coffee on, if not to drink it.

Natalie came down soon after. In her flannel nightshirt, with her hair tousled, her eyes puffy with sleep, she was again the little girl with whom he had passed so many early mornings, telling stories of the sack of Troy, the Peloponnesian War, Antigone and Polynices, Odysseus and

Penelope. Wildly inappropriate tales, some of them, for a small child, stories of slaughter and mayhem and betrayal. She had adored them.

"You hungry? Want me to make you a pancake in the shape of an N?" He meant it as a joke, but the offer came out sounding unexpectedly sincere.

She smiled. "It's been a long time since I had one of those."

"Oh!" he said, mildly panicked now that she seemed to be taking him up on his foolish offer, wondering if he had the wherewithal, either in his pantry or in his constitution. "I—I'm sure I could—"

"I'm not hungry," she said.

"Ah," he said, absurdly disappointed.

"How are you feeling, Grandpa?"

"I'm feeling much better." He looked at her. "Did you sleep well?"

"Not really."

"Was the bed—"

"The bed's fine. I don't sleep well in New York, either." She went to the counter, poured herself a cup of coffee, splashed in a little milk from the refrigerator. When she turned back to him she was holding a slip of paper.

"This is for you," she said. She handed him a check, folded in two. When he opened it, he saw that she had made it out to him in the amount of five hundred dollars.

"It's what you gave me and Daniel. For our wedding. I'm returning it."

"Honey, that's crazy. This is just five hundred bucks more you'll have to pay inheritance tax on." He crossed to the woodstove, opened the door, and tossed the check into the blaze.

"So much for that part of my plan," she said, sounding so lost that he almost regretted his action.

"What plan is that?" he said. "Returning your gifts?"

"Don't you think I should? Since the marriage lasted only three months?"

"You want to know what I think? I think that if your little shit of a husband leaves you for some dolly after you gave him twelve years of your life, you are entitled to enjoy the modest consolation of an automatic bread maker. Or a five-hundred-dollar check from your grandfather."

She nodded, a small, childlike nod of submission that made his heart ache.

"I guess I need a new plan," she said.

That was when she started to cry. Softly, for a long time, saying nothing about the grandfather she would soon be losing or the husband she had already lost. He patted her on the back and then, when she showed no sign of stopping, went to try to find her a box of Kleenex. He had forgotten to restock. He considered bringing her a roll of toilet paper, then remembered that in his bedroom he had a drawer full of old linen handkerchiefs, ironed flat. As he peeled one off the stack, he saw in the drawer a little pouch of worn black velvet. He hefted it, remembering with a faint pang the weight of it against his palm. At one time the contents of the pouch had been a kind of obsession. Now the velvet pouch was just one of the things stuffed into his dresser drawers. He wished there was a way to help Natalie understand the flimsiness, the feebleness, of objects, of memory, even of emotions, in the face of time with its annihilating power, greater than that of Darius of Persia or Hitler of Germany. But she would just have to live long and lose enough to find out for herself.

He feared what Natalie might do after he died, with no job to distract her. He imagined her sitting alone in the midst of a Maine winter, growing ever more depressed, losing the last of the spark that had made her the delight of his life. He weighed the cinched pouch of velvet in his hands for another moment, then took it with him back in the kitchen. He handed her a handkerchief and then, as she wiped her eyes and blew her nose, tipped the contents of the pouch into his palm. He caught hold of the gold chain. The gold-filigreed pendant dangled. It bore the image, in vitreous enamel, of a peacock, a perfect gemstone staring from the tip of each painted feather.

She flinched when she saw it, as if it were not a pretty little art nouveau bauble but something hideous to contemplate.

"Ugh," she said.

"What's wrong?"

"I wish I'd listened to you. You didn't want me to wear it at the wedding, and I did anyway. And now I'll think of him every time I look at it and feel ashamed."

"That hardly seems fair. After all, I had this necklace long before you and Daniel were even born."

"Did you buy it for Grandma, or did she inherit it?"

"Neither. It was mine."

"It wasn't Grandma's?"

"No."

"Are you serious? Why did you tell me it was hers? That's the only reason I wore it!"

"I never told you it was hers. Why would I tell you that, when it wasn't?"

She narrowed her eyes, trying to remember.

"Huh," she said, as if to concede the point. "Well, whose was it? Your mother's?"

"No."

"So whose?"

"Well, that's the thing. I don't know." He could see the glimmer of interest in her eyes, a revival of the spark that had, until recently, always flickered in the eyes of Natalie Stein. He was going to feed that small fire with whatever tinder came to hand. "That's why I need your help."

One

SALZBURG

1945–1946

· 1 ·

THEY FOUND THE TRAIN PARKED on an open spur not far from the station at Werfen. When they pulled up to the siding in their jeeps, Captain Rigsdale jumped out with a show of alacrity, but Jack hung back, eyeing the train. More than forty wagons, both passenger and freight. The nature of the cargo was as yet undetermined, but in this green and mountainous corner of the American Zone, a string of boxcars was never something Jack felt eager to explore.

Fencing the train were enemy troops uniformed in ragged khaki. They carried FÉG 35M rifles, but they had flagged their right sleeves with strips torn from white bedsheets, and they displayed no apparent satisfaction with their prize. By the side of the rails, a woman crouched over a wooden bucket filled with soapy water, wringing out a length of white cotton shirting. Two small boys took turns leaping from the door of one of the passenger cars, marking the lengths of their jumps with pebbles and bickering over who had leaped farther. They spoke a language unknown to Jack, but he assumed, based on what Rigsdale had told him, that it was Hungarian.

"Come on, Wiseman," Rigsdale called over his shoulder. "You're supposed to be fluent in gibberish."

"Yes, sir."

Jack climbed down from the jeep and followed Rigsdale toward the train. He had never worked for this particular captain before, but by now he was used to receiving sudden assignments to the command of senior officers tasked with undertaking excursions into obscure and doubtful backwaters of the Occupied Zone. Jack had a gift for topography and a photographic memory for maps. He had a feel for landscape and a true inner compass, and in his imagination the most cursory and vague of descriptions, a two-dimensional scrawl on a scrap of paper, took on depth and accuracy. This aptitude, which in civilian life had meant little more than always knowing whether he was facing uptown or downtown when he came up out of the subway, had found its perfect application in the war. Even during the confusion of battle, command had always been able to rely on Wiseman's company to be where it was supposed to be and, even more important, to be moving in the right direction, something not always true of the rest of the division. This spatial acuity, along with his fluency in German, French, Italian, and (less usefully) Latin and ancient Greek, kept him in demand with the brass, who contended among themselves to have him attached to their commands.

"What're they saying?" Rigsdale said.

"I don't know, sir."

"Well, figure it out, goddamn it."

"Yes, sir."

One of the enemy soldiers ducked back into the passenger car from which the boys were leaping. Jack lifted his rifle. A moment later, a portly little man in a gray suit, complete with vest and watch fob, emerged from the same carriage and stepped down, wiping his mouth with a handkerchief, still chewing a mouthful of something. Like the guards, he had tied a scrap of white fabric around his upper arm.

The man hurried over to the half-dozen American soldiers standing by their two jeeps, his expression at once servile and calculating, as if they were potential customers of undetermined means. He extended his hand to shake Captain Rigsdale's, seemed to think the better of it, and instead gave him a crisp, theatrical salute.

Rigsdale kept his own hands tucked by the thumbs into the webbed belt at his hips.

"Captain John F. Rigsdale, U.S. Army, Forty-Second Division. You the conductor of this choo-choo?"

The man shook his head, frowning. "No English. Deutsch? Français?"

"Go ahead, Lieutenant," Rigsdale said, motioning Jack forward.

"Deutsch," Jack said.

The man's German was fluent, although the Hungarian accent made the language sound softer, mellifluous, the *r*'s rolled on the tongue rather than the back of the throat, the emphasis placed on the beginning of the words. Jack's accent had its own peculiarities. Beneath the elegant High German cultivated by the Berliner refugee who had taught his German classes at Columbia University, Jack spoke with a touch of the Galicianer Yiddish of his maternal grandparents. His father's parents, of authentic German Jewish stock, had never to his knowledge uttered a word in that language.

"His name is Avar László," Jack told Rigsdale. "He's in charge of the train."

"Ask him if he's a military officer, and if so why he's not in uniform."

He was, Avar said, a civil servant, the former mayor of the town of Zenta, currently working for something he called the Property Office.

"Ask Mr. László why the hell his men haven't turned their arms over to the U.S. government," Rigsdale said.

"Avar," the Hungarian said in German. "My surname is Avar. Dr. Avar. László is my first name."

Jack asked Dr. Avar if he was aware that the terms of surrender required that enemy soldiers turn over their weapons.

Avar said that he was aware of the order, but regrettably the guns were necessary to protect the train's cargo. He said his men had been fighting off looters since the train's departure from Hungary. In May they'd been in a shoot-out with a group of German soldiers, and recently they'd been dealing with increasing problems from the local population, whose greed was inflamed by rumors of what was held in the wagons.

"Tell him I'm deeply sorry to hear how hard his life has been lately and that the U.S. Army is here to unburden him of all his sorrows," Captain Rigsdale said. "And his guns, too."

By now a small group of civilians had descended from the passenger carriages. One of them stepped forward and conferred with Avar, who nodded vigorously.

Jack translated. "They want us to know that nobody's given them any provisions. Avar says they've been starving." Jack looked doubtfully at the vigorous guards, the men in their neat suits, the plump-cheeked children. "Starving," he supposed, was a relative term.

The captain said, "Tell him they'll all be fed once they get to the DP camps. Now I want to have a look inside the cars. See what all the fuss is about."

Avar led them to the first of the cargo wagons, its doors officially sealed with bureaucratic wallpaper bearing an elaborate pattern of stamps and insignia. Jack looked down the row of boxcars. Some of the seals along the train remained intact. Others looked tattered, torn away. What that proved or didn't prove, he wasn't sure. There was no way of knowing whether the seals had been put there six months or six hours before.

At the door of the first cargo wagon, Avar hesitated. He conferred in Hungarian with one of his colleagues, a lanky, elderly gentleman with an extravagant mustache waxed to points, before making his wishes known to Jack.

"What now?" Rigsdale said.

"He's asking for a receipt."

"The fuck he is."

"To show that we assume protection of this property on behalf of the Hungarian government."

Avar didn't need Jack to translate the look on the captain's face. Puffing up his chest, the little man asked Jack to remind his commanding officer that the cargo of the train was Hungarian state property, and therefore he, Avar, with all due respect, could only turn over the custody of said cargo if assurances were made that it would, in due time, be returned to the government of Hungary.

"Lieutenant, please remind Mr. Avar that the government of Hungary just got its ass handed to it, and suggest to him, if you would be so kind, that he, his men, and his whole damn country are now under the authority of the Allied forces. I am not going to give him a goddamn receipt, and he should please open this motherfucking door now, before I use his fat head as a battering ram."

In as formal a German as he could muster, Jack said, "Captain Rigsdale reminds you that he speaks with the full authority of the United States Army, and requests that you delay opening the boxcar no longer."

Avar glanced at his guards, and Jack silently cursed the military command that had sent six men to disarm sixty. Though he never made vocal his disapproval, he had learned by hard experience that a soldier rarely lost money betting against the wisdom of the brass. The institutionalized idiocy was one of the many reasons that for nearly all of the past year and a half since his enlistment Jack had hated the war, hated the army, hated even the civilians who all too often seemed to despise their American liberators far more than they had their German conquerors. The only people he didn't hate were the men with whom he served in the 222nd Battalion of the 42nd Infantry, the Rainbow Division, none of whom he'd known for longer than a year and all of whom he loved with a devotion he had never felt before for anyone, not even the girlfriend who had predictably broken his heart in a letter a mere three weeks after he received his commission. He was especially fond of the men of H Company, whose dwindling ranks he had led on a relentless slog through the torn-up landscape, through France and across the Siegfried line until they reached Fürth, where the battalion commanding officer, after a grueling exchange with a recalcitrant local farmer, had decided that he needed the assistance of an aide conversant in German and transferred Jack away from the men who were all that he cared about in this miserable war. His many attempts to return to his company defeated, Jack was left stewing in his loathing and waiting to earn enough points for a discharge. Even considering the battle decorations he'd received at a recent cluster muster, he was three points shy of the eighty-five he needed to be sent home. Best possible outcome, eighty-two points put him in Salzburg for three more months. Worst possible, he was heading to the Pacific.

The Hungarian having failed to respond to his order, Jack repeated, "Please open the boxcars."

Across Avar's face seemed to pass the entire history of his benighted people in this interminable war: pride, belligerence, bravado, defensiveness, anxiety, despair. And, finally, resignation. He removed a large iron key from the inside breast pocket of his suit jacket, inserted it into the heavy padlock, and, with a grunt, sprung the lock. When he pushed the door back, the seals tore with a pop like the bursting of an inflated paper bag. The door rumbled open on its runners.

The boxcar was heaped with wooden cases and crates. Some of the cases had iron hinges and clasps; others were nailed shut. Toward the back of the car they stood in orderly stacks, but many of those nearest the door had been pried open and were piled haphazardly one upon the other.

"Pull a couple of those over here, Lieutenant," Rigsdale said. "Let's see what we're dealing with."

Jack climbed up into the car and dragged over an open crate. He dug through the straw and pulled out a teacup decorated with a pink rose and a scattering of green leaves. The gilt-edged handle came off in his hand.

"*Vorsicht!*" Avar said.

Jack gave a meaningful glance at the jumble of open boxes. No one else had bothered to take the care that Avar seemed to expect of him.

"Try another crate," the captain said.

The next crate contained a pile of expensive-looking camera equipment, none of it padded with straw or excelsior. Some of the lenses were cracked. What, Jack wondered, were these Hungarians doing riding around the Austrian countryside with a trainload of household goods?

Captain Rigsdale ordered Avar to open another boxcar. This one contained mainly rolls of carpets. Most were stacked neatly, but someone had been pilfering those nearest to the door; smaller carpets had been unrolled and draped over the piles, and there were muddy boot tracks everywhere.

"Looters," Avar said.

"After the treasure," Captain Rigsdale said after Jack had translated. "All this must have been on its way to the *Alpenfestung.*"

Among the strange ideas held in common both by the Allies and the defeated German troops was the chimera that, hidden in the mountains of southern Bavaria, defended by one hundred thousand SS officers, the Nazis had erected a final stronghold. Although there was no more evidence for the existence of this national redoubt than there was for that of the city of Atlantis or the valley of Shangri-la, everyone on both sides seemed to be sure that it was there, hovering high above them, a Valhalla for the desperate Germans and an anxiety dream for the Allies, many of whom had a hard time accepting that their mythic Teutonic-warrior opponents had not fought to the end predicted by their death's-head insignia.

"Strange kind of treasure," Jack said, holding up a crystal liqueur glass. "Sir, this doesn't look like bank assets. It just seems to be a lot of, well, stuff."

"Let's keep looking," Rigsdale said.

Avar led them through the train, a car at a time. He showed them crude pine crates of bed linens and fur coats, cases of men's pocket and wrist watches, of women's jewelry. Jack opened up a box full of evening purses, most of them beaded or decorated with silver chains. Another of silver sugar basins, silver teapots engraved with monograms, bronze statuettes of men on horseback. In some cars they found heaps of leather wallets alongside silver cigarette cases, heavy musty-smelling furs piled on top of brightly colored Oriental carpets, tangles of costume jewelry, paintings of all sizes stacked one upon the other. The contents of other cars had been painstakingly sorted, the radios neatly loaded into wooden crates, the silver candlesticks separated from the vases, the sets of china plates and porcelain platters carefully packed.

In the fifth car, Avar opened an unlocked small wooden casket with brass hinges. It was full to the brim with small misshapen loaves of gold and gold coins stamped with mysterious insignia. This indeed was treasure, like a child's imaginary pirate's trove, lustrous in the sunlight.

"You see?" Avar said in German. "Untouched since we left Brenn-bergbánya."

"Where is Brennbergbánya?" Jack asked. "Is that where you came from?"

"This train was loaded in Brennbergbánya. Before that we did the sorting and organizing in the Óbánya Castle in Zirc. Before that most items were stored in the warehouses of the Postal Savings Bank."

"But who does it belong to?"

One of Avar's companions said something in Hungarian.

Avar said, "All property belongs to the people of Hungary. It must be returned to the people of Hungary."

When Jack translated this, Rigsdale said, "Tell him the American government is not in the business of stealing anybody's property." Rigsdale pointed at the small casket. "Is this all the gold?" he asked.

There was more gold, Avar told them, but they had distributed it throughout the train to make it more difficult for looters to find. There were also a small number of precious gems. Avar had done his best to protect the most valuable property, but there had, as he'd said, been loot-ers. And also government officials had removed much of it.

"U.S. government?" Rigsdale asked.

"No," Avar replied. "Hungarian government."

"Wait a minute," the captain said when Jack translated Avar's response. "Hungarian government officials have been here?"

No, not here in Werfen, Avar said. But before the end of the war, there had been individual government officials who had taken items from the train. He had tried to keep an inventory. He would show them.

"Anything else of value in this car?" Captain Rigsdale barked.

Avar opened another case. "Watches," he said. "Gold. Gold plate. Very valuable. And you see? Also untouched."

In another car, Avar pulled out an old steel box, unlocked, that appeared to contain mostly envelopes.

Jack crouched down next to the box and pulled out an envelope. It was torn open and empty. "What does this say?" Jack asked, showing it to Avar.

"It is a name," Avar said. "Korvin György. This is an address in Kolozsvár, a city in Transylvania." He pointed to another line. "And this says, 'Gold ring set with diamonds. One karat.'"

"Where's the ring?"

Avar shook his head. "When we did the sorting, we removed the items from the envelopes. And also, we usually removed the precious stones from the jewelry."

"Why?" Jack asked.

"So we could protect what was most valuable."

Or, Jack thought, to make it easier to sell.

The rest of the steel casket was filled with pages of paper covered in ornate and spidery handwriting, liberally decorated with accents and umlauts.

"Inventory," the Hungarian said. "With names."

It was while going through a boxcar that contained household silver—cutlery, tea services, platters and bowls, candlesticks—that Jack caught on to the origin of the treasure on the train. Up to his elbows in a crate his superior officer had instructed him to open, he grabbed hold of a heavy silver candelabra. For a moment he wasn't sure. But there were four arms on either side, and one in the middle. He disentangled the menorah from the other silver pieces in the crate and then dug out a silver cup decorated with Hebrew writing. A kiddush cup like the one his grandmother had on her mantel. Without seeking Rigsdale's permission, he grabbed another crate and split it open with a crowbar. In this one he found a silver breastplate and crowns that looked very much like the ones that had decorated the Torah from which he had chanted on his bar mitzvah at Temple Emanu-El on the Upper East Side of Manhattan, nine years before.

"Everything in this wagon is silver?" Rigsdale asked Avar.

Avar gazed at him blankly.

"You know, silver? Wiseman, ask him if this car's all silver."

"Captain," Jack said, the only evidence of his distress the beads of sweat collecting on his lip. "All this stuff is Jewish, sir."

"What do you mean?"

He held up the Torah breastplate, pointing to the Hebrew words. He picked up the caps for the Torah handles. They were hung with silver bells that tinkled in his trembling hands. "This is from a synagogue."

He turned on Avar. "Where did you get this?" he said. "And this?"

Avar looked blank but not quite blank enough.

"This is stolen from Jews!" Jack said. He pawed through the pile of silver, yanking out candlesticks and kiddush cups, waving them, piece after piece, at the man.

Avar let loose with a string of German, but Jack was far too upset to understand more than a few phrases—"civil servant," "official government business." Avar shrank into himself, like a turtle hiding beneath its bureaucratic shell.

"What's this 'Property Office' that you work for? What property?" Jack shouted.

Avar raised his chin defensively and informed Jack that he was an employee of the Jewish Property Office, a division of the Hungarian Ministry of Finance, and that it was in his role as an employee of that department that he had protected this property on behalf of the Hungarian government.

"Wiseman!" Captain Rigsdale said. "Get down here. Now."

Jack willed his body to still, his breath to even out.

"Yes, sir," he said and leaped lightly to the ground.

"Your orders are to translate, Lieutenant. That is all."

"Yes, sir."

"Do your job."

"Yes, sir."

"Now, what the hell is going on?"

It was important that the Americans understood, Avar said, that he and the other officials on the train were civil servants, tasked with carrying out the law and protecting the assets under their control. These assets had come from the banks.

And before that? Captain Rigsdale pressed him.

Avar admitted that the valuables had been collected from the Jews of Hungary by the commissioner for Jewish Affairs.

"Why?" Jack asked.

"Why?" Avar repeated. "To help in the war effort." He himself was responsible only for the transport of the property, not for its collection. The Jews had turned in their property to the banks; the banks had turned it in to the Jewish Property Office; officials from the office had sorted it and loaded it into the boxcars, at which point it had been turned over to him. He had protected the property, he told them, at great risk to his life.

As Jack translated this last for Captain Rigsdale, he wondered at Avar's confidence that the danger to his life had passed.

Rigsdale said, "Ask him if there's anything else he needs to show me."

"Moment," Avar said, and spun on his heel. Jack thought how easy it would be to lift his weapon, fire off a single bullet, and send the man crumpling to the ground.

Avar returned a moment later with a small suitcase, which he balanced in the opening of the boxcar and unsnapped. In the suitcase were bundles of currency in a rainbow of colors. Hungarian pengő, U.S. dollars, British pounds sterling, Swiss francs, reichsmarks. Even a small banded-together stack of green-and-yellow bills: Palestinian pounds. Jack had never seen those before. Avar opened a small sachet and poured a handful of colored gemstones and pearls into his palm.

"That's what we've been looking for," Rigsdale said. Avar put the gems back in the sachet, tied it closed, and tucked it into the suitcase. Then he buckled the suitcase and, with great solemnity, handed it to the American officer.

On Captain Rigsdale's orders, Avar's men turned over their ammunition. Rigsdale sent a GI to the station to bring back the stationmaster and a few railroad workers to uncouple the passenger cars. Arrangements were made to escort Avar and the rest of the Hungarian civilians to a DP camp. Rigsdale ordered the now-unarmed guards to accompany the train to Salzburg, under the guard of a few GIs. Then he turned to Jack.

"You. With me."

Jack followed Rigsdale to the jeep. Rigsdale, though he'd ridden beside the driver on the way to Werfen, swung himself into the backseat. Jack began to climb into the front when the captain barked, "With me."

Rigsdale didn't speak for the first part of the journey back to Salzburg, and Jack remained silent beside him, waiting for the inevitable reprimand and busying himself with trying to clean a smear of dirt from the knee of his trouser. Though he loathed all things military, Jack was punctilious about his uniform. Whenever possible, he kept it clean and tidy, his collar and cuffs crisp, his shirttails tucked tightly into his webbed belt. Unlike many of the other U.S. Army officers and certainly the men, he refused to slip into slovenliness, even when covered with battle filth. He tried to shave every day, had done so even during the long weeks of battle, when the possibility of bathing was as remote as the idea of going home. The more furious he became at the perverse machinery of the military, the more his belt buckle gleamed, as if to prove that it wasn't he who was unfit for the service but the service that was unfit for him.

When they reached the outskirts of Salzburg, Rigsdale said, "That was quite a performance, Lieutenant."

No reply seemed called for, so Jack provided none.

"You need to remember something, soldier. This is a war, not a crusade, and you're an American soldier, not a rabbi."

"Yes, sir," he said, the only evidence of his furious embarrassment the flutter of muscle in his clenched jaw.

2

FOR JACK'S SINS RIGSDALE gave him a deuce-and-a-half M35 truck and put him in charge of unloading the train. Twenty-five Hungarian POWs, a half-dozen GIs to guard against looters and black marketeers, and one truck to unload 1,500 cases of watches, jewelry, and silver, 5,250 carpets, thousands of coats and stoles and muffs of mink, fox, and ermine, crates of microscopes and cameras, porcelain and glassware, furniture, books and manuscripts and tapestries, gold coins and bullion, the few remaining precious gems, the liturgical objects, the stamp collections and silver-backed hairbrushes; all the items, valuable and less so, that constituted the wealth of the Jews of Hungary, 437,402 of whom had been deported to Auschwitz over the course of just 56 days almost exactly a year before.

One of the GIs offered to organize more transport, but Jack had seen too much of what passed for organization among his fellow soldiers. In his unit's first days in Austria, his men had "organized" everything from alcohol to bedding, from guns to eggs to radios. Once, two corporals had even organized a Volkswagen and gone joyriding. It took them an hour to realize that the strange sound they had been ignoring in the backseat was the mewling of a baby in its basket. Jack had tracked down the frantic mother and returned the baby. His CO had kept the car.

"Come!" Jack called out in Hungarian from the back of the truck where he was loading a cargo of furs and carpets. As his captives were uninterested in learning any English beyond the words "Lucky Strike," and as they resisted even the German their superiors spoke fluently, he'd had no choice but to acquire a few words of their language.

One of the Hungarian soldiers popped his head into the back of the truck. Jack indicated to him that he should grab an end of a rolled carpet. It still surprised the POWs to see Jack pitching in with the heavy work, humping out the crates and boxes one at a time, heaving them into the bed of the deuce-and-a-half, then running them over to the old Wehrmacht warehouse where the army had decided to store the contents of the train. It wasn't that he was looking for extra work or trying to set an example or, God knew, looking to give the POWs a break. On the contrary. He would have been happy to see every last enemy soldier put to hard labor cleaning up the streets and countryside instead of lying around the POW camps while the civilians did all the work. He was just looking to get the damn job over with as quickly as he could.

The carpet securely lodged, Jack headed deep into the truck to see how much more could fit into the load. He winced at the musty odor of the furs and remembered how every spring his mother would pack up her mink stole and sheared-beaver coat, even the rabbit muff she'd had since she was a girl, and deposit them at the French dry cleaner to be put in cold storage for the summer. Fur wasn't meant to be kept baled up in a metal boxcar parked on a sunny railroad siding. He worried that the warehouse wasn't much cooler. Who knew what state the furs would be in when they were finally sent back to where they belonged? Half drunk on the musk rising out of an armload of moth-eaten minks, he heard a commotion, a woman's voice, a bark of laughter, shouting. He lifted the canvas flap and peered out.

One of the POWs had a young woman by the arm. He was trying to drag her away from the train. She shouted at him, scrabbling at his hand. The POW was laughing at her. The woman's face was alight with fury.

"Hey!" Jack yelled.

The Hungarian POW looked up, surprised. He dropped the woman's arm. She slapped him across the face, the slap sounding flat and feeble in the hot afternoon. Now the other POWs started to laugh. The GIs just stood there, looking mildly interested in the proceedings, for a change. A corporal named Sully called out, "I think they know each other, Lieutenant."

"I do not know this man," the woman said, in English.

She rubbed at the arm the Hungarian had been gripping. Her cotton blouse had been worn so long and washed so many times that what had once been a floral print, perhaps, was now no more than a faded smear of pink on a ground of grayish white. The woman checked to make sure that its tired seams had not given way beneath the Hungarian's thick fingers.

She had the unmistakable look of a survivor of the camps. Even months after their release, they were thinner than the other DPs, let alone the Austrians, who were only now beginning to experience the kind of food shortages the rest of occupied Europe had suffered throughout the war. The woman's face was gaunt and shadowed, her frown severe, but her hair was growing back in a riot of cheerful red curls.

"Can I help you, ma'am?" Jack said, jumping lightly down from the truck. *"Gyerünk vissza dolgozni!"* he said to the POWs. Of all the Hungarian phrases he'd learned, "Back to work!" was particularly useful, since the Hungarians' interest in finishing the task of unloading the train was severely hampered by their desire to continue to receive U.S. military rations. They knew that once this work was done, they'd be sent to a POW camp.

"This train," the woman said, "it is from Hungary?" Her voice was low, husky. Her accent had a British inflection. She pointed to the white letters painted on one of the boxcars: MÁV HUNGARIA.

"Are you Hungarian?" he asked.

"Yes," she said. "From Nagyvárad. In Transylvania."

One of the Hungarians called out something.

The woman's face softened for a moment, but then she seemed to marshal her anger and spat out a sentence whose tone of vituperation was unmistakable. The young Hungarian flushed and turned away, dragging self-consciously on his cigarette.

"Back to work," Jack said again. He lifted his hand to his sidearm. "Now." The Hungarians turned back to the boxcars, making their usual show of great effort. He asked the woman, "What did he say to you?"

"He says he is also from Nagyvárad."

"And what did you say to him?"

She narrowed her eyes and cocked her head, sizing Jack up. In a tone brittle but bright, even cheerful, she said, "I ask him did he guard the ghetto there, maybe he helped my grandmother onto the train for her trip to Auschwitz."

Before he could stop himself, Jack laughed. There was nothing funny about what she had said; it was the audacity of this woman. She was no ruined wraith. She was all wire and sparks. As he covered his mouth in shame at his outburst, her eyes widened, and then she laughed, too. Darkly, bitterly, a laugh almost—but not completely—wrung free of joy.

"I'm so sorry," he said. "I didn't mean . . . it's just—his face. You shut him up good."

"Time for him to shut up, I think," she said. "Time for them all to shut up. Now, this Hungarian train here. There are people on this Hungarian train or only soldiers?"

"It's a cargo train. There were some people on it, but not the kind of people you're looking for."

"You know what kind of people I am looking for?"

He did not normally blush. It was rare that he embarrassed himself, and around women he tended to be remote rather than tongue-tied. But something about this woman made him feel like an awkward child with an ungovernable mouth. It was curious, since she was much younger than he had initially assumed—perhaps no older than himself.

"I mean there are no Jews."

"You think I am looking for Jews?"

She let him hang there, flustered, trying to figure her. It was true that all kinds of people had gone to the camps: homosexuals, Communists, prostitutes. But the woman had mentioned her grandmother. In the awkward silence Jack became conscious of the gazes of his men upon him. They had to be surprised to see their cool and unflappable CO looking so decidedly flapped.

"Excuse me," he told her. He turned to his men and gestured with a thumb toward the Hungarians. "Sully, take the truck and three of these bozos on over to the warehouse. Get unloaded and then get back here, fast. The rest of you: patrol. You remember how to do that, right?"

Steadied, now, Jack turned back to the woman.

"This is a secure area, miss," he said. "I'm afraid I can't let you stay here."

"Yes," she said, without moving. She watched as two of the Hungarians kicked a long roll of carpet out of one of the boxcars like lumberjacks rolling a felled log, then struggled to lift it onto their shoulders.

"So," she said. "No Jews. Only carpets."

"Miss, you cannot stay here," Jack said. "I'm sure you must have somewhere you're supposed to be."

"I have a pass," the woman said, reaching into the pocket of her skirt. She thrust a scrap of thin blue paper covered in smeared ink at him. "I stay at the Hotel Europa, but today I have a pass. You see?"

"That's fine, I don't need to see it."

When he had first arrived in Salzburg, Jack had done a week of guard duty at one of the DP camps. The inmates there were mostly forced laborers awaiting repatriation back to their native countries in the East, who must have felt as though they had changed one warden for another, a hair more lenient, more generous, but still armed. None of the American guards had any MP training, and they chafed against the constant checking of passes, the breaking up of endless arguments over firewood or cooking oil, or, more disturbingly, over the nationality and background of the well-fed individuals with SS haircuts who, in those early days and weeks, had tried to hide themselves among the crowds of refugees. It was hard to do the work of a jailer without feeling like one, to imprison people without treating them like prisoners. He had often found himself furious with the attitudes of the replacements in his command, boys who had never seen a camp or fired a shot in battle and who were as disgusted by the bedraggled DPs as they were enamored of the plump and eager Austrian girls. The Austrians were clean; they were hardworking; they lived in pretty little houses painted in sherbet colors. The DPs, crowded together with few possessions, fewer legal sources of income, nothing to do but fear the future and trade on the black market, repelled the American soldiers. The replacements would make jokes about typhus and lice as they kept at arm's length the half-starved children who milled around them, calling "Candy! Candy!" By the end of a week of this, Jack had been ready to court-martial half the soldiers under his command, though he feared that what made him so angry was a suspicion that their attitude was uncomfortably similar to his own. Though it shamed him, he knew that he, like his men, flinched when he saw the survivors of the camps, and avoided speaking with them, or even looking at them. This girl was, he thought, the first camp prisoner with whom he'd had more than the most cursory of contact.

The young woman put her pass back in her pocket and stared over his shoulder at the train cars.

"Did someone tell you the train was here?" he asked.

"I am passing by only. I saw the Hungarian writing, and I thought maybe there's someone on this train. But I found only them." She waved at the Hungarian soldiers. "And you."

It was time to get back to work. If he drove the men hard enough, they could finish before dark. He must send her on her way.

"Is it your family that you're looking for?" he said.

Her face grew slack, her animated frown dissolved, her bright and furious gaze lost its focus. She looked at once like a little girl and like an ancient crone, blind to anything other than the past. But she allowed herself only a moment before she shook her head and steeled her jaw. She looked at the growing pile of items that the Hungarians had heaped, stacked, and scattered on the ground.

"Where are you taking all this?" she said.

"To a secure facility, where it can be stored pending investigation."

"Okay," she said, as though granting him permission.

Jack started to tell her that this was a restricted zone and he must return to work, but she was already going. She walked with a slight limp, a small hitch in her step, but she moved quickly.

"Miss!" he called, but by then she had crossed the street and couldn't—or pretended not to—hear him.

3

THE NEXT DAY AFTER Jack finished his duties, he gathered a stack of C rations, opened them, and sorted through the M units, discarding the ones that contained chopped ham or frankfurters, and swapping in extra cans of chicken and vegetables, which had the virtue of being not only marginally more kosher but also more palatable. He added as many packs of Brach's fudge disks, Jim Dandee cookie sandwiches, and vanilla caramels as he could find. He shoved everything into a sack and set out on foot for the Hotel Europa.

He was not so foolish as to expect it to be easy to find a nameless young woman among the thousands of displaced persons who had taken refuge in Salzburg, but he had allowed himself to imagine some kind of lobby, a desk clerk with a registration book. Failing that, there would be U.S. Army guards, one of whom was sure to remember a decent-looking young redhead with a quick temper and a ready command of English.

The main entrance was blocked by rubble, heaps of shattered bricks and paving stones, splintered boards, the kind of disaster zone that had by now become so familiar. In the courtyard, groups of shabby men gathered, smoking foul cigarettes and trading in information and goods in a babel of tongues. As he crossed the courtyard to the lobby where, in better days, a reception desk had surely stood, Jack witnessed a brisk trade in sacks of cucumbers and potatoes, bread and cabbages, and of course the ubiquitous packages of Chesterfields and Luckies. A brace of game birds changed hands, too small to be ducks, too colorful to be pigeons. No one bothered to hide his activities from or even take notice of the American officer in their midst. He was taken aback by their brazenness, but when he found the GIs ostensibly guarding the place, he understood. The American soldiers were themselves busy selling off the contents of their C rations and of the packages their mothers and girlfriends had so lovingly sent them from home.

There were so many girls in the camp, the sergeant in charge told him. And most of them had already learned enough English to communicate at least a little bit.

"Red hair," Jack said. "Curly. And thin. Very thin." He had been ready to come up with some bogus reason for his visit, but the sergeant in charge at the Hotel Europa clearly did not care about the rules against fraternization, even less about Jack's business.

"Feel free to look around. Word of warning, though, sir. Some of these people, you stick your head in their room, they act like you're coming to murder their mother."

Jack was tempted to remind the man that the experience of having a soldier walk into their houses and murder their mothers was a familiar one to a fair number of the people currently residing in the hotel, but the sergeant had three bronze battle stars on his chest. Jack wouldn't be telling him anything he didn't already know.

They were interrupted by furious shouts from across the courtyard. A woman barreled through the crowds, assuming—correctly, it seemed—that anyone unlucky enough to find himself in her path would give way.

"Aw, shit," the sergeant said.

The woman had an apple face on a potato body, a thin braid of colorless hair circling her head. "Come!" she said.

"What now, Maria?" the sergeant said. "Why you all worked up this time?"

Her English was insufficient to allow her to explain. She just kept repeating, "Come! Come!" until finally the sergeant called over two of his men and told them to escort the lady upstairs and find out what was wrong. Jack, curious, accompanied the men across the courtyard, none of them moving fast enough to suit Maria, who kept stopping and waving at them to catch up, with a flick of her hand, the way you'd call a dog to heel.

She led them through a door, its glass replaced with panels of scarred timber that had somehow managed to evade the cooking fires. A stairway looped upward with vestigial elegance, and at its center rose an elevator shaft, enclosed in lacy wrought iron. It was heaped with trash, including a baby carriage missing all but one of its wheels. As they climbed up the staircase circling the defunct elevator shaft, birds nesting in the walls took off with a great flutter of wings, startling Jack, though not the others.

There were three rooms on each floor, and most of the doors were open as a concession to the thick July heat. Jack saw that the rooms had been divided into crude cubicles, with each living space separated from the others by a strung-up blanket. Six, seven, up to a dozen people were crammed into each room, lying on bunks of crude lumber or sprawled in one of the few remaining chairs. Children chased one another through the halls. When the soldiers and their furious escort reached the fourth floor, the door to the first apartment opened, and an elderly woman walked out. Jack looked past her into the apartment and saw a couple kissing. They were standing, the woman leaning against a wall, her face turned to the door, the man's hands planted on either side of her head. She opened her eyes just as Jack looked in. She stared at him, impassive. He turned quickly away.

Maria stopped in front of the last apartment on the floor, poked her head through the open doorway, and immediately she began yelling in some Slavic language.

"Fucking DPs," the older of the two GIs muttered.

"Hey, Lieutenant," the other one said in a thick Southern accent. "You speak the lingo? Think you can figure out what the hell's going on here?"

"Not my job, Private," Jack said, but now Maria had switched to broken German, and he was curious to find out just whom she was threatening to throw down the stairs.

He pushed into the room and found her towering over what he took, at first, for an elderly man, hunched at the waist, propped up by crutches fashioned from two lengths of broken board. The man's body shook with the effort of staying upright. Huddled behind him were two small boys, one of them in tears.

Jack said, "Is it the children you plan to throw down the stairs, Maria? Or the man with the canes?"

Maria looked surprised at his German, though unembarrassed that her threats had been overheard. "They don't get out, I throw them down all three." Her accent was thick, her grammar terrible, but she had no trouble making herself understood.

"This room is for this men!" Maria said, pointing to the back of the room, where Jack now noticed two men sitting at a small table, filling the air with the smoke of their cigarettes. They acknowledged his presence with barely a glance. They appeared to have been harvested from the same potato field as Maria.

The *KZler* was lucky Maria was here, she told Jack. Otherwise the rightful residents might have taken the interlopers' eviction into their own hands, and then all three would be crying, not just the little louse.

"Louse?" Jack said.

"It's what she calls the children," the man with the makeshift canes said softly, also in German. Jack saw now that he was not elderly at all. He was hardly more than a boy himself. But his face was gray and creased, and he was missing most of his teeth.

"Take them away!" Maria said to Jack.

Jack kept his temper, and turned to the ruined young man. "She called you a *KZler?*"

"Buchenwald."

Jack asked the young man if it was true, what Maria had said about him and the boys trying to move into the room.

"You are calling me liar?" Maria said, shouting again.

"Silence," Jack said, his voice soft but clear. Maria folded her arms over her chest and glared, pressing her lips into a thin white line.

The man said, "I lived in this room with six others from Buchenwald, but when I received word, four days ago, that my nephews had been found in Vienna, I went there, to fetch them. When I returned, I found the other men who shared this room gone. These two had taken their place. I have asked for another room. The administrator says there is none to be had. He says that since there are now only these two, the room can also accommodate me and the boys. These gentlemen have other ideas." The man struggled with his canes, trying to turn around without falling. "In any case, I am fully prepared to deny myself the pleasure of their company." He turned to Maria. "Find me another place, and we will go."

Maria smiled. "You go," she said. "The American will take care of you." She called something out to the two men at the back.

"Where are you from?" Jack asked Maria.

"Ukraine," she said.

"And your friends? They're from the Ukraine, too?"

"Yes."

"What are you doing in Salzburg? How did you end up here?"

Maria's smile faded. "Forced labor," she said.

"Liar." The voice, harsh and angry, came from the doorway, and Jack knew before he turned around who had spoken.

"You are looking for me?" the redheaded woman asked Jack, in English.

"This one!" Maria said. "Take this one away! Put in prison where she belong!"

Jack ignored her. "What's going on here?" he said to the redhead, in English.

"Maria is *Kapo* of this stairway. While this gentleman was away, she evicted the other Jews from this apartment and turned it over to her friends. People are afraid of her, so they do what she says. For some reason, this gentleman seems less afraid than most."

"You called her a liar," Jack said. "Are you saying she wasn't a forced laborer?"

"Perhaps she was. Perhaps the women here who survived Ravensbrück, and say this lady was a guard there, are mistaken."

Maria caught the name, and her face fell. "No!" she said in German. "Not Ravensbrück! Forced labor! I am prisoner, too."

"What is Ravensbrück?" Jack asked.

"A camp in northern Germany," the redheaded woman said. "For women only."

By the time the war had ended, it was as though someone had picked up the crazy quilt of Europe by its corner and shaken it, sending people tumbling to all ends of the continent. There were millions of forced and slave laborers conscripted from Poland and Russia, Denmark and Holland, from every corner of the Third Reich's empire. Joining in these streams of humanity winding through the rubble left from the war were anti-Communist eastern Europeans fleeing the advancing Russian army, hundreds of thousands of Germans and Austrians forced by Hitler's armies to evacuate rather than surrender to the advancing enemy, and Volksdeutschen, the ethnic Germans who had celebrated Hitler's invasion of their countries and eagerly assumed dominion over their neighbors and who now abandoned their homes in fear of reprisal. Former concentration camp prisoners constituted only a very small fraction of the humanity packed into the DP camps, and in and among them hid concentration camp guards like Maria, trying to sneak back home before their crimes came to light.

"If it's true, why hasn't she been denounced?" Jack asked.

"She has. More than once. But your military government, they like her. She is disciplined. Efficient. She keeps the others in line."

He turned to Maria. "Where is your room?"

"Ach! Never mind," Maria said, her voice saccharin sweet. "No problem. They stay. We go."

Casually, without menace, Jack shifted his body to block the door.

"She lives on the ground floor," said the redhead. "Behind the staircase."

"That'll do," he said.

He called the GIs in and ordered them to help the crippled man and the two small boys down the stairs. He took Maria by the arm and frog-marched her down ahead of him. She refused to unlock the door of her apartment, but he saw the key tied to a loop on the webbed military belt that she wore where her waist would have been, had she had one. With a snap of his wrist he yanked the key free and unlocked the door himself. This room, unlike any of the others, still had its hotel furniture. Two large beds made up with actual sheets, even pillows, a dresser missing only one drawer, a cupboard, a table and two chairs, even a scrap of carpet.

By the time the GIs showed up with the crippled man and his nephews, Jack had tossed all of Maria's belongings—her clothes and her stacks of linens and blankets, her extra boots and her packages of soaps and cans of kerosene, her sacks of potatoes and flour, her side of cured meat, her cooking pots and dishes—out into the hall. He left the beds, complete with their linens, the dresser and the cupboard, the table and the two chairs.

"This is your room now," he said, handing the key to the young man from Buchenwald. Jack slung the sack of C rations he carried onto the floor, opened it, pulled out half of what he'd brought, and dumped it on the bed. Maria stood in the hallway kneading her skirt in her hands, keening bitterly.

The man hesitated, but the boys ran into the room. The smaller one threw himself onto the bed and rolled on it like it was the first fresh snowfall of the winter.

"They will punish me," the man said. "As soon as you leave."

Jack pointed at the GIs. "These men will protect you." To the soldiers he said, "These three are now your responsibility. Anything happens to them, and you'll have to answer to me. Got that?"

"Yes, sir," said the Southerner. He then winked solemnly at the older boy, who tried out a tentative smile.

Out in the hall, Jack picked up the largest of Maria's bundles.

"Come," he said to her, but she buried her face in her hands.

"Help me carry her things up to her new room," he told the GIs. Jack took the steps two at a time. When he reached the fourth floor he saw that the Ukrainians had closed and locked their door. Jack, his arms full, kicked at the door with his heavy boot. When they did not imme-diately open it, he kicked it again, and it splintered around the lock. He nudged it open the rest of the way, now with the toe of his boot, and handed Maria's bundle to one of the startled Ukrainians. On his way back down the stairs, he passed the GIs each with a sack of potatoes over his shoulder.

"Old Maria's losing her mind down there," the Southerner said.

The redhead sat one step up from the bottom, chin in hands, watching with cool fascination as Maria muttered dark syllables in her sinuous mother tongue, weeping and furious.

"She says she will go to the senior camp administrator," the redhead said. "She will report you to the military police."

"Good," Jack said. "Tell me. What's your name?"

"Ilona. Surname Jakab." Ilona Jakab looked at the bundles of food and clothes piled on the floor around Maria and said, amused but without apparent rancor, "She has done well for herself."

"If you like," Jack told Maria, in German, "I will post a guard outside the door to your new room, to protect your possessions until you return with the camp administrator and the military police. At that time, we can discuss in more detail your grievances and in particular your experiences as a forced laborer, which I have no doubt were terribly painful."

Maria howled something, scooped up a blanket and a basket of apples, and ran up the stairs, her U.S. Army leather and rubber shoepacs thudding on the slick wooden treads.

Ilona glanced after her and nodded, a satisfied smile crossing her face for an instant. Jack flushed, gratified at the implied compliment.

She stood up, brushed the grime of the step from the back of her skirt. She began to walk out the door, and as she passed him Jack reached out a hand, hesitating before he touched her arm. She looked back but did not stop, and he followed her out into the bustling hotel courtyard.

"Wait," he said. He pushed the sack in her direction. "I brought these for you."

"Why?"

"Why?"

"Yes, why. Why do you bring me a present?"

"It's not a present. It's food."

"So why do you bring me food?"

"Because you look hungry. Are you?"

"Am I hungry?"

"Yes."

She considered the question. "I am always hungry."

"I heard on Rot-Weiss-Rot this morning that the bakeries have started making rolls and croissants again. Would you like to go get some fresh bread?"

She shook her head. "I think we have had enough excitement for today."

"How about I go get some for you?"

"Another day, perhaps. I am tired now."

"Of course," he said. Resilient as she seemed, she must tire easily. She had, after all, only just begun to recover from the hell of her life over the past months or years.

She put out her hand, and he shook it. Her palm was cool and dry, despite the heat of the day, but it felt swollen, the knuckles red, the nail of her right thumb cracked down the middle.

"Good-bye," she said.

"Wait," he said, keeping hold of her hand. "Is there anything you need? Can I help you with anything?"

She pondered this question for a moment. Then, instead of answering, she said, "You know my name, but I do not know yours."

"Wiseman Jack," Jack said.

She laughed. "You answer like a Hungarian."

"Yes."

"But you are not Hungarian. Your family, I mean."

"No. My mother's parents came from Russia, my father's great-grandparents from Germany."

"But Wiseman Jack, you are a Jew, no?"

"Yes," he said. "I am a Jew."

"So this is why you helped the Jewish man and his nephews."

"Yes. I mean, no. Anyone would have helped."

She laughed darkly. "You are a funny man."

"No, I'm not."

She sized him up with a single, raised brow. "Perhaps not. And yet you make jokes."

"I really don't."

"To say anyone would help is a joke. No one helps. No one ever helped."

"No. I guess not." He bit his lip. "Please."

"What?"

"Please. Is there anything I can do for you?"

"What is it you want to do?"

He stared, flummoxed. He had no idea.

She gave him a reprieve. "Thank you, Jack Wiseman. If ever I need anything, I will come to you."

· 4 ·

JACK SHARED HIS BILLET in an apartment house off the Hoftsallgasse with two other officers, Phillip Hoyle, a lieutenant fresh out of West Point, and another named David Ball, who did something in the OSS about which Jack was careful never to ask. Ball was from Philadelphia, a gawky man with beautiful hands and long, delicate fingers who planned after his service to disappoint his mother's dreams of his career as a concert pianist and instead go to medical school. Ball's brief was mysterious and his movements furtive, but part of his duties, Jack knew, included the pursuit and apprehension of former members of the local Nazi Party. One day about two weeks after the incident with Maria, Ball was sent to arrest the former mayor of a small village about twenty miles from Salzburg. The burgomaster's wife, tipped off to the Americans' arrival, had hung signs in English throughout her home that read WIPE YOUR FEET and NOT TO TOUCH.

"I wouldn't even have bothered with a search of the house," Ball said, "if it weren't for those damned signs."

It was beneath a floorboard in the kitchen that Ball's soldiers found the steel box that now lay on the rickety table in the kitchen of their billet.

"Jesus," said Hoyle. Neither Ball nor Jack liked Hoyle, though Jack's loathing was more pronounced, stemming as much from the fact that Hoyle had served in battle not a second longer than it took to earn a dubious Distinguished Service Cross before being pulled back to protect his valuable brass hide, as from the twenty-two-year-old West Pointer's greedy and craven nature.

"What are you going to do with it all?" Jack said.

It was a record, written in food, of the advance of Hitler's armies across Europe: tins of potted French foie gras, packets of Dutch chocolate, Spanish sardines canned in oil.

"Eat it, of course, you fucking idiot," Hoyle said. "Foie gras, Jesus Christ!" He took his knife from his pocket and picked up a can, but Ball lifted a restraining hand.

"No. It's evidence, Hoyle."

"Then what'd you bring it here for?"

"It was a moment of weakness. But seeing you salivating over it has brought me to my senses."

"If you take it back, some corporal in the evidence room is just going to boost it."

"True enough," Ball said, looking like he might be on the verge of another moment of weakness.

"I know what to do with it," Jack said.

"He's going to take it to that red Jewess of his," Hoyle said.

"I've seen the lady," Ball said. "She could stand to put a little meat on her bones."

Jack carried the strongbox down to the Hotel Europa, self-conscious at the value of his burden in a city undergoing ever-increasing food shortages. For weeks now, he had been bringing bread and C rations, cans of Spam, margarine, and other nutrient-dense items to Ilona and to the young man from Buchenwald, whose name was Rudolph Zweig. Jack sweetened his packages with chocolate and hard candies for Zweig's nephews, Josef and Tomas. Rudolph expressed his gratitude so fervently that he made Jack uncomfortable. His eyes were often wet with tears when he opened the boxes and bags, and once he tried to kiss Jack's hand. Ilona greeted his deliveries with reluctance and skepticism, even verging at times on an outright irritability ("You again?") that he found amusing and much easier to tolerate than Rudolph's damp hand-kissing.

Today, Jack poked his head through the open door of the room Ilona shared with half a dozen other women, on the third floor of the wing of the building opposite from the one where Zweig was now comfortably and safely ensconced, Maria and the other two Ukrainians having disappeared within days of Jack's first visit. Ilona was sitting on the edge of her cot while one of her roommates made up her face. The other woman wore a stained and baggy coverall. Her patchy hair was held back by a bright scrap of blue-dotted muslin, and her mouth was done up in the same garish maraschino red that she was now busy applying to Ilona's lips.

The woman scolded Ilona in Hungarian, rubbed away the smear she'd made when Ilona had smiled. Then she turned to the door to see what had inspired the grin. "Oh-ho."

"Hello," Ilona said to Jack.

Until that moment he had not noticed how she'd changed over the past couple of weeks. She had filled out. Her features had softened. And now two slashes of cherry red had transformed her abruptly from the object of his pity to a woman he might conceivably, indeed almost certainly, want to fuck. He thrust the box at her, tongue-tied, suddenly at a loss, no longer a benefactor with provisions but a suitor with a gift.

The box was so heavy that the makeup artist had to help Ilona ease it to the ground. She lifted the steel lid. All the women in the room craned forward to look.

"Foie gras!"

"Caviar!"

They cooed and sighed and exclaimed as Ilona pulled out tins and jars and packets. "My God, Jack," she said. "Are you trying to give us gout?"

He wondered if she was, in her own bitter and broken way, flirting with him.

"I like your lipstick," he said.

"It's Luba's," Ilona said. She switched to German. "Luba, this is Jack. Maybe if you harass his Hungarian POWs he'll bring you some sardines, too." Luba giggled.

"You'll never guess where Luba got the lipstick," Ilona said.

"Where?" he said.

"Bergen-Belsen!"

At the look on his face, all the girls in the room burst out laughing.

Luba said, "After we were liberated, the British Red Cross came to inspect. We had nothing. People were still dying every minute. I remember seeing once a woman with a scrap of soap, washing herself from a cistern in which floated the body of a dead child. But the Red Cross came, and then, a few days later, ten crates of lipstick arrived, no one knows how or where from. We have no food, no bandages, but lipstick we have. And my God, so much! Boxes, boxes, boxes. We were so happy. All of us wore it all the time. Woman squatting in the corner, emptying her bowels from dysentery, but her lips! Perfect red. My friend she dies holding her lipstick in her hand. Most important thing she owned."

Ilona said, "In the camp everyone is just a bald head, a scrap of cloth, a number. But"—she smacked her lips together—"you put lipstick on and you are a person. A human."

"You look beautiful," Jack said.

"Maybe not beautiful," Ilona said. "But I look a little more like myself."

"Come to dinner with me tonight," he said.

The women in the room clucked and cooed and made a great show of turning away to allow them a semblance of privacy.

"Is that an order?" she asked, and he still couldn't decide if she was flirting with him or not.

He took Ilona to a place called the Salzburger Café, one of the few restaurants in the city whose menu could be relied on to feature meat. The menu offered reassuring promises of *entrecôte de boeuf* and *lammkotelett*, but Jack had been in the area for four months without seeing a cow or a lamb, and it was his view that the remnants of the once-splendid German cavalry brigades, now roaming freely through fields and forests outside the city, nightly met their fate in the kitchen of the Salzburger. He debated keeping his theory to himself, but in the end he guessed that Ilona would see the bitter humor in it.

She laughed. "I hear rat is quite tender," she said. "When the horses are gone."

She pored over the menu as if it were the Sunday *Times,* reading the name of each item aloud, regardless of whether it was available. When the food came, she dispatched it with a terrible ardor. She licked sauce from the tines of her fork, from the flat of her knife.

"I have gained new respect for horses," she said. "Also for Austrian chefs."

Jack was less enamored of the dark fist of horseflesh sitting clenched and bloody on his plate. He found it gamy and tough, ribboned with strings of fat, so at a certain point he just laid his fork down and got his pleasure from watching her go at it. After she had cleaned her plate she belched and then covered her mouth with her hand. It was the first time he'd seen her blush. Then her eyes drifted toward his plate, and he saw hunger fight its way through the embarrassment. He passed it across the table toward her, and she cleaned that, too, sopping up the gravy with a piece of the white bread that had suddenly become available in the city, the bakers catering to the tastes of their American occupiers. When there was nothing edible left anywhere in the vicinity of their table, Ilona pushed back her chair, settled her hands on her belly, and smiled sleepily, looking, with her yellow-green eyes and red hair, like a contented ginger cat.

"You save any room for dessert?" he asked.

She blushed again. "Maybe a little. Do they have coffee?"

"They have something they call coffee. What it is, I don't know."

When the waiter had served their strudel and the watery brown liquid he insisted, despite all evidence to the contrary, on calling coffee, Ilona managed to slow down, lingering over the dessert.

"The Red Cross nurses who come to the DP camp keep saying be careful, be careful," Ilona said. "They say our digestions are not used to protein, to fat. And it's true; at first I got sick sometimes. But now?" she patted her belly. "My stomach is like the horse I just ate. Maybe I'll go home and eat your foie gras, too."

"My grandmother used to make strudel like this," Jack said. "Actually, I think it was her cook. But she used to say it was her grandmother's recipe."

"This is your German grandmother?"

"Yes. I mean, generations back. But they'd been in America so long they weren't really German. They were barely Jewish. They had a Christmas tree every year."

"My family is like your father's, I think. Only just a little bit Jewish. We celebrate every year Christmas. In America, there are many Jewish army officers?"

"Some," he said. "I wouldn't say many."

Jack had been one of only three Jews in his officer training course. Early on, the NCOs had targeted the Jewish officer candidates for special mistreatment, and their fellow OCs, relieved to find scapegoats for their misery, had eagerly joined in. Kleinbaum had washed out after only a few days of the abuse. Finkelman, a wiry little graduate of NYU law school, had responded to the attacks by growing steadily more belligerent. By the time he and Jack received their bars, Finkelman had been involved in at least a dozen scraps. He was saved from being shit-canned from the course only because his victims were too embarrassed to complain that a skinny, four-eyed, Jewboy shrimp had cleaned their clocks. Jack had never run from a fight, but he did not consider truculence to be a sustainable philosophical approach to life, and so he had chosen to survive officer training by keeping his mouth shut and his head down. He made no friends, but neither did he, unlike Finkelman, lose any teeth.

"And it's okay, life for a Jew in your army?" Ilona asked.

"It's fine," he told her, and indeed things had improved once he joined the Rainbow Division and found himself in the company of a fair number of Jewish enlisted men and even a couple of other Jewish officers.

Despite the ease with which many of his men and fellow officers tossed around words like "kike" and "sheeny," he would not have described them as anti-Semites. True, the running joke about "Abie and Sadie," who managed, despite rationing, to get tires for their car and sugar for their tea, depressed him, as did the fact that when conditions got particularly bad he frequently heard GIs complaining that the only reason they were being forced to endure the misery was because they were fighting Hitler for the sake of the Jews. But the men's antagonism was born of ignorance—Jack and the others in the division were the first Jews many of them had ever met. So he was generous with his forgiveness of them and stingy in his praise of the Jewish enlisted men. He was harder on the Jews in his command than on the Gentiles, holding them to a higher standard of comportment and conduct in a way that was, he supposed, a kind of secret favoritism, as though he believed in his heart that more could be expected of a Jew than of his Gentile brother-in-arms.

Ilona said, "Both my great-grandfather and my grandfather were officers in the Hungarian Honvédség; you know what this is?"

"No."

"The Hungarian unit of the Austro-Hungarian Army. They fought for the emperor. They both had the rank of *ezredes*. In German, *Oberst*."

" 'Colonel.' "

"Yes. My grandfather would be higher, even, than *ezredes*, but he died in the Great War. His regiment, the Twentieth Nagyvárad, was very brave. Many were killed. My mother said we must be glad he was dead because if he had lived to see his men turn on him, it would have broken his heart."

Jack considered posing the question that had been on his mind for so long, the question he both wanted and dreaded to ask.

Perhaps sensing the reason for his silence, perhaps following the unknowable trend of her own thoughts, Ilona said, "My mother is dead. Also my father."

"I'm sorry," Jack said.

"Why are you sorry? You didn't kill them."

"It wasn't an apology," he said. "Sometimes when you say you're sorry, it just means that you are sad."

She said, "Ah. Sad. Not sorry. It is my English. I didn't understand. So now I am sorry. But not sad. What's the word? Apologistic."

"Apologetic."

"Yes. Apologetic. I am apologetic."

"You don't need to be. Ilona . . . what . . . Will you tell me what happened to your parents? To your family?"

She shrugged. "The usual. Ghetto, train, Auschwitz, selection."

Her large extended family had remained together as long as they could, she told him, all the way to the ramp at Auschwitz, but only she and her older sister, Etelka, had been directed to step to the right. By the time the two girls had been processed into the camp, the rest of her family, her parents, her aunts and uncles, a passel of cousins, her grandmother, every last Jakab of Nagyvárad, had been transformed into the grease and smoke that coated the inside of Ilona's and Etelka's nostrils and settled in a dingy film on their skin.

The girls were sent from Auschwitz first to Dachau and then to one of the Kaufering satellite camps in Landsberg. They had clung to each other until only a few weeks before the war's end, when Etelka had been taken from the morning count without warning. It was only days later that Ilona found out that her sister had been moved to a different satellite camp, near Obermeitingen, and not, as Ilona had feared, sent to the gas.

"I have been looking for Etelka since liberation," Ilona said. "Everyone that was there in Obermeitingen, I ask them."

Jack didn't ask the question, but she answered it anyway.

"I know she's alive. Etelka was an athlete. Before the war, she was a champion fencer. Then came the anti-Jewish laws, and she could no longer compete, but she still trained at home with our uncle Samu. She only stopped when we went to the ghetto. She's so strong! There was a time in the munitions factory when our job was to unload iron beams from a train and carry them two hundred meters up a hill to the smelter. She always took the rear, where the load was heaviest, because she was so much stronger than I. Also, she was a medical student before the war, and in the camps she was like a doctor to so many people. Even sometimes the *Kapos* came to her if they were hurt. When she helped them, they would give her food. If I can survive, so can Etelka."

"How will you find her?"

"We had agreed, if we were ever separated, we would meet in Salzburg."

"Why here?"

"We used to come here many times as children on our way to Bad Gastein, where my father liked to take the waters."

In her smile, Jack saw flickering to life the city as it was before the war, as he had never seen it. Whimsical alleyways and squares where there were now rubble-strewn paths. The elegant wrecks in front of the Müllner church brought back to life, buildings reconstructed behind what were now mere façades. The listing balconies righted on the Grecian reliefs that held them up, the statues' heads restored. Gone in her smile were the orderly piles of rubble, boulders separated from blocks, flat pieces of stone stacked up by size like planks fresh from the sawmill. Gone were the bundles of wire like tumbleweeds or balls of hair hanging on telephone poles beside ruined buildings. And the richly costumed people, the men coming in from their fields in their lederhosen and jaunty feathered caps bedecked with whisk brooms, the dirndled women wrapped in embroidered aprons, not wooden-faced folk enacting an insincere pastiche of history, a parody of tradition, but pleasant, simple, generous people. He saw in Ilona's smile a Salzburg that was not merely a picturesque corpse but a pretty, vibrant place, full of music and joy.

She said, "We even met here our English governess."

"You had an English governess?"

"You think all Hungarian girls speak such good English? Miss Richards was with us six years as a governess, then she married my uncle and became our auntie Firenze. She would have gone with us even to the ghetto, but my father forbade it. When I find Etelka, we will go home to Auntie Firenze in Nagyvárad."

The waiter came by again, obviously eager for them to release the table to one of the other young couples who waited impatiently to be seated. They were everywhere in Salzburg, American soldiers and their Austrian girlfriends, cheerfully violating the rules against fraternization and providing steady business to the city's newly opened cafés and bars.

"Well," Ilona asked, neatly folding her napkin, "shall we walk?"

"Would that be all right for you?" he said, recalling her limp. "Would you prefer to take the streetcar?"

"I like to walk. Especially after a meal where I have eaten everything but the tablecloth and the flowers in the vase."

"I saw you eyeing the flowers," he said. "Frankly I was a little worried for them."

She laughed and took his arm. They meandered along the east bank of the Salzach, until they rounded a corner at Mozartsteg and came face-to-face with Lieutenant Hoyle, Jack's roommate. Hoyle had his arm slung around the waist of a girl, young, giggly, no more than fourteen or fifteen years old. Her lips were painted with an inexpert wobble of clown red that reminded Jack uncomfortably of Ilona's lipstick. She staggered along on a pair of high-heel sandals at least a size too big, as if she'd borrowed them from an older sister or even her mother, a little girl playing dress-up as a cheap whore.

When they saw each other, the two men stopped, each taking careful inventory of the other's date, drawing all the likeliest conclusions.

"So," Hoyle said. "Looks like we got a couple of out-and-out fraternizers here, eh, Wiseman? Couple of flagrant violators of the rules."

Hoyle was right; by the book, a dinner date with an of-age DP was the same as raping an Austrian child.

"Looks that way," Jack said.

"Good thing there's a loophole."

"Is there?"

"Yes, brother, there is." He gestured for Jack to lean closer and whispered loudly so that the girls would easily be able to hear. Jack smelled booze on his breath. "Technically, now, it ain't fraternizing, if you don't talk while you fuck 'em."

Ilona gasped.

"You can go to hell, Hoyle," Jack said, grabbing Ilona's hand and pulling her around the other couple and down the street.

"Pig," he said once they'd left the other two behind. "Ilona, I'm so sorry."

Ilona said, "You are always so sorry, Jack. This also is not your fault."

"I know. I just . . ."

"You don't want me to feel like a Chocolate Girl?"

"No! Of course not."

"But why not? Some of those girls, they support their whole families with gifts from their GIs. You know the price of American cigarettes on the black market? So high! And that meat you give me in the can?"

"Spam?"

She laughed. "Spam. Ridiculous. We eat for three days from what I get for this Spam of yours. You gave me a beautiful meal tonight, Jack. And lovely company. And we will do this again, yes? Not just because I want another meal but because you like me, right?"

"Yes. I like you."

"Okay. I like you, too. You may kiss me if you want."

He stopped and turned to face her. She was tiny; her head would fit snugly beneath his chin. He bent over as she lifted her face, and he brushed his mouth against hers. The lipstick had all but rubbed away, and her lips felt hot, chapped. When she didn't resist, he flicked his tongue between them. Though she didn't return the kiss, she allowed it, and he moved closer, pressing her body against his. His cock got hard and to spare her its importunements he kept his hips shifted back and to the side. He was not like Hoyle, he told himself. This was different. Finally she put her hands on his chest and pushed him gently away.

"Okay," she said. "Enough."

"I'm sorry."

"Stop apologizing!"

He started to apologize for that, too, but caught himself just in time.

"I like you very much, Ilona. Not only because you're beautiful, but—"

"Shh," she said, squeezing his arm. "You don't know, Jack. I am not good for you."

"Of course you are!"

She seemed to consider saying more but thought the better of it. They walked for a while in silence. Finally, she spoke. "It is a beautiful night, and we had a lovely meal. And a sweet kiss. That's enough, don't you think? For now."

For now, he thought as he walked back to his billet. For now.

· 5 ·

IN THE HARDT FOREST, Jack had taken a 7.92 x 57 mm Mauser round to the shoulder, a clean shot through the deltoid that missed bone and arteries and left two neat holes. The wound had obliged him to spend only three days away from his unit and on his return had given him little pain or trouble, through bad weather and hard fighting. He had remained on equable terms with the holes in his shoulder, in fact, until now. Captain Rigsdale had turned responsibility for the Werfen train over to the Property Control Branch of the Reparations, Deliveries, and Restitution Division and, with it, Jack himself. Though he'd protested, petitioning to be returned to his unit, the army had decided to leave Jack there, in charge of the contents of the train. Jack's latest CO, Lieutenant Colonel Clancy K. Price, had ordered him to complete a preliminary inventory and reorganize the property. The unloading and cataloging of the contents of the train required that Jack spend ten hours a day hunched on a stool over a desk fashioned from a door and two sawhorses. Pain radiated from his shoulder to his neck. It forked like lightning down to the small of his back. He needed a goddamn chair.

He went by the book, through the usual channels. He approached the Rainbow Division support battalion, and when he was told they couldn't help him, he turned to the Quartermaster Corps and from there to the engineers. It seemed to be the case that there was not a serviceable desk chair in the entire Occupied Zone. Any chair that had survived the winter without being chopped into firewood had long since been looted or commandeered by the U.S. Army Air Corps, whose postwar mission appeared to require a remarkable amount of sitting. In the meantime Jack reported every day to the warehouse and set his back on fire.

Under his organization plan, all furniture recovered from the train was stored in section C of the warehouse, at the back, between furs and household goods. There were two hundred sixteen chairs in section C. Jack had counted every one.

He considered a fancy ball-and-claw mahogany side chair with a torn pink silk cushion, a leather-and-aluminum wheeled desk chair that he discovered the hard way had a sprung spring aimed at the center of his left buttock, a high-backed oak office chair that seemed too regal for the task, before settling at last on what he took for a plain kitchen chair, with black lacquer paint that would resist scratches and eighteen holes punched in the back, for ventilation, he supposed. It did not promise or indeed provide any padding or back support; it was plain, the simplest chair he could find. He figured it for the cheapest, though years later he would see the chair's twin in a museum exhibit of the works of Josef Hoffmann, the noted furniture designer of the Vienna Secession, and realize that he couldn't have chosen a more valuable chair if he'd tried.

Jack sat a moment in the straight-backed chair, trying to decide whether the relief that sitting afforded exceeded the trouble it gave to his conscience. He was no saint. Like all the soldiers in the victorious armies—in victorious armies since the dawn of war—Jack had done his own share of souveniring. Rolled in a couple of towels in his duffel, back in his billet, were two Lugers, one of them engraved with an elaborate oak-leaf design. On the windowsill next to his bed stood an eight-inch-high marble bust, "liberated" from the home of a minor Nazi Party official in Anzenbach near Berchtesgaden, of Tacitus, whose *Dialogus de Oratoribus* had been the subject of Jack's undergraduate thesis at Columbia. Taking the guns and the bust of Tacitus had caused him only minor pangs, but this was different. He took his responsibility as official custodian of the contents of the Werfen train seriously, and that was part of what troubled him as he carried the black lacquered chair out to his makeshift desk in the front office, sat down, and felt his shoulders unknotting. But mostly what troubled him was the thought of the murdered Hungarian Jew whose kitchen chair might be the only remaining trace of his ever having existed.

"I'm sorry," he said to the ghost that haunted the chair. "But my back is killing me."

"Even when you are alone, you apologize."

Jack leaped to his feet, his cheeks burning, as if caught in the midst of committing a bestial and unforgivable act.

"You're here," he said, gratuitously.

"Am I not permitted?"

"No. I mean, yes. Well . . . actually, no, you aren't supposed to be here, but it's fine. It doesn't matter. Nobody in this place gives a damn but me."

"I think that may be true," Ilona said, with what might have been tenderness or pity.

He came around from behind the desk and took her hands in his.

"I'm glad to see you," he said. "Come on in. I can probably manage a cup of tea."

"Tea would be nice."

She looked around her for a place to sit, and Jack quickly steered her outside to where his men had set up a tiny field kitchen with a Coleman pocket stove and a cache of tea bags, powdered coffee, and milk. He pulled an overturned bucket up to the stove, cleaned it of dust, and offered it to her. Private Willie Streeter, a sweet-tempered New Yorker who was Jack's favorite by far of the men under his command, offered to prepare the tea, but Jack insisted on doing it himself. When the water had boiled, he put a tea bag and a dollop of sweetened condensed milk into a metal mug and handed it to Ilona.

"Thank you," she said. "It was so crowded in the Europa, I couldn't be there no more."

"Anymore."

"Anymore. I thought I would come to meet you here, instead of waiting for you to pick me up. I hope it's all right."

They had a date; they were—though it was a New York verb, an activity too dumb and innocent and tinged with swing music to apply to anything Ilona Jakab could or would ever consent to engage in—dating. David Ball had gotten them tickets to the first night's performance of the reopened Salzburg Festival. Neither Jack nor Ilona took much interest in Mozart, but it was a tough ticket to get. Only a very few Salzburgers would be in attendance, and no DPs at all, beyond the musicians drafted to replace those subject to the denazification laws.

"It's fine," Jack said. "I'm glad you came. I know you've been curious about this place."

"Curious," she said, quoting him back to himself, not quite ready to agree to the description. Given all that she had been through, it did not surprise him in the least that she chose to maintain or simply could not help feeling a distance between them, a gap of experience that no amount of physical closeness, intimate talk, or mutual affection could bridge. But he was and remained surprised to find that she should most often manifest this distance in the form of irony, teasing, a tinge of mockery in all her replies. She carried the cup of tea back inside the arcing shadows of the warehouse. He followed.

"Curiouser and curiouser," she said. But her eyes as she took in the stacked boxes, crates, and pallets were not detached or ironic. They were huge in the darkness, avid and sad. "Everything is from the one train, the day I met you?"

"Almost everything," he said.

"Silverware."

"Lot of that."

"Jewelry?"

"Yes."

"Paintings, statues."

"Some."

"What else?"

"All kinds of personal property. Furs. Housewares. Gold."

"Furniture?"

He felt her guessing, blindly, at the shame in his heart.

"Every kind of thing somebody might want to take or hold on to," he said.

"It's like a treasure train."

"I guess you might say that," he said. Apart from the relatively small quantity of gold bullion and gems handed over by Avar, there did not appear to be all that many items of great value on the train—no Leonardos, no trunks spilling over with diamonds—but the sheer quantity of the loot was overwhelming, and in the aggregate its value must be considerable. A single gold-filled watch was perhaps not worth more than fifty or sixty dollars, but if you multiplied that watch by a thousand or ten thousand?

"And it all came from Hungary?"

"The man who turned the train over to us was a Hungarian named László Avar. He told us that he worked for the Jewish Property Office."

"The Jewish Property Office," she repeated, and this time there was no hint of mockery or teasing. She murmured a few words in Hungarian, then said, "Yes. I know them."

"What I don't understand," he said, "is how this stuff came to be on this train in the first place. Avar said his Jewish Property Office got it from the Hungarian banks. But how did the banks get it?" He regretted the question as he uttered it. He could never decide if beneath Ilona's apparent fragility lay a fundamental strength or if the opposite was true. Maybe she only appeared strong but would shatter with the wrong word.

"They took it. Everything we had, they made us turn in to the bank.

First was telephones. I even remember the day. March twenty-seventh, 1944. I know because it was Etelka's birthday. As a present to her, the government passed a law saying Jews were not to own or use telephones. How do you think we found out about the law?"

"How?"

She gave a bitter laugh. "On the telephone, of course. My uncle Oskar rang us with the news."

She said that her father had not wanted to spoil Etelka's birthday celebration, so he had waited until the following day to go to the bank and turn in the telephone.

"He waited in the queue all day. Who knew there were so many Jewish telephones in the city of Nagyvárad?"

Within a couple of weeks the Jews of Hungary were ordered to purchase an official form on which they were to declare all possessions whose worth was in excess of 10,000 pengő, and then turn all of it over to the banks that had collected their telephones.

"One day it was bicycles. Then radios. Then gold. Even my parents' wedding rings. My father was a grain dealer. All around Nagyvárad there are farms. Wheat, everywhere wheat. My father would buy wheat from the farmers, sell it all over Europe. His warehouse was far too big for him to carry down to the local branch of the Royal Hungarian Postal Savings Bank. So they were kind enough to come one day and collect his keys. You know, before they confiscated his business, he sold wheat to the army, even to the Germans, right up until 1944. The SS who killed my father, maybe after they went back to the barracks and for dinner, they ate bread made from his wheat. How funny it all is, Jack, isn't it?"

"Ilona—"

"Every day they took something different, and every day we waited in queues. All of us waiting so patiently to give up our possessions to the bank."

Ilona walked down one of the aisles that Jack had created out of the pallets and crates. She knelt down beside a small stack of empty suitcases on which the owners' names were chalked in large clear letters.

"They told us, put everything in packages and envelopes, write your name on everything. They gave us receipts with lists of what we turned in. My father kept these receipts in his billfold. He was terrified that if he lost the receipts, when the war was over he would not be able to put in a claim. He carried those papers all the way to Auschwitz, to the gas."

Jack caught himself just before he could tell her how sorry he was.

"What will your army do with all these things?" she asked.

"They'll return them, eventually."

"Return them," she said, and now the mocking tone was back again. "I wish them luck."

In fact Jack had often wondered how the owner of any specific item in the vast store would ever be identified. His soldiers brought him anything they found with writing on it that might indicate to whom the objects belonged, but aside from the documents initially handed over by László Avar, there was little to connect most of the items with the people from whom they had been taken. More often Jack and his men found references to cities, a stack of empty silver picture frames stamped with the name and address of the silversmith, or labels in the collars of fur coats embroidered with the names of shops or dealers. Even if there were survivors who came looking for their belongings, Jack worried about how anyone would ever find, for example, a specific set of silver Shabbos candlesticks among the tens of thousands that had filled the train. Which of the thousands of gold watches belonged to a father, which lynx coat from among the thousands belonged to a mother, which album of those filling the sixteen huge crates of stamp albums belonged to a son? How would anyone ever know?

The door of the warehouse burst open with a bang, and in stormed Lieutenant Colonel Price.

Resisting the urge to shove Ilona behind a shelf, Jack instead took her arm and led her up to the front of the warehouse.

"Colonel," he said, steeling himself to face the music.

The colonel's tie was askew, his face purpled with agitation. He was clutching a sheet of paper and thrust it toward Jack. "As if we weren't already up to our necks in bullshit!" he said. "Now I've got this to deal with." He noticed Ilona and snatched back the paper.

"Lieutenant Wiseman," he said. "There's a civilian in the warehouse."

"Yes, sir."

"A female."

Jack stood, paralyzed, trying desperately to come up with an excuse, any excuse to justify his flagrant violation of the rules, the one against fraternization, the one against allowing a civilian in the warehouse, the entire scaffolding of military regulations, mandates, and injunctions that he was violating every time he held Ilona's hand. It was not that he was afraid but rather that he hated the idea of exhibiting such a failure of control to his superior officer. But he could think of nothing.

Price stared at Ilona, who gazed back, a glint in her eye.

"This warehouse is off-limits to unauthorized personnel!" Price said.

"This is what your lieutenant here keeps telling me," she said. "He has refused to allow me, a representative of the Hungarian Displaced Persons Property Reclamation Authority, access! I wish to make a formal complaint."

Price looked confused. "A complaint?"

"Yes! I demand access on behalf of the HDPRPA."

HDPPRA, Jack thought, though thankfully Price didn't notice the jumbled acronym. Jack could not help but stare admiringly at his girl. He never would have expected her to be such an accomplished liar.

Price blustered, "This is a U.S. Army facility, miss! You can't demand anything here."

"You and your subordinate will be hearing from the governing board of the HRDRPPA," she said, and flounced out the door of the warehouse.

"Jesus Christ," Price said. "That's all we need right now." He handed Jack the paper.

The document was entitled "Requisition Memorandum" and read:

1. The Commanding General directs that you give first priority to obtaining without delay the following listed household furnishing:

    a. Chinaware (all types necessary for formal banquet and other meals). Sufficient for 45 people.

    b. Silverware (same qualifications as above and to include serving forks and spoons). Sufficient for 45 people.

    c. Glassware (to include water glasses, highball glasses, cocktail glasses, wine and champagne glasses, and liqueur glasses). Sufficient for a formal banquet involving several kinds of wine for 90 people.

    d. Thirty (30) sets of table linens, each set to consist of 1 tablecloth and 12 napkins.

    e. Sixty (60) sheets, sixty (60) pillowcases, and sixty (60) large bath towels.

2. The General desires that all of the above listed items be of the very best quality and workmanship available in Land Salzburg.

"What does he think this is?" Price said. "Wanamaker's?"

Jack was not used to having senior officers commiserate with him over the arbitrary demands of their superiors, and for a moment he enjoyed the unexpected camaraderie.

"Goddamn it," Price said. "We'd better make sure he gets all this crap today."

"I'm sorry, sir," Jack said. "I don't understand. How do you want me to fill this requisition order?"

"What do you mean 'how'?"

"Where am I supposed to find all this stuff?"

"Lieutenant, are you dense? Fill the requisition order from the warehouse."

"Respectfully, sir. The only items like this in the warehouse belong to the Werfen train."

"You think I don't know that? You think I didn't tell that to the son of a bitch who handed me this memo? Just fill the order, Wiseman."

Jack glanced over at the chair he'd just appropriated and cringed. He steeled himself and said, "The property on the train isn't enemy property. It didn't belong to the Hungarian government officials who turned it over to us. They stole it."

"Lieutenant, however they got it, there's no question that what we've got here are enemy assets, and if our commanding general wants to borrow them to furnish his billet, if he wants to turn us into a team of glorified shop clerks running around filling his orders, there's fuck all we can do about it."

"It's Jewish property, sir. The Hungarians stole it from the Jews. We can't just give it away. They'll want it back, sir." He thought of Ilona's father, going to his death clutching a sheaf of irrelevant documentation. "They have receipts."

"Who has receipts? The commander of the train?"

"Not Avar. The Hungarian Jews, Colonel. When the Hungarian government made them turn over their property, it gave them all receipts."

"How do you know that, Lieutenant? How are you such an expert on the practices and policies of the Hungarian government?"

Because I've been fraternizing. Because that beautiful young woman you just chased out of here is a Hungarian Jew, and her parents' wedding rings might be lost among the other hundred thousand gold bands filling the crates and boxes stacked floor to ceiling in this miserable warehouse.

"Research, sir."

"Lieutenant, this is the army, not debate club. You'll get these items together and escort them personally to General Collins's house, and you'll do it today. Is that clear?"

Price left with the same aggravated bustle in which he'd arrived. When the senior officer was gone, Jack went to his desk, grabbed the chair, and strode back into the warehouse to the aisle full of furniture. He heaved the chair on top of a huge pile of crates and then returned to his desk to find that Private Streeter had already put his hard stool in its place. Without a word, he sat down, his back flickering with pain, and began going over the list.

The silver was easy; there were any number of sets in their original cases. He pulled three: two plain sets, without engraving or scrollwork, and one that came in an intricately carved wooden box decorated with a coat of arms and the Latin motto GRANDESCUNT AUCTA LABORE. Jack sketched the design in the left margin of the account book in which he had decided to record in accurate detail every item loaned by the murdered Jews of Hungary to General Harry Collins. Someday the industrious heirs to this grand coat of arms might come looking for their fish forks, and God help him but it eased Jack's conscience to think that his care and precision might help them track their property down.

He had more difficulty with the china requisition. Finding a matching service for forty-five was impossible. Surely only the fabulously wealthy would need to serve that many people at one time. He tried to cobble together a single set from four or five others, but who knew there were so many different china patterns in the world? This one with blue flowers, that one with pink, this one with Chinese gazebos and dancing girls. In the end Private Streeter took upon himself the task of finding two or three sets of dishes that would, as he said, "complement" one another even if they did not match.

Jack sat with the glassware, noting each Ajka crystal goblet, each cut-glass decanter. Then he moved on to the linens. He easily found the desired table and bed linens, but spent an hour in a grim, jaw-clenched silence, combing through boxes of textiles, trying to find the set of sixty capacious bath towels the general required to wrap his colossal behind.

Private Streeter finished wrapping the china he'd chosen and joined Jack in pulling various cloths from the chests. The private opened up a length of stiff, shiny cotton and smoothed it across his lap. "You know, sir, maybe nobody packed towels."

Jack could not help but imagine Ilona's family packing up their linens to deposit at the bank and choosing, for whatever reason, not to include the towels. Perhaps they couldn't bear to part with them. Or perhaps the Jewish Property Office had simply forgotten to include towels on the list of items to be relinquished.

Streeter continued, "Or maybe towels are just different in Europe. Maybe they don't look like towels do at home. Maybe they don't have terry cloth over here."

Jack paused to consider this. The farmhouses he'd passed through in the French countryside had often not even had bathrooms, let alone towels. But as they pushed their way through Germany, they'd passed many nights in ordinary middle-class homes that were at once familiar and strange. The furnishings were not unlike those of his own parents, but the houses were full of goods that no one in America ever bothered with. The feather beds, for example. Even the poorest of German farmers' wives slept on a feather bed and beneath a down-stuffed quilt that put Jack's mother's pricey innerspring mattresses and Hudson Bay blankets to shame. What joyless Puritan impulse had convinced his great-grandparents, emigrating from Germany, to leave this luxury behind? Why hadn't he grown up cosseted by goose feathers?

But had there been towels in those German houses? He couldn't remember.

"Maybe this is a towel," Streeter said, holding up a length of white fabric edged in rickrack.

Jack assessed the cloth. It was smooth and stiff and hardly seemed designed to absorb water. And it was too pretty to be used to dry a man's ass, even a general's. But then the monogrammed sheets with their intricately embroidered borders seemed far too fine to sleep on.

How had he ended up here, kneeling in a sea of white linen, plundering booty stolen from Jews just like Ilona? He felt as though the train had been loaded with the limitless property of the Jakab family, as if the crystal and the dishes and these towels, if that was what they were, had been stolen from Ilona herself.

"Screw it," Jack said. He massaged his temples where a headache had begun to pulse beneath his skull. "We'll say they're European towels. The general's from Chicago. What the hell does he know?"

Lieutenant Colonel Price had ordered Jack to make the delivery himself, and so he did, despite his headache. He chewed up a handful of aspirin, ignoring the bitter taste, and threw the bottle into the glove compartment of the truck.

Hollywood Harry, as the general was known to those who were less loyal and admiring than the men of the Forty-Second, had taken as his billet the former home of an Austrian nobleman, an early adherent of the Nazi Party. Thanks to the intercession of the archbishop of Bavaria, a Nazi sympathizer who had wormed his way into the good graces of Patton's military government in Munich, the baron had escaped trial, though he'd lost his home to the American occupation forces. Before surrendering his house, the baron had been careful to strip the place bare. He took with him into his exile in his protector's Bavarian villa every stick of furniture, every dish and spoon, every painting, every wall mirror. He had his servants tear the curtains from the windows and rip up the carpets from the floors. He pried paneling from the walls of the many receiving rooms and even removed a number of the floorboards in the servants' quarters. This last was mysterious to the Americans on their arrival at the palace. Some posited that the baron had simply taken the floorboards to burn as firewood in his new accommodations, although as he had also ordered that the house's woodbins be cleaned out, one could assume he already had a fair stock of that.

General Collins's staff had been beating the Austrian bushes to furnish their boss's deplumed estate, and the arrival of the Hungarian train struck many of them—not excepting the general himself—as providential. The cook and the other household servants, abandoned by the baron to face the fate that his furniture and bibelots were spared, set to work at once, unpacking the crates as fast as Jack and his men could carry them in, spreading out the loot on a massive Biedermeier dining table that had been too big for the baron to self-pillage.

One of the silver services was Austrian, from the late eighteenth century, and as the cook opened its ornamented case, she whistled through her teeth. "Lovely!" she said. Then she held up a fish server and turned it over in her hands, frowning at it in a way that might have been critical or maybe just puzzled.

"What is it?" Jack said. "Is there a problem?"

"It's lovely," the cook said. "But see below the coronet? It is engraved with an *H*. Not a *C* for 'Herr General Collins.' The guests of Herr General will be confused."

Jack considered explaining to her the true provenance of the silver, suggesting as well the likely fate of the Hymans or Hirschorns or Herzfelds, but he knew what her response would be. Bewilderment. Perhaps sympathy. And most definitely defensiveness. She would have seen nothing, have heard nothing, have known nothing about the fate of the Jews. None of the Austrians would admit to having known anything. If pressed, they might acknowledge that they understood the Jews to have been deported, resettled in the East. They themselves had disapproved of this, they would assure their American interrogators. They had personally been on good terms with any number of Jews, but then what could a mere citizen do? Even to express opposition to the Nazi regime had meant denunciation, imprisonment, death. In this regard the Austrians only echoed their German cousins, but somehow it bothered Jack more. Austrians were always so eager to remind Americans that they had been Hitler's first victims, so reluctant to recall the way they had welcomed their invaders with roses and confetti.

Jack said, "You can just tell them that *H* is for 'Herr General.'"

"Ha!" A raucous voice rang out across the high, vaulted ceiling of the room. "Very clever, soldier."

General Harry Collins was all jaw, with a deep cleft chin and a smile that, though thin-lipped, was amiable and approachable. He never bothered to affect the smoldering scowl, borrowed from Patton, that was almost universal among the brass in the ETO.

Jack stood at attention, permitting himself to give no outward sign of how furious it made him to watch Herr General make a slow, appraising circuit of the table, taking stock of the loot.

"Very nice," Collins said. He picked up a crystal wineglass and held it to the light coming in through the French windows. He set it back down on the table, licked the tip of his right index finger, then whirled it slowly around the rim until it keened. He looked up and down the length of the table and frowned. "No champagne glasses?"

"Yes, sir," Jack said. "Ninety champagne glasses, as instructed."

"Where are they?"

"They are here!" the cook said triumphantly, pulling a champagne glass out of a crate, trailing a shower of excelsior. She took a corner of her apron and polished the glass, but her beefy arms and plate-sized hands were better suited to boning a haunch of beef or beating a glossy meringue, and under the pressure of her fingers the crystal shattered.

"*Gottverdammt!*" she muttered.

"That's no problem, sir," Jack said. "I will send someone over with a replacement, pronto."

It seemed to him that his voice soured as he said it, and he hoped that the general would not hear or otherwise sense his disapproval of the expropriation of the train and its contents. Indeed Collins turned, his eyes narrowing as he looked Jack over with the same amiable avidity he had brought to his inspection of the looted silver, linen, and china. He pointed to the Rainbow insignia on Jack's uniform.

"You're one of mine. What's your name?"

"Wiseman, sir. Lieutenant Jack Wiseman, Two Hundred Twenty-Second, sir."

"Wiseman. Wiseman. What company?"

"H Company, sir."

"H Company. Wiseman, yes, Lieutenant, I've heard about you. Mickey Fellenz once told me he could drop H Company blindfolded and ass over elbows in the middle of the Sahara, and a week later you'd have them back at Camp Gruber without a grain of sand in their undershorts."

"Thank you, sir," Jack said, feeling the flush of blood in his cheeks, and just like that he felt his outrage slipping away. Was this all it took to make him forget Ilona's father, the receipt for his stolen business burned to ash in the ovens of Auschwitz? A compliment from his commander? A word of praise, the fact that the general knew who he was, even remembered his name? Was this enough to make him forget the responsibility he'd assumed over the contents of the train, the responsibility he felt toward the vanished owners of the property? Apparently so.

"Wiseman," the general repeated. "Son, would you by any chance be of the Jewish persuasion?"

Jack stiffened. "Yes, sir, as a matter of fact I am."

"Well, that's just swell. Terrific!"

"Sir?"

"Come on into my study, son. There's someone I'd like you to meet."

Jack followed the general into a spacious room lined with empty bookshelves that had been spared the ministrations of the baron's zealous crowbar. The room was otherwise, typically, bereft of furniture but for two matched leather armchairs, from one of which rose Rabbi Eli Bohnen, one of the Rainbow Division's chaplains.

General Collins said, "Rabbi, I believe this young man's one of yours."

Jack knew Bohnen though he had never sought the man's counsel or ministry. Jack was such a confirmed unbeliever that at first he had not even bothered to have himself listed as "Hebrew" in the army rolls, changing his mind only because the lack of designation subjected him to constant importuning by the chaplains of various evangelical Christian denominations, who were desperate to save his soul before he lost his life on the battlefield. But Bohnen made it his business to get to know every Jew in the unit, no matter how disaffected or irreligious, and so he and Jack had spoken a few times. He was a thoughtful man, friendly without being pushy, with a trace of Toronto in his accent. No matter Jack's lack of interest in the practice of his putative religion, he could not help but like the rabbi.

"Indeed he is," Bohnen said. He had long ears and a firm chin, a small mouth that broke into a ready, easy smile. "Lieutenant Wiseman, how've you been?"

"Can't complain, Major."

Collins said, "The rabbi here's been filling me in on the situation in the DP camps. It's a terrible thing, Wiseman. A cruel thing."

"Yes, sir," Jack said.

"And more of the poor bastards coming west every day."

"Yes, sir."

"You were there with us at Dachau, weren't you, Jack?" Bohnen said.

"Yes, sir."

"All those emaciated, diseased, beaten, miserable shadows of human beings. I still have nightmares about it."

"Yes, sir," Jack said. He refused to allow his mind to wander back to the things he had seen when his unit had been among the first to liberate the camp.

"Our brothers, Jack. Our poor broken brothers. I tell you, when I saw that place I felt like apologizing to my dog for being a member of the human race."

Jack's throat closed around his words, and he could only nod.

Bohnen said, "There's nothing left for the survivors of the camps. Their families are dead. They've lost everything. They don't belong in Poland and Romania anymore. And the one place they do belong won't have them."

Confused, Jack said, "Where's that, sir?"

"Why, Palestine, Lieutenant," Bohnen said, looking mildly offended. "Of course. Eretz Yisrael."

"Ah," Jack said. "Sure."

"The British won't let them immigrate to Palestine. Not legally, at any rate. So they come here, looking for our protection."

"It's a tragedy, is what it is," General Collins said. "A tragedy on top of tragedies."

Rabbi Bohnen said, "A righteous man can do only one thing in the face of such compounded tragedies."

Again, though he could see that Bohnen expected him to be following right along, Jack was clueless as to what the rabbi had in mind. It did not seem to him that, faced with the horror of Dachau, the shame and squalor of the DP camps, a righteous man would know his ass from his elbow. But he did not say as much. Instead he just tried to look politely patient, waiting for Bohnen to let him off the hook.

"Lend a hand, however he can," Bohnen said.

Jack agreed that this was indeed incumbent on all righteous men. He wondered if evicting an old Ukrainian bat from her apartment and smuggling Spam and powdered lemon drink to Ilona and the Zweigs counted as lending a hand.

The general said, "Shouldn't you be in Vienna, Wiseman? With the rest of the Two Hundred Twenty-Second?"

"I've been reassigned, sir. To the PCB of the RD and R."

"You due to rotate home soon, Lieutenant?"

"No, sir."

"Not enough points?"

"Not yet, sir."

Collins said, "Given any thought to signing on for another six months?"

"I'm considering it, sir." Jack had, in fact—much to his surprise—given it some thought. For more than a year, his every waking moment not devoted to keeping himself and his men alive had been spent contemplating his return to New York, but now suddenly, at the ass end of it all, he was starting to dread the thought of leaving. He had stopped throwing away the memoranda encouraging him to extend the period of his service, though he'd yet to reach a final decision about signing on for another hitch. That decision, he had come to understand, was not in his hands at all, but, like his heart, was in the hands of Ilona Jakab.

"You bet I have, sir," he said.

"That's encouraging news, son," the general said. "We need every one of you old-timers. Men who know what we're doing here, what we fought for. Too many of these young replacements have a hard time remembering who the enemy was, do you find that, son? Among your men? Do you find that they're so green they can't tell friend from foe?"

Jack was so thrilled to have the general express this, Jack's own worst frustration, that he could not keep himself from nodding in vigorous agreement. "I try to make sure they know the difference, sir."

"Good for you. You're a fine officer, Lieutenant Wiseman. I'm proud that you're a Rainbow."

"I'm proud to be a Rainbow, sir." Jack knew that the distinctions between divisions were meaningless, that he would have developed the same camaraderie under fire if he'd been in the 101st Airborne or the 119th Infantry. He had known from the beginning that it was to his men that he both owed and felt loyalty, and to his fellow junior officers. Not to the brass, and not to a division, an accident of classification. Nonetheless, in his chest expanded a bubble of pride and pleasure. As idiotic as it was, he felt at that moment proud to wear the rainbow on his sleeve, proud to serve under Major General Harry Collins, proud to be recognized and valued.

"The war may be over," the general said, "but I'm afraid we're in this for the long haul, and it's men like you that we'll be relying on to get us through."

"Thank you, sir."

The general dismissed him, and as Jack turned crisply on his heel, Rabbi Bohnen said, "Let me walk you out, Lieutenant Wiseman."

As they passed through the gracious entryway, Jack glanced at the dining room, where the cook and her assistants were still exclaiming over the bounty he'd brought. Their exuberance caught him up for a moment, and he hesitated, reminded once again of the shameful errand on which he'd come.

When they reached his truck, the rabbi put a restraining hand on his arm.

"Jack," he said. "What I said inside about lending a hand. I wonder. If your hand was needed, would you lend it?"

"Sir?"

"If I were to call on you someday to help our poor Jewish brethren, could I count on you?"

And though he didn't know for what he was being asked, or even if the question was actual or rhetorical, Jack said, "Yes, sir. Of course, sir."

"I knew it," the rabbi said. "I knew you were a righteous man."

Jack thought of all he had done in battle, of the dozens, maybe hundreds, of men he'd killed, of the orders, rules, and regulations he followed no matter what he thought of them, followed them because they were his job and his duty. And yet, despite all that, though "righteous" was not a word he had ever used to describe himself, he realized at that moment that righteous was all he'd ever wanted to be.

· 6 ·

MONTHS PASSED, THE WEATHER TURNED, and Jack continued to spend his evenings and rare days off with Ilona and his days as a glorified quartermaster's clerk, processing requisition orders from U.S. generals throughout Land Salzburg, all of whom, it seemed, were in need of carpets and china, linens and tableware. He filled the orders and kept his records, periodically expressed his objections to his superior officer, and waited for someone to do something about it all. And then, finally, one day it seemed about to end. He was sitting at his makeshift desk, writing a letter of recommendation for Private Streeter, who was applying to pharmacy college in Albany in anticipation of his release, when the warehouse door creaked open, and Lieutenant Colonel Price strode through, a crowd of civilians in his wake. There were five in all, a small clutch of older men in brushed and mended suits and hats, and one younger man, taller than the others, elegantly attired, with watchful eyes. Bringing up the rear was Rabbi Bohnen.

"Lieutenant," Price began, "I'm going to need you to—"

"If I might have a moment?" Rabbi Bohnen said. "I'd like to introduce Lieutenant Wiseman to our guests."

Not used to being interrupted by an officer of lesser rank, but nonetheless respectful of the chaplain's role, Price pressed his lips together and nodded.

"Lieutenant Wiseman, this is the delegation from Hungary, emissaries of the Jewish community of Budapest come to review the contents of the train."

Finally! Jack thought. *"Jó napot,"* he said.

The Hungarians exclaimed and began speaking to him in a rush of Hungarian, but Jack had to hold up his hand. "That's about all I know," he said.

"It's more than I do," the rabbi said. "Jack, I also want to introduce you to Gideon Rafael, a member of the political department of the Jewish Agency, from Eretz Yisrael."

Gideon Rafael was the first Jew from Palestine that Jack had met. He looked nothing like the sunburned orange growers, the socialist hikers in climbing shorts, who populated the Palestine depicted in the pages of his grandparents' Yiddish newspapers. Broad across the shoulders, dressed in a crisp white shirt and an impeccable gray flannel suit, Rafael looked every inch the European diplomat.

Price took over at this point and instructed Jack to show the Hungarians through the warehouse. Before they set off, however, he pulled Jack aside.

"You got your wish, Wiseman. But . . . well. Discretion. The better part of valor and all that."

"Yes, sir," Jack said, understanding that he was to make no mention to the visitors of the items decorating the living quarters of the brass. He didn't care. Now that these men had arrived, it would not be long before everything would have to be returned and sent on its way, back to Hungary where it belonged.

He led them to the first aisle. He pointed out the crates and boxes, and the Hungarians pressed forward, reading the tags and chalked markings, murmuring to one another. At one point one of them gasped and, with a shaking finger, traced a name scrawled on a leather suitcase. He was slightly younger than the rest, his bald pate covered with an ink-black velvet yarmulke. Rafael bent over the man, and they spoke together. Jack tried to grant them a modicum of privacy, but the quarters were close, and he could hear what they were saying.

"Not my own family," the man told Rafael. "My son-in-law's cousin. From Debrecen."

Rabbi Bohnen, standing next to Jack, lifted a handkerchief to his eye and dabbed.

"Sir," Jack said, softly, "should I open the case?"

Bohnen considered this for a moment. Then he asked the question of Rafael, who in turn asked the Hungarian.

"No," the man said. "Not this one."

The leader of the group of Hungarians, a small man with a neatly trimmed white beard and a pair of gold pince-nez perched in the crease above his nose, said, "But perhaps another box?"

Jack moved a few yards down the aisle. He stopped before a section in which he'd put crates of silver religious objects, chose one, and pried it open with his knife. He removed a silver goblet from the box. The cup was tarnished, and he wiped it clean on his handkerchief before handing it to the leader of the Hungarians. The man held it reverently, his rheumy eyes filling with tears. He murmured something, and his bald colleague turned to Rafael. "Rabbi Mendlowitz asks where are the Torah scrolls."

Before Rafael could translate, Jack replied in German, "I'm sorry, sir. We found dozens of breastplates and silver handle covers, but no actual Torah scrolls."

At this news the elderly Hungarian shook his head, his wet eyes spilling over.

Rabbi Bohnen took his hand and patted it.

For a moment they all stood silently, honoring the elderly man's grief. Then Rafael turned to Jack. "Where have you stored the more valuable items? Jewelry? Watches? That type of thing."

Jack took them to the far corner, beneath the boarded-up windows, where he'd put the crates of jewelry and gold watches. He opened a casket of each. One of the Hungarians knelt down, sorted quickly through the watches, and then turned to the jewelry. He affixed a jeweler's loupe to his eye and began picking pieces up one at a time, holding them close to his loupe and turning them over in his fingers. After a few moments he murmured something to the leader of the delegation. An intense conversation ensued in Hungarian. The members of the delegation seemed upset. The small white-haired man turned to Jack.

In German, he said, "These items are not as valuable as we expected. The watches are gold, yes, also some of the chains. But where are the gemstones?"

Rafael asked Jack, "Are they stored in another location?"

Jack left the men for a moment and returned with the casket of gold bullion, the briefcase of currency, and the small velvet bag of gems that Avar had turned over when first the Americans assumed control of the train. "This is what we have," Jack said.

"This is all?" Rafael asked, weighing the pouch in his hand.

"Yes."

"Are there other crates of jewelry?"

"Yes," Jack said, "but most of what we have looks like it was dismantled, the stones pried out. Given how many chains and settings we've found, it's clear there should be more. In fact, we found very little in the way of valuable jewelry, gold, or currency. The Hungarian in charge told us that the crates with the most valuable items were removed from the train by his superior officer Colonel Árpád Toldi during the final days of the war."

Price interrupted. "The gems and gold stolen by Toldi were found in the French Zone. The French are in control of those items."

"Yes," the leader of the Hungarian delegation said. "Our government is in negotiations with them for the return of that property."

Jack wondered if the Hungarians had heard what David Ball, his OSS-officer roommate, had told him, that the French had only discovered the valuables because the Austrian peasants whom Toldi had chosen to guard the caskets of loot instead turned up at their village markets with fistfuls of diamonds with which to barter for bread, their wives festooning themselves in gem-encrusted diadems and tiaras to milk their cows and pull turnips from their fields.

Price said, "We'll make sure that you receive a copy of Lieutenant Wiseman's inventory. But rest assured, everything we received when we seized the train is here in the warehouse."

Everything but what's in the homes of the brass, Jack thought, but didn't say. Moreover, there did not exist a complete inventory of the contents of the train. Yes, he had inventoried and accounted for everything requisitioned by his superior officers, but the rest? There was just so much. There were at least five hundred crates full of silver bowls, dishes, and vases alone. The kind of inventory he would have liked to make would have itemized every item in every crate. But to do so would have taken far more manpower than he'd been allotted. It was all he could do to roughly organize the property.

All told, the visitors spent four hours in the warehouse, and by the time they were finished, Jack was exhausted. But he was also conscious of a huge weight being lifted from his shoulders. Finally, he would be rid of his nearly unbearable responsibility.

He escorted them out to the two long black cars that waited in the street in front of the warehouse. He held the doors open, and one by one they piled inside. The leader of the delegation was the last of the Hungarians to enter the cars, and before he did so he motioned for Jack to bend over to him. He placed his gnarled hands on either side of Jack's head and murmured a prayer. The tune was not one Jack recognized, but the words were the same as the prayer with which his mother's father had blessed him and his younger brother over Shabbos dinner.

"May God make you like Ephraim and Menashe," the rabbi sang in Hebrew, blessing Jack as Joseph had blessed his grandsons, Jacob's sons, two boys who grew up as Jack did, in the Diaspora, subject to the temptations and dangers of exile.

In Yiddish, because German seemed at that moment a sacrilege, Jack thanked the rabbi, who pressed his lips to Jack's forehead before getting into the car.

As Jack closed the car door, Rabbi Bohnen, who had watched the exchange, said, "A blessing from such a rabbi is a very great thing. I'm proud of you, Jack."

What was there to be proud of? Jack thought. That he'd kept the warehouse well organized so the brass's pillaging was easier to accomplish?

"You've been a good guardian," Bohnen said, as though reading his mind. "Their property has been safe with you."

And even Jack, so adept at self-criticism, had to admit that this was true. He'd done a fair job of limiting theft, as well as could be expected given the limited staff he'd been assigned. He'd kept careful track of every requisition. Bohnen was right. He had been a good guardian. And now the Hungarian property was going back where it belonged, to be dispersed among the surviving remnant of Budapest's Jews. He allowed himself to experience a flush of contentment, a hint of hope.

Within moments, it was gone.

"I didn't want to give you this while they were still here," Price said.

"Sir?"

Price handed him a file of requisition orders. For Medical Corps officer General Edgar E. Hume: eighteen rugs, tableware and silverware, table linen, and glassware. For General Howard's Vienna apartment: nine rugs, one silver set, and twelve silver plates. For Brigadier General Linden: ten rugs. For Major General McMahon: two hundred pieces of glass and porcelain tableware.

Jack opened his mouth, but Price lifted his hand. "I don't want to hear it, Lieutenant. Fill the orders."

And with that Jack's sense of accomplishment and hope was gone. He was powerless against the military, like a polar bear standing on a melting ice floe, the sea lapping ever closer.

THE WOMEN WHO SHARED Ilona's room knew him, and they smiled at his attempt to greet them in their own tongues. His *"Jó napot"* sounded pretty good, but at his polite and friendly *"Achuj"* the Polish women bent over at the waist, wiping the hilarious tears that streamed from their eyes. He wouldn't know what it was about his accent that amused them so until many years later, when he'd try it out on a waitress in a bar in Little Poland in Greenpoint, who'd also bend over, clutching her belly and wheezing, until she wiped her merry eyes and told him that he hadn't in fact wished her a good day but rather called her a prick.

He was under the impression that Ilona's roommates were a ribald bunch, and he was relieved, as ever, that he didn't understand enough Hungarian to know what they were saying as they teased him.

This afternoon, weeks and weeks after the visit from the delegation that Jack had foolishly imagined would signal the end of his job and the return of the contents of the Werfen train, he had left newly promoted Corporal Streeter in charge of the warehouse, unable to bear another moment there. He needed to see Ilona. He found her sitting on her bed, darning a sock. The sock was blue, but the thread was black. Jack wished he'd bought her a pile of spools in a rainbow of colors. Her skirt was rucked up above her knee. She was not wearing tights, and in the chill of the room the reddish-gold down on her legs stood erect. A considerable share of Jack's nocturnal rumination was devoted to the as-yet-unanswered question of whether the color of her bush also ran to strawberry blond or something closer to the auburn of her head. She caught him staring at the heart of the mystery. He started to avert his gaze, then mastered the impulse and returned her fixed gaze.

They looked into each other's eyes for a moment, and then she did something astonishing. Subtly, almost imperceptibly, she shifted her legs apart. It was no more than an inch or two, so little that one who was not obsessed might not even have noticed. Jack caught a glimpse of pink thigh and white panty, and then it was over. She put down her darning and stood up.

"More presents!" she said when he handed her his daily offerings. "Soon I will be the richest Chocolate Girl in all of Land Salzburg." Then as if she regretted the joke, she lifted her hand to his cheek. "Thank you," she said sweetly. She was not often sweet, a sardonic smile more frequently on her lips than a gentle one, so when she allowed herself to be like this, it melted his heart.

"Listen, Jack, I have something to tell you," she began, but now the other girls had come over to see what he'd brought.

"Later," she told him, and unwrapped two chocolate bars and passed them around. When she pulled out the pairs of Gotham Gold Stripe nylon hose, one of the women said something in Polish, and the others burst out laughing. A Hungarian woman fingered the nylon and murmured something to Ilona, who pressed a pair into her hands.

Ilona said, "She says she must have them to wear when she gets off the train in Budapest so she will be beautiful for her husband." Though the woman spoke no English, Ilona lowered her voice. "Her husband is a Christian. They divorced in 1944, when the Jewish laws were passed, and she is worried that he won't take her back. She heard that he and her son survived the war in Budapest, but they have not answered her letters."

Son of a bitch, Jack thought, cursing the man, though not aloud.

From somewhere the Polish women had scrounged a bottle of nail polish, and they went back to painting one another's nails. The Hungarian woman returned to her packing. Jack noticed that some of the other Hungarians were also collecting their bags.

"Are they leaving?" Jack asked. He felt a sudden flash of anxiety. Were all the Hungarians leaving? Was Ilona leaving, too?

"In three days there will be a train from Vienna to Budapest. Everyone must go to Vienna tomorrow morning to get travel permits to go home."

Jack's heart sank. "Oh. I mean, well. Is this good-bye?"

She frowned for a moment and then laughed. "No. You silly boy. I'm not leaving Salzburg. How could I leave without Etelka?"

How long, he wondered, would she wait? Though he wished for the sake of the woman he loved that her fantasy were true, Jack was sure that if Etelka had survived, by now her name would have appeared on some list, somewhere. He had gone with Ilona again and again to the offices of the Red Cross and of the United Nations Relief and Rehabilitation Administration, searching through the lists of names for Etelka's. Along the way Ilona had come across names of others of her acquaintance, mostly on lists of the dead, but once or twice on those of the living. But she had yet to find her sister's name. Wherever they went in the city, Ilona scanned the crowd, peering at faces. She even chose activities based on the possibility that her sister might be there. As if Etelka would have come to Salzburg and gone for a hike up the Untersberg before searching for her sister or registering with the Red Cross. *Your sister is dead,* Jack wanted, and feared, to tell Ilona. She died on one of the forced marches with which the Nazis had tortured the last surviving prisoners. Almost everyone had, after all.

Jack was stuck in the untenable position of both believing that it was best for Ilona that she acknowledge this truth, that she accept it and begin the unbearable task of moving on, and knowing that her fruitless search was what kept her here, with him. Otherwise she would leave, move on out of this graveyard back home to Hungary. To layer ambivalence upon ambivalence, he also feared that it was the search for Etelka, the inability to move on, that kept Ilona from being with him wholeheartedly. Ilona's delusion about Etelka's survival allowed them to be in each other's company but kept her from falling in love with him as he had fallen in love with her.

They left the room and walked down the stairs, Jack's arm looped around Ilona's shoulders, holding her close. They had been together nearly six months now, and he'd proven the seriousness of his commitment by extending his service for another six months in order to stay with her in Salzburg, but this—the bones of her shoulder, the brush of her lips across his, the flavor of her mouth—was the only access she allowed him to her body. The hours they spent together in the cinema or at the Marionetten Theater, in cafés, on blankets spread on the chilly banks of the Leopoldskorn before the snow began or, now that the ground was too wet, in darkened doorways, had become the venue of a single ongoing wrestling match, gentle and infuriating.

The rain was coming down in its perpetual Salzburg "strings," the *schnurlregen* for which the city was so infamous, and they decided to ride the streetcar rather than walk. The military had lifted the ban on fraternization in September, and for the last few months they'd been allowed to walk freely through the city, to go to movies and frequent cafés, to ride the streetcar without worrying about being discovered by an MP in a bad mood. The car was half empty, and so they were able to sit together.

"What was it you wanted to tell me?" he asked, trying not to dread her response.

"I received today a letter from my aunt Firenze," Ilona said, and showed him the thin blue envelope. "She is in Budapest, trying to arrange transport back to England. She says there is nothing left for us in Nagyvárad. She invites me to go with her to her old home. In Manchester."

Jack felt his chest constrict with anxiety, with loss, as though he were already missing her, even as he felt her next to him, her thigh pressing against his. "Do you want to go to Manchester?"

"I don't know. Before the war I never imagined living anywhere but Hungary. In the cemetery in Nagyvárad are the graves of my great-great-grandparents, maybe even further back than that. My grandfather said we could trace our family back a thousand years, all the way to the Khazars. But now Nagyvárad is gone."

"So what will you tell her?" he said. "Your aunt Firenze."

"I don't know." She slipped her hand into his. "Maybe we are not so different after all, you and I. Maybe I'm like you a soldier who can't leave her post. I have to wait for Etelka, just like you have to stay and guard the train until it is returned to its rightful owners."

He felt a stab of shame. If she knew what had happened today she would be horrified at the comparison.

Ilona folded the letter and put it back in its envelope. "After Etelka comes, and after your work is done, after that, we'll see."

They had arrived at their stop, and Jack jumped down from the streetcar and lifted his hands for her. Surprised, she leaped into them, and he spun her around, placing a kiss on her lips as he set her on the ground.

"You are so silly, Jack!" she said, laughing.

Together they crossed the road to the movie theater, where the marquee read DR. EHRLICH'S MAGIC BULLET.

"Are you sure we should see this?" he asked. He loved Edward G. Robinson, but he was less enthusiastic about the idea of passing an afternoon with his girl immersed in the biography of the man who had discovered the cure for syphilis. "Do you know what it's about?"

"I know, yes. My sister, Etelka, I told you she was a medical student. This is exactly the kind of movie she would go to."

The theater was dark and murky but, unlike the theaters of his childhood in Manhattan, was gloriously, impeccably clean. Though he enjoyed not having to wonder whether it was popcorn or something more disgusting that crunched beneath his shoes as he walked down the aisle, he missed the smell of butter and the din of a few thousand children left to their own devices for an entire day's worth of cartoons, newsreels, and features in the RKO Roxy or the Rivoli.

He maintained an impassive expression as Ilona scanned the crowd, looking as always for her sister's face. She settled down only once the screen flickered to life. Halfway through the second reel, the lights, such as they were, came on, but the projectionist did not stop the film.

The crowd murmured in protest, and Jack amused himself imagining what the response would have been in New York. The shouts of disgust, the boxes of popcorn flung at the screen. Four Austrian policemen in their Wehrmacht uniforms, stripped of insignia and dyed a streaky blue, came down the dimly lit aisles and stood in front of the screen, the looming intent scowl of Robinson projected on their own pale faces.

"Out, out!" the officers shouted in German. "You lazy pigs. It's time for work, not play!"

"What the hell?" Jack said. He looked around but realized that he was, as far as he could tell, the only American officer in the theater.

The policemen spread out through the theater. They walked slowly up the aisles, stopping periodically and hauling out a young man or woman, berating them as shirkers and layabouts and sending them out of the theater. The policeman closest to Jack and Ilona was rotund, with a face full of acne scars and a uniform slightly more official looking than the others'. He carried his nightstick in his hand, slapping it against his palm and using it to prod and push at his victims.

When he reached Ilona and Jack, he stopped. He jutted his chin at Ilona and said, "You! Why are you not at your job?"

"I am exempt," she said.

"DPs are not exempt! Show me your papers!"

Ilona pulled a folded piece of paper out of the leather change purse Jack had bought her at the PX. It was her brand-new refugee permit, received only a few days ago from the UNRRA office in the Chiemsee-hof Palace.

"Put that away," Jack said. "This isn't Nazi Germany. You don't need to show him your papers."

She hesitated. "In the newspaper yesterday was an article complaining about how people are going to the cinema instead of working to clean up the city. Perhaps now they begin arresting people."

"It's their mess," Jack said. "Let them clean it up." To the police officer, in German, he said, "She's with me."

The officer hesitated a moment and then shrugged and joined his colleagues and the small, bedraggled group of frustrated cinephiles they had assembled at the back of the theater. Batons at the ready, the police herded their charges out the door.

The projectionist turned out the lights and Edward G. Robinson was denounced, exonerated, and ultimately died, but Jack had difficulty paying attention. When the lights went up, he led Ilona swiftly through the crowd, trying to get away as quickly as possible. When they reached the street, dark now, he said, "It's cold. You want to get something to eat?"

She nodded and shrugged deeper into the warmth of the wool coat he had had his mother send from New York. It was one of the few things that he had given Ilona that she hadn't passed on to another, ostensibly more needy, DP. They walked through the old city, bundled up against the biting wind and the flurries of snow. They walked into the Getreidegasse, and soon they were ensconced at a table in a corner of the gaily lit Café Mozart.

Though he didn't usually, today he ordered a piece of cake for himself as well. The whipped cream tasted funny; it had, he thought, gone off. That the café had cream at all, not to mention flour and sugar, in a time of increasing food shortages, spoke to a great Austrian capacity for ingenuity, at least when it came to sweets. Ilona was either too polite or too hungry to complain. Only once she'd licked her finger and used it to blot up the last crumbs of cake did he say, "Listen, Ilona. I have something to tell you."

"Today is a day of news, I guess."

He took a deep breath, and told her the miserable thing he'd spent the day trying to forget, the thing he knew he owed it to her to say. "Price came into the warehouse with a memo. The stuff on the train isn't going back to Hungary after all. Not anytime soon, anyway." Jack bit his lip, waiting for her angry reply, but then suddenly conscious of a feeling of resentment. Why should he be afraid to tell her? It wasn't her property. What right had she to make him feel bad about it? But at once he knew he was being irrational. She wasn't making him feel bad. He was doing that all by himself. And he should feel bad. It was terrible what his army was doing. Criminal.

"What happened?" Ilona said, every bit as shocked as he expected her to be. Though not angry. Not yet. "Weeks ago you said the Hungarian delegation had come!"

"I don't know," Jack said. "There's some debate going on between the Hungarians and the Jewish Agency. Price wouldn't tell me much."

"What is there to debate?" she said. "It is simple. The property belongs to Hungary. Give it back. End of story."

He sighed and said, "Nothing's ever that simple."

"Of course it is."

"Think about it, Ilona. Who are we going to turn over the property to? The Hungarian government? They're a defeated enemy. We aren't about to give them a huge pile of loot."

"You give it to the people it belongs to."

"How? You want the U.S. military to just roll into Budapest and set up a commissary? Give it out to people on the street?"

"There are receipts, Jack! Many people have receipts."

"Most of the people who got those receipts are dead, you know that. And even the ones who aren't, how many of them managed to keep hold of their receipts?"

"You could do what you said you were going to do! Give the property to the Hungarian delegation, the representatives of the Hungarian Jewish community."

"There's some kind of problem with them. Some kind of dispute between them and the Jewish Agency. It could take years to resolve." And by then, he knew, it would all be gone, chipped away, looted in spoonfuls and by the yard.

He waved his empty coffee cup at the waitress, whose frown was as starched as her crimped apron.

Ilona said, "It is not simple. I know that. It is all very complicated. But this is not complicated: my parents are dead. Don't you think the U.S. Army should give me back my bicycle?" Her face was pale, and she was trembling. With anger or sadness he couldn't tell. Both, he thought.

"I swear to God, Ilona. If I could find your family's things in that mess, I would give them back to you. I would give it all back to you, whatever my bosses say."

"I know," Ilona said.

He imagined bringing her back to the warehouse and searching together through the crates and boxes until they found her parents' wedding rings, her father's watch, her bicycle.

Ridiculous. Even if by some miracle her family's property was there, and even if it was possible to search through crate after crate of identical gold bands and identify two among tens of thousands, most of his time nowadays was spent keeping people out of the warehouse to protect its contents from pilfering. He could hardly hand anything over to her when he'd threatened his own men with court-martial for the same.

"I'll get you a bicycle," he said.

"I didn't mean it about the bicycle. It was symbolic."

"I know. But still. You could, you know, ride around the city looking for Etelka." And just like that he handed to her another helping of the false hope he knew it was so bad for her to indulge in.

Her pallor lifted, and she shifted her chair closer to his. She rested her head on his shoulder. He put his arm around her and pulled her close.

"I know it's not your fault," she said.

He kissed her there, in the middle of the café, under the furious eye of the prim and bitter waitress. She not only let him but kissed him back, harder and more urgently than ever before, and he was conscious of having won something from her and ashamed at what it had taken to do so.

8

HE ORGANIZED HER A BICYCLE. Ball's promotion to captain had come with access to a jeep and driver. It was a small matter to convince David not to turn in the bicycle he'd been using but to hand it over.

"I should tell you," Jack said. "I'm not planning to use it for military purposes."

David laughed. "Honestly, Jack, I couldn't care less. I'm just glad not to have to ride that thing anymore. A bicycle is a ridiculous means of transport in a city where it is always either raining or snowing. I'm surprised you want it."

"I'm going to give it to someone," Jack said.

"Your girl?"

"Yes."

"Good for you."

"I'm taking a piece of military equipment and giving it to her."

"Oh, for God's sake. Half of Salzburg lives on American rations. Pry off the damn USAF tag, paint the bicycle pink. No one will notice or care."

So that's what Jack did, quashing his too-easily-agitated conscience. It was a Westfield Columbia, with heavy-duty rims and spokes. He painted it bright red, a color more suited to his girlfriend's fiery nature, adjusted the brakes, oiled the chain, clamped a tire pump to the frame, and wrapped a chain and lock around the seat. He rode it to the Hotel Europa, then carried it up the three flights of stairs to her room. He knew the moment he walked in that something was wrong; the room was silent. One of Ilona's roommates, the only other Hungarian to have remained with Ilona in Salzburg when the others left, rushed up to him, took his arm, and, whispering incomprehensibly in his ear, pointed to where Ilona lay on her iron cot, curled up in a ball, her knees tight to her chest and her arms folded at her belly. She clutched each arm with the hand of the other so tightly that the tips of her fingers were white and her nails left angry red slivers of moon in the flesh that had all too recently grown plump and healthy.

He set the bicycle against the wall and allowed himself to be led to her bedside.

"What happened?" he asked the other woman.

She answered in Hungarian, and he cursed that impossible language with its *cs*'s and its *sz*'s, devoid of cognates to any language he knew.

"Ilona," he said, kneeling at her side. "Ilona?"

She opened her eyes.

"Ilona, what happened?"

She looked at him, but without interest or recognition, like you might glance at a crack in the sidewalk as you stepped over it. She closed her eyes again.

His hand hovered in the air over her head. He wanted to touch her, to smooth her hair and cup her cheek in the palm of his hand, but he was afraid she might flinch.

He put his hand back in his lap. He knelt next to the bed, still and quiet, listening to her breathe, until one of the women brought him a stool. He sat on the stool and rubbed his knees where they ached from the floor. He extended one leg, and his stiff knee cracked, a gunshot in the quiet room. Ilona's eyelids flew open. After a moment, she closed them again.

He would just sit here next to her. He wouldn't bother her. He wouldn't touch her or speak to her or force himself on her in any way. He would just sit here and wait and show her by waiting that he would always be here, that she could trust him never to leave her alone.

He listened closely for her breath, matching her inhalations and exhalations with his own. He was not sure how long he sat; his sense of time was not as honed as his sense of direction. It might have been an hour, maybe more, maybe less.

The Hungarian woman came over with a tin cup of hot water in which she had mixed some of the soluble coffee Jack had given Ilona the last time he saw her. This woman was older than Ilona, anywhere between thirty and fifty, or perhaps a brutalized twenty-five. Her hair had grown back only in patches, the rest of her skull red and peeling, inadequately covered with a triangle of grass-green cloth. She had beautiful eyes, though. Deep and dark, with long sooty lashes. She set the cup of coffee on the floor next to the bed and began murmuring to Ilona. Gently she pulled Ilona up until the girl was sitting, bent over, her arms still wrapping her body, all the while murmuring in Hungarian, her voice low and rhythmic, like a song. She took Ilona's hands and cupped Ilona's cheeks, her fingertips pressing gently into the bruised circles under her eyes.

Ilona opened her mouth in a wide O, and Jack waited for her inevitable tears, but instead she sagged silently against the woman's wasted bosom. The woman cocked her head at Jack, motioning him over with her chin. He shook his head, but she shifted Ilona's weight to one of her arms and with the other grabbed his shirt, pulling him to her. Awkwardly, the placket of his shirt gripped in her iron hand, Jack moved from the stool to the bed. In one fluid motion, the woman transferred Ilona from her arms to his. She rose to her feet and walked swiftly away.

Ilona leaned on him only for a minute before lifting her head. She rubbed her eyes with the heels of her hands.

"Etelka is dead," she said flatly.

His emotions upon hearing the inevitability for which he'd been waiting for weeks and months were complex. He felt at once terribly sad for Ilona and relieved that the charade would end. He was both afraid and excited about the future that now opened before them. Would she leave Salzburg and return to Hungary? Would she go to England, or would she stay with him, come home with him? And through this complex fabric of emotions was woven a ribbon of something strange, even ridiculous. He was conscious of a peculiar disappointment, as if he, too, had been hoping against hope that Etelka could have survived.

Though he knew it was the last thing he should say, the last thing she'd want to hear, Jack said, "I'm sorry."

9

DURING THE EARLY SUMMER of 1937, when Ilona was ten years old and her sister, Etelka, was nearly twelve, the family Jakab repaired to Bad Gastein so that Mr. Jakab could relieve the pain of his arthritic knees in the restorative radon baths. It was the last of their yearly trips to this mountain village a couple of hours south of Salzburg. In March of 1938, Hitler invaded Austria, and they were no longer welcome. But in that last glorious summer, they took a suite of rooms at the Grand Hotel de l'Europe, one each for the parents, one for the girls and their nanny, and a sitting room for the mornings when they wished to enjoy their breakfast and the newspapers without changing out of their robes and slippers. It was their last family vacation, and Ilona remembered it as their last period of careless happiness, a year before Hungary's new anti-Jewish laws changed their lives, four years before the first Jewish massacre in Hungary, twenty thousand refugees murdered in Kameniec-Podolsk.

The Grand was the queen mother of Bad Gastein's spa hotels. A colossal Jugendstil confection of arched windows and ornate balconies, it dominated the landscape of the town. While Mr. Jakab occupied his mornings soaking in the waters and inhaling the toxic vapor that might eventually have killed him, had he only lived long enough, his wife and daughters hiked through the alpine meadows and up to the town's waterfalls. The little girls wove garlands of wild daisies and brilliant purple gentians. In the afternoon the family promenaded along the main road or played croquet on the great lawn of the hotel.

In Nagyvárad their father was often distracted by his business concerns, but in Bad Gastein, Ilona and Etelka enjoyed hours of his undivided attention. They dined beneath the gilded ceiling of the hotel dining room, long languid meals untroubled by discussions of fluctuating wheat prices and the effects of the weather on crops. The family Jakab had last been truly happy in Bad Gastein, and so it was there that Ilona asked Jack to take her when she found out that Etelka was dead. Jack agreed right away, thinking it possible that distraction might be an adequate substitute for comfort and a fond memory a way to feel anguish and still survive.

The Grand Hotel was the first thing they saw upon arriving in the town. To his surprise, Ilona had no interest in exploring the lobby. Instead, she led him out onto the expanse of packed snow and earth that had once been lawn. He tried to argue that it was too cold for a picnic, but she told him that her sister had always loved to picnic on the lawn, so picnic they would. She spread a tarp on the ground, opened a can of Spam, and sliced it, arranging the processed meat on pieces of bread and dotting the sandwiches with a tiny bit of the precious black-market mustard for which she had traded six U.S. Army oat bars and two packets of cigarettes. For dessert he had finagled a jam roll, and this she cut in two equal pieces.

He finished eating before she did. He leaned back on his elbow and watched her. She took large, methodical bites, chewed them gravely, and, upon swallowing, immediately opened her mouth for another. She ate no less than normal, finishing her own sandwich and the half of his that he offered, but she took none of her usual pleasure in her food. She was just chewing and swallowing, and taking another bite.

At this altitude the air was thin and crisp and smelled of snow. The sun shone overhead, and he tipped his head back to warm his face. Ilona, pale and freckled, hid from both the cold and the glare of the winter sun beneath a floppy U.S. Army winter cap. The hat was too big, and the buckled earflaps drooped to her neck as though she'd taken cover beneath the flap of a tent.

She looked, he thought, like the tomboy she had been. She had told him stories of how she and Etelka had passed the long summer days at their family cottage in Siófok on Lake Balaton, riding ponies through the countryside, bathing in the lake, and sleeping outside on a blanket spread on the grass in the garden, staring at the stars. He wished he could have known her then, the cosseted daughter of a wealthy family that spent their summers in the mountains and their holidays in elegant spas. He wished he'd been able to see her home in Nagyvárad, to understand how her family had lived, to know what paintings decorated their walls, what food they ate, what the view was from her bedroom window. He wished he had known her before she was broken and her world was broken. But perhaps part of what he loved about her was her very brokenness. After all, it was Ilona as she was right now with whom he was obsessed.

"Are you finished?" Ilona asked him.

"Yes."

She gathered up the remains of their sandwiches. He stilled her hands and put his arm around her, moving her close to his side. She stiffened for a moment and then relaxed against him. He pressed his lips to her hair. As deep as her grief was, he felt able to relieve her of its burden. Or at the very least share it with her.

He said, "Is it very different from what you remember?"

"Everything is different," she said.

Something about the way the thin winter sun warmed the fabric of his pants suddenly made him conscious of a stirring in the folds of his army-issue boxer shorts. He froze, willing his erection to subside, but the increasing intensity of his attention only served to make matters worse. This had happened to him before when out with Ilona, but only in circumstances where it had been easy to disguise. He'd hidden his boner beneath restaurant tablecloths, shoved his fists into his pockets and bent over slightly while walking, flipped onto his belly when stretched out on the grass. None of these maneuvers was available to him now. He sat on the freezing ground, his legs out before him and crossed at the ankle, the fabric at the crotch of his pants bunched as if strategically to magnify not only the rise but the rising as his penis shifted and waved and grew.

He was so embarrassed he shut his eyes and thus missed her reaction. He thought, after what she said next, that it was not too much to assume that she might have looked at him fondly, patiently, even if, the day she found out about Etelka's death, it was too soon to expect a smile.

She stood up. "Come," she said, holding out her hand.

He grabbed the tarp and the remains of their lunch and let her lead him back to the truck. The canvas flap was pinned up. She climbed into the back, unsnapped one side of the canvas, unrolled it, and lowered it to meet the tailgate. Then she lowered the other side of the flap and disappeared behind this fallen curtain into the mysterious dark of her intentions. He wanted to spring up into the truck like a pole-vaulter, but was that what she really wanted? Was she even in her right mind? What kind of a man would take advantage of a girl who had just found out that every last person she loved was dead?

He hovered, knotted up by his own ambivalence. Who was he, he thought, to decide what was best for her? Of course she wanted him now, in the wake of what had happened, because only he could comfort her. He was all she had. This was the justification he clung to as he climbed into the truck and let the canvas fall closed behind him.

Later in his life he would remember little of what followed. He would forget the way the pale green light seeping through the seams of the canvas bathed Ilona's skin like the sheer gossamer of a bridal veil, hiding her scars and pocks, the patches of discoloration and dryness on her back and legs. He would forget the heat of her body in the freezing air, the surprising heft of her ass, the dry rasp of her vagina as he pushed into her, her suppressed whimper, or the way she locked her heels around his waist and pulled him deeper inside. He would forget that she bit him, leaving a mark on his shoulder that took weeks to fade. He would forget how quickly he came, how, when he pulled out, his semen pulsed onto her belly as he buried his face in her neck.

He would remember only what happened after. The way she got to her feet and wiped herself with a corner of the tarp that had served as a picnic blanket. He would remember the way she slipped her dress over her head, wrapped herself in her coat, and, looking down at the bed of the truck as she searched for her shoes, said matter-of-factly, "There is no blood."

Was she wondering at the lack of blood or telling him not to bother to look for any? He could not ask and would never learn if he had been the first man she'd lain with, or if there had been others before him, back home in Nagyvárad or, as horrible as it was to imagine, in her year in the camps.

"Come here," he said, sitting up. "Come sit with me."

She hesitated and then sat down next to him, and he was conscious of the contrast between them, his body, naked below the waist, her clothed one.

"Are you okay?" he asked.

"Yes."

"Was it . . . good?"

She brushed her lips against his, and he relaxed. It was enough of an answer, he thought.

"Should we see the rest of the town?" he said.

"I want to go back."

"Okay."

As he pulled away from the hotel, she lifted her foot into her lap, pulled off her shoe and her sock, and shook out a pebble. He had never before seen her bare foot, so it was the first time he understood the source of her limp, the slight hitch in her step. Her foot was ruined. Her pinkie toe and the one next to it were gone, and in their place was a lumpy purple-red scar. Her first and second toes had no nails, and the nail beds were puffy and swollen. Without their nails they hardly looked like toes, just small appendages of flesh and bone. Her middle toe, however, was perfect. It was long and slender, curved slightly, with an opalescent shell of a nail.

A thick, gray callus stretched from her heel up to the back of her ankle. It was cracked at the joint, revealing tender red tissue.

"Wooden shoes," she said. "Mine were too small." She ran her fingers lightly over her toes. "And then frostbite. The American doctor who cut off my toes told me I was lucky not to have gangrene."

"I'm sorry," Jack said.

"Again with the apologies. What do you think, Jack? You are Hitler? You are Horthy Miklós? It's your fault what happened to us?"

The harshness of her tone shocked him. All he could think to say was "Who is Horthy Miklós?"

"Horthy, our regent. Who was supposed to protect us. He murdered us, not you. You liberated us. It's not your fault my family is dead. It is your fault I am alive."

He realized then that he had misread her terribly, that what had passed between them had not been Ilona seeking comfort in his arms but just another punishment she had inflicted on herself.

She owed her survival only to happenstance, but he was willing to take responsibility for the deaths of her parents and sister. He had not come in time. He had not joined the army until 1944, until after he'd graduated from college and received his commission. He'd waited until it was convenient, as the world had waited, choosing to let the Jews of Europe be a carcass thrown as a sacrifice to distract the wolf while the hunters took their time readying their bows.

She kneaded her foot.

"Does it hurt?" he said. "I have some aspirin in here." He reached across her to the glove compartment.

"No," she said. "Not really. Not anymore. Why do you keep aspirin in your truck? Does your head hurt?"

"Not today."

"When?"

"I don't know. A while ago."

"A while ago you had a headache?"

"Yes."

"Why did you have a headache?"

"What do you mean 'why'? I just had a headache. I get headaches."
But he did remember why he had the particular headache that had led him to throw a bottle of aspirin into the glove compartment of his truck.

She shook her head, the gesture somehow maternal, like a mother disappointed in her child's lie. She waited. Jack could not bear the silence and foolishly filled it with words. "I was angry."

"And when you are angry you get a headache?"

"Yes. Sometimes."

"What made you angry?"

"Nothing."

"How was it nothing? It was enough something to make a headache."

"I had to do something I didn't want to do."

"What?"

"It's not important."

"Nothing is important. It's all just days and work and here and there. But if you are so angry it gives you a headache, I want to know why."

He took advantage of a dip in the road to concentrate on unnecessarily shifting to a lower gear. The gears ground against one another, and he swore under his breath.

She said, "What did you do? Did you punish someone?"

"No."

"Did you kill someone?"

"No. Jesus. No."

"So what happened, Jack, that made you so angry you had to take aspirin for your head?"

"General Collins requisitioned a massive pile of crap for his house. That's all."

"What?"

"What do you mean 'what'?"

"What did he requisition?"

"Just, you know. Dishes and glasses. Silverware. Stuff like that."

She considered this. She squeezed her foot again and then reached down for her shoe.

By the side of the road lay a carcass of a cow. One of its legs stuck up in the air, and a blackbird perched on its hoof. As they drove by, the bird turned its dark bead of an eye on Jack. He scowled, and as if in answer the bird took off into the sky with a flap of its blue-black wings.

She said, "Your general requisitioned this from you?"

"From Price. But, yes. I filled the order."

"From your warehouse."

"Yes."

"But, Jack, the only things in your warehouse are from the train."

"There's other stuff in the warehouse."

"There is?"

When he had arrived at the warehouse with the train from Werfen, he had found a small amount of other goods stored there, mostly works of art that had been looted by the Nazis. He had marked those items and put them in a separate corner of the vast space.

"Yes."

"So you gave him this other 'stuff'?" Her voice added quotation marks around the word, and he wasn't sure whether it was because it was unfamiliar or because she thought it an offensive term to use about the belongings of dead people.

He didn't answer.

"Jack? You gave the general other things from the warehouse, yes?"

It would be so easy to lie. But he wanted to tell her. He hated keeping what he was doing a secret from her, and he wanted her to know. He needed her to know.

"I gave him things from the train."

She stared at him, aghast.

"I had no choice, Ilona. I had to fill the requisition order. But I wrote it all down. I've written everything down, and the generals will give it all back. I'll collect it myself."

"The generals? There have been more than one?"

"Yes."

"How many?"

"A lot."

"A lot of the generals have taken things from the warehouse? Things from the Hungarian train?"

"Yes. But I told you. I'm keeping an inventory. I write everything down, and I'll get everything back."

"When?"

"When what?"

"When will you get it back?"

"When it's time for the U.S. Army to turn over the property."

"And when will it be time? You yourself told me that your army has decided that the Hungarian delegation gets nothing. When will it be time, Jack, to give it all back?"

"I don't know."

"You don't know? Those are *my* dishes and *my* glasses and *my* silverware. My bracelets and my candlesticks and my . . . what? My fur! And my bicycle, Jack. They took my bicycle. Give it back to me! Give it all back!" Her voice rose steadily until by the end she was shouting. He thought of the cherry-red bicycle that he had brought her this morning, how happy he'd been when he'd painted it. How happy he'd imagined she'd be when he gave it to her.

This had, he knew, nothing to do with the train and its contents, or the secret he'd kept from her about the generals and their requisitions. Ilona knew the limits of his authority. This had only to do with her sister. And with the foolishness of his delusion that he had and could provide her with any comfort.

He pulled over onto the shoulder of the road. The truck rattled and shook on the rough gravel. He braked, stretching his arm out over her chest, to keep her from being flung forward into the windshield.

She was crying now, her whole body heaving. He had never seen her cry before, and it frightened him. He kept his arm across her chest, as though to protect her from a pending impact, and felt her breasts rise and fall. He tried to make himself reach out his other arm and clutch her to him. He wanted to smooth her hair and lick the tears from her eyes. He saw himself doing this so clearly, he felt her bird bones and the curls of her hair, he tasted the salt of her tears on his tongue. The image was so vivid that when she gave a last sob and wiped her nose and eyes with the back of her hand, he felt as if it was he who had soothed and comforted her, as if it was he who had dried her tears.

He sat back in his seat, took an ironed handkerchief out of his pocket, and gave it to her. She rubbed her face clean and blew her nose. She folded the handkerchief into a small square and held it in her hand as if trying to decide what to do with it.

He said, "I'll give it to the laundress."

Wordlessly, she dropped it into his hand.

· 10 ·

JACK SET ABOUT GETTING DRUNK the way he did most things, with method and a sense of purpose. He began immediately after taking Ilona home, before he'd even left the Hotel Europa. When he pulled up in front of the hotel, she said, "I don't want to see you anymore."

He felt like he'd been punched in the stomach. No. Not punched. Shot. Her words were like bullets tearing through skin and muscle. She leaped down and he tore after her, begging her, pleading with her to wait, to stop, to talk to him.

In the courtyard he grabbed her arm, and she shook him loose.

"If you touch me again I will call out for help."

"No. No. Please," he said. If he had been a different kind of man, he would have dropped to his knees, flung his arms around her ankles, kissed her ruined feet, begged her to stop, to be who she'd been yesterday, last week, last month.

"I'm sorry," she said gently.

"Is it because I let them take the property?" he asked, though he knew it wasn't. Or not merely. "I can get it back. I'll just go and take it."

"It is nothing you did, Jack. I don't want you, that's all."

He watched her walk away, her hip swaying with her faint limp, the light from the bare courtyard bulbs catching her red curls, making them glow. And then she was gone. He turned and saw two men haggling over the price of a glass bottle of murky brew.

"How much?" Jack said, stepping between them.

The seller smiled and flicked his fingers at the buyer, who threw up his hands and stomped away, muttering under his breath. The seller held up four fingers, then put two to his lips, miming smoking a cigarette.

Though he didn't smoke, Jack always carried cigarettes to trade. He fished a crumpled pack out of his breast pocket, but the dealer shook his head, drew a square in the air, and again held up four fingers.

"Four packs?" Jack said, not bothering to speak German.

"*Ja.*"

"Bullshit," he said. He searched his pockets until he found an unopened pack. He held it out to the man.

"*Nein, nein,*" the man said, insistently waving his four fingers.

"Ah, go to hell," Jack said, turning away.

"Okay," the man said, scurrying after him. "Okay, okay."

Jack lobbed him the pack of cigarettes and snatched the bottle. He climbed into the truck, and before turning the key in the ignition, pulled out the cork with his teeth. He spat the cork out of the window; he had no intention of needing it again. He took a long slug and gagged. The only thing what was in the bottle had in common with actual schnapps was the fire it lit at the back of his throat. It was fit only for a machine shop, for the stripping of furniture. By the time he reached the street where he lived, he had managed to choke down enough to cause him to stumble and fall as he was getting out of the cab of the truck. The bottle slipped from his grasp and shattered on the ground. The resultant blast of fumes burned his eyes and left him coughing.

"Shit," he said, halfway to laughing. Without getting up, he wiped dirt from his hands and checked the knees of his trousers for tears.

An elderly Austrian couple walking by on the sidewalk passed him where he sat in the street. The woman clucked, shaking a finger. Her husband seemed about to offer Jack a hand, his expression more tolerant, but the wife took his arm and hustled him away.

"Welcome," Ball said as Jack staggered into the apartment. He was sitting at the dining room table with a bottle of authentic Sporer schnapps and a water glass. Ball filled the glass more than halfway and lifted it in a mock salute.

"*Prost!*" he said, and knocked it back. He smacked the glass down on the table, wiped his mouth with the back of his hand. "Grab a glass and join me, Lieutenant Wiseman. That's a direct order."

"Sir, yes, sir," Jack said, holding on to the back of a chair to steady himself.

"Already in your cups, are you, laddie?" Ball had spent part of the war attached to a British intelligence unit with a Scottish cryptanalyst, and when he was drunk the ghost of that sodden Glaswegian returned to haunt his companions.

"When did you get home?" Jack asked.

Ball pushed back his sleeve and made a great show of looking at his wrist where his watch should have been.

"That information appears to be classified," he said. He picked up the bottle and held it up to the light. "Strictly need to know."

Jack found another glass and joined Ball at the table.

"There's a wee canny bairn," Ball said, and filled his glass. "And what're you drinking to, tonight, Hamish me lad?"

"Nothing," Jack said. He took a long sip of schnapps, light and mellow, with just a hint of fruit. Smooth going down. "Tonight Hamish the wee bairn is just drinking."

"Fair enough," Ball said, and drained his glass. "As for me, tonight I am drinking to the good people of Munich," Ball said. "May their black Nazi hearts burst in their motherfucking chests."

"To the people of Munich," Jack agreed, and drank.

With an unsteady hand, Ball spilled more booze into their glasses. "And to our fellow pricks and SOBs in the good old U.S. Army."

"To all of us pricks and SOBs. What did we do now?"

Ball had been sent to Munich to investigate a rumor that had made its way to the OSS via an informant who regularly reported on the moods and activities of his fellow camp survivors.

"Are you sure I should be hearing this?" Jack said.

"Oh, who cares?" Ball said. "I ask you, Jack, at this point, who the fuck cares?"

The Munich Housing Office had assigned a number of apartments in what had once been a retirement village for members of the Nazi Party to a group of Jewish survivors of the camps. When the Jews attempted to move in, they found the apartments still occupied by their original tenants. Not only did the retired Nazis refuse to leave, they responded to the eviction order with lusty cries of "*Heil* Hitler" and threats of violence. When the bewildered Jews sought the assistance of a passing group of American soldiers, the GIs instructed the Jews to shut up before somebody put them back in Dachau where they belonged. Or so, at least, went the rumor.

"Couldn't be true, right?" Ball said. He rolled his glass between his palms. "Baseless slander." He took another long gulp of the schnapps. He put on the voice, a patrician South Carolina baritone, he used when impersonating his commanding officer. "'A hysterical canard concocted by a paranoid people so accustomed to persecution that they see anti-Semitism under every rock, Captain Ball.'"

"It was true," Jack said, gulping down his drink, refilling it from the bottle. He was stinking drunk and found that he quite liked it.

"Of course it was true," Ball said. "But that is nae the point of my tale, laddie. The point is that when I went to interview the director of the Munich Housing Office, to find out what happened, I couldn't conduct said interview, because said director, Lieutenant, was busy enjoying the hospitality of our fine military police, who had arrested the director of the Munich Housing Office, you see, because they said he issued the eviction order against the retired Nazis without the right stamp."

Each took a long pull from his glass.

"Now," Ball said. "Your turn."

Jack managed a garbled recitation of Ilona's rejection.

"Oh, Hamish," Ball said. "You sad, sorrowful thing."

Ball stood up. He grabbed the table to keep from swaying. "We need to go out."

"Out?"

"Yes, sir. Out we go."

They barely made it down the hall stairs. Had they not run into Hoyle on the first-floor landing, they might well have admitted their incapacity, given up, and fallen asleep there in the hall. But in a rare moment of camaraderie, Hoyle threw an arm around each roommate and, one on either side, helped them down the stairs, up the road, and across the bridge over the river. Their goal was a bar where Hoyle claimed it was possible to get laid for the price of a beer and a pack of cigarettes.

"Have you ever been laid, Wiseman?" Hoyle said.

"Let me see. Yes, Lieutenant Hoyle, I believe I have. I believe that I got laid earlier this afternoon, in fact." And for a moment Jack enjoyed pissing on the memory.

" 'Earlier this afternoon'!" Hoyle bellowed, clapping Jack on the back. "You know, for a stuck-up Jew prick, you're not so bad."

"For a stuck-up West Point prick, Hoyle, you're . . . well, you're a stuck-up West Point prick," Jack said, and Hoyle roared even louder.

By now they had reached the bar of the legendarily low-priced women, a dismal, underground room furnished with little more than a beer tap, a row of stools, and a fat bartender who stared at them with a sullen expression and a filthy towel draped over his shoulder. There were no women in the place at all, at any price. There were only a few men, each sitting alone and nursing a beer.

Jack was furiously disappointed. He'd been intent on erasing the afternoon with an encounter the uglier and more meaningless the better.

"Whiskey!" Hoyle said, slamming his fist on the counter.

"No whiskey," the bartender said. He pronounced it *vis-key*, with a pause between the syllables.

"Yes, whiskey!" Hoyle said.

"Beer," the bartender insisted, taking three earthenware steins from beneath the counter. He filled the glasses with a thick, dark brew and scraped off the foam with a knife. Jack watched the foam subside. Once the level of the beer had dropped below the lips of the steins, the bartender filled and scraped them again. Jack reached for one of the steins, but the barman shook his head, filled them a third time, scraped the foam, and only then slid one across the counter to him.

There was not enough food in the city to feed even half the population, people scrambled for bread and milk, and Ilona greeted the cans of Spam he brought her as though they were filet mignon, but the bars had reopened, and the beer was good, even though they sold it at prices only the Americans could really afford. He licked the foam mustache from his upper lip.

"S'good," he muttered to Hoyle.

"Damn right, it's good," Hoyle said, taking a long swallow, then holding one hand over his belly and belching loudly.

Jack snorted into his glass, sending foam all over the counter.

"Laddies," Ball said, reviving his brogue. "Laddies, to us! Long may we rule."

Jack and Hoyle hoisted their glasses in the air. "To us!" they shouted.

Jack clicked his stein against Ball's, but by now he was far too drunk to have any sense of distance or strength. He knocked Ball's stein hard enough to send beer sloshing over the sides, drenching both his arm and his friend's.

Nearly hysterical with laughter, Ball smashed his stein against Jack's with enough force to shatter the earthenware. Ball stared at his palm. Blood beaded up along a long gash.

"Fuck," he said, loudly. "Fuck my fucking hand."

"*Schwein.*"

Jack swung around on his stool. At the far end of the bar, a man sat hunched over a glass.

"What did you say?" Jack said, politely, in his impeccable German.

The man raised his head to look at Jack. He had dark hair, thick eyebrows, and fleshy lips. His shirt was unbuttoned, and his undershirt was stained. His sleeves were rolled up over his meaty biceps. He scratched his throat, tugging down the collar of his undershirt. Whether or not he had meant to reveal the twin lightning bolts tattooed on his neck, Jack didn't know or care. Jack sprang off his stool and down the length of the bar. Before the man had time to react, Jack had him around the throat. He pulled the man off his stool and punched him in the face. The Nazi's nose splintered and smeared under his fist. Jack danced back, lifting his fists to protect his face. The man staggered around, blood pouring down his shirt. Jack kicked the Nazi's legs out from under him. The Nazi fell so hard he made the glasses on the bar jump.

"Who's a pig?" Jack shouted, aiming a kick at his stomach. "Goddamn Nazi! Who's a pig?" The man curled up, protecting his belly. Jack kicked him in the ass.

"Let me in," said Hoyle, pushing Jack aside. The man spread his hands on the floor and tried to get up. Hoyle stomped on his fingers, laughing as he went down with a groan.

"Get up, you Nazi pig," Jack said, grabbing the man by the shirt collar and heaving him to his feet. "Stand up and fight."

The man swayed. He grabbed the bar to steady himself and then cried out at the pain of his swelling fingers, broken beneath Hoyle's heavy boot.

"Say you're a pig," Jack said.

The man moaned and searched blindly for his stool.

"Say you're an SS pig!" Jack repeated. He balled up his fist and readied it. "Say you're a goddamn Nazi pig!"

Jack realized that he was speaking English.

He switched to German. "Say you are a Nazi swine."

"I am a Nazi swine," the man said immediately.

"Say you're an SS swine."

"I'm an SS swine."

Jack tried to think of something else to make the man say. He looked over at Ball, who shrugged.

"Hit him again, Wiseman," Hoyle said. "Hit him and then tell him he got the shit beaten out of him by a Jew."

The man's legs buckled. He fumbled for the stool and sat down, leaning his good hand on the bar. Jack watched him for a moment and then felt the cocktail of moonshine, schnapps, and dark beer bubble in his belly. He clasped his hand over his mouth and ran for the door, bursting out onto the sidewalk. He aimed for the gutter but instead spewed vomit all over a dun-colored Volkswagen parked at the curb.

· 11 ·

THE COMPOUND HUMILIATIONS OF Ilona's rejection and his own horrible behavior in the bar served to shut Jack down. He did his best to become a mindless functionary, a soldier with a job about which he felt nothing, without a personal life or care. When he woke in the morning with an erection from a half-remembered dream, he tried to replace thoughts of Ilona with those of other women, like his old girlfriend or some of the prettier WACs who had lately shown up in Salzburg. But he still put most of his allotment of cigarettes aside for Ilona. He frequented the PX on the Getreidegasse, purchasing things he knew that she liked or items he thought would be useful to her in trade. For himself he bought nothing other than the most basic necessities. His parsimony made him feel good, and occasionally he allowed himself to imagine her face when he presented her with this hoard, proof that he hadn't shirked the responsibility he'd assumed for her care.

As the weeks passed, he often thought of Rudolph Zweig's little nephews and felt guilty. He sent packages with his most trustworthy soldier, but the last one came back unopened. Zweig and the boys were gone; they'd moved on. Jack fretted terribly about them, despite Ball's assurances that things had improved substantially for the Jewish DPs recently. Though his friend promised that the Jewish DPs' daily calorie ration had been increased, Jack was plagued by the thought that without his help all those for whom he'd assumed responsibility would go to bed hungry.

In this period Jack also received an overdue promotion to captain, though it had little effect on his day-to-day life beyond a marginal increase in pay. If anything, his job became more tedious. Now it consisted primarily of protecting the contents of the warehouse, not from looters or thieves, or even from the requisitions of the brass, but from his own men, who were finding it harder and harder to keep from slipping things into their pockets. He supervised his apathetic GIs on their halfhearted patrols and warned them again and again, but he couldn't be everywhere at once, and he knew things were disappearing from the warehouse.

He felt a mounting sense of impotence, like a man trying to carry sand in a sieve. He had tried to hold on to the property in the warehouse, but between the senior command's requisitions and the men's pilfering, it was dribbling away. He had tried to care for the Zweigs, and they were gone. And Ilona, though he tried not to think about her, she had slipped through his fingers, too.

One afternoon, Corporal Streeter, finishing his very last week as a soldier in the U.S. Army, called Jack over. "I found something you're going to want to see."

They had long ago gone through the boxes and crates looking for ones of particular value, but somehow they'd missed a small leather case, a lady's jewelry box, full of gold watches.

"Look at the lining, sir. Of the box."

The lid of the case was lined with pink silk on which the name of a store and an address were stamped in gold lettering.

"I remember you said to tell you if we found anything from Nagy-várad."

For the whole long period of their relationship, Jack had searched desperately and fruitlessly for anything at all from the town of Ilona's birth. He had known that at least some of the paintings and furs, silver menorahs and tureens, must have come from this former city of twenty-five thousand Jews, but he could find no discernible trace. And now, when he'd stopped looking, here it was, a case of gold watches. He couldn't know, of course, if the watches themselves came from Nagyvárad or only the jewelry case. Perhaps the watches had been placed in the case by the Jewish Property Office when it had sorted the property at the Óbánya Castle, before they loaded the train.

"Where was this?" Jack said.

"I found it at the bottom of a crate full of cameras. I was having a heck of a time finding one with an intact lens to fill General Lorde's order."

Jack lifted out the watches one at a time and studied them, trying to decide if any of them might once have adorned the wrist of a prosperous grain merchant. One of them looked expensively plain, a simple case and a heavy gold band, in a way that he thought might do for the purposes of self-flagellation, remembering Ilona and the way she used to talk about her father. He lifted it out, and saw lying beneath it a pouch of black velvet. He opened the little velvet bundle, and found a piece of women's jewelry, a large pendant decorated with an enamel painting of a peacock in vivid purple and green, with white accents. The metal was intricately filigreed, the work of an accomplished metalsmith, and the tip of each peacock feather was inset with a gem.

He knit the braided gold chain through his fingers. He imagined the woman who had worn it, against the pulsing hollow of whose throat it had once grown warm. Had it been a gift from her husband, her father, her lover? Had she known Ilona? Was she dead? He eased the pendant back into its velvet pouch, tucked it back in among the watches, and closed the case. He wrote GOLD WATCHES on a paper label, dabbed the back of the label with mucilage, and pasted it to the front of the case. Then he carried it to the corner of the warehouse that he had reserved for the more-valuable property and set it on top of a stack of other boxes containing watches.

And then, as if thinking of her had conjured her presence, Ilona walked in the door. She had changed in the weeks of their separation. Her hair was longer, and she wore it pinned back from her face. She had on the wool coat his mother had sent, belted tightly at the waist, and when she removed it she revealed a new white blouse and a pale blue cardigan embroidered with rows of tiny flowers around the neck. Her pants were black wool and looked like they'd originally been a military uniform but had been altered to fit her small waist and round hips. Her lips were shell pink and moist from her lipstick, and he thought she might have powdered her nose; the freckles were smoothed over. He liked the lipstick, it reminded him of the first time they kissed, but he wanted to take out his handkerchief and rub the powder away.

Though he was happy to see her, at once realizing how much he had longed for her all these past weeks, he was conscious of a darker emotion, a complicated brew of guilt and shame, anger and hurt.

"Ilona" was all he could say.

She leaned across the improvised desk and kissed his cheek. He resisted for a moment and then gave in to his impulse and in two steps had rounded the desk and pulled her into his arms. He kissed her on the mouth, tasting the wax of her lipstick.

"You missed me, Jack," she said. She leaned her face on his chest, and he linked his hands around her waist. He rocked back and forth on his heels.

"Yes," he murmured into her hair.

"I, too," she said, pulling away. "I missed you, too."

"How are you, Ilona?" he asked. "You look good."

"I am well. Many things are different for me. I moved. And I have a job."

"You moved?"

"They moved all the Jews out of the Hotel Europa, so I am now in the Muelln Camp. It's good there. Not so comfortable, but we are all Jewish there. No more Marias from the Ukraine."

"And you're working?"

"I am a kindergarten teacher."

He smiled.

She pulled away, but returned his grin. "Perhaps you don't think I am suited to this job?"

"Not at all." He couldn't bear not to be touching her, so he took her hand. He saw that her broken thumbnail had almost grown out. "I'm sure you're a great teacher."

"I am only an assistant. I take them for long walks in the mountains to strengthen their legs. And I am learning with the children. We have a teacher from Palestine who has come to teach us Hebrew. Do you know Hebrew?"

"A little."

"I am finding it surprisingly easy to learn. You should come study with us. Perhaps it will be even easier for you. You will recognize words from synagogue."

"I learned Hebrew in college. My family isn't much for synagogue."

"Of course. You told me this. My family was the same. In Nagyvárad we were Yom Kippur Jews, you know what that is?"

"I guess I do."

"But now I study Hebrew," Ilona said. "It took Hitler to make me a good Jew."

He laughed, but it was out of politeness. Even in its bitterness the joke was spoiled for him by the knowledge of the kind of Jew the war had made out of Jack Wiseman. Could a religious identity be crafted from anger and disgust?

"Can I take you to dinner?" he asked. "To that restaurant you like near the Mozarteum?"

"Today I can't stay, but Saturday is Erev Purim, and there will be a big celebration in the evening. Will you come?"

"To Muelln?"

"Yes."

"Okay, sure."

She kissed him good-bye on the cheek, but he turned his head and pressed his lips to hers. For a moment it seemed like she might wriggle away, but then she relaxed in his arms. He ran the fingers of his right hand through her hair and gripped her skull in his hand, kneading it gently with his fingertips. His left arm circled around her. He fingered the strap of her brassiere, wishing he could push it aside and hold her breast in his hand.

"Don't go yet," he said. "I have something to show you."

"What is it?"

"Most of the stuff here isn't labeled, but some is, and all along I've kept my eye out for property from your town, from Nagyvárad. You won't believe it, but just today we found a case. The name of a jeweler was printed on the inside lid. Csillag and Dux."

A sad smile. "My family used to shop there sometimes. I remember my uncle bought my aunt Firenze's wedding ring there. I helped him choose it."

"Do you want to see it?"

"What's in it?"

"Watches and some jewelry. Although I don't know if what was in the box actually came from Nagyvárad at all. The Jewish Property Office did a lot of sorting and reorganizing before they loaded everything on the train."

She stood still for a minute, biting her lip.

"Okay, yes. Show me."

Jack took her back into the warehouse, to the corner where he'd placed the case. He took it down, balanced it on a wooden crate, and opened it. For a moment she just looked at the case, at the printed name and address on the silk, at the heap of gold watches. Then she picked up the velvet pouch and dumped the contents out into the palm of her hand. She stared at the peacock pendant.

For a moment, Jack allowed himself to imagine that everything they had together and lost was there again, to hope that the pendant, and by extension the one who had shown it to her, had laid a claim on Ilona. A claim she was willing to honor.

"Do you recognize it?" he asked eagerly.

"No," she said.

"You don't?"

"Nagyvárad is a large town. And people from the countryside come to shop there. This necklace could have belonged to anyone from the district, or like you said, from anywhere in Hungary." She dropped it back into the little velvet bag and the bag into the case. She turned away. "Anyway, peacock feathers bring bad luck. Who would wear such a thing?"

"Do you want to look through the rest of the case?"

"What's the point?" She walked quickly away, up through the aisle of crates and boxes, past the stacks of paintings, until she reached the front of the warehouse, where she waited for him.

When he caught up with her, she said in a voice of brittle, false cheer, "So I will see you on Purim?"

"I shouldn't have showed you that. I'm so sorry."

"You don't need to be sorry. I'm okay. I'm fine. It's only . . . for a moment I hoped that by some miracle you found something of mine. Or something of my parents'. I was just disappointed. But even if you had found something that belonged to me back then, I don't know if I would want it. All that is the past. And I am done with the past. I don't want anything from the old world."

"I understand. Of course."

She seemed to gather her energy and gave him another kiss on the cheek. "I'll see you Saturday."

"See you Saturday," he said, and watched her go.

THE ROAD LEADING INTO the camp at Muelln was lined with oversized tombstones. Cut with crude artfulness from cardboard and plywood, they were inscribed, in gay lettering, with the dates of the birth and death of Adolf Hitler. The walls of the barracks were hung with painted banners depicting the late Führer in various tortured poses, some of the caricatures verging on the obscene. Stuffed effigies recognizable by their bristle-brush mustaches hung by their ankles or their necks from every lamppost. A boy of about ten years stood in front of a makeshift fire pit in which blazed a small but merry flame. The boy was holding a book and offering passersby the opportunity to tear out a page and fling it into the fire. Jack watched one man shove a page down the back of his pants before crumpling it up and lobbing it into the flames. The boy laughed so hard he doubled over and wiped tears from his eyes. When he stood up he noticed Jack and waved to him.

"Look!" he said in English, turning the volume so that Jack could see its cover, with the black-lettered title: *Mein Kampf*. "You want wipe your ass with Haman's book?"

"Hitler is Haman?" Jack asked.

"Hitler is the biggest Haman of all!"

Jack remembered a proverb his grandfather used to mutter when reading the newspaper: So many Hamans, and only one Purim.

The closest Jack had come in his life to celebrating the holiday of Purim was to eat the three-cornered *hamentaschen* his *bubbe* used to make. But if the wild revelry going on right now in the DP camp was what Purim was like, he had had no idea what he was missing. The roadways and paths of the Muelln camp, a former army barracks, were teeming with people in costumes and masks. It was like Halloween, except here the adults dressed up, too. There were jesters and queens, leopards, witches, and Cossacks. One young man had scavenged most of an SS uniform, complete with cap and death's-head insignia. He had padded out the seat of his gray jodhpurs with a pillow, and he carried a wooden paddle that he offered to passersby, inviting them to land a hefty wallop on his behind. With every blow he would fling himself down into the dirt, feigning agony, howling for his "Mama Adolf" to save him.

Jack passed a booth featuring a huge plywood tombstone that read HERE LIES HITLER, MAY HIS NAME BE BLOTTED OUT. People took turns climbing up a painter's ladder, dipping brushes into a bucket of black paint, and slapping paint over their tormentor's name.

As Jack watched the crowd stream through the pathways, in their motley and ghoulish giddiness, he felt his own spirits lift. Somebody handed him a tin cup filled with some unholy brew of K ration lemon-drink powder and grain alcohol. He drank it all and searched the painted faces for Ilona's. He doubted he would find her in her room, even if he could bully his way through the crowd to get there. He mooched a refill of his cup from a passing girl with a pitcher and climbed up onto the roof of a porch of one of the barracks, where he could see the parade that was about to begin.

The camp orchestra led the way, a battered hodgepodge of clarinetists and violinists, bassoonists and saxophonists, many of the finest lights of European classical music, playing a raucous version, half polka, half circus, of John Philip Sousa's "The Liberty Bell." They flung their legs about in a parody of the goose step as the spectators clapped their hands along with the music. Next came the Muelln Football Club in homemade uniforms, their muscular legs extending from their shorts, followed closely behind by a team of teenage gymnasts, boys and girls, turning cartwheels down the parade route. Jack peered at the next group to be sure that his eyes were not clouded by alcohol. There was no mistaking the small group of tiny people, waist-high adults bedecked in matching lederhosen, the women with their hair hidden beneath cloth caps. The Seven Dwarfs, but without their Snow White. Every group in the parade carried a gaudy hand-lettered banner: the needleworkers' union, the trade school students, the hospital staff. A group of young people wearing shorts and sandals inadequate to the March cold bore a banner proclaiming themselves members of the youth group Betar; another group was members of Kibbutz HaShomer HaTzair. A group of scouts attempted a valiant if hopeless simulacrum of a color guard, each scout desperately waving his or her own homemade version of the flag of the Zionist movement, a blue Star of David on a white background between two horizontal blue stripes. Then came the kindergarten, the children hopping delightedly from foot to foot, running this way and that, barely able even to keep to the parade route, let alone march. In their midst, laughing joyously, was Ilona. A gaily patterned kerchief covered her head, and she wore a matching apron. She'd braided her hair in two pigtails that stood out crookedly from beneath the kerchief. She'd drawn large freckles across her nose and painted a bright red cupid's bow over her pale lips. She wore two different striped stockings, one red, one black.

Jack swallowed the last of his drink, climbed down from the roof, and ducked through the crowd until he caught up with the parade. He called to her. At the sound of her name she scanned the crowd.

"Ilona!" he shouted again. He wormed his way through the crowd until he reached the edge of the parade. She disentangled her hand from that of one of the small children who clung to it and waved him over. He plunged in. He wanted to take her in his arms, but the parade in which they both now marched propelled him forward.

"Ilona!"

She smiled. "Happy holiday, Jack," she said in Hebrew.

"Happy holiday to you, too!"

They had by now reached the end of the parade route. A bearded rabbi stood on a stage erected in the middle of what had been the mustering grounds of the barracks that once occupied this site. The rabbi lifted his hand for silence, and despite their varying levels of intoxication, the large crowd quieted. He took a small leather-bound volume out of the pocket of his suit jacket and began to chant the first chapter of the Book of Esther. Jack wondered how many of the assembled crowd actually spoke Hebrew and how many merely listened for the name of the diabolical enemy of Israel. Each time the rabbi chanted "Haman," the crowd erupted in boos and hoots. Children banged cymbals fashioned of pot lids or beat sticks together. By the end of the rabbi's reading, the crowd was delirious with a rage-fueled joy.

The speakers came next, various camp dignitaries and officials, who decried the beast of Germany and recalled the Purims of previous years, when there had been little hope that the prophecy of Ezekiel would come to fruition, that the dry bones of Israel would live again. Some spoke in Yiddish, others in German, still others in a Hebrew sufficiently simplified that Jack had no trouble understanding it.

The speeches showed no sign of winding down, and Jack was wondering how he would get Ilona alone when she grabbed his hand.

"Come with me!" she said.

She stopped to whisper in the ear of one of the other kindergarten teachers, turning over her charges, Jack figured. She moved quickly, snaking her way through the crowd. At times there were so many people Jack couldn't see her ahead of him, but she held fast to his hand, and he trusted her to lead him along. They broke free and ran down a path between two barracks to a door by the barbed-wire fence that marked the boundary of the camp. They ducked inside.

The barracks had been organized into rows of cubicles demarcated by piles of furniture and makeshift plywood walls. She led him to a tiny cubicle in the middle of the barracks. Though there were small windows cut into the walls, the light barely penetrated so far inside, and so it was in murky half-light that she stripped off her clothes. He watched her, trembling. When she was naked, she lay back on the small cot. With a groan, he fell on top of her, fumbling at the buttons of his pants, the grain alcohol swirling in his belly. Her body trembled as he traced his tongue along the scars, pocks, and pleats that ravaged her beautiful, pale skin.

It was over almost as soon as it had begun, but for long moments afterward, he lay on top of her, his lips pressed into the side of her neck, murmuring her name.

She wrapped her arms around his neck, planted a wet kiss on his mouth, and said, "Come, Jack. There's someone I want you to meet."

· 13 ·

THE MAN WHO OPENED the door to them was short, with bushy black eyebrows from which a few wiry white hairs stuck up like antennae. More tufts of hair poked from the open collar of his shirt. The effort of producing such plenty had exhausted his follicles, however, and his pate was hairless and polished to a high shine, mottled with misshapen freckles. He greeted Ilona with a nod but raised his caterpillar brows in Jack's direction.

"Jack Wiseman," Ilona said. "My friend."

"A pleasure to meet you, Captain Wiseman," the man said, extending his hand. He had a thick eastern European accent, but his English was good.

Jack, dressed in civilian trousers and shirt, wondered how the man knew his rank.

Ilona said, "Jack, this is Aba Yuval. He is a member of the Jewish Brigade."

When he'd first read about the Jewish Brigade in his grandfather's Yiddish newspaper, Jack had not known whether to feel pride at their exploits or insulted by their segregation from the main body of British armed forces. Would he have wanted to be part of a specially designated, separate brigade of Jews in the U.S. Army? It was hard even to imagine such a thing coming to be, until he thought of the colored soldiers.

He followed Ilona into the room and immediately snapped to attention. Rabbi Bohnen, in uniform, sat on a wooden chair at a small table in the center of the room.

"Captain Wiseman," the major said. "Happy Purim to you!"

"Sir."

" 'Sir' is for soldiers. You should call me rabbi."

"I'm a soldier, sir."

"Yes, of course you are, son. You are a soldier. But you are also a Jew. And also a righteous man, aren't you?"

It was no easier now to answer the question than it had been the first time the rabbi had posed it, months before, no easier, in fact, even to discern the truth behind the question. Jack felt as though the rabbi was trying to tug on a string in his heart, a string labeled "Jew." But that string was tangled and frayed from disuse. Nothing happened when you pulled it.

The rabbi got to his feet and patted Jack on the arm. "These are fine men, Captain Wiseman. I hope you'll help them in any way you can."

On his way out the door, the rabbi shook hands first with Yuval and then with the third man in the room. This man sat on the edge of a cot, his legs crossed elegantly one over the other, smoking a cigarette. Unlike Yuval, who was dressed casually, in a well-worn shirt and a pair of army fatigues, this man wore an impeccably tailored suit, the cuff of his pants breaking cleanly over a pair of canary-yellow socks.

He smiled blandly at Jack, who struggled to get a read on him.

Jack looked from one man to the other and then back at Ilona, who was busy pulling at a loose thread on the apron of her Purim costume. Why had she brought him here?

Yuval said, "In the Yishuv we are not so formal. We use first names. May I call you Jack?"

Jack didn't reply, instead he looked again at Ilona, who still refused to meet his eye.

Yuval continued, "We have a situation, Jack. You know the conditions in the DP camps, yes?"

Jack looked around the room. It appeared to be the residence of a single person, and though the cot was narrow and there was a paucity of personal belongings, it was a room, not a cubicle. Yuval's "situation" seemed better than most.

The man continued, "In Germany it is worse even than here. At least here, in Land Salzburg, your command is sympathetic to the plight of the Jews. Your general sends Rabbi Bohnen to help us. But in Germany the military government appoints SS to high positions and lets them abuse the few Jews who survive. Your General Patton, he refused to arrest the SS because he said it would be silly to get rid of the most intelligent people in Germany. Instead, he packed the Bavarian Provincial Administration full of Nazis. Even now, we haven't managed to weed them out. They have a saying in Germany, 'Too bad you weren't a Nazi, then maybe you'd get somewhere.' You've heard this?"

"No." But Jack wasn't surprised. Ball had recently told him that a survey of U.S. troops reported that 59 percent of them believed that Hitler had done a lot for Germany. Given his experience with the replacements, Jack thought the figure was an understatement.

"The Germans will never stop killing the Jews," Yuval said. "Even when the Allied victory was inevitable, even as the Wehrmacht prepared to surrender, German civilians murdered the remnant of the camps, those who were led on forced marches through the countryside. I met a man once who told me that he was chased by a gang of boys—boys, Jack—who screamed at him, 'We're going hunting, to shoot down the zebras!' You know why 'zebras'?"

"No."

"Because of the striped uniforms."

At this Ilona moved closer to Jack, slipped her hand in his. He knew she was thinking of Etelka. He almost forgave her for ambushing him with these men.

"What do you want from me?" he asked Yuval, though the question might as easily have been directed at her.

Yuval said, "We understand that you have access to a truck. A U.S. military truck."

At the thought of the truck and what had happened in the back, Jack flushed.

"There is a truck at the warehouse where I work," he said.

"A U.S. military truck."

"Technically it belongs to the Allied civilian authority."

"It is our hope," Yuval said, "that you will make it possible for us to, let us say, borrow your truck."

"Nothing doing."

"Sorry?"

"I'm afraid I can't do that. Like I said, it belongs to U.S. Forces, Austria."

"But it is under your command, yes?"

"Yes."

"So where you command it," Yuval said, pleased by his own logic, "that's where it goes."

Was this what it was about? Was this why Ilona had come to him? Was this why she had made love with him? As incentive? To get him to turn over his truck? He was furious and humiliated and wanted to leave, to run, to escape his anger and shame.

"Sorry," Jack said, turning to the door. "The truck's not mine to lend."

The way Yuval blocked the door was elegant, without apparent force or effort, but as surely as a brick wall. "Okay, so you do not lend it to us. You just park the truck in an unguarded place, leave the key, walk away. And don't come back for it for a day. That's all."

"Oh, that's all, is it?"

"That's all."

"And what, if you don't mind my asking, do you need a truck for?"

The man in the yellow socks shook another cigarette loose from his pack, affixed a small cardboard holder to it, and lit it with a shiny silver lighter. He blew two thin streams of smoke from his nostrils. He held the cigarette like a woman, between his index and middle fingers. He spoke in a refined and cultivated German accent. "Captain Wiseman," he said, "you are a Jew."

It was not a question, so Jack did not bother to answer it.

"I was at Auschwitz," the man continued. "Not long after liberation. You know of Auschwitz?"

"Yes."

"As difficult as it is for the Jewish survivors in Germany and here in Austria in the terribly overcrowded DP camps, it is worse in Poland. Those who have tried to reclaim their homes have been threatened. Some of them have been killed. They survive the camps, and find their way home at last, and there they die, on their own doorsteps, killed by their own neighbors. It is a terrible dilemma, don't you think?"

"What is?"

"What to do with all these Jews. Hitler killed so many of them, but still some remain. Perhaps one hundred thousand, perhaps a million. No one is sure. Neither is anyone sure what to do with them. Will your government take them, do you suppose? Will Mr. Harry Truman say, *Please, half-dead Polish Jews, come to New York. Come to Missouri.*"

Jack remembered sitting as a teenager at his maternal grandparents' kitchen table, watching his normally stoic grandfather weep over the fate of the German Jewish refugee passengers onboard the *St. Louis,* turned away from Cuba, rejected by the United States, and sent back to their grim fates in Hitler's Europe.

"I doubt it," he said.

"You doubt it. I, also, doubt it. So then, what will become of them, Captain Wiseman? Their villages are gone. Even their cities. What remains of Jewish Vilna, Jewish Warsaw? Jewish Bucharest or Jewish

Berlin? You know as well as I do. So, then. What will happen to all these Jews?"

"I don't know."

"And, like you, your government has no answer."

"If they do, I'm not privy to whatever it is."

"Ah, that is where we differ, you and I. You see, I am privy to the answers of at least some in your government. Right now, it is costing your government millions to feed and house the Jews who are pouring into the American Zone. It's costing, and nobody wants to pay for it. Your president, he wants to spend his money rebuilding Europe, turning Germany and Austria into allies against the Soviet Union. The British are your allies, and thus there can be no official policy that contradicts them, but some in your government agree with me that the Jewish remnant should go far away, as far as Palestine, to settle the land of Israel."

"I see," Jack said. "And so you're planning on driving them there, a hundred thousand Jews, in my truck."

The man smiled.

"Only a few of them," Yuval said. "And only to Italy. After that we use a boat."

Jack had never told a woman to fuck off, and he wasn't about to begin, but as Ilona chased him through the camp, calling his name and begging for him to stop, to talk to her, he was sorely tempted. Instead he ignored her and would have made his escape had he not run into the crowd of revelers, only just now dispersing, the speeches having finally come to an end.

"Goddamn it," he muttered, trying to make it through the throng.

"Please, Jack!" Ilona said, catching up to him. She grabbed his arm with both her hands. "Why are you running away from me?"

He shook her off. "I'm not running away."

"Yes, you are."

"Tell me, Ilona, did you invite me here today because those men told you to?" He glanced quickly around to be sure that none of the passersby could hear him. He bent his head and hissed in her ear. "Did you sleep with me because they told you to?"

She dropped her hands and glared at him, her face red. "You dare to say this to me? You go. Go now! I never want to see you again."

He thought of her hand stealing into his at the mention of the murderous German boys and their hunt for the "zebras," and he hesitated, wondering if his anger was justified.

"Ilona, tell me the truth. What happened today, in your room. In your bed. Did they tell you to do that?"

"I am not a prostitute. And those men are not . . . I don't know the word. They are not men who own prostitutes."

"Pimps."

She frowned. "That's not the word."

"Yeah, it is."

" 'Pimp'?" she said. "That is a ridiculous word. It's like a joke."

"Ilona!"

"Jack, I came to you because I missed you. I took you to my room because I was happy."

"And why did you take me to meet those men?"

"Because your rabbi asked me to. I told him you were coming today, and he told me to bring you to meet the men from Palestine."

Jack wanted so badly to believe her. And he did. He did believe her but for one worm of doubt that wriggled and gnawed and poisoned what he wanted so desperately to feel. And then another small hand slipped into his, and he jumped. It took him a moment to recognize Tomas Zweig. It had only been a matter of weeks since he had last seen the boy, but in that time Tomas had grown at least a few inches. It was as though his body had hibernated during the long years of the war and was now doing its best to catch up.

"Tomas!" he said. The boy smiled and allowed his hair to be tousled. In German Jack asked, "How are you? How are your brother and your uncle?"

"They are well. Are you well?"

"I am."

The boy turned to Ilona. "Uncle sent me. He wants you to bring Jack to see him."

When Jack and Ilona arrived at Rudolph Zweig's room, they found a convivial group sharing a holiday meal of small green apples and slices of hard yellow cheese.

Rudolph leaped to his feet and said, "I am so glad Ilona has brought you to me! I wanted to tell you when we left the Europa, but it was so sudden."

"How are you?" Jack asked.

"Very well." Rudolph looked like a different person. Though his back was not entirely straight, he had discarded one of his canes. His cheeks had filled out. He looked impossibly young.

Tomas's older brother, Josef, had also shot up and filled out. The boy gave a stiff little bow, a remnant of the punctilious manner instilled by a governess long forgotten. He greeted Jack with a hearty "Shalom!"

Jack raised his eyebrow at their uncle. "He speaks Hebrew?"

Rudolph said, "Both boys are learning. As am I. They have taken Hebrew names." He gripped the shoulder of the older boy. "Josef is now Yossi, and Tomas calls himself Zvi."

"Zvi?" Jack said. "And what about you. Have you changed your name, too?"

"Why not?" Rudolph said. "A new name for a new life. Reuven Ben Ari. In honor of my father, Leopold. Yossi and Zvi's grandfather. We will now be sons of the lion, all of us."

Ilona said, "Reuven, Yossi, and Zvi are planning on immigrating to Palestine as soon as they are strong enough. They are the only members of their family to survive, and they cannot return to Berlin alone."

Not long ago, Rudolph told Jack, he had been asked by the UN Relief and Rehabilitation Administration to fill out a questionnaire about his immigration goals. He, like 18,700 of the 19,000 other Jewish DPs who filled out the questionnaire, listed "Palestine" as not only his first but also his second choice.

Ilona said, "In the Fürth DP camp near Nürnberg, when a UNRRA worker said they must put a different destination for their second choice, a quarter of the DPs filled in the word 'crematorium.'"

"There is nowhere else for us," Rudolph told Jack.

Was this true, Jack wondered. Had Hitler proven to the Jews that there were only two places safe for them, the first an ancient and misbegotten spit of land surrounded by enemies and the other no place at all?

Tomas, now Zvi, said, "We are going to walk over the Alps!"

Jack looked doubtfully at Rudolph's remaining cane.

Ilona said, "In the winter the trip is perilous. Reuven does not like it when I say this, but he isn't strong enough to make the journey. I tell him he must wait for spring."

Rudolph said, "They say that as time passes, it will only get harder to cross. The British are putting pressure on the Italians. No one knows how long the route from Salzburg will be open. If we don't go now, we will lose our chance."

Jack said, "Who is 'they'? Yuval? The other guy?"

Rudolph said, "You have met Aba Yuval?" He beamed. "A great man. A hero. The Yishuv, the Jewish community in Palestine, they sent not just Yuval but also Hebrew teachers, scout leaders. To help us prepare. Everyone is trying to get to Palestine."

Jack turned to Ilona. "And you? Are you trying to get to Palestine?"

"I don't know where I'm going. Maybe England to my aunt Firenze. Maybe Hungary. Maybe Palestine. Maybe someplace else."

"Where?" he said.

She shrugged and smiled.

And then, despite all his efforts to the contrary, he felt a tug on the tangled and frayed string in his heart, the one the rabbi had first pulled. He recognized what the rabbi had been telling him. He was a soldier but also a Jew. And now, here, in this place, with this impossibly brave young man and his impossibly brave boys, Jack understood which came first.

14

JACK AND YUVAL WALKED along the pathways of the DP camp, dodging groups of children playing in the squares of dirt that might have once been lawns and men gathering in small groups, smoking cigarettes and talking. Everywhere they walked Yuval was greeted with waves and cheers, though as soon as people realized that he and Jack were deep in conversation, they allowed a respectful distance.

"When we are ready, we will send Ilona," Yuval told Jack. "You'll give her the keys and show her where you park the truck."

"No," Jack said.

"No?"

"I'm not giving you the truck."

"Then why are you here?"

He had come on his own to see Yuval. Though Ilona knew of his decision, he had not wanted her to accompany him. "I will drive the truck."

"You will drive the truck."

"Right."

"To the Italian border."

Despite Rudolph Zweig's admiration of the man, Jack did not trust Yuval. He didn't trust him to protect USAF property, and, more important, he did not trust the man to protect the truck's cargo. Whatever the pugnacious Jew's assurances, Jack could not be sure that that cargo was as precious to Yuval as it was to Jack himself. There was, as ever, only one person Jack trusted. Himself.

"I don't care if you're taking those Jews to Tierra del Fuego," Jack said. "You want my truck, I'm driving it."

"Ridiculous," Yuval said.

"And yet fact."

"First of all, if you are caught, you will be court-martialed."

"That's my business."

"It will be my business if your arrest causes an international incident.

You think the U.S. Army will continue to turn a blind eye to our operations if they find out we're using GIs as drivers?"

"I don't know, and I don't care. You want my truck, well then, I'm going to drive it."

Yuval muttered darkly, harsh words in Hebrew, something about Jack being the son of a something. A whore, perhaps. Because he didn't trust Yuval, Jack had kept his familiarity with the language a secret, and so he did not ask. Though he didn't understand it all, he was surprised to find how similar the language the Jews from British Mandated Palestine spoke was to the biblical Hebrew he had studied in the Columbia University Classics Department. Yuval's accent was more glottal and rougher edged than that of Jack's Hebrew teacher at the university, an effete Englishman named Peters who seemed, if anything, to be an anti-Semite and who made no effort to pronounce Hebrew words any differently from English ones; but with practice and exposure Jack was finding Yuval and the other Palestinian Jews in the DP camp easy enough to understand.

Jack said, "And second of all?"

"And second of all what?"

"First of all, I'll be court-martialed. And second of all?"

"Second of all, how do I know what kind of driver you are?"

A doorway opened, and a woman stepped out and hurled a bucket of water directly in their path. Jack leaped aside, but Yuval was too slow. The sudsy water drenched his trouser legs and his boots.

"Oh, my God!" the woman cried in Yiddish. She switched to Hebrew. "I'm so sorry, Aba. What a terrible mess. Please, come in the laundry, and I will find you some dry pants."

Yuval gave her a reassuring smile. "It's no problem, madam. I needed a bath."

She giggled and went back inside.

Yuval turned to Jack. "Well. You've got good reflexes. I'll give you that."

Jack was supposed to drive the refugees to a spot a few kilometers from the Italian border, where they were to be met by guides who would lead them across the border and over the Reschen Pass, where another truck waited to take them south. The night before the trip, when Jack arrived in Yuval's room to discuss the plan, he had been surprised and happy to find Ilona there. She had been so busy with work and classes that they hadn't seen each other for a few days.

"I have wonderful news," she said. "Reuven is finally strong enough to make the journey. He, Zvi, and Yossi will be going with you tomorrow."

Yuval said, "This is a complicated transport. There will be almost a dozen children among the refugees."

Jack objected. The journey was too arduous, he told Yuval. Children wouldn't be able to tolerate hours stuck in the airless cold in the back of the truck, and they couldn't be expected to walk four or five kilometers through the snow over the border to the truck waiting on the other side. Yuval scoffed, reminding Jack that these children had survived far worse than a ride in an unheated truck and a short alpine hike. Moreover, if they waited until spring when the snow cleared from the passes, they'd be expected to walk the whole way, not cut the journey short in a truck.

"The truck is a magic carpet compared to the spring hike," Yuval said. "They will have only to manage the short walk across the border."

"And if they can't make it to the border?"

"They'll make it."

"And if they get caught?"

"If they get caught, the Italians will send them back, and we'll try again. And again. And again, until we get them through."

Jack might have continued to object had not Ilona taken up the cause. "They have been training for months," she told him. "All of them. Even the children."

"It's just too hard," he said.

"Please, Jack. If they wait and the border closes, it will break their hearts."

Eventually, he agreed, but only on condition that he be allowed to drive the group all the way across the border to Italy where the second truck waited, so that they would not have to hike at all. "There's a tuberculosis sanatorium in Meran, in the South Tirol," he told Yuval. "We'll disguise the refugees as TB patients on their way to take the cure."

"And if we get stopped? How will we explain the presence of an American officer?"

"I'm the official medical escort."

"And I will be the Red Cross nurse!" Ilona said. Before Jack could protest, she said, "There is no way the Red Cross would send TB patients without a nurse in attendance."

Jack had to acknowledge that she was right, and Yuval, impressed perhaps by their mutual strength of purpose, did not bother to muster arguments in opposition to either Jack's plan or Ilona's refinement.

The road through the mountains was rutted and buckled, and a skin of ice had formed over the puddles in the deeper potholes. Had the choice been his, Jack would have driven much more slowly to avoid sending the passengers hurtling around the rear of the truck, but every time his foot touched the brake, Yuval growled at him to "move it." With every bump, Jack imagined the people in the back tumbling over one another, the children jerked from side to side, banged together like a load of empty milk bottles.

The road smoothed out, and Jack shifted up a gear. Yuval propped his M1 between his knees and fished a pack of cigarettes out of his shirt pocket. Both the weapon and the cigarettes were American made. Had these also come from the Jewish Agency, Jack wondered. Or was General Collins so eager to rid himself and the American Zone of the ever-increasing burden of DPs that he was supplying the Jews with weapons to guard their escape through the Alps to Italy and their run on the British blockade of Palestine?

Yuval lit his cigarette. Jack rolled down his window against the acrid smoke, glancing in his side mirror. The clouds were heavy, and there was only a faint sliver of moon. They had timed the trip for this day, when there would be just enough light to see the road without the aid of headlamps but not so much as to risk being noticed. But their plans had been complicated by the threat of a storm, and for most of the drive the toenail moon that was all Jack had to light his way had been lost behind streaky gray clouds. It was only because his eyes were sharpened by hours of peering into the gloom that Jack noticed the shadow on the road behind them.

The cold night air was like a slap across his cheek as he stuck his head out the window and looked back. There was no mistaking it. They were being followed.

"What is it?" Yuval said.

"There's something coming up behind us."

"A truck?"

"Smaller than that."

"Step on the gas!" Yuval said.

Jack looked back again, gauging the distance between himself and the approaching vehicle. Gently, he pressed his foot down. The truck rattled beneath him, picking up, but slowly, too slowly. The road was poor, the load was heavy, and the deuce-and-a-half wasn't made for speed. He looked out the window again. The vehicle behind him was still far enough back that it appeared little more than a smudge or shadow in the road, but it was growing closer.

"Move it!" Yuval said.

Instead Jack lifted his foot off the gas and shifted down.

"Faster!" Yuval said.

Jack slowed still further. He snapped his headlights on.

"What the fuck are you doing?" Yuval shouted.

"We can't outrun them," Jack said.

"The border is no more than ten kilometers away! Just go, go!"

"The border is eight kilometers," Jack said. "But they'll catch us long before that." He glanced back again. He could make out the silhouette of the vehicle behind them. It was a Willys jeep, American. By now both vehicles were traveling at a sedate thirty miles per hour, and Jack used the excuse of a huge pothole in the road to slow down still further.

"You'd better tuck that rifle under the seat," he said.

Yuval jammed his gun beneath his seat and covered the protruding butt with his haversack.

The jeep was right on their tail.

"Roll down your window," Jack said. "Stick your arm out and wave them by."

After a moment's thought, Yuval did as Jack told him.

The jeep pulled up next to them. Jack obligingly slowed. He glanced over but could not make out the jeep's occupants. They rolled along side by side for a moment, before the jeep pulled out ahead of them, slowed, and stopped.

Cursing, Jack ground the gear into first and brought the truck to a shuddering halt.

"Stay here," he said to Yuval.

He yanked open his door and hopped down.

"What's up, fellas," he called out, with a joviality that no one who knew him would ever have recognized.

A pair of GIs leaped from the jeep as he approached, their rifles cocked and ready.

"At ease!" Jack called.

When he was close enough for them to make out his double silver bars, the soldiers snapped to attention and saluted.

Casually, Jack returned the salute. "What can I do for you boys?" he asked.

"We've got orders to patrol the roads, sir," said one of the men, a sergeant. He was young, about Jack's age, his stripes newly minted. Still, he gave off an air of competence and military precision that under other circumstances Jack would have admired.

"For what?" Jack asked. "Smugglers?"

"Yes, sir," the sergeant said. "But mostly for refugees."

"Refugees?"

"We're supposed to keep them from crossing the border, sir."

Jack shrugged. He reached into his pocket and pulled out a pack of cigarettes. He tapped out three, gave the men each one, and lit his own. Then he held out his lighter. The unfamiliar smoke was harsh in his throat, and he stifled the urge to cough.

"Well then," he said. "I will surely keep my eyes open for refugees."

"Thank you, sir," the sergeant said, handing back the lighter and taking a long drag on the cigarette. "Only, hope you understand, I hafta ask. What have you got in the truck, sir?"

"Refugees," Jack said.

The two GIs glanced at each other.

"Kidding," Jack said. "TB patients. Taking them to a hospital in the South Tirol." He stuck the cigarette in his mouth, one eye closed against the smoke, and fished around in his pocket. He pulled out a scrap of paper and pretended to read it. "The Meran Sanatorium."

"You're escorting them yourself, sir?"

"You bet your ass I am, soldier," Jack said.

"Uh-huh. Only, I don't know. Seems like an unusual job for a captain. If you don't mind my saying so."

Jack eyed the sergeant. The man was tall, with a face that was saved from being pretty by a mass of acne pits and scars decorating his cheeks. He gazed blandly at Jack, and Jack smiled back.

"Well, you're right, Sergeant," Jack said. "But the bunch of candy-ass drivers that the army in its wisdom has seen fit to saddle me with? Not one of them was willing to drive a truck full of raging tuberculars. Go figure. Bunch of chickenshit motherfuckers."

"They refused an order, sir?" the young private said. At the sergeant's baleful look, he cast his eyes to his boots.

Jack said, "I could give every one of the bastards a yellow ticket, but do I need the paperwork? No, Private, I do not. So I decided to 'lead by example,' if you know what I mean."

"Mind if we take a look, sir?"

"Sure, Sergeant," Jack said. "Go 'head. But it's your funeral. Literally."

The sergeant strode over to the truck, the private lagging behind. As they approached the cab, Yuval leaned his head out.

"Nothing to worry about, Doc!" Jack said cheerfully. "Sergeant here just wants to make sure we're not smuggling refugees over the border." He turned to the sergeant. "That's the doc. He's responsible for the patients."

Yuval opened the door and jumped down. He extended his hand to the sergeant. "Dr. Lehrman. Franz." He was laying his German accent on a little thick, Jack thought.

The sergeant shifted his weapon and grudgingly shook Yuval's hand.

"How'd you get yourself a military escort?" he asked Yuval.

"Are you kidding?" Jack said. "Hollywood Harry wants these SOBs the hell out of Land Salzburg, that's how. Excuse the French, Doc."

"Not at all," Yuval said.

"All right," Jack said. "Let me introduce you to my cargo."

"I'd prefer you didn't," Yuval said. "The air is too cold for them."

"If you're worried about the cold, why are you traveling at night?" the sergeant asked.

"You are an inquisitive motherfucker, aren't you, Sergeant?"

"It's definitely in my nature, sir."

"We're traveling at night because that's when I want to travel, son," Jack said, doing his best impression of a superior officer growing impatient with a recalcitrant subordinate. "And I'd like to get on my way, so if you'll follow me . . ."

He led the way around to the back of the truck. He felt a familiar ache in the pit of his stomach, the anxious flutter he'd felt immediately before leading his soldiers into battle, the same flutter he'd felt when he'd asked Ilona out for the first time. He whipped the canvas curtains open, revealing the crowd huddled in the back of the truck. Rudolph was sitting on the bench closest to the rear opening, and when Jack opened the curtain he lifted his hand to shade his eyes from the glare of the sergeant's flashlight. Ilona, wearing a Red Cross smock, a jaunty nurse's cap, and a navy cape lined with red, sprang down from the truck.

"Captain!" she said in a British accent so impeccable it was all Jack could do not to laugh. "Shut the curtain immediately! The patients will catch their deaths."

"It'll just be a moment, ma'am," Jack said.

At that moment little Yossi began coughing. The sergeant shifted the flashlight, catching him in its beam. The young boy held a white hand-kerchief to his lips. His hacking was so realistic that Jack wondered for a moment if the boy might not, in fact, be ill. Then he pulled the cloth from his mouth, revealing an ugly smear of red blood.

"Jesus!" the private said, backing away.

"You see!" Ilona said, indignantly. "We must get them out of the cold!"

Jack let the flap drop. "Shit," he said, wiping his own mouth in a dis-play of nervousness. "What the hell was I thinking, making this ride myself? It's a fucking plague truck. I'm going to court-martial every last fucking one of those bunk lizards when I get back, if I don't cough up both my fucking lungs before that." He turned on the sergeant. "What's your name, soldier?"

"Walther, sir. Robert."

"Okay, Sergeant Walther. You about done here? I want to get this damn thing over with. Rumor has it there's a bar in Bruneck where the girls are almost as pretty as the booze."

Walther gave the truck a final suspicious look and then shrugged. "Yes, sir."

"So move your goddamn vehicle, Walther," Jack said.

Walther hesitated, and Jack wondered if he'd gone too far, but Wal-ther said, "Yes, sir."

Jack swung back up into the cab of the truck and gave an impatient tap on his horn. The two GIs got into their jeep and pulled it off the road. Jack drove away, sending up a spray of gravel as he passed.

Yuval said, "You appear to have a gift for subterfuge."

They passed the last eight kilometers to the border in silence. Jack reprised his irritable captain persona for the Austrian and Italian border guards, who seemed only too happy to accept the forged paperwork he thrust at them. An hour's drive past the border, on an unmarked cow path that Yuval was surprised Jack had so little difficulty finding, the second truck was waiting for them.

A man and a woman were leaning against the bumper of the truck, both of them bundled into white parkas that looked, Jack thought, suspiciously like U.S. Army issue. They greeted Yuval in Hebrew. It only took a moment or two for Jack to adjust to their accents and to understand at least some of Yuval's explanation for their delay.

Jack opened the flaps of the truck. "Cute trick," he said to Rudolph in German. Rudolph accepted Jack's hand; the leap to the ground was still too much for him to manage on his own. "How did you do it?"

Once he was firmly on the ground, Rudolph pushed up his sleeve, revealing a white handkerchief knotted around his wrist about three inches above his palm. He untied the handkerchief. Beneath it lay a gash about an inch long, still oozing blood.

"You couldn't have pricked your thumb?" Jack said.

Rudolph laughed. "Ilona figured we needed more blood than that."

"Probably right. You'd better get that sewn up once you get where you're going."

"I will," Rudolph said. "Jack?"

"Yes?"

"Thank you. For everything."

"Don't thank me yet," Jack said. "Send me a letter when you get to Palestine." If you get to Palestine, he thought.

"I'll send you a crate of oranges."

"Not milk and honey?"

"That as well."

As Ilona helped the refugees settle themselves in the second truck, Jack leaned against the hood of his, staring up. The clouds had cleared, and there were so many stars it looked as though a shaker of salt had spilled across the velvet sky. He entertained himself by identifying as many constellations as he could.

He listened as Yuval gave his colleagues a series of detailed instructions, including information about which of the refugees were likely to need extra help should walking become necessary and which could be relied upon to assist others. Yuval recommended that certain of the refugees, including Rudolph, be looked to as leaders.

"That one?" the woman in the white parka said, looking at Rudolph. "He can be trusted?"

"As much as any of them," Yuval said.

"Is this batch as bad as the others?" the woman said.

Jack stiffened. He listened, growing ever more furious, ever more still.

"They're all the same," Yuval said.

The other man sucked his teeth loudly. "*Ai,* Yuval. We're going to end up regretting this. Imagine the hell if every one of the DPs in the camps ends up coming to the Yishuv."

The woman said, "All this filth, just as it is."

That was more than Jack could bear. Had she not been a woman, he might have punched her. Instead, he leaped up, strode over to her, and, in stilted biblical Hebrew, told her that she disgusted him. He wanted her to cower; he wanted to see her bend her head in shame. Instead, she laughed.

"Where did you study Hebrew? In cheder?"

"What is wrong with them?" Jack said to Yuval, switching to English.

Had Yuval rebuked his colleagues, Jack might have dismissed them as callow, ignorant youth, like the U.S. Army replacements who sucked up to the Austrian burghers and their daughters and treated the DPs like dirt. But Yuval said, "Captain Wiseman, your job is to drive. Understanding the complicated political situation is perhaps above your pay grade."

"Above my pay grade?" Jack said, his voice growing softer as his fury rose. He did not want to frighten Rudolph and the boys or the other people now climbing into the back of the second truck.

"Tzipi and Micha are doing their job. It's time for you to do yours. Let's go."

"We're not going anywhere," Jack said.

Yuval shrugged. "It's your truck. I care little what time we return. I am not the one who risks court-martial." He switched back to Hebrew and told his colleagues to help the rest of the DPs into the truck and get moving.

"No one is getting moving until I say so." In a smooth motion Jack pulled his sidearm from its holster. Tzipi began to raise her weapon, but Yuval put up a restraining hand.

"What do you want, Jack?" he said.

"How can you speak about them like that?"

"As I said. The situation is complicated."

"Why don't you explain it to me. Help me boost my pay grade."

"In Palestine our life is work and war, and our people must be strong and brave. These people"—Yuval jerked his head toward the truck where the refugees waited, unable, Jack hoped, to hear the conversation between the two men—"these 'survivors' . . ." He said the word as though it were a curse, not a miracle. "You think they are strong and brave?"

"Who could possibly be stronger?"

Yuval gave a derisive click of his tongue. "What happened in Poland could never have happened in Palestine. No one could have slaughtered us in our synagogues, in our fields. There would have been no Jewish councils fulfilling the Nazis' demands for bodies. Every Jewish boy and girl in the Yishuv would have taken a gun and shot every German soldier they saw. Even if we had lost, we would have lost fighting. That, my friend, is strength. That is bravery."

"These people survived unholy misery, unimaginable torture. You know what proves their strength? They're alive. That's all the evidence we need."

"Yes. They are alive," Yuval said. "Why do you think they are alive when so many others are dead?"

"Because they managed by some miracle to hold on to the thread of life. If the war had lasted a few more months, they wouldn't have made it."

"Millions died," Yuval said. "Millions. These DPs who survived, I don't ask what they did, what they stole, or who they killed so that they of all the millions would live." He lifted his hand to silence Jack's protest. "Whatever they did, maybe some of them have the strength and courage to live in the land of Israel. I don't know. I hope some do. But most of them are broken people. And in our new land, with all our enemies, we have no room for broken people."

For a miserable moment, Jack saw the DPs through Yuval's eyes, the way they shuffled and scurried through the camps, the way many of them froze on the sidewalk when a black car approached, their eyes darting as though searching for a place—a hole, a burrow—in which to hide. The tears that came so easily to many, even the men. Their diffidence and exhaustion when asked to work, and the prickly rage with which they greeted any suggestion of anti-Semitism, real or imagined.

He pushed these ugly thoughts from his mind and said, "So why are you bringing them? You say you don't want them, but yet you go into the camps and convince them to immigrate. You train them, for Christ's sake. You've got Ilona traipsing up and down mountains with all these broken children. Why bother, if they're so damaged?"

Yuval shrugged. "We are at war. Now with the British, soon with the Arabs. You're a soldier. You know only some battles are fought on the field. Other battles are fought at sea, and others in the newspapers."

"The newspapers?"

"We will have our land, Jack, because Hitler showed the world that we have no other choice. We are owed. And these people, they are evidence of that debt. Evidence for everyone to see."

"You make me sick," Jack said. "They're people. Not objects to be used to serve your ends."

"I make you sick, do I?"

"Yes."

"You, my friend, have the luxury of a sensitive stomach. We in the Yishuv can afford no such delicacy. But there is an irony here, you know."

"What irony?"

"You guard so conscientiously that treasure train. And for whom?"

For the Jews of Hungary, Jack wished he could reply. But of course by now he feared that was no more than the vaguest and most unlikely of hopes.

Yuval smiled. "You guard the train for *us.* Someday soon, your government will give it all to us, all the gold and the diamonds and precious artworks, and we will use them to pay for this very operation of which you so disapprove. We will sell it all to buy boats and supplies and weapons. The Yishuv will owe you a great debt, Captain Jack Wiseman, which we will repay by fighting and surviving the next time you and yours allow yourselves to be herded like lambs to slaughter."

For a moment Jack imagined lifting his weapon, considered how many shots he could get off before Tzipi or Micha sent a bullet crashing through his skull. Then he shrugged and turned away, allowing himself only one final indulgence. "I hope you won't be disappointed," he said over his shoulder as he walked away. "There's not that much in the way of gold and diamonds."

Ilona's shadow in the sliver of moonlight looked odd, hunchbacked, but it wasn't until he was by her side that he realized she was wearing a haversack on her back. And even then it took a moment for him to understand what it meant.

"You can't," he said.

"I'm so sorry."

"Did you plan this all along?" She bit her lip, and he could see that she was trying to decide whether to lie to him. "Just tell me the truth," he said.

"Yes. I owe you that much. I knew I would go after I found out Etelka was dead, but it was only recently, when Reuven became determined to make the trip, that I decided to go now. He needs my help."

"Yeah? And who's going to help you? Those guys over there?" He jutted his chin in Yuval's direction. "Do you even know what they are? Those people who have trained you and pushed you and convinced you that Palestine is the only place for you? They're not your friends, Ilona. They're not your protectors or your heroes. They're just using you. They think you're the dregs of European Jewry. You can't trust them."

"What is a dreg?" she asked.

"You know. Dregs. Like what's left over in your coffee cup."

She smiled her bitter smile. "Yes. The smear in the bottom of the cup. That is what we are. All that's left."

"You don't understand. It's an insult. It's the worthless part that's left over. The dirt."

She sighed and adjusted the straps of her haversack. What did she have in it, he wondered. Had she packed any of the things he'd given her?

"Do you know what I think about at night?" she said.

I think about you, he wanted to say. "I have no idea what you think about, not at night, and not during the day, either."

"At night, as I try to sleep beneath a Wehrmacht woolen blanket dyed a horrible red, like dried blood, I wonder if I might not be the only Jewish survivor of Nagyvárad. I wonder, were they all killed? All the doctors and lawyers, wheat dealers and manufacturers, chiefs of police, members of the city council, teachers, beggars and housemaids. Are they all gone? Am I all that is left? One twenty-five-year-old woman from twenty thousand?"

"I'm sure there are others."

"Maybe. Maybe not. You say I cannot trust Aba Yuval. But he and the others from the Yishuv offer to the last Jew of Nagyvárad the possibility of a homeland."

Jack groaned in frustration. "They don't care about you or any of the other DPs. They're capitalizing on the world's guilt to force the British to give them Palestine. You're just a pawn in their battle with the British."

" 'They.' Who is 'they,' Jack? Isn't 'they' also you? Aren't you also a Jew?"

He refused to let her tug on the thread that had led him so astray. "They're not me. And they aren't you, either. It isn't about Jews and not Jews. It's about them using you, using immigration, as a weapon of war. Don't you see? They know the British are going to enforce the blockade.

They know none of the boats are going to get through. Rudolph and the boys and all the other DPs are basically hostages. Worse than that. The best thing that could happen in Yuval's eyes is if the boats to Palestine are fired on! If the British sink a ship full of concentration camp survivors there will be a huge outcry, and they will have no choice but to cave in to international pressure."

"Reuven."

"What?"

"His name is Reuven. You keep calling him Rudolph, but his name is Reuven."

"How can you not see this? He's being used. You're all being used."

"Maybe you're right. Maybe we are being used. And maybe we will die. But at least this time we die standing. We die on our feet. Not crawling in the mud."

"I don't understand you."

"Of course you don't understand. How could you? You are a lucky boy from America. You don't know anything."

"I know what happened to you."

"Do you?"

"Yes."

"You think you know. But you don't really know how I lived for almost a year."

"Yeah, well, I spent a year getting shot at by Germans, and you know what? That was no goddamn picnic, either."

Even as he said it, Jack knew that if this was the game they were doomed to play, he had already lost. In the hierarchy of horrors, as dreadful as his were, they were far down the list. Jack imagined a chart. Color coded, with rows and columns, figures and values. Picking up his first sergeant's helmet after a mortar blast and finding inside the rubbery gray remains of the man's brain was worth a few points, he supposed, but fewer than inhaling the dust of your mother's burned body. Being stripped of your clothes, forced to wear nothing more than a dead woman's torn blouse, the shredded shirttails barely covering your ass as you stood at attention hour after hour, the sun raising blisters on the top of your shorn scalp: ten points. The blood of your final menstrual period dripping down your thighs as you waited to be selected for death or another day of starvation? Another five. Scrambling to dig a foxhole in the frozen dirt while mortar shells whistle down around your ears: two points, at most. Taking cover beneath the dead body of your best friend?

Four more points. Or perhaps five. If there were actuaries in the world who could accurately assess the worth of a man's life, surely someone could determine the value of his misery.

He said, "The people Yuval works for, in Palestine? The Jewish Agency people? These are the very same people who are telling the U.S. government not to send the property from the train back to Hungary. They're the same people, do you understand? You were so angry at them. You said they were stealing your bicycle."

"No. I said you were stealing my bicycle."

"We aren't stealing anything." He paused. "Okay, yes. The U.S. brass are stealing stuff from the train. But they'll give it all back." Even as he said it, Jack knew this was at best a pathetic hope, at worst a bald-faced lie. When had the brass ever given anything back?

He continued, "It's not the U.S. Army's fault that the property hasn't been given back. If it weren't for the Jewish Agency, we would have sent the train back to Hungary by now. Your friend Yuval's bosses are telling the U.S. Army to sell the contents of the train and give them the money instead of sending it back to Hungary."

"You don't know what you're talking about. Why would they do that?"

"For the money! You think this huge immigration project of theirs is free? Yuval and his buddies are buying trucks and boats and weapons. They've got to bribe every Italian bureaucrat between the Alps and the Mediterranean. Not to mention what it costs to feed and train all the refugees in the camps along the way. Yuval's American cigarettes alone cost more than your bicycle."

"You know where I think my bicycle is, Jack?"

He sighed.

"I think a nice Romanian lady in Oradea is right now riding my Jewish bicycle home from work. Maybe she works in a bakery stolen also from Jews. Maybe she lives in a house stolen from Jews. Or maybe not. Maybe she has lived all her life in her house, and it is only her sister who stole a Jewish house. This kind Romanian lady, she took only a Jewish bicycle."

"Ilona!" Yuval called. "It's time to go."

Urgently, Jack said, "The Romanians are horrible. And the Hungarians, they're horrible, too. I don't think you should go back there. But Yuval and the rest of them aren't your answer. Palestine isn't your answer. You don't need to become a martyr. Come with me instead!"

"Come with you where?"

"Home. To New York."

"You want me to come live with you in New York City?"

"Yes."

"Because in New York City they love so much the Jews?"

"New York is full of Jews."

Tzipi and Micha swung up into their truck, slamming the doors. He had no time.

Ilona said, "You know what the Hungarians called Budapest before the war?"

"No."

"Jew-dapest."

"It's different. Please, Ilona!"

"In New York I will not be the dregs of Europe?"

Jack tried to imagine his parents seeing Ilona for the first time. His fastidious father pursing his narrow lips at the sight of her crippled foot, his warm but neurotic mother reduced to tears by the crooked tattoo, the number A11436 etched in blue on the freckled skin of her arm, a few inches below the crease of her elbow. He thought of the girls he'd dated in college, the bookish ones in their headbands and plaid kilts, with whom he'd exchanged chaste kisses in the library stacks, the jolly AEPhi girls in their green-and-white sweaters, with their bouncing curls and their sturdy legs. The racy downtown girls, their mouths tasting of cigarettes and red wine, who'd occasionally let him slip his fingers beneath the elastic of their panties as they necked in the dark corners of bars and cafés. Would these girls be Ilona's friends? What would all these cheerfully clueless people make of this dark and lonely girl with her bitter laugh?

He said, "In New York you'll be my wife. Ilona. Marry me." He belatedly dropped to the ground, on one knee.

"My God, Jack! Are you okay?"

"I'm fine."

"You fell."

"I didn't fall. I'm kneeling. Ilona. Please. Marry me."

"Oh, get up. For God's sake, get up."

He scrambled to his feet, wiped the dirt from his knees. He felt ridiculous.

"Jack," Ilona said. "I am not a foolish girl."

"I know that," he said.

"I know what Yuval and the others are doing. I know they are fighting a battle for Palestine and that we are a weapon in this war. I know they look at us and think, *Why are you alive when so many others are dead?* I know they wonder, Did this one steal bread? Did that one betray his friends? Was this one a *Kapo*, is that why she is alive? I think the same. I ask the same questions. I know I'm not the best of my family. My sister, Etelka, she was much finer than I. She deserved more than me to live. So I am alive, and I am not the good one."

"That's not true!"

"No," she agreed. "Or maybe yes. The others, maybe they're not the good ones, either. Or maybe they are. I don't know."

"I love you, Ilona. I love you, and I want to marry you."

"Once I was like you. I lived in a gossamer world, a tissue of lies, where things like love mattered. And that was all just blown away. Shredded and torn and destroyed. I don't want to go with you to New York, where even you cannot promise me it is not the Jew-dapest of tomorrow. I want to go to Tel Aviv and live where everyone is Jewish, and if your neighbor steals your bicycle it is because he is a thief, not because he is an anti-Semite."

"The British will never let you get to Tel Aviv."

"Of course they will. You said so yourself. The world will not let them kill Hitler's victims. They will not fire their guns on the few who survived."

"They will!"

"Maybe once. Maybe they'll kill one of us. Or two. Or ten. Maybe they will even kill me. But eventually we will win. Eventually they will have no choice but to give us the land."

"Okay, let's say you're right. You're still risking your life for people who despise you."

"Everyone despises us. This maybe is the only lesson I have learned. Every single person despises the Jews, even the ones who say they don't. Even the Jews themselves." Again the bitter laugh. "Except Yuval and the others from Palestine. They despise us, but they don't despise themselves. That is the miracle. A Jew who doesn't hate himself."

"I don't despise you. I love you. And you love me. I know you do."

"I don't even know what that means anymore. How can I?"

"Are you saying you never loved me? You lied to me? You really did come to the warehouse and take me back because Aba Yuval needed an American military truck to smuggle DPs across the border? You made love to me to get my truck?"

The second truck started up, the engine gunning. She glanced over at it. In the faint moonlight her skin shone pale, and he imagined he could see the flutter of her pulse in her throat. He allowed himself to believe that she was fighting back tears, but when she looked up at him, her eyes were dry.

"I'm sorry," she said.

He laughed then, a dark and bitter bark that he had learned from her. "Are you sad or apologetic?"

He left her there, walked around his truck, and swung himself into the driver's seat. He wanted to look away but couldn't, and so he watched as she crossed to the second truck, pulled aside the canvas curtain, and climbed inside. He waited for her to look back, to acknowledge everything that had passed between them, but she never did. So much did he loathe the idea of spending even another minute in Yuval's presence that he considered leaving him in the rutted field in northern Italy to make his own way back to Salzburg. But in the end Jack did, as always, the honorable thing.

Two

BUDAPEST; ISRAEL

2013

15

IT WAS NOT UNTIL they were knee to knee at a small table in the Central Kávéház that Amitai asked her name.

"Natalie," she said, then hesitated. "Stein."

"You're not sure?" he said.

"It's Natalie Stein."

"Because you sound like a woman who has given an alias."

She had hair the color of blood oranges, a head of coils and ringlets that shone bright amid the neobaroque splendor of the coffeehouse. She had bunched her curls up on top of her head as though to banish them for being so outrageous, affixing them with a cracked tortoiseshell clip. Her skin was pale and dappled with freckles that were the same color as her hair, like shoes dyed to match a dress. Amitai allowed his eyes to follow the trail of freckles to the point at which they disappeared into the deep V-neck of her shirt. Indeed he could not prevent them from doing so.

"It's just that I recently changed it. It was Friedman for a little while, but now it's back to Stein."

"Divorce?" he asked. She looked barely thirty, at least a decade younger than he was. It surprised him that someone so young could have already made such a serious mistake.

"Yes."

"So am I. Though my ex-wife is still Shasho. But then her maiden name is Cattan, which in Hebrew means 'little,' and she always resented the irony."

"She's not little?"

He smiled. "She is beautiful and shapely and thus, like all women who do not look like survivors of famine, despises herself."

"You think all women despise themselves?"

"I think a woman who has the kind of body a man enjoys invariably hates it."

He thought it best not to mention that it was the surprise discovery of Natalie's heart-shaped ass, admirably *gadol,* that had inspired his invitation to join him at the coffeehouse, rather than discuss their mutual business in the relatively more professional setting of Pétér Elek's small shop off Váci Utca, on the Pest side of the Danube.

"And what kind of body does a man enjoy?" Natalie asked.

Though Amitai was not vain about his good looks, neither was he averse to taking advantage of the power conferred by them. He possessed a pair of electric blue eyes behind a tangle of long, dark lashes, lips so lush that they flirted with prettiness, and a square jaw with the barest hint of a cleft. Women always flirted with him, and so he was not surprised that Natalie's words were flirtatious, as was the tip of her tongue as it delicately licked a bit of *dobos* torte from her fork. Yet there was something halting about her tone as she flirted, as if she were attempting to converse in a foreign language. For a moment it seemed she was batting her eyes at him from behind the layers of sponge cake, chocolate buttercream, and caramel, but then she gave that up and, with a small sigh, shoved a huge forkful into her mouth.

The waiter returned with two silver trays, each outfitted with a cup of coffee, a glass of water, and a cookie in a paper wrapping. He wore operetta livery, all brass buttons and gold frogging, but his cuffs were smeared with chocolate sauce. Amitai removed the cookie from the tray the waiter set before him and placed it on the edge of Natalie's saucer.

"You're not hungry?" she said.

"I don't have much of a sweet tooth. How is your cake?"

She licked caramel from the prongs of her fork. "Mm," she said. "So? You were saying?"

"What was I saying?"

"You were telling me what kind of body men like."

"Was I? Actually I don't think I was. There is not one kind of body all men like. Different men like different things. But most men, I think, prefer women who are shaped like women, not like small boys. We like hips and breasts."

"Your wife had hips and breasts?"

"I think perhaps I have talked too much about my ex-wife. Tell me instead about the necklace. It belonged to your grandmother?"

It was the necklace—an unusual pendant, decorated with an enamel painting of a peacock, the tips of its feathers set in alternating stones of amethyst and peridot—that had brought them, and their kneecaps, together. Two days earlier, Amitai had received an urgent e-mail from his friend Pétér Elek, a dealer in jewelry and art, informing him that he might have a lead on a painting that Amitai had been pursuing for the past few years. A young woman, Elek said, had visited his shop seeking information about the history of a pendant she had inherited. Elek had recognized the piece as similar, if not identical, to the one worn by the woman depicted in the painting. This was Amitai's first break in the hunt for the *Portrait of Frau E.* Two days after Elek's call, he was on a plane bound for Budapest.

When Elek had buzzed Natalie into his tiny, poorly lit shop, hair ablaze, cheeks flushed from the river-bottom chill of the Budapest winter, Amitai was caught off guard. He had been so focused on the mysterious necklace that he had not bothered to try to imagine its owner. If he had, experience and a reflexive pessimism would have led him to expect a wealthy Upper West Side matron with a hint of a mustache and comfortable shoes, relieving her empty-nest tedium with the hobby of genealogy. Recovering from his initial shock, he had proposed to Natalie that they adjourn to the Centrál, to discuss their mutual interest over coffee and cake, so as to allow Elek privacy in which to haggle with the mistress of a minor Russian oligarch over the price of an emerald-encrusted diadem.

Now Natalie said, "The necklace was my grandfather's, not my grandmother's."

Why, Amitai wondered, the distinction?

"It is a family heirloom? From his mother, perhaps?"

She busied herself with her cake. "He . . . got it during the war. He was an officer, a captain in the U.S. Army. He was in the infantry."

"But American forces never fought in Hungary."

"He served in France and then, after the war, in Salzburg. During the occupation. That's where he . . . found the necklace."

Amitai took note of the difficulty she faced in coming up with the right verb to describe the means by which the necklace had come into her grandfather's possession. He wondered how many synonyms and euphemisms for "looted" she might resort to before she would be willing to face the truth.

"In Salzburg," he said. "But you're sure the piece is Hungarian?"

"Yes. At least, I know that its owner must have been. She was from a place called Nagyvárad, which I guess is now called Oradea? It's just over the border into Romania, but it was part of Hungary at the time."

An odd coincidence, he thought, that Natalie had told her story to one of the few people who might know how a Hungarian heirloom could end up in the possession of an American soldier serving in Salzburg in 1945. Amitai was disappointed by the admission, not because it revealed her grandfather's criminality, though it likely did. He was disappointed because if the necklace could have been traced to a relative of Natalie's in Hungary, he would have been that much closer to learning the identity of the Frau E. who had posed for the portrait and thus, perhaps, its current whereabouts. Now he feared he had come all the way from New York for nothing.

"Mr. Elek told me that you're an art dealer?" Natalie said.

"Of sorts."

Amitai worked for his paternal great-uncle, Jacob Shasho, who had initially founded the firm of Shasho & Sons as a means of profitably disposing of the remnants of his collection of art and artifacts salvaged during his escape from Aleppo, Syria, in 1947. Shasho & Sons had expanded into a vast mercantile empire and now included real-estate holdings and various retail and wholesale businesses. Amitai had joined the firm after finishing his military service and emigrating from Israel to New York. Under his leadership, Shasho & Sons' art and artifacts department had shifted away from the appraisal and sale of Middle Eastern art and decorative objects to their current specialty, the reclamation and sale of art lost in the Holocaust, and had consequently become substantially more profitable.

Natalie said, "And so, what, a necklace like mine is in a painting that you own?"

"A painting that I am searching for. The necklace in the painting is very much like yours. Identical, I think."

"How do you know, if you've never seen it?"

"I have seen a photograph of the painting. The artist was named Vidor Komlós. You have never heard of him, I am sure."

"No."

"His work has been lost since the war. Komlós was a friend of the great Bauhaus artist László Moholy-Nagy, who took a photograph of the painting."

Amitai scrolled through his phone until he found a black-and-white photograph. The vantage point was from above and at a distorted angle, but it was still easy to make out that it was of a young man with wild curly hair, wearing work clothes and holding a painting. The painting, though visible only in part, was of a woman, drawn from behind, nude on a wooden chair with a rattan seat. The woman was posed twisting at the waist to look over her shoulder, face and chest to the viewer, eyes downcast. Her head, however, was not human. It was the head of a peacock.

Amitai showed the picture to Natalie, then had her zoom in on the pendant that dangled from the plumed throat of the peacock woman. Even in a blur of low-res pixels, it was unmistakably identical to the one Natalie wore.

"It's my necklace!" she exclaimed.

"One of the things that's exciting for me, seeing your necklace, is the color. The purple and green. Perhaps these give some indication or clue of the palette used by Komlós in the painting."

"Is it valuable, the painting? Is that why you're looking for it?"

"Possibly. The photo is fairly well known, and for many years people have wondered about this painting and the young man who was holding it. It was not in the style of Moholy-Nagy. It is reminiscent of Max Ernst's work, so there was some speculation it might be his. But I have established with reasonable certainty that the man in the photo is Komlós. Correspondence between Moholy-Nagy and Komlós was discovered not long ago that makes it clear that this painting was Komlós's *Portrait of Frau E*. And that makes it very interesting."

"Why is it more interesting if it was painted by someone unknown?"

"Komlós's peacock head is reminiscent of a character in the work of Max Ernst, Loplop, a bird. Loplop was in many ways Ernst's alter ego. When he wrote of Loplop, Ernst said he first received visitations by the bird in 1930 and began after that to paint and draw him. But the Moholy-Nagy photograph was taken in Berlin early in 1929, before Loplop first appeared. Also the Komlós painting, a nude with the head of the bird, shares something with Ernst's *The Robing of the Bride,* which was painted many years later. I wonder, did Komlós know Ernst? Had they met before Ernst created Loplop? Who influenced whom?"

"Do you own other Komlós paintings?"

"No one does. The works of Komlós have been missing for nearly seventy years. But lately a mythology has grown up around Komlós because of the Moholy-Nagy photograph, because of the idea that he might have inspired Ernst."

"What happened to Komlós?" she asked. "Why were all his paintings lost?"

"Unlike his friend Moholy-Nagy, Komlós did not escape to the United

States at the outbreak of World War Two. He remained in Hungary, and like most Jewish men, he was conscripted into the labor service. He died on the Russian front."

"And his paintings?"

"Lost during the war. However, in the letter to Moholy-Nagy, Komlós wrote that he made a gift of the bird painting to its muse. That is why, when Elek told me of you and your necklace, I had hoped that I might find this model, and that by finding her, I would find the painting."

Though he had refrained from allowing his voice to reveal the extent of his disappointment, the girl was more observant than he'd given her credit for, and she said, "You had hoped. You don't anymore."

"You said your grandfather was in the American army in Salzburg."

"Yes."

"And that's where he got the necklace."

"Yes."

"So then he took it from the Gold Train."

She lost her grip on her cup, splashing coffee into the saucer. He took hold of the saucer with one hand and with the other steadied her wrist. He tipped the spilled coffee back into the cup.

"You know about the Hungarian Gold Train?" she asked.

"I specialize in art and artifacts lost during the Holocaust," he said. "So yes, I know about the train. If the necklace came from the train, then, unfortunately, its owner, this mysterious muse of Vidor Komlós, was a Jew. This suggests that the painting which Komlós presented to her was likely confiscated along with the rest of her property. In that case it, like every other painting on that train, is gone."

"The paintings from the train can't have just disappeared," Natalie said. "Some of them have to be somewhere."

"The U.S. Army stored the paintings somewhere in Salzburg, that much we know. But what nobody knows is where, though many, including me, have searched."

"Well, maybe the painting wasn't on the train. Maybe just the necklace was. Maybe the peacock woman hid the painting. Or maybe she survived, and her heirs still have the painting."

Amitai said, "Elek tells me that you are searching for the rightful owner of the necklace?"

"Yes."

"Why?"

"To return it."

"Why do you want to return it?"

"Why? Because my grandfather . . ." Her voice trailed away, and all at once he felt impatient with her evasiveness.

"Stole it?"

"Yes. And I guess it bothered him for a very long time. He was not a bad man; in fact he was a very sweet, kind, gentle man. He was a classics professor, not a thief." She pushed her curls off her forehead. "He died a couple of weeks ago."

"I'm so sorry for your loss."

"Thank you." Her eyes swam, and she blinked a few times. "Anyway, he asked me to return the necklace for him."

"But surely he knew that he was asking the impossible?"

"Not impossible. Just, you know, difficult."

"And you are, what?" he said. "A woman who enjoys a challenge?"

"Don't miss a trick, right?" she said. "That's your shtick, isn't it? Mr. Perceptive. See right through people like you're X-raying a painting."

"That is one of my shticks," he agreed. "I have one or two others."

"If you were to find the painting, what would you do?"

"In the unlikely event that the painting was not on the train, you mean? Then it depends."

"On what?"

"Well, if it is as you suggest, and the painting is in the possession of a descendant of the owner of your necklace, who was in fact the model for the painting, then I would congratulate that person on his or her good fortune and go back to New York."

"And if someone else has it?"

"Then it becomes a question of provenance. If the person in possession can prove he purchased the painting before the war, I might try to buy it, depending on the price. But that is not usually the kind of art I deal in."

"Why not?"

"I am not interested in artwork with legitimate provenance, only art stolen during the Holocaust."

"And in that case, what? You sue?"

"Not usually. People have had a limited success with this kind of suit, but not here in Hungary. Here the government has consistently ignored international norms and precedents regarding the repatriation of property. And, anyway, neither my firm nor I is interested in lawsuits. That is not our style. We look for compromise."

Natalie said, "What kind of compromise?"

"We convince the individual in possession that it is in his interest to allow us to sell the work and give him a portion of the proceeds. The rest we turn over to the rightful heirs." Less Shasho & Sons' 40 percent commission, he refrained from adding.

"You give a percentage to the very people who stole the property? How is that fair?"

In Amitai's experience the glorification of abstract notions of fairness and justice was a characteristic found primarily among children and Americans. But this was another observation that he kept to himself.

"Most of the time, those who actually did the stealing are long dead. But still, it's true, you're right. My solution is not, strictly speaking, fair. But it is often the only way to repatriate the object."

"What kind of objects have you 'repatriated'?" He was familiar with the hint of scorn in her voice. It was one adopted by many who learned of his profession.

Again he scrolled through the images on his phone until he found a photo of a brooch, worked in a tulip design, inset with dozens of diamonds.

"Things like this," he said, showing her the image.

"Beautiful!" she said. "Who did it belong to?"

"A couple named Patai from here in Budapest."

"They must have been very happy to get the jewelry back."

"Zoltán Patai and his wife, Bertha, died in the winter of 1945, of starvation and exposure, but there was a brother, Albert, who immigrated to Argentina before the war. It is Albert's grandson who is my client. And yes. He was very happy."

The Argentinian heir had indeed been very happy with the outcome of the case, though he never set eyes on the brooch but only on the check from Shasho & Sons, a windfall from a great-uncle he'd never even known existed. The heirs rarely saw the objects Amitai retrieved. As Jacob Shasho said, "We are not a charity, nor a firm of private detectives." Shasho & Sons did not represent people who longed for their grandfather's lost Degas statuette because it reminded them of their mother's years as a ballerina and who planned to display it in a special cabinet constructed in their living room. The firm represented people who recalled with sufficient detail the items in their relatives' collections, who ideally had some documentation backing up these claims of provenance, and who wanted nothing more than to sell the objects to the highest bidder.

"It can't have been easy to track down that brooch," Natalie said.

"Easy? No."

In recent years, Amitai had come to realize that there was an even more lucrative way to approach the business. He began now with the property itself, not with the owner. He determined what specific types of work were selling well in the current art market and then researched lost Jewish collections. For example, the sale of Gustav Klimt's portrait of Adele Bloch-Bauer for $135 million, one of the highest reported prices ever paid for a painting, and the consequent resurgence of interest in works of the period, had inspired him to begin searching for lost Hungarian collections. The Jews of Hungary, particularly of Budapest, had been financially secure, many of them even wealthy, during the height of the Art Nouveau or Jugendstil, and they had thus acquired a large amount of valuable artwork, virtually all of which was then stolen from them during the war. More important, although a great number of them had been murdered—at least half a million—relative to the Jews of other countries there were more survivors, particularly in Budapest where the wealth was concentrated. This combination of stolen wealth and living heirs made Hungary uniquely suitable for his purposes. Though great wealth had been acquired by certain of Poland's and Ukraine's urban Jewish communities, the thoroughness of the decimation of the Jewish populations of those countries made their stolen art irrelevant. What point was there in discovering that a provincial Polish museum was in possession of a valuable Renoir that could be traced to the private collection of a Lemberg banker and art collector, if that man and every single member of his extended family had been shoveled into the pits at Bełżec?

In the case of the brooch, Amitai had discovered the existence of an intact archive of a distinguished Viennese jeweler, and Elek had acquired for him through means not entirely legitimate a digital catalog of all the holdings of the Budapest Bedö-Ház, a museum devoted to the art of the Magyar secession movement, the Hungarian version of the Austrian Jugendstil. Amitai had cross-referenced the two lists. It was meticulous, tedious work, comparing descriptions of rings and brooches, diadems and necklaces. His work was always like this: vast expanses of featureless failure out of which there would appear, from time to time, a solitary mast flying like a flag, the promise of treasure. Eventually he found in the jeweler's archive a reference to the sale in 1934 to a Herr Patai Zoltán of Budapest of an exceptionally valuable brooch that matched a description in the Bedö-Ház archive. Then it was simply a matter of tracking down the lucky nephew and convincing the Bedö-Ház that a quick and quiet sale was preferable to a noisy public scandal.

Natalie said, "Well, will it be that much harder to find out what happened to the painting? I mean, if my necklace can lead us to the model?"

"I have been looking for a long time," he said. "And though I'd hoped your necklace would lead me to the painting, I fear now I've learned only that the worst is true. I've learned that the painting was likely on the train, and so it's gone."

"You can't know that for sure. Don't you think it's worth looking? I mean, since you've spent so much time already?"

"I fear not."

"You strike me as a man who enjoys a lost cause."

She took him by surprise. How could she know that he always felt most comfortable among the uncomfortable, most at home among the homeless? This, more than anything perhaps, explained the passion of his search for Komlós's painting. There were many lost paintings, after all, many dead artists. And many of those other lost paintings by dead artists were likely to be more valuable than this particular one. Yet this was the search that consumed him. There was something about Komlós, about the extent to which the man had been so effectively erased from the earth, virtually all shadow he'd cast gone with him, that interested Amitai enough to make him drop everything and fly across the world at the smallest glimmer of hope.

"How do you mean?" he said.

"Well, for three years you've been looking for the lost painting of a lost artist on behalf of whom? His lost relatives?"

He had hoped Natalie would not ask him about his client in the Komlós case. It had taken him nearly a year of concerted effort to find any surviving relative on whose behalf he could claim the artwork. Jill Gillette, the widow of a second cousin of the artist, was as close as he had come. Attenuated as the relationship was, Ms. Gillette was in possession of genealogical evidence of the connection, which made her a perfectly adequate client. Still, not one of whom he was eager to brag.

He said, "I know Komlós's relatives. They're not lost."

"Even better. I've now given you the chance to search for the lost owner of a found necklace on behalf of a found relative. Simple, right?"

She spoke with her hands moving emphatically in the air. Her cuticles were torn, and she had a hangnail on her thumb. He thought she might be a nervous woman, high-strung. The kind of woman he had sworn not to pursue anymore.

"Right," he said. "Simple."

16

PÉTÉR ELEK WORE HIS silver hair long, slicked back from his high fore-head and falling past his collar. His mustache and beard ended in a hussar cavalryman's sharpened points. He exuded a kind of vintage urbanity; he was a Budapest flaneur, down to the paisley cravat tied around his throat and fixed with an onyx tie pin. He bent over Natalie's hand and planted upon it a kiss. She blushed.

"Forgive me for being busy when you first arrived," he said.

"Did you make the sale?" Amitai asked.

"Did I make the sale, what kind of question is it? 'Did you make the sale?' Please." He winked at Natalie.

"Don't insult the man," Natalie said.

"I have time now, if you wish," Elek said to Natalie, "to examine the necklace more thoroughly."

Natalie unfastened the pendant and handed it to him.

"Mm," the elderly man murmured, "such a lovely warmth the gold retains. You must be quite hot-blooded. It's the red hair, no doubt."

Amitai laughed. "Oh-oh. Look out," he said. "I must warn you, Elek is a notorious ladies' man."

"Really?" Natalie said. "And who's going to warn me about you?"

Elek pulled a square of black velvet from the hip pocket of his suit pants and spread it across the top of one of the glass cases. He aimed a task lamp at the cloth and positioned the necklace at the center of the bright bluish spot of light. He screwed a jeweler's loupe into his eye and examined the pendant, angling it this way and that.

"As I told you when you first showed me the necklace, my dear, I would call it more Art Deco than Jugendstil, although the enamel work, the use of semiprecious rather than precious stones, this is indeed emblematic of the Art Nouveau."

"Can you tell who made it?" Amitai said.

"The enameling reminds me of some of the early work of Lajos Kozma, before he devoted himself to architecture. You see how the pea-cock is made of geometrical patterns? This is very typical Kozma. The subject matter is unusual, though. In Hungary the peacock feather is an omen of ill fortune, and so one doesn't generally see it used decoratively. The colors are also not Kozma's. He most often worked in yellow, blue, red, and gold. I have never before seen him use purple, white, and green. They are not so beautiful, these colors together, I don't think. Not harmonious. So they must mean something, no?" Elek continued examining the pendant, flipping it over, bringing it close to his eye and away again. "But Kozma, he is a man who likes to sign his work, so if it is his, where is the signature?"

Elek reached beneath the counter. He dug around in a drawer until he found a leather case in which were arrayed a selection of tiny screwdrivers. Moments later he grunted "ah!" and held the pendant out for the other two to see. The back and front were separated, joined by an infinitesimal hinge. It was not just a pendant, but a locket. Inside the locket was a tiny photograph.

Amitai laughed, delighted both by the intricate workmanship and by Elek's skill in discovering it.

"As I thought. Kozma," Elek said. "See, his signature is here."

Elek passed the loupe to Natalie and directed her attention to a swirl of calligraphy on the inside of the locket, opposite the photograph. In spidery letters it read KOZMA LAJOS, surname written first in the Hungarian manner.

Natalie peered at the photograph on the other side of the locket. After a few moments she offered Amitai the loupe, and he held it to his eye. The tiny sepia-toned photograph depicted what Amitai took to be a woman and a child in front of a glass-fronted building draped with flags. The child, a girl in a ruffled white dress, had been posed standing on top of a wooden box. On either side of the figures dangled two long white banners inscribed with characters too small for Amitai to make out, even with the loupe.

"I can't read what's on the banners," he said.

Natalie took back the pendant and the loupe. "One's in Hungarian, so I don't know, but the other's in English. It says SEVENTH INTERNATIONAL WOMAN SUFFRAGE CONGRESS, JUNE 15–20, 1913." She brought the tiny photograph closer to the loupe, squinted. A tendril of hair fell forward, and she jammed it impatiently behind her shell-pink ear. "I thought it was a little girl."

"It is a little girl," Amitai said.

"I don't think so," Natalie said. "She has a big head, an adult-sized head, and her hair is up in a bun. A little girl wouldn't have worn her hair like that. She's a dwarf."

Amitai and Elek each took another look and agreed with Natalie's revised assessment.

"Sharp eyes," Elek said, with only a hint of lechery.

"This will make our search much easier," Amitai said. "We just go to the National Széchényi Library and ask to see the archive of the Suffrage Congress of 1913. Surely there was no more than one dwarf in attendance."

He took a closer look now at the other woman, whom at first he had taken for the mother of the child. She was thin and fair haired, and possibly quite beautiful.

"Do you think that's her?" Natalie said. "The model in your painting?"

"It's hard to tell, since she has the head of a pretty girl and not a peacock. But it's certainly not impossible." He handed her the necklace. "A very good day's work."

As Natalie reached back to reclasp the necklace, Amitai saw that the skin on the underside of her arms was pale and smooth. No freckles.

He continued, "Justifies a celebratory dinner, don't you think?"

"All right," she said. "Sure. Mr. Elek, I hope you'll join us?"

"I'm afraid not, madam. As much as I would love to. My wife waits for me at home."

"Well, you could bring her, too," Natalie said.

The two men exchanged a glance. Between a sharp-eyed jeweler and a gray-market art dealer much can be said without a word being spoken.

Elek said, "You are very kind. Indeed my wife, when properly rested, can be quite a lively dinner companion, but she will be tired at the end of a long day of working. I will see you again, perhaps, before you leave Budapest. When it is time for you to purchase a souvenir of your visit, you will return, yes?"

"Of course!"

Amitai steered Natalie out of the store. He flagged down a cab. "Please take us to the Hotel Gellért," he told the driver.

"To the hotel?" Natalie said, nonplussed, whatever flirtatious tone she had previously allowed herself now gone.

"They have a very fine restaurant," he reassured her.

· 17 ·

THE STUFFED CABBAGE for which the hotel restaurant was justifiably famous tasted fine, better even, from a room-service tray. They ate in bed, the tray balanced on a pillow between them. Modest after the fact, Natalie twisted the white sheet around her body, covering her breasts. Her curls, liberated from their restraining clip, dangled fetchingly around her face.

If Amitai had thought their quest was anything more than a mutual fools' errand he would not have complicated their relationship with sex. But as it was, there was no point in denying himself the pleasure. Even so, it was unusual for him to have brought a woman to his own room. After his divorce, he had come to value his privacy obsessively, and made it a point always to go to a woman's apartment or hotel room rather than invite her to his. The home he had shared with his ex-wife, like the homes of most of the members of the close-knit community of Syrian Jews in Midwood, Brooklyn, was always spilling over with relatives and friends, friends of relatives, relatives of friends. When Jessica was not entertaining all of her female cousins over Turkish coffee and pastries or hosting a baby shower for a sister-in-law, she was serving dinner to thirty members of her immediate family. He and Jessica had been expected to report at least once a week to the respective homes of her parents, her aunts and uncles, and at least one of her seven siblings. And on the rare Sabbaths or holidays when Jessica's family did not demand their presence, his own extended family did. Even more than escaping the suffocation of a marriage to a woman with whom he had nothing in common beyond the accident of their mutual Syrian Jewish ancestry, he had longed to get away from the crush of familiar humanity in Midwood. The delightful solitude of his Manhattan bachelor's apartment was still, three years after his divorce, a singular pleasure. He had never once allowed a woman even to visit. When traveling, he generally extended this prohibition to include his hotel rooms. And yet he'd invited this young woman to his room without any hesitation at all. Moreover, he thought, she appeared to be preparing to stay the night. He tested out the idea in his mind. Why, he wondered, didn't it bother him?

"Eating in bed always makes me think of my grandfather," Natalie said. "When I was a little girl, I would stay with my grandparents at their summerhouse in Maine. My grandfather used to wake me up every morning with tea and toast on a tray."

"You miss him very much," Amitai said.

"Yes."

"You were very close?"

"Yes. Unusually so, I guess." She took another bite. "My husband used to hate it when I'd eat in bed."

"You are only recently separated, yes?"

"How did you know?"

"You called him your husband."

"Oh. Right. What about you? How long have you been divorced?"

"A few years," he said.

"How long were you married?"

"Also a few years. And you?"

She shrugged. "Well, that's a difficult question to answer."

"How can it be difficult?"

"We got married in June."

He raised a quizzical eyebrow. "This past June? Half a year ago?"

"Nearly eight months," she said defensively.

"And how long have you been separated?"

"Five months."

"You were married for three months?"

"Yes."

"Okay."

"But we were together for twelve years before we got married. We met in college."

"Ah."

"Yup," Natalie said. "Together for twelve years. Married in June. And in September he left me."

"For another woman?"

"How did you know?"

"This is often why men leave, I think."

"Is that why you left?"

He considered this. There had indeed been other women, but he had assuaged his guilty conscience by considering them the result of the unhappiness of his union, rather than its cause. Eventually he had used the excuse of infidelity to end his marriage, but upon engineering his escape had immediately broken off with the woman with whom he had happened to be sleeping at the time. He said, "My wife and I didn't like each other much."

Natalie said, "I guess that's a good reason. My husband and I broke up because his girlfriend got pregnant."

"Also a good reason."

She laughed. "I am developing a theory of relationships. Would you like to hear it?"

"I would."

"It's called the Principle of One-Third. Each and every love affair lasts for precisely one-third longer than it should. If you've been together for three years, then the last year was a waste of time, more pain than pleasure."

"And if you've been together for thirty years?"

"Shame about that last decade."

He laughed. "Okay, then. What about a week?"

"You should have gotten out midmorning on the fourth day. I'm telling you, the theory works for every relationship. The only problem with the Principle of One-Third is that it's only once the relationship is over that you know how much time you've wasted. You don't know that the last decade was pointless until you've been with someone for the whole thirty years. And you definitely don't know that your husband will start fucking an ERISA lawyer in year ten until you get to year twelve and realize that the last four were a farce."

He considered her theory with due seriousness and found it, on the whole, to be sound. Certainly it had been during the last year of his three-year marriage that he had felt the most miserable, as sex had become a perfunctory necessity, devoid of desire and timed to Jessica's ovulatory cycle. By then their conversations had devolved into an endless series of meta-arguments, arguments about who had started the argument, arguments about what they were really arguing about, about whose apology was less insincere. He applied Natalie's one-third rule to some of the women he'd been with since his divorce, and it held up. And what about one-night stands? Should he have crept from the beds of those women after a few hours of lovemaking, instead of occasionally allowing the rendezvous to last through breakfast? He briefly considered seeking clarification from the theory's proponent, another one-night stand in the making.

Instead he said, "Tell me something about yourself that has nothing to do with your ex-husband."

"I told you, I met Daniel in college. I have barely had an adult experience that doesn't involve him. This is the first trip I've taken without him. I don't own any clothes that he didn't buy with me. I'm still using tampons from the wholesale-size pack he picked up for me at Costco last summer."

"I would hope so," he said. "Otherwise I would suggest you see a doctor."

"Shut up."

"Surely, though, even when you were together, you weren't always in his company. Did you work in the same place?"

"No."

"What do you do?"

"I'm a lawyer."

"What kind?"

"I work in the litigation department at a big firm. Two blocks from the big firm where Daniel practices."

Again, the ex-husband. Amitai gave up. "He is a lawyer, too?"

"Yes."

"So you even went to law school together?"

"Sort of. We lived together, but we went to different schools. He went to Boston University. I went to Harvard."

"You are smarter than he is."

"I got better grades, that's all."

"This is something so curious to me about women. If it were Daniel who went to Harvard he would say, 'Yes, I am smarter.' But because you are a woman, you say only 'I got better grades.'"

"You think that's gender related?"

"Men are more confident than women."

"Maybe some men are more confident than some women."

"Maybe most men are more confident than most women."

"Okay," she said. "I think I can give you that."

"Now, you must take my advice, and when people ask you about your ex-husband, you must say, 'He was a nice man, but not smart enough for me.'"

She laughed. The sheet fell, revealing her breasts. She tugged it up but did not completely cover herself. "Now it's your turn. Tell me something about yourself that has nothing to do with your ex-wife. Tell me what you did before you became an art dealer."

"Before that? Nothing."

"Where did you grow up?"

"In Israel."

"Where?"

"On a kibbutz."

"Really? That's cool. I've always wanted to go to a kibbutz."

She had always wanted to go to a kibbutz, Amitai thought, and he had always wanted to leave. His parents, immigrants from Syria, were the lone Levantine Jews on Kibbutz Hakotzer, the only Mizrahim amid hundreds of Ashkenazim. They had come as teenagers, assigned to the kibbutz by the agency responsible for dealing with the wave of unaccompanied minors who had arrived in Israel in the aftermath of the War of Independence. From the very first, the two young Syrian Jews had longed to disappear into the larger kibbutz community, to be engulfed rather than merely acculturated. As a small boy, Amitai had also wished to assimilate, to be just like all the other children, but by the time he was ten or eleven he had been able to recognize something his parents still did not. Vanishing wasn't possible, not on a kibbutz founded by German immigrants who dismissed the Mizrahim of the city as ill educated, inclined to criminality, a less-cultured, less-intelligent Jew. As a teenager his blood had boiled at the insults, both great and small. The nickname given his darker-skinned brother—Kushi, its closest equivalent in English a word so offensive that liberal white Americans referred to it only by its first initial. The way his father's name was never put up for discussion when it was time to appoint a new head of the furniture factory, no matter his seniority. That the Shashos were considered in most ways exceptions to the rule of Mizrahi inferiority was itself an insult. It was no accident that his parents had married each other three years after arriving at Kibbutz Hakotzer. Who else would have had them?

"You moved from the kibbutz to New York?" Natalie asked.

"First I was in the army."

"What did you do in the army?"

"Nothing special. Infantry." Back home, one of the first questions people asked of one another, especially men, was where they had served. A general sucking of teeth and raising of eyebrows would greet his admission that he had been a member of Golani's elite commando unit. Even the most diehard peaceniks were impressed. To his relief, Americans rarely knew enough to ask for details.

"Were you an officer?"

"Yes. But not very high. Just a lieutenant."

"How come you didn't stay in the army?"

"Nobody stays. You do your three years, one more if you have the bad judgment to sign up for an officer's course, and then you leave to climb Annapurna or El Misti."

Another sin of omission. It was true that most soldiers, even officers, mustered out as soon as their first period of duty was over, but in fact Amitai had planned to make a career in the army and would have done so if not for the events of September 27, 1993, when he had lost both the unimpeded use of his left arm and right leg and his faith in his country.

She reached over and traced the scars on his shoulder, the first so obvious a gesture she'd made, though he'd seen her notice his limp when they walked from Elek's store to the coffeehouse, and again when he'd shifted her weight from his right thigh while they made love. In summer, Amitai tanned to a nearly Bedouin brown, and in winter, as now, he faded to a more sallow shade of olive. Black thatch covered his chest, forearms, and legs. But his graft had left a square of pale, smooth skin that she now covered with the palm of her hand. "Did you get these in the army?" she asked.

"Yes."

She was sensitive enough to recognize the finality in his tone and did not try to pursue the topic. "So where did you go after the army?" she said. "Nepal or Peru?"

"I climbed the Great Hill."

"Where's that?"

"You know El Misti and not the Great Hill? The Great Hill is in your hometown. In Central Park."

"That's not a hill; it's a picnic ground." She smiled fondly. "The Great Hill. I haven't been there since I was a kid."

"It's very beautiful, you should go back."

"Maybe you should take me there." His silence caused her to blush furiously. "I was just kidding," she said. "I know this is a one-night thing. I'll be sure to get out before the extra one-third kicks in."

He saw that now might be the right time to change the subject. "Tell me about the locket," he said. "Why was it so important to your grandfather that you return it?"

She sat up in bed, pulled up the sheets, and tucked them firmly under her arms, covering herself. "I always assumed the necklace belonged to my grandmother," she said. "I don't know why. I'd never seen my grandmother wear it."

In fact, she had never seen the pendant at all until the summer after her grandmother's death, when she had been helping her mother clean out the piles of clothing, cosmetics, papers, and other bits and pieces that had accumulated during the decades of summers her grandparents had spent in their small cottage on the coast of Maine. Her grandfather had left them to the task, not because he couldn't bear to do it, she thought, but because her mother had wanted the job for herself.

Her mother made four piles: a small heap of things to throw away, a larger one to donate, a third for Natalie's grandfather, the last what she wanted to keep for herself.

Natalie remembered her mother finding the necklace in a velvet pouch in her grandfather's top dresser drawer and adding it to the pile of things she intended to keep. When Grandpa Jack came in to check on their progress, he saw the pouch and snatched it up, as if it contained dirty pictures, compromising letters.

"What is this doing here?" he said.

Natalie's mother said, "I'd like to have it, if you don't mind. It's so pretty. I never saw Mom wear it, but I'm sure she would have wanted me to have it."

"It wasn't hers to give," he said.

Then he returned the pouch to the dresser drawer and chased them out of the room. Natalie's mother had been furious, though Natalie didn't understand why.

"My mother never wore jewelry at all," Natalie said to Amitai. "Only her wedding band."

" 'Wore'?"

"She died six years ago. My father wears her ring now, on top of his."

"She must have had large hands, for your father to wear her ring."

"She did. Much larger than mine. I have his hands. Stubby little fingers."

He held his hand up to hers, his long fingers against her small ones. "I am sorry for your loss," he said.

She smiled. "You're so formal. But thank you."

On the weekend of her wedding, which had taken place at her grandfather's summer cottage in Red Hook, Maine, Natalie found herself wishing she had something of her mother's or her grandmother's to wear. "I needed something old, something borrowed, and something blue," she said. "So I asked my grandfather if I could borrow that pendant."

"It's not blue," her grandfather had said, only half joking, clearly reluctant to let her wear it, even for an hour. "And, anyway, peacocks are bad luck."

"He was like Bilbo with the ring," she told Amitai. "He didn't want to give it up. It wasn't like him to care so much about a thing like that. Eventually I wore him down, but I could tell he wasn't happy about it."

Despite her grandfather's reluctance, she wore the pendant, though it was too long and dangled far past the neckline of the ill-fitting 1950s prom dress she had paid seventeen dollars for at the Goodwill in Ellsworth, Maine. She had not seen the necklace again until months later, when her grandfather had been diagnosed with pancreatic cancer, and she had rushed up to Maine to facilitate his insistence on dying in his own bed on, as he said, his own terms.

"The day before he died he asked me to do something for him. I remember he took my hand in his. He had these big, freckled hands. Like my mom's. He poured the pendant into my hand and closed my fingers around it. He told me the necklace hadn't belonged to my grandmother. Or even to him. He told me he'd stolen it."

As a young army officer at the end of World War II, Natalie's grandfather told her, he had been assigned to guard the contents of a train full of plunder. It was his job to protect the property from looters of all kinds, and he'd failed. More than that, he had looted it himself.

"The Hungarian Gold Train," Amitai said.

"Yes. He stole the pendant from the train. I asked him why, and he said it reminded him of a girl he knew. Someone he was in love with."

"It was hers?" Amitai asked.

"No. But she was from Nagyvárad, too. I guess he took it thinking it might have belonged to her or to someone she knew. But it didn't. He tried to give it to her, but she didn't want it. And then he just kept it."

"What happened to the girl?"

"They broke up, and he never saw her again. He told me that he couldn't bear to die knowing that he'd kept the necklace. He asked me to find out who the necklace had belonged to and to return it for him."

"And *I* am the one with a thing for lost causes?" Amitai said.

She shook her head. "I know. It's an almost impossible task."

"Not just impossible. Also pointless."

She stiffened, and he reached out a soothing hand. "Forgive me. Sometimes in English I am too blunt."

"Are you less blunt in Hebrew?" she said.

"No." He smiled. "But in Hebrew it doesn't matter. I only meant that even if the woman who owned the necklace did not die during the war, then she is by now anyway dead."

"I know. But her heirs might not be. Especially if they lived in Budapest. There were many Budapest Jews who survived."

"Yes, this is true."

"It's just . . . he never asked very much, my grandfather. He took care of everyone around him. My grandmother, my mother. Me. He was generous without ever letting you even notice he was giving you something. He was just a good man who felt like he'd done a terrible thing. And I promised him I'd at least try to fix it."

"What he did was hardly terrible. If he hadn't stolen the necklace from the train, it would have been lost like everything else."

"Yes, but then he wouldn't have felt like a thief."

He said, "One theft does not make a man a thief."

"You know that, and maybe I know that, too. But that's not the way he saw things."

How Amitai envied the moral certitude of those who had never had to confront the pain of ambiguity.

She continued, "He said he'd made so many mistakes in his life. That he hadn't held on to the people he cared about, which was ridiculous. He and my grandmother were married for more than forty-six years. And while his relationship with my mom wasn't the greatest, it wasn't terrible. And I don't know anybody who is as close to their grandfather as I was. I couldn't figure out what he meant."

"He was sick, Natalie," Amitai said. "He was dying. He wasn't making sense."

"I don't know. He seemed like himself. Weaker. But he was all there. And he knew exactly what he wanted me to do for him."

"To return the necklace he stole."

"Yes. I promised him I would, and it seemed to relieve his conscience, somehow. That day we watched a movie together, and I read to him a little bit from this book of Greek myths for children that he used to read to me when I was a little girl. I made him some soup that he couldn't eat, and then he went to sleep." She paused then, as if remembering. "When I kissed him good night he called me Ilona."

"Ilona?"

"Yes."

"And who is Ilona?"

"The girlfriend. The one from Nagyvárad."

"So perhaps he was not as all there as you thought?"

She shook her head. "Then he said I was his beautiful red-haired girl. He always loved my hair. My grandmother used to say he had a thing for redheads, that her hair was why he married her. She was a student in his Ancient Greek history class at Wellesley. He noticed her hair on the first day of class, and by the end of the semester they were engaged. I always figured that the scandal was why he left Wellesley for Columbia."

"Very romantic."

"I always thought so. She even converted for him. She was Irish. My mom didn't have red hair, though. I guess it skipped a generation."

Amitai wrapped one of her fiery tendrils around his finger. "It is very beautiful, your hair."

"When I went in with his tea and toast the next morning, he was dead."

"You found him?"

"Yes."

"That must have been very hard."

"You'd think so. But it wasn't. He was gone. It wasn't him anymore. Just his body. My dad flew up that afternoon, and we buried him the next morning, just the two of us and the undertaker. When my grandfather put up my grandmother's headstone, he'd put up one for himself right next to it. Hers had her name, Florence Wiseman, and the dates of her birth and death, 1930 to 1997. His said JACK WISEMAN 1922—and then just empty space. It was like that for sixteen years, waiting for him."

"Your mother? Is she buried in the same place?"

"No. She wanted to be cremated. Which drove my grandfather crazy. He was the least religious man in the world, but he kept telling her when she was dying that Jews shouldn't be burned up in ovens. I guess because of his experiences during the war."

"Was he at the camps?"

"He would never talk about the war, so I don't know what he did. I don't even know if he was in battle. I tend to doubt it. He spoke a lot of languages, so he probably was just a translator before they assigned him to guard the Gold Train." She gazed at the scars on Amitai's shoulder. "You know," she said. "He had scars on his shoulder. One on the front and one on the back. He said it was a training accident. But I wonder . . ."

"You wonder what?"

"Nothing."

She was quiet for a moment, and Amitai said gently, "Your grandfather? He died only a couple of weeks ago?"

"What day is today?"

"Tuesday."

"Fifteen days. We were lucky it's been such a warm winter in Maine. Usually in that part of the country you have to wait until the spring thaw to bury people."

"Your grandfather died fifteen days ago, and right away you boarded a plane to Budapest?"

"First we had the shivah."

"I think you are an impulsive person."

"So they tell me. Though I prefer to think of it as 'spontaneous.' Anyway, I had to come. I promised my grandfather. And I'm glad to do it. My grandfather knew me better than anyone. He knew that this kind of project was sort of made for me."

"Why?"

"I've always been interested in the Holocaust. Ever since I was a kid in Hebrew school, and they showed us those movies. You know the ones the Nazis made to document what they were doing? I remember one photograph, I must have been about eleven or twelve when I saw it for the first time, sometime before my bat mitzvah. It was of a man who had crawled under the wall of a barracks or a fence, something like that. He died before he could get all the way through, and the photograph is just of his face and of his hand by his cheek. Do you know it?"

"If I've seen it, I don't remember."

"I used to be obsessed with that photograph. Wondering why he didn't make it, how close he got to getting away. I read so many books when I was a kid, young-adult novels about the Holocaust. And then eventually I read *Night* and Primo Levi's memoirs. All that stuff. In college I majored in Holocaust studies."

Every once in a while, Amitai's work put him in contact with a certain type of Holocaust-obsessed American Jew, the kind who spent holidays touring the camps of Poland and Germany, and Sundays watching all nine and a half hours of *Shoah* for the thirteenth time. Ironically, given the way Amitai earned his living, he himself felt detached from the history of the Holocaust. As a Jew of Syrian descent, his connection to the decimation of the Jews of Europe was not personal. During World War II, the Free French in Syria and Lebanon had defeated the Vichy forces and their Nazi allies. While the Jews of Europe were being murdered, Amitai's parents were playing soccer with Muslim playmates, eating chicken with apricots, miniature meat pies, and date cookies prepared by their mothers, aunts, and grandmothers, praying in synagogues dating back, some said, to the fifth century, and in all ways living the lives their ancestors in Aleppo had lived since the time of the Romans, all but untroubled by the war.

But it was not merely the divide between the Ashkenazi and Mizrahi that led to Amitai's detachment. Though the Israeli origin story was inextricable from the Holocaust, it was also in aggressive opposition to it. The surviving remnant of European Jewry was not rescued, they were "raised up" from the abyss, led to the summit by a different kind of Jew, the indomitable and pugnacious Israeli. Inherent in this lesson, necessary to it, was an unacknowledged but nonetheless palpable contempt for those who died without fighting, who trudged meekly to the ovens. The German Jewish founders of the kibbutz on which Amitai was born had abandoned the comforts of their bourgeois German homes for the pestilent swamps and unforgiving deserts of Palestine before Hitler had fully seized power. They considered themselves pioneers, not survivors. The few elderly kibbutzniks with numbers on their arms spoke little about their experiences, except on Holocaust Remembrance Day when they came to the children's classrooms to recite the lesson of "Never Again."

Natalie said, "My ex-husband? All four of his grandparents were Holocaust survivors. His mother's parents got out of Germany in time, but his paternal grandparents were both from Poland and ended up at Auschwitz. Daniel's father was born in a DP camp."

"Ah."

"Ah, what?"

"You have always been fascinated with the Holocaust, and you married a child of survivors."

"A grandchild of survivors. But yes. I get your point. But I didn't marry Daniel because he was the grandchild of survivors."

Who knows why we marry whom we marry, Amitai thought. He had ended up with Jessica because he had been eager for a home, a community, after leaving the kibbutz and Israel. The American branch of his family welcomed him warmly, but they had strict rules about whom he was permitted to marry. In 1935, the leading Syrian rabbis of New York issued a document known as the Edict, proclaiming that no member of their community was permitted, on pain of excommunication, to marry a non-Jew, even one who had undergone an Orthodox conversion. Every successive generation of Brooklyn-based Syrian Jews vowed never to accept a convert or a child born of a convert into their midst and to expel any child, no matter how beloved, who married such a person. Amitai's immediate family, the Shashos of Kibbutz Hakotzer, were Israeli, and thus not technically governed by the Edict, but once Amitai moved to New York, Jacob Shasho, the family patriarch, informed him that as he was now a Syrian Jew of the New World, he was subject to its rules. Had Amitai wanted to marry an outsider, the Edict would have required evidence of genealogical purity going back at least three generations. The rules were so restrictive that they had their intended result: by far the easiest path for a Syrian Jew was to marry a person from the same community. And so Amitai had married Jessica, whose family was from Aleppo, like his. After their divorce, his uncle Jacob made it clear that Amitai was permitted to look no further than their own community for a replacement. Amitai had so far refused the attentions of no fewer than three of his ex-wife's first cousins. He had no grounds to criticize another person's idiotic reasons for having married the wrong person.

He said, "Did you ever meet your ex-husband's grandparents?"

"Just his Polish grandmother. But we were close." Natalie paused, as if to consider her words. "I mean, I was as close to her as she would let me be. She wasn't an easy woman to be close to. Daniel couldn't stand her, not that he ever really tried. He used to say she grossed him out." She shook her head. "He was such a shit. She couldn't bear loud noises, especially when she was sleeping, and she used to have these wax ear-plugs that she'd leave all around her room. I mean, I admit they were disgusting, little pink balls with greenish earwax stuck to them. But Daniel never bothered for a minute to consider why she needed them. Why she couldn't stand noise. He didn't make the slightest effort."

"And you did?"

Natalie shrugged. "She spoke English, but by the time I met her, she had kind of regressed to speaking Yiddish. I studied Yiddish in college, so I was able to communicate with her in the language she was most comfortable with. She'd tell me stories about her family. I tried to ask her about the camps, but she wouldn't talk about the war at all."

"Okay, so Natalie. Tell me. What if you cannot do what your grand-father asked. What if you can't find the heirs to the locket? What will you do if you fail?"

She pleated the sheet between her fingers. "I don't know. But I have to at least try. And anyway, how hard can it be? We're looking for a suffragette dwarf."

"The painting is of a woman of normal size. So I think it is not the dwarf we are looking for, but her friend."

"The dwarf will lead us to the other woman. And suffragette dwarfs don't just disappear off the face of the earth."

Surely, he thought, someone who had majored in "Holocaust studies" understood that in Hungary, in the first half of the twentieth century, all sorts of people disappeared off the face of the earth, even suffragette dwarfs and their bosom friends.

18

EARLY THE NEXT MORNING, Amitai descended through the opulent decay of the Gellért's lobby to its basement. After navigating a venerable and intricate bureaucracy—securing an admissions ticket, a towel ticket, a ticket for a massage, this key available from that clerk, that key from this clerk—he was eventually permitted to execute a shallow dive into the most beautiful swimming pool he had ever had the privilege of enjoying. For a few moments, he kicked lazily, gazing up at the glass vault of the ceiling, then settled down to business with a strong and serviceable freestyle. He had large hands that plowed deep furrows in the thermal-heated water. His kick was smooth and had a lot of muscle behind it. But the wound in his shoulder, though healed twenty years ago, gave his left arm stroke a hitch as it came up out of the water. The wound in his leg, where bits of shrapnel still lurked and made periodic, painful journeys to the surface, caused his right leg to be slightly weaker than the left. Yet even without lane markers, he kept to a straight line, and when he reached the wall his flip turns were crisp and wakeless.

Compensating for his injuries enough to swim true and turn cleanly required intense concentration, and at the end of his sixty laps Amitai was shaking with exhaustion and had not thought of Natalie, of the balsam smell of her hair, the salt taste of her tongue, for a full forty minutes. Happily spent, he returned to the men's section of the baths, settled himself in a corner of the vast soaking tub, and draped a damp cloth over his eyes. He was close to drifting off when he was awakened by a great splashing and loud voices complaining in Hebrew about the heat of the water. He pulled the towel down farther over his face in a vain effort to avoid the fate that he knew awaited him. The cloth slid down his forehead and tumbled free. He reached to catch it, but it was too late; across the soaking pool, one of the ultrasensitive Sabra detectors his countrymen all carried around in their heads began urgently to klaxon. He closed his eyes, as if with an infantile hope that, if he did so, Dror Tamid might disappear.

"Shasho? Amitai Shasho?"

Amitai opened his eyes.

"Hello, Doctor," he said.

"Please!" Tamid said. "Dror!"

"Hello, Dror."

It was not much of a coincidence that he and Dror Tamid would bump into each other in one of the former capitals of European Jewry, considering that they were both in the business of exploiting the region's history. Dr. Tamid was not, like Amitai, a dealer in lost and stolen art but a historian of the Holocaust, a professor at Bar-Ilan University, who periodically led tours on behalf of Yad Vashem. When Amitai had first begun dealing in Holocaust art and had felt the need to educate himself, he had taken one of Dr. Tamid's tours, imagining that it might prove to be a more entertaining alternative than embarking on a course of dense, relentless reading. After the second day in Auschwitz, which had followed a whirlwind visit to Treblinka, to the Nazi processing center in Lublin, and to the Majdanek death camp, Amitai, under the influence of too much vodka and the ghosts of too many dead Jews, had found himself unable to refrain from posing a question to their tour leader, the eminent Dr. Tamid. What, he asked, was the point of elevating the history of Jewish calamity to such fetishistic heights? Wasn't it a kind of idolatry?

Tamid had been furious but also, momentarily, flummoxed, unable to give any answer beyond the familiar quotation from Santayana, "Those who cannot remember the past are condemned to repeat it."

"Never again!" Amitai had said, raising his glass.

The doctor raised his glass, in relief and agreement, not realizing that what Amitai meant was *Never Again will I take such a tour.*

From then on, Amitai had studiously avoided the Jewish tourist destinations of vanished greatness and terminal horror. Though his work had taken him frequently to Prague, for example, he had never visited the famous Jewish cemetery with its snaggled headstones nor the medieval synagogue, the Alt-Neu, with its fantastical attic tenant. He had spent long weeks in Warsaw and Kraków, in L'viv and Lublin, negotiating for the return of works of art, jewelry, and, in one remarkable instance, six vials of frozen horse semen from a stallion descended from a champion bred by one of Poland's few Jewish noblemen, but had never again felt the need to stand beneath the ARBEIT MACHT FREI sign at Auschwitz or genuflect before the seven heroically sculpted figures of the monument of the Warsaw Ghetto Uprising. In Amsterdam, he passed by the perennial line of tourists waiting to troop through Anne Frank's hiding place without ever bothering to take his turn.

Tamid said, "What brings you to Budapest, Amitai? What are you looking for now? Diamond tiaras? Abstract expressionists?"

Amitai smiled blandly.

"It's Komlós," Tamid said. "You have a lead on Komlós."

"Komlós?" Amitai said. "The artist?"

"Don't pretend with me!" Tamid said, floundering across the pool, through thigh-high water, to hover over Amitai.

What crime, Amitai wondered, had he committed that deserved the punishment of having to sit in such close proximity to the genitals of a man he despised? He smiled politely, heaved himself out of the tub and took his towel from its hook on the wall. He walked swiftly out of the room to the locker area, where he dried off and dressed, wondering all the while at the source of Tamid's information. Could Elek have betrayed his confidence? No. Though Elek relied on Tamid to steer clients both to his shop and to his consultancy business, he shared Amitai's antipathy for the man.

Amitai strode up the stairs, through the lobby, and up to his room. When he entered, he found the bed empty. Steam poured from the open bathroom door, and he heard Natalie humming over the noise of the shower. He poured a cup of coffee from the room-service tray and sat on the edge of the velvet armchair, sipping, his lips puckered against the sour, cold brew.

"Hey," she said, when she walked out of the bathroom. She was wrapped in a thick terry robe, her face flushed from the steam, her hair in soaked tendrils on her shoulders. "I hope it's okay that I ordered room service. Of course I'll pay for it."

"Please. It's fine." He drained his cup in a single gulp, and then, trying to maintain his habitual calm, asked, "Do you, by any chance, know a man named Dror Tamid?"

"Dr. Tamid? Yes! Wait, do you know him? He's here, you know. In Budapest."

"I know him." He did not bother to conceal how little pleasure he derived from this particular acquaintanceship. "How do you know him?"

"He was a visiting professor at Brandeis when I was a junior. I took his seminar Eichmann and the Topography of Extermination."

"Did you tell Tamid about your search, that you are looking for the owner of your pendant?"

She tilted her head to the side and squeezed the water from her hair. "Sure. He's the one who recommended that I see Mr. Elek here in Budapest, rather than go straight for Nagyvárad."

"And did you also tell him that you would be meeting with me?"

"I sent him an e-mail the other day, when Mr. Elek told me about you and your painting." She put down her towel. "Are you upset? Is there something going on between you and Dr. Tamid?"

In the years after Amitai's misbegotten participation in Tamid's Highlights of the Holocaust tour, he and the topographer of extermination had continued periodically to bump into each other, never with very felicitous results. A number of years ago, Tamid had even managed to queer one of Amitai's deals. Amitai's client in that case had passed the years of her adolescence as the concubine and galley slave of a group of Polish partisans who had brought nearly as much energy to the task of mopping up those few Jews who managed to survive the liquidations of the ghettos as they did to attacking the German army. After Amitai spent eight months and nearly ten thousand dollars tracking down the woman's father's collection of Chagall drawings, Tamid, knowing full well the extent of Amitai's investment, convinced the woman's children to have their mother declared mentally incompetent and thus void her contract with Shasho & Sons. Amitai was then forced to watch as the fruits of his labor were promptly—again at Tamid's urging—donated to the Israel Museum in Jerusalem, in return for a large tax deduction for his former client's eldest son and the honor of having a urinal in the museum dedicated, with an informative plaque, to the memory of the old woman's father. (It might, in retrospect, have been a library nook or a bench in the lobby, but Amitai preferred to remember that Dr. Tamid's interference had resulted in the bartering away of his profits in exchange for a porcelain piss pot.) To his knowledge, the drawings, which were charming and technically interesting, had been shoveled into the museum's vast archive and never put on display.

"I don't get upset," he said.

Natalie's attempt to suppress her smile served only to annoy him more than an actual grin would have. "I didn't mention you or Komlós by name," she said. "Only that Elek said there was an art dealer interested in my pendant because of a painting. But I suppose he guessed?"

"It's not a problem."

"Is he looking for Komlós's painting as well?"

"Everyone with interest in the field is looking for Komlós's painting. But again, it is no matter."

At this point, he had invested nothing more than a plane ticket and the price of a few nights in the Hotel Gellért in this latest dead end in his search. The best thing he could do was cut his losses and leave. There were other artists, other paintings. There were even other jobs. He indulged for a moment the fantasy of asking his uncle to transfer him to a different branch of the company. Why should he not sell real estate, like his cousins? Or electronics?

Natalie said, "Well, it obviously is a 'matter.'"

There were other artists, other jobs, and other girls, too. Lots and lots of other girls.

She sat down in a chair, tucking her bare legs up beneath the terry robe. She wrapped her hands around a cup of coffee. The robe slipped off her shoulder. Even wet, her wild curls tumbled prettily over her pink skin.

He said, "Come, shall we go to the Castle Hill? I am not sure when the Széchényi reference libraries close for lunch."

19

IT TOOK ONLY A few minutes in the Széchényi Library for Amitai and Natalie to discover that the bulk of what they needed was available online, in an archive meticulously translated and uploaded by the reference staff of the New York Public Library.

"I spent a thousand dollars to fly to Budapest," Natalie said, exasperated, "and the papers I'm looking for are a mile from my apartment."

"I once spent a month in the Czech Republic on the trail of a Degas statue," Amitai said. "Only to discover that my client's father had given it to his pregnant mistress when he sent her to America after the Nazi annexation of the Sudetenland. I eventually found it in a cardboard box in her daughter's basement in Hackensack, New Jersey."

"Seriously?" Natalie said. "What did you do?"

"I introduced the half sisters and organized the sale."

The huge cache of photographs from the Suffrage Congress that had been archived by the NYPL included pictures of the delegates arrayed on the steps of Parliament, of the mayor of Budapest greeting the attendees, of Boy Scouts who had served as city guides, and, in a photograph captioned "Mrs. Rózsa Schwimmer and colleague at Mrs. Megyeri's villa in Budapest," of a stout yet elegantly dressed woman in a platter-sized ostrich-feather hat, standing on a set of sweeping white marble steps between two pillars on which cherub archers stood on tiptoe. Standing beside the famous suffragist, looking equally elegant in a pleated tunic over a fitted sheath, was the unnamed colleague, the top of whose plumed toque just reached the underside of Mrs. Schwimmer's formidable bosom.

"Holy shit," Natalie said. "Amitai, oh, my God, it's her."

"Probably."

"It is totally her!"

Her exuberance was at once charming and disconcerting. Amitai was used to carrying out his business in an atmosphere if not of secrecy, then certainly of discretion. He glanced around. They were sitting side by side on a small settee in the Gellért's lobby with his laptop open on the table in front of them. The waiter caught his eye and winked.

She snapped open the locket and held it up to the screen of the laptop, looking back and forth at the tiny face emerging from the pixel blur of the scanned photograph to the tiny portrait on a scrap of ancient photo paper, scratched and faded. "I can't believe we found her!"

"Madam," the waiter said, appearing at Natalie's elbow with a small plate of apricot *kiflie*.

"Thank you," she said, with an effusive grin, her excitement over the photograph spreading to everything and everyone in their vicinity.

"I don't know," Amitai said when the waiter had gone.

"Okay, first of all, what are you saying, there were two beautiful dwarfs who attended the International Woman Suffrage Congress in 1913?"

"Perhaps there was an entire dwarf delegation."

"It's definitely her," Natalie said. "She's got that same incredible pompadour."

"So who is this Schwimmer of whom our lady is the unnamed colleague?"

A quick search found that Mrs. Rózsa Schwimmer had been one of the organizers of the congress. She was the editor of the Hungarian feminist magazine *The Woman,* the founder of the Hungarian Feminist Association and of the Women's Peace Party, and Hungarian ambassador to Switzerland. In 1921, she had fled to the United States in response to the Jewish purges in her homeland. It was her papers that had been donated to the New York Public Library to create the archive they were searching.

"Let me see what I can find out about the women's magazine," Natalie said. "Maybe there will be some reference to Schwimmer's colleague." She clicked rapidly through a few links. "Damn it! It's all in Hungarian."

"Perhaps I can help?"

They glanced up to find the waiter hovering.

"I am not only a waiter but also a student. I have a master's degree in English literature, and I am applying now to graduate schools in America. I can translate for you."

After first making sure no other patrons were waiting for his attention, the waiter sat down with them, took the laptop, and began searching. Very quickly he turned up an article from the February 16, 1913, issue of Schwimmer's magazine about a lecture at the Men's League for Women's Suffrage, at which a Miss Gizella Weisz, described as "Mrs. Rózsa Schwimmer's diminutive and talented young secretary," presented on behalf of her employer a letter praising the Men's League's efforts in combating the transport of Hungarian girls to Russia and Turkey for the purposes of sexual slavery.

"It must be her," Natalie said. "Otherwise why reference her height at all?"

"Gizella Weisz," Amitai said. Could it be that he was finally closing in on the painting that had obsessed him for so long? No, he reminded himself sternly, chances were still that it had simply disappeared along with the rest of the contents of the Gold Train.

"That's her," Natalie said, gazing down at the picture in her locket. "She's got the most beautiful face."

"She is beautiful," Amitai agreed. "Now who is that equally beautiful woman beside her?"

At this point Krisztián, their waiter-cum-translator, was forced to abandon them to serve a group of Japanese tourists. They resumed their study of the NYPL photo archive, searching through hundreds of scanned images for the other young woman, the willowy one with the fair hair and the full lower lip. Though they found no photograph that was clearly of her, they did find one of a group of young women holding posters on long poles, each with the name of a different language. They wore light-colored dusters over their white dresses, sashes across their chests, and what appeared to be white sailor caps. The young woman holding the sign that said DEUTSCH must have moved just as the film was exposed, because her face was blurry. Her hair was tucked up under the sailor cap so that its color could not be distinguished, but nonetheless Natalie insisted that she resembled the photograph in the locket.

"Possible" was the most Amitai was willing to allow. Though he could not help but be affected by Natalie's enthusiasm, he tried to remain calm. It was never useful in his business to rush to conclusions, to allow optimism and enthusiasm to overwhelm caution and skepticism.

Unfortunately, the photograph was captioned only "Pages at Cong., 1913," with no other identifying information, and nowhere in the index of archived documents was there a list of the names of the young women who had acted as congress pages.

Krisztián returned. "I'm off work," he said, pulling out a chair. "Maybe I can help you more?"

"You're being so helpful, Krisztián," Natalie said. "How can we repay you?"

Krisztián appeared to consider the question.

"How about money?" he suggested.

Amitai swiftly negotiated a fair price for Krisztián's time. He then directed the young man to search through the online archives of the various Budapest dailies from the period, searching for references to Miss Gizella Weisz.

They found one article from March 1913 in a magazine called the *Magyar Genius,* a society column that recorded that Gizella Weisz, a "girl dwarf," had attended a performance at the Royal Theater of the play *The Yellow Lily* as the companion of Mrs. Schwimmer.

Krisztián changed his search to the term "girl dwarf," and found a second hit in a newspaper called *Magyarság*, from the issue of August 15, 1913. This was a front-page story, prone to a certain tone of alarm, reporting that on the previous night a gang of foreign ruffians, including a female dwarf, had stampeded the royal box at the Budapest Royal Opera House during a performance of Sándor Szeghő's one-act opera *Erzsébet Báthory*. Thankfully, the writer said, the king himself had been absent, though a member of the royal guard was injured during the fracas.

This was big news at the time, reported in all the papers that Krisztián searched. "According to the right-wing papers," he said, "shots were fired, a banner demanding universal suffrage was hung from the box, and the conspirators dumped onto the crowd pamphlets calling for the assassination of Franz Josef and the redistribution of wealth. The left-wing papers describe it somewhat differently. They agree about the banner, but they make no reference to gunshots. One reprinted the pamphlet, which says nothing about assassinating the king. It says only that the monarchy should give way to government by the worker."

"It must be Gizella," Natalie said. "What do the articles say about her? What exactly did she do?"

"You see here?" He pointed to the screen on which was reproduced a page of newsprint. "This paper is, what do you call? A scandal paper? It writes about sexual affairs and divorces. That kind of thing."

"A tabloid?" Natalie said.

"Yes, exactly. The headline is 'Bolshevik Girl-Dwarf and Conspirators Wreak Havoc on Opera!' It says she used her sexual perversions to distract the guards."

"What kind of 'sexual perversions'?"

Krisztián dutifully scrolled through the rest of the article, looking for prurient details with the air of a biologist counting fruit flies.

"They do not say," he said at last.

Amitai said, "I imagine that in 1913 any hint of sexuality at all from a dwarf would have been considered perverse."

Krisztián said, "Only this paper talks about perversions. The others say only that she was a conspirator. They do not say sex."

Natalie said, "So, what, this 'sexual perversion' thing is just the tabloid being dramatic?"

"Probably."

Amitai said, "Let's figure out what happened to Gizella, if it is her, after she and the others were arrested. They went to prison, I assume? Were they executed?"

Krisztián continued searching. After a few minutes he said, "Okay, well, I find here information that the others from the conspiracy were sentenced to hard labor after a big trial. Very public, you know? It was even covered in other countries. But I don't find anything about the girl dwarf. It is like she disappears from the case."

Amitai said, "Schwimmer was politically powerful. There was that picture of her with the mayor of Budapest, remember? And she later on became an ambassador. She must have used her clout to get Gizella off."

"Also maybe just the judge cannot believe this little girl dwarf is really such a criminal," Krisztián said.

"Don't call her that," Natalie said. " 'Girl dwarf.' "

"Why not?" Amitai said. "You did."

"I know, but it's insulting. We shouldn't call her a dwarf. She was a 'little person.' "

"No, I'm quite sure she was a dwarf," Amitai said. "You can see in her picture, her proportions are not normal."

"I know. I mean, yes, she had dwarfism. But I'm pretty sure we're supposed to call people with dwarfism 'little people' now."

Amitai said, "You think 'little person' is less insulting than 'dwarf'?"

"It's not what I think. It's what they call themselves."

"This particular dwarf has been dead a very long time. I think probably when she was alive she was relieved to be called a dwarf and not something ugly."

All the while they were talking, Krisztián kept up his search, stopping only periodically to blow a lock of lanky hair out of his eyes.

Krisztián said, "Gizella Weisz's family called themselves 'Lilliputs.'

I mean, I think they are her family. The articles said the girl . . ." He paused, then continued. "The little person . . . girl . . ."

Amitai laughed.

Krisztián flushed but plowed on. "The girl little person was from Transylvania, so, look. I search for dwarfs named Weisz in Transylvania, and here is a whole family of them from Tășnad."

"Transylvania!" Natalie said. "Is Tășnad near Nagyvárad?"

"I don't know. Maybe one hour? Two hours?" Krisztián said. "Transylvania is very large. The Weisz family, they were singers and performers."

"Performing dwarfs?" Natalie said.

"Performing little people," Amitai said.

Krisztián said, "They had a family troupe."

"Like a circus?" Amitai said.

"Some places they call them circus, but I think not so much circus as performance, in a theater, you know? Singing, dancing. Comedy."

"Vaudeville," Natalie said. "Gizella's family were vaudeville performers."

Amitai laughed. "So, Natalie, when you decided to find the owner of your necklace, did you ever dream she would be a radical socialist, performing Lilliputian? Or, more accurate, the friend of a radical socialist, performing Lilliputian?"

Natalie ignored him. "So Gizella was from Romania? She wasn't Hungarian?"

Krisztián said, "This part of Transylvania, it goes back and forth. Before World War One, it is Hungary. Afterward it is Romania. Then it is Hungary again; now it is Romania. There are people in Hungary now, you know Jobbik? The fascist political party? They want it back again. Because it is all, you know, the ancient kingdom of Hungary."

It seemed to Amitai that Krisztián did not sound entirely averse to the proprietary claims of the party he'd described as fascist.

One long night, his face plowed into the grit of a Lebanese hillside, his clothing soaked with blood—his own and that of the mangled young men beside him—had cured Amitai of humanity's fetish for homeland. Whatever reflex or impulse that made a man care enough about such things to vote or demonstrate, to pick up arms and die, had been erased in him as thoroughly as the Jews had been erased from eastern Europe. Now he craved only the anonymity of the immigrant, to be a man with a vague accent in a city of vague accents.

Natalie said, "But Gizella must have been Hungarian, right? Otherwise wouldn't the papers have said something about her being Romanian?"

"Well, it seems she was a Jew," Krisztián said.

"But a Hungarian Jew or a Romanian Jew?" Natalie pressed.

Krisztián said, "Like I say, parts of Transylvania are sometimes Hungarian, sometimes Romanian. But Gizella is always just a Jew, you know?"

It was the casualness of his tone that caught Amitai and Natalie off guard, the phrase spoken without awareness of its meaning or power. *Always just a Jew.* Natalie looked away, a flush creeping up her neck, as if she were somehow ashamed, not of Krisztián, Amitai thought, but of herself.

Gruffly, Amitai said, "The Weisz family probably spoke Hungarian, Romanian, Russian, German, and Yiddish. But I'm sure they considered themselves Hungarian, like most Transylvanian Jews at the time." He ignored Krisztián's doubtful look and instructed him to continue searching the Hungarian newspaper archives. While Krisztián worked, Amitai shifted closer to Natalie and draped an arm casually around her shoulder. She shot him a grateful smile.

"There were seven Weisz siblings," Krisztián said, "all of them dwarfs."

"That seems almost too perfect," Natalie said.

Of those seven dwarfs, five had been girls, Krisztián told them. The two elder Lilliput sisters played the violin, one of the younger ones played a drum set, another a half-sized cello. The brothers performed on tiny accordions, and the youngest girl played a miniature pink guitar.

"And Gizella?" Amitai asked. "What did she play?"

"This is from the newspaper *Debreceni Független Újság*," Krisztián said. "From November sixteenth, 1933." The ad announced the performance of the Lilliputs in the Csokonai Theatre in Debrecen. There was a small photograph of the troupe, each one holding an instrument.

"Is this her?" Krisztián said, pointing to a small woman standing next to a miniature cymbal, a single drumstick in her hand.

Natalie flipped open her locket and compared the photograph. "I can't tell," she said. "They all look so much alike."

The five women, though separated widely in age, were strikingly similar in appearance. They had wide lips painted in a shade of red so dark it appeared black in the old newsprint, heavy brows, and angular cheekbones. Their noses were long and narrow, flared slightly at the nostrils. Three had dark hair piled high on their heads, one a short bob. They were exotic and striking, even beautiful.

Krisztián said, "According to this article, Gizella was the third of the sisters. Bluma, the eldest, was born in 1886, Franziska sometime after. Then Gizella. The newspaper reports of the Opera House incident give that girl's age as twenty, which means, if it was Gizella, and it seems it must have been, she was born in 1893. That would make her approximately forty in 1933, at the time of the performance advertised here."

"The woman in this photo doesn't look forty," Natalie said.

Amitai said, "The violinists Bluma and Franziska would have been approximately forty-seven and forty-five years old when this picture was taken, but they look much younger, too."

Krisztián said, "The woman at the drums and the woman with the guitar look far younger than the others, so they are Judit and Gitl. That leaves only the one at the cymbal. The one with the short hair. She must be Gizella. Perhaps it is an old photograph? Or perhaps they just look young? The women of Hungary are very beautiful, even the old ones." He glanced at Amitai from the corner of his eye, as if to verify that the Israeli had noticed his granting of nationality to Gizella and her sisters. Amitai wondered if, absent their previous discussion, Krisztián might have complimented the beauty of Jewesses, which was, he had been told many times during his visits to Hungary, renowned.

Amitai said, "Does the advertisement give any details about the performance?"

" 'The world-famous Lilliput Troupe, players to kings and emperors, presents a program of love songs and popular tunes,' " Krisztián quoted.

" 'Kings and emperors'?" Amitai asked.

Krisztián smiled. "An exaggeration, I think. In Hungary we never called Franz Josef emperor. Hungary was itself a kingdom, and thus he was our king."

"You did very good work, Krisztián," Amitai said. "You're even a better research assistant than you are a waiter."

"Do Americans tip their research assistants like they tip their waiters?"

"Perhaps. But then I'm Israeli, not American," Amitai said, giving the young man the amount they'd agreed on, then, a moment later, the extra twenty euros he'd always planned on adding.

20

WITH A SECOND NIGHT TOGETHER, Amitai and Natalie turned a one-night stand into something else, something out of the ordinary in Amitai's postdivorce life. He'd only rarely been with the same woman more than once, and never two nights in a row. But he had not wanted to let Natalie leave the hotel after they finished with Krisztián, had urged her to come upstairs to celebrate their successful day. She had been as eager as he, and in the morning he'd found himself for the first time not even craving the solitude of the swimming pool. In the elevator she looped her fingers through his. He used to hate it when Jessica did that. His hand had always immediately begun to twitch restlessly, eager to escape. But he found himself enjoying the feeling of Natalie's cool, smooth fingers in his hand and did not let go until he had to open the taxicab door for her.

Krisztián had agreed to meet them at the library of the Department of Justice. Out of his waiter's tuxedo he looked much younger, and he'd added to the impression by putting gel in his hair and fashioning it into something that looked more like a porcupine's pelt than a hairstyle. At the library, a young female reference librarian, made cheerfully cooperative by the lucky coincidence of her sharing Natalie's name, handed them a thick dossier, the official records of the trial of the opera house conspirators. The Hungarian Natalia helped Krisztián read through the documents, and it was she who discovered the letter from the Office of the Prosecutor to the judge, informing him that a decision had been made not to prosecute a "girl dwarf" by the name of Miss Gizella Weisz for her involvement in the affair.

Krisztián said, "It is because she was, how do you call it? Retard?"

The Hungarian Natalia corrected him, "A mental defect."

Gizella Weisz, secretary to the most famous Hungarian feminist of the age, was described in the prosecutor's letter as "defective of both body and mind," a woman in possession of a "child's shape and naïveté."

"They actually said she was mentally retarded?" Natalie asked, aghast.

Natalia said, "Yes. The prosecutor says because Gizella is mentally retarded, she is not responsible. He says to release her, but on condition that she go to family in Transylvania. She becomes like a child, you know? She must live with her family, and if not with her family, in an institution."

"So, basically they took away her right to self-determination?"

Krisztián and the librarian shared a glance, neither sure what Natalie meant, only that this information made her angry.

Amitai said, "Clearly she was not retarded, or she could not have become Mrs. Schwimmer's secretary. Therefore the prosecutor did what needed to be done to justify her release. Actually, she was a very lucky woman. The others were sentenced to years of hard labor. With her physical limitations, she would have died. Mrs. Schwimmer must have intervened to save her life."

"We should look for a connection, maybe, between the prosecutor and Mrs. Schwimmer," Krisztián said. "His name is Einhorn Ignác. Also a Jew, right? Just like Gizella and just like Schwimmer. Maybe they all know each other. Maybe they go to synagogue together!"

Natalia slapped Krisztián on the arm, and let loose a stream of irritable Hungarian, to which the young man replied in a voice that seemed genuinely confused. After a brief exchange he turned to Natalie and Amitai and said, "I am very sorry if I seem to be anti-Semite, because I am not. Only I am, according to Miss Natalia, an idiot, and I did not know that there were very many Jews, before, in Budapest, and just because one is a Jew does not mean one knows all other Jews. Although, may I say, my mother's concierge, she is a Jew, and she is also the relative of my colleague at the university, so you see, two of the only Jews I know, know each other. But again, I apologize because, as Miss Natalia insists I must say to you, I am an idiot."

He looked to Natalia to see how he had done. She nodded, satisfied.

"No, that's good thinking," Natalie said. "It can't hurt to explore the connection."

"But why?" Amitai asked. "What's the point? We are looking for the other young lady, remember? And we know she is not Mrs. Schwimmer. Obviously, she is not the prosecutor. At any rate, this prosecutor, he is just a factotum. Mrs. Schwimmer had friends high in the government who arranged for this document to be submitted on Gizella's behalf."

Natalie pushed back her chair, crossed her arms over her chest, and glared at him like an angry child. "Well, then what do you want to do? Because I can't think of where to search next."

Amitai rubbed his forehead. As much as Natalie wanted to find the woman in the photograph in her locket, he wanted to find the painting more. He had, after all, been searching for years to Natalie's few days. But he had been doing this work for a very long time and knew the seduction of fascinating stories and exciting leads, most of which turned out to be worthless. The sensible course of action, having discovered that Natalie's locket had been taken from the Gold Train, would have been immediately to concede defeat. If the woman's property had been confiscated and ended up on the train, then it was gone. And yet he hadn't quit. Out of hope, perhaps, or out of curiosity about and attraction to Natalie, he couldn't tell. Still, he was a professional and should not be wasting his time.

"Perhaps I am not so much the fan of lost causes as you'd hoped," he said.

Natalia, the Hungarian clerk, interrupted. "I will bring you the file of Einhorn Ignác, yes? You look. Maybe you find in there something."

More out of politeness than because he shared Natalie's naïve hopes, Amitai agreed. And so it was that an hour later he was forced to eat crow, albeit only a small portion.

Natalia translated the final entry in Einhorn's file. "Dismissed from the prosecutor's office in 1939 pursuant to the second anti-Jewish law. Moved with his family to his birthplace of Nagyvárad!"

"Nagyvárad!" Natalie said triumphantly.

She was all for packing up and setting off for Nagyvárad immediately, but Amitai convinced her that it would be better, first, to consult with the Jewish library at the Dohány Street Synagogue. He had worked in Romania before and tried to find information there, and while the Hungarian Jewish library was hardly a model of organization, it was better than anything he had ever found in the country next door. Moreover, the archivist herself, Anikó Vázsonyi, possessed admirable powers of recall and had often in the past surprised him with her capacity to pluck crucial bits of evidence from beneath teetering stacks of moldering books and folders.

It was Friday evening, however, and Mrs. Vázsonyi observed the Sabbath. When Amitai called, a message cheerfully informed him that she would not be back at work until Monday.

"So what should we do?" Natalie asked.

They had thanked the reference librarian, tipped her well, dismissed

Krisztián, who had to hurry back to the hotel for his shift, and now stood awkwardly at the taxi stand.

"We have to wait," Amitai said.

"Okay." Natalie fumbled around in her bag, extracted her wallet. "I guess I should get back to my hotel."

He nodded. Then, "Is it nice, your hotel?"

"It's all right. Nothing like yours."

"The Gellért is very nice. The pool especially."

"Well, I'd better get going."

"Do you like to swim?"

"Do I like to swim?"

"As I said. The pool is very nice. If you like to swim, you could swim at the Gellért."

"Now?" she asked. "You want to go swimming now?"

"I usually swim in the morning. But I suppose if you wanted we could swim now. There are mineral baths also. To soak."

"Amitai, what are you asking me?"

What was he asking her, he wondered. Not to join him for a swim, as much as he enjoyed swimming.

"If your hotel room is not very nice, you could stay with me at the Gellért," he said.

"You want me to stay with you because my hotel's a dump?" she said, gently teasing him. "Is that why?"

"Yes. I mean, I would like you to stay with me. If you want. But if you don't, no problem."

"No problem," she said, laughing.

He glanced up at the sky. The perpetual drizzle cooled his flushed cheeks.

"Yes, Amitai," she said. "I'd love to stay with you. At your big, fancy hotel."

"Excellent," he said. He lifted his arm and, with a curt gesture, waved over the first taxi in the line.

AFTER RETRIEVING NATALIE'S BELONGINGS and checking out of her
indeed dumpy hotel, they walked through the door of the Gellért to find
Dror Tamid sitting on one of the lobby's sofas, in the midst of a heated
conversation with Péter Elek. The day before, after his chance encounter
with the Israeli in the baths, Amitai had considered moving hotels. But
he would have missed the Gellért's pool too much, and more important,
his pride would not allow him to be driven away. Now he steered Natalie
briskly through the lobby, in the vain hope that they would not be noticed.

"Amitai Shasho!" Tamid called out in English. "You're still here in
Budapest."

"A classic Tamid insight."

Tamid blinked, struggling against his innate tone deafness to irony.

"And with my lovely former student. Natalie! How are you?"

"I'm fine, Dr. Tamid," she said, glancing quickly at Amitai.

"Our friend Mr. Shasho isn't getting you into any trouble, I hope?"

"On the contrary," Amitai said. "It's the other way around."

He nodded at Elek, and turned to cross the rotunda toward the bank
of elevators, but Tamid held up his hand.

"And you know, of course, Péter Elek."

To Amitai, Elek's smile seemed somewhat embarrassed.

Tamid continued, "Elek, it is our friend Amitai you should be arguing
with, not me."

Natalie turned to the Hungarian. "Why should Amitai argue with
you, Mr. Elek?"

"I'm sure he should not," Elek said.

Tamid, who had not bothered to rise, said, "Elek and I were debating
the proper disposition of the Herzog Collection. Do you know about
this, Natalie? It was amassed during the early part of the last century by a
very wealthy man, a Budapest Jew, Baron Mór Lipót Herzog. Just now it
is the subject of a large and important lawsuit, one that has caused quite a
little diplomatic fracas between the Hungarians and the Americans. And
also a diplomatic fracas between me and my friend here."

Elek again smiled, pretending, Amitai thought, not to take offense. "Come, Dr. Tamid," Elek said. "There is no 'fracas' between us. I readily acknowledge the right of the Herzog family to compensation. I merely regret the loss of even more of Hungary's art treasures to the West. Our country has already lost so much of its cultural patrimony. First during the Depression of the 1930s, when so many collectors were forced to sell and so few in Budapest were able to buy. And then again during the war, when first the Nazis and then the Soviets looted both the museums and the private collections."

Amitai gazed in wonder at his friend, who had helped him over the years extricate so many individual pieces of his country's patrimony. Was Elek blustering for Tamid's sake, or was he suddenly admitting a hitherto unacknowledged objection to the very work in which Amitai was engaged?

As if in answer to the unasked question, Elek said, "This is not a small quantity of jewels or an assortment of valuable coins or stamps or even a single painting. Baron Herzog's is one of the last great collections remaining in Hungary. If the family prevails in its lawsuit, all that will be lost to us, too."

Tamid said, "Baron Herzog's collection was stolen by the Arrow Cross, the same villains who murdered his son and drove the rest of his family from the country. Is his family not entitled to the return of his property?"

Amitai tugged gently at Natalie's arm, urging her away, but she resisted. She was interested, it seemed, in the debate. He had been carrying her suitcase, and he set it down with a sigh.

Elek said, "As I have told you before, Dr. Tamid, you and I are in agreement on this point. Like you, I find it offensive that Herzog's El Grecos hang in our fine arts museum, their provenance unacknowledged. And unlike my government, I feel restitution is appropriate. But am I not entitled to regret my country's loss? First we were raped by the Nazis, then by the Soviets—"

"It is not rape if the woman consents," Tamid said. "You and I both know how Hungary spread its legs for Hitler. You bent over for Eichmann like a Moldovan prostitute, with a smile on your face."

Amitai felt Natalie stiffen next to him. Softly, in Hebrew, he said, "Enough, Dror."

In English, Tamid snarled, "Why enough? It's always 'enough' when it's us, but to them no one says 'enough.'"

"It's enough," Amitai said, in English, "because Elek is a Jew."

Like a surprising number of the citizens of Budapest—like Budapest itself—Péter Elek concealed a Jewish history, a secret narrative that was written not in his face, a set of Slavic planes and angles, but in the tiny stature that brought him barely to the tip of Amitai's chin. A Jew who grew up in Pest, mere blocks from the great Dohány Street Synagogue, he had survived the war because his mother managed to obtain false documents for herself and her son. She had taken an apartment in a non-Jewish neighborhood in Buda, where she masqueraded as a decent Hungarian Catholic woman. But the son, unlike his mother, carried between his legs the evidence that could betray them both. His mother was afraid to have him leave the safety of the apartment, even to go to school. So for two and a half years he had played the role of invalid, confined to his bed. Elek attributed his diminutive size to those years. He once told Amitai, "I went to bed a ten-year-old boy, and a ten-year-old boy I remained, in my body if not my mind."

At one time Amitai might have been astonished by the strange good fortune that had allowed Elek to survive. But if you worked in his business long enough, you came to realize that every Holocaust survivor represented, by definition, a story of miraculous happenstance, desperate subterfuge, random salvation. Those of whom no such story could be told were dead.

"I am Hungarian," Elek said now. "But yes, my family is of Jewish descent."

Tamid scowled. "Worse then. Of all people you should understand and have sympathy."

Elek bristled, finally indulging Tamid with the fracas that the Israeli had been so eager to provoke. "For whom should I have sympathy? The Herzog family? Aristocrats whose gold allowed them to escape in comfort and safety while the rest of Jewish Budapest tried to keep from being shot and thrown in the Danube? A gang of robber barons who got out with millions and lived to produce a gaggle of squabbling spoiled heirs? Those are the people with whom I should have sympathy? And what about those who were not able to go to America in 1944 when Eichmann came? What about those like my family, who lost everything, though it was so little? To my mother, a new pair of shoes was worth more than an El Greco to a Herzog. Where is her compensation? Why is it you do not argue on her behalf but only on behalf of the wealthy?"

Tamid said, "The rich always benefit more than the poor, Elek. You must have learned that as a small boy, back in the days of communism. At any rate, that is not a question for me but for Mr. Shasho. I am myself an advocate for all survivors, be they rich or poor, with property or without. It is Mr. Shasho here who helps only the rich."

Ordinarily, Amitai would have refused to tolerate this fraught and hysterical conversation for even a minute. But Natalie's presence prevented him from walking away. She looked at him now, as if to say, *Defend yourself!* and he wanted to. He wanted to crack Tamid across the nose.

Tamid continued, "If Amitai were representing the Herzog heirs, he would by now have arranged a quick and quiet sale, proceeds to be split evenly between thief, victim, and dealer alike, and no one the wiser, isn't that right, Amitai?"

Amitai wondered if he would have been able to accomplish what Tamid claimed. Could he have negotiated a deal with the Hungarian government by which the works would be sold and the proceeds divided? Not, he thought, if Hungary was keen to see its museums and private collections rival those of her fellow European states. Amitai's successes would always be quieter and smaller. Not national galleries but regional museums, not major collectors but minor pilferers, not El Greco but Komlós.

Amitai shot Natalie a glance. Was Tamid's attitude toward him making her regret her decision to join him? Tamid had after all been her professor. She shared the Israeli's emotional investment in the Holocaust, and it was his counsel she'd sought before coming to Budapest.

Natalie said, "This is your fight, Dr. Tamid. It has nothing to do with Amitai." She turned to Amitai. "Come on. Let's get me checked in."

She grabbed his hand and strode off. Gratitude toward a woman was a new sensation for Amitai. Over his shoulder, his delight all out of proportion to the events, he said, "I'm afraid the Herzog fortune is too rich for my blood. I'm strictly small-time."

22

AMITAI HELD THE DOOR FOR Natalie and ushered her into the crooked stairway, last carpeted during the Brezhnev era, that led up to the attic of the Dohány Street Synagogue. Mrs. Vázsonyi waited for them in the dark and muddled room that was, he had frequently been promised, only awaiting adequate funding before it would be transformed into a model library. With every successful Hungarian venture, Shasho & Sons wrote a check to assist in these efforts, but so far Amitai had seen no change. Still, though the room itself was a disaster, the woman managing it was brilliant, and he greeted her warmly.

"Did you bring it?" she said. Mrs. Vázsonyi dressed for her job as if for a gallery opening, swathed in chic black, red lipstick, glittery drops dangling from her ears.

"Don't I always?"

He reached into his bag and took out two huge plastic bottles. Natalie raised a curious eyebrow, and he winked at her.

Years ago Mrs. Vázsonyi had complained to him about how impossible it was to tame her head full of wild frizz. He'd gone home and asked his then wife how she solved the same problem and ever since had been providing Mrs. Vázsonyi with hair conditioner and gel, a New York City brand, designed specifically for a Jewess's curls. The way to a woman's heart, it seemed, was through her hair.

"Bless you, you wonderful man," Mrs. Vázsonyi said. "I was almost out."

"It's you who are wonderful," Amitai said.

"I am," she agreed. "Sit!"

The only chairs other than hers were covered in heaps of files. Natalie hesitated, but Amitai dumped the papers on the floor and motioned for her to do the same.

"Okay," Mrs. Vázsonyi said, lighting a cigarette. She clenched it between her teeth and leafed through a sheaf of documents. "I found your man. The attorney Ignác Einhorn was a decorated officer in the

Magyar Honvédség, and also a member of the Hungarian Olympic team."

"He was in the Olympics?" Natalie said, surprised.

"There have been many Hungarian Jewish Olympians," Mrs. Vázsonyi said. "In some years before the war, upwards of thirty percent of the team was Jewish."

Natalie laughed. "That's certainly not true in the States."

Mrs. Vázsonyi seemed disappointed by the athletic ineptitude of America's Jews. "Your Mr. Einhorn seems to have been a star of the prosecutor's office with a promotion to judge all but guaranteed, but with the enactment of the second anti-Jewish law in 1939, which included a purge of Jewish civil servants and government employees, he was dismissed."

After his dismissal, Mrs. Vázsonyi continued, Einhorn had removed, with his wife, Nina, and their two adult children and their grandchildren, to Nagyvárad. Their son and son-in-law were drafted into the labor service. Between May 25 and June 3, 1944, the inhabitants of the Nagyvárad ghetto were deported to Auschwitz. The elder Einhorns, their daughter, and their grandchildren were all killed. Their son-in-law died, like Vidor Komlós, of starvation, overwork, or a bullet on the Russian front. Imré, the son, survived the torment and depredations of the labor service and returned to Nagyvárad after the war, only to be beaten to death on the streets of that city two days after his arrival. "There is no evidence or testimony in the archive," Mrs. Vázsonyi said, "but I expect that he was killed when he tried to reclaim the family house."

"Like what happened in the Polish village of Kielce?" Natalie asked.

"Very similar, in fact," Mrs. Vázsonyi said, with a look at Amitai that signaled mild surprise. He imagined that she had dismissed Natalie as one of his conquests. Though he'd never before brought a woman with him to the archive, he'd nonetheless acquired in the archivist's mind the (fair and accurate) reputation as a ladies' man. She continued, "But I found no record of accusations of blood libel, nothing about a pogrom. Though, at this point, in late 1945, the city was again part of Romania, and the record is not as comprehensive as it might be if it were still a part of Hungary. Even so, were I a betting woman, I would wager that what happened was personal. The young man came back to his home, the ones who had taken it were not willing to return it. In that time, people were killed for a good deal less."

Mrs. Vázsonyi leafed through the file until she came to a large black-and-white photograph, creased and tattered at the edges. She unclipped it from its backing and passed it across her desk. Amitai and Natalie leaned in to look. It depicted a youthful man dressed in an ornate Hungarian military uniform, complete with high leather boots and gold braid. To his left and slightly in front of him stood a boy of three or four years, his fair hair curled around his ear, dressed in a flowing white shirt trimmed at the cuffs and collar with lace, short pants, and shoes that buttoned up the side. Just behind the boy, with her hand on his shoulder, stood a good-looking blond woman with a serious face, dressed in a sacklike flapper's shift that struggled but failed to conceal her curves. Older, plumper, sterner, she was unmistakably the young suffragette from the picture in Natalie's locket.

"Nina Einhorn," Natalie said.

"Frau E.," Amitai said. "For 'Einhorn.'"

"I can't believe she was killed." Natalie sounded stunned, even grief stricken.

Amitai said gently, "But you already knew she was dead."

"Of course I knew," Natalie snapped. "The picture in the locket was taken a hundred years ago. I didn't think I'd find some one-hundred-twenty-year-old crone in an old-age home. I just, you know, I guess I just hoped that she hadn't died in the war along with her entire fucking family."

Mrs. Vázsonyi grimaced and raised an eyebrow. Amitai tried to put a comforting arm around Natalie, but she shook him off.

"Mrs. Vázsonyi," Natalie said, "can you find out if any of her family are still alive? Maybe she had brothers and sisters who survived the war? Their children? Even, I don't know, a cousin?"

"I can look. There will be some record of her maiden name. And if her family is from Budapest and not the countryside, it is very possible that they survived. At least some of them."

"Okay," Natalie said, resolutely cheering herself up. "This is good news, not bad. We now know who the girl in the picture with Gizella is. Her husband was a prosecutor, and she must have convinced him to intercede on Gizella's behalf. We've connected the dots."

"Not all of them," Amitai said, a gentle reminder to Natalie that though they had the search in common, their goals were different. "Do you have any other information about Nina, Mrs. Vázsonyi? I am curious if she moved in artistic circles."

The archivist glanced around the jumbled room, narrowing her eyes at various heaps of documents. "The Israelite Women's Artistic Society," she said, yanking loose a sheaf of disintegrating card stock from a pile of similar documents. She leafed through the pages. "Yes, Nina Einhorn was a member, indeed. Her name is listed as a subscriber to the newsletter. Also, here, in August 1922 she donated to a fund established to provide paints and canvases to needy artists."

"Could Vidor Komlós have been one of those needy artists?" Natalie asked.

The archivist said, "Mr. Shasho's mysterious artist? Maybe. I don't know. It doesn't say. But it's certainly possible. Why not?"

"All the dots," Natalie said. "Nina Einhorn lived in Nagyvárad. The locket was from Nagyvárad, so it must have been hers. She was a patron of the arts, and a supporter of artists. She has got to be the Frau E. of the portrait." She looked at Amitai. "So? Now can we go to Nagyvárad?"

He was closer than he had ever been before to the painting for which he had been searching for so long. But with the prospect of an end to his search in sight, he allowed himself a hint of uncertainty. Why, when the world was full of lost treasures, had he been searching so hard and so long for this one? What was it about Komlós or this painting that compelled him so? And what would he do if he found it?

"Yes," he said. "Now we can go to Nagyvárad."

23

THOUGH THE PROPERTY RECORDS of the city of Oradea, once Nagy-várad, were not as thorough and complete as those of some comparable cities, there was enough information to lead Amitai and Natalie to the house on Strada Costache Negruzzi, a house that had been occupied since 1944 by the Varga family, and before that by the Einhorns. Amitai parked their rental car a block away from the house. Natalie was about to open the door, when he stopped her.

"I wonder," he said. "Would you mind very much if I went alone?"

"Alone, why?"

"These negotiations can be very delicate. I don't want to intimidate him by outnumbering him."

This excuse sounded as lame to his ears as he could tell it did to hers. The truth was he didn't want her to see him at work, to witness his Dale Carnegie pitch, his false smoothness. His outright dishonesty. He wanted her to think of him as an upstanding art dealer, not as a kind of con artist.

She seemed to sense the urgency of his request. "Okay," she said. "I'll wait in the car."

Had Attila Varga's appearance matched his Transylvanian ancestry, his violent family history, and the implied savagery of his given name, he would have come to the door of his villa accompanied by the scrape of a heavy tread, by the sound of rattling chains, by the clanking of massive bolts drawn back, by the loud grating noise of a long-disused key turning in a lock. He would have been clad in black from head to foot. The steely hand he offered to Amitai would have been cold and clammy. His face would have been aquiline, his nostrils arched, his lofty domed forehead bare of all but scant wisps of hair, and his mouth cruel, with perhaps just the slightest suggestion of sharpened fangs peeping from the parting in his fish lips. But Varga looked more like Santa Claus than Count Dracula. A faded, dissolute Santa Claus, maybe, running short of cheer and goodwill toward men but squat and portly, with a tangled white beard, yellowed at the corners of his mouth, and watery blue eyes, in one of which the role of elfin twinkle had been taken over by a fiery-red sty. His handshake, proffered with a hint of grudgingness, was warm and limp.

"Mr. Varga!" Amitai said, his voice full of false conviviality. "Do you speak English?"

"Yes."

"Wonderful! Otherwise I would have had to return with an interpreter!"

"What do you want?"

"First of all, I must say that I am so very glad to meet you."

"To meet me?"

"Yes! I have come to Oradea to offer you a once-in-a-lifetime opportunity. May I come in?"

Amitai pressed forward, but Varga crossed his arms over his chest and blocked the door. "What you want?"

"To give you the chance to transform what I know is a very awkward possession into a not-insubstantial pile of cash. Dollars, Mr. Varga. Or euros. Whatever you like."

Those words had the magic effect they always did. Varga's frown faded, and after a moment he stepped back through the door, indicating with a jut of his chin that Amitai should follow him.

"Dollars for what?" Varga said.

Amitai began an imperceptible assessment of the value of the furniture in the entry hall. A mirror framed in walnut, the glass cracked but the starburst inlay intact (1930s approximately, could fetch as much as two thousand if authentic), an oaken chest of the type used to hold a young girl's dowry linen (popular in American antique shops but insufficiently valuable to justify the cost of shipping), a laminate IKEA bookcase (worthless), a hat rack screwed to the wall (at least one hundred years old, decent oak, but homemade, worth a hundred, max).

"I am looking for artwork," Amitai said. "Paintings."

Varga's eyes narrowed. "What paintings?" he asked, warily.

Amitai doubted that Varga would recognize the work of Moholy-Nagy, let alone understand the value added to the painting by its presence in a photograph by a great artist, but he had nonetheless taken the precaution of cropping the photograph so that he could show the man an enlargement of the painting out of context. He watched Varga's face as he looked at the print and was rewarded by a widening of the eyes, a flicker of rapacious grin.

"Why you look for this?"

"You recognize it," Amitai said. "Very good."

"Maybe. Maybe not. Is valuable?"

"Maybe. Maybe not," Amitai echoed, smiling. "Shall we sit down?"

Varga led him into a sitting room off the entryway. Again Amitai did his swift and undetectable inventory. Two sofas (twenty to twenty-five years old, torn upholstery, worth less than the cost of removal), another IKEA bookcase (sigh), two American movie posters in metal frames (as much as a hundred dollars if the *Scarface* was original), an Oriental carpet (finally! classic turn-of-the-century Tabriz, slight change in dye lot at one end but excellent condition, at least fifty thousand dollars).

Amitai sat on one of the sofas, Varga on the other.

"Okay," Varga said. "How much this painting?"

"Do you have it?"

"How much?"

"Is it here? May I see it?"

"How much?" Varga repeated, raising his voice.

"That depends. There is the problem of ownership."

"What problem?"

"A court of law would find that the painting belongs, by right, to the heirs of the artist, Vidor Komlós, or to those of the model, Nina Einhorn." Amitai watched Varga's face, satisfied by the flash of recognition at the second name. He decided to take a small risk. "The Einhorns were the prior owners of this house," he said.

"This house has been in my family for generations," Varga said gruffly.

This, Amitai knew, was perfectly true. The Varga family had maintained diligent possession of the house they had stolen, all through the long decades of Communist nationalization, the brutalities of the Ceauşescu regime, the upheavals and disruptions that followed its fall.

"Three generations," Amitai agreed. He smiled pleasantly. "Your grandfather"—he rapidly considered and rejected other formulations, before settling on the anodyne—"moved in during the war, after the Einhorns were deported."

Varga crossed his arms over his chest. "The Jew sold house to my grandfather. He pay good price."

"Did he? Excellent. If the case were to go to court, you'd have the transfer of title to show the judge."

"That is not how we do in Romania. No paper."

Amitai shook his head regretfully. "That's a shame. Now that Romania is part of the EU, any lawsuit would be governed by European laws and courts. And they would expect to see a legitimate and verified transfer of title. Especially in a case involving the Holocaust."

That word, uttered for maximum impact, had its desired effect. The stout little man began chewing anxiously on his beard.

"I fear," Amitai continued, "that a lawsuit in this case might have a very negative outcome. And that is something, I assure you, Mr. Varga, that my firm and I work very hard to avoid."

He outlined, briefly, the terms of the standard arrangement offered by Shasho & Sons.

"I get ten percent?" Varga said furiously.

"Yes."

"And the rest? Who get?"

"The legitimate heirs."

As always, it was less a negotiation than a progression through a Kübler-Rossian series of stages of grief and loss, and throughout Amitai remained patient, unruffled. First there was intransigence ("There is no painting!"), then dismissal ("I give you nothing!"), eventually hate speech ("I know better than to haggle with a Jew"). As Varga grew steadily more angry and insulting, Amitai only grew calmer. The Romanian demanded that Amitai leave his house.

"I call police," Varga said. "I know mayor! Police do what I say."

Relieved to have achieved with such relative ease the penultimate stage (anger, immediately preceding resignation and acceptance), Amitai said, "I wonder how much the mayor will like the idea of the EU standing on his neck?"

An expression of anxious doubt crossed Varga's face. It was time to let him stew.

"With your permission, Mr. Varga, I will call you tomorrow so that we can continue our conversation about the Komlós painting."

Varga stepped around him to open the door. He held it wide. "You want, you do. But my painting? I give never!"

Amitai gave no hint of his relief, his joy, at the confirmation that indeed Varga had the painting. It was here, in this house. And it was only a matter of time before it was his.

"I'll just leave my card." He snapped open his silver card case.

Varga crossed his arms over his chest, making as great a show of refusing the card as Amitai had of proffering it. Amitai placed it on a small occasional table (cheap plywood veneer). He walked out the door, but though Varga was holding it open and clearly wanted Amitai to leave, he did not step sufficiently aside, and Amitai's hip brushed against his great belly. Only then did Amitai have to fight to maintain his composure. The sensation of the man's body against his own caused him to feel a flash of disgust, veined with fury.

The door slammed behind him, and he stood for a moment, shaking. Once he was calm he set off down the street, whistling. He had sunk the hook.

24

"HOW COULD YOU JUST stand there and listen to that? 'Haggle with a Jew'? Fuck him! He was the one trying to fleece you!"

Natalie drained her shot glass and sputtered and coughed. Amitai handed her a napkin. They were sitting at the bar of their hotel, an American chain so generic that but for the Romanian beer on tap they might have been in a Ramada Inn in Duluth.

She was feeling frustrated because her own expedition, to the main post office, had been a failure. There were no Einhorns to be found in any of the local telephone directories. It did not come as a surprise to either of them, but the utter absence of the name had angered and depressed her.

"It's a poker game," Amitai said. "He tries to bluff me, I try to sandbag him."

"A game? His grandfather most likely murdered Nina's son, stole their house, their property. This guy is a Jew-hating pig, living in a house he knows is stolen, waking up every morning in a stolen bedroom, cooking his dinner in a stolen kitchen. He and his whole family are criminals."

Somewhat to his surprise, Amitai found that her outrage made her even more attractive. He lifted her hand to his lips and kissed her palm.

She let it linger for an instant, then snatched it away.

"I don't understand why you're not angry. Have you completely lost your capacity for outrage?"

He wondered if perhaps all the years of effort he had expended mastering the difficult angles of his profession, bridling his temper, controlling his emotions, had caused those emotions finally to atrophy. As if to prove this very point, without even meaning to, he shrugged.

"I don't even have definitive proof yet that Varga has the painting. What would you have preferred that I do? Storm inside and search the house?"

Before she could answer, her eyes widened. Amitai turned to follow her gaze out of the bar to the reception desk, where, carrying a suitcase, handing his credit card to the clerk, stood Dror Tamid.

"Christ," Amitai said. "We have to find another hotel."

"No. Screw him," she said. "Hello, Dr. Tamid," she called out in a saccharine tone. Tamid joined them at the bar, looking innocently pleased to see them. She continued, "If I didn't know better, I'd think you were following us."

In Hebrew, Amitai said to Tamid, "I do know better, and I know you're following me."

"You didn't want to be followed, then you shouldn't have told the concierge at the Gellért where you were going. You think you're the only person interested in Vidor Komlós?" Switching to English, Tamid turned to Natalie. "May I join you?" Without waiting for permission, he sat down on a stool beside her. "Bartender! A Coca-Cola."

When the bartender had handed Tamid the drink, he raised his glass in Amitai's direction. "To a genuine war hero." Then he turned to Natalie. "Did you know that your friend was a war hero?"

She shook her head. "I don't think he's the type to brag about something like that."

"Well, he should. He most absolutely should brag. Our friend Amitai won the Medal of Valor."

Amitai fought and lost a brief battle just to let the error stand. "That is not the case."

"But it is!"

"I won the Medal of Courage. It's less."

"Less what?" Natalie said.

"Just . . . less."

Tamid said, "How many people in all of Israel's history have won the Medal of Courage, Amitai Shasho? One hundred? One hundred and fifty?"

"A little over two hundred."

Tamid laughed. "See? He knows. 'A little over two hundred.' Still very impressive when you consider how many Israelis have served in the defense forces over the past sixty-odd years. Ask him what he did, Natalie."

Amitai watched her fighting her own battle, struggling with her curiosity, not wanting to oblige Tamid, out of loyalty, he hoped, to him.

"I'm sure he'll tell me if he wants me to know."

Tamid nodded, as if this struck him as a reasonable reply.

"Or," he said, "you can simply look on the Internet. There is a very comprehensive website complete with English translation. It will tell you all about our Israeli war heroes, including Amitai Shasho, and then, after you have read what he did, you can be as confused as I am. We can wonder together how a man capable of such courage on behalf of his country and his people can then turn his back on them so completely."

Amitai stood up. He dropped a bill on the table. "That'll cover your drink, too, Tamid, plus a tip." He said to Natalie, "He's a notoriously lousy tipper."

Amitai went right into the bathroom as soon as they reached their room. He filled the tub as hot as he could bear and sank in until just his head and the knobs of his bent knees were above the surface. He soaked for a while, using his toes to turn on the hot tap as the water cooled. When he got out, his skin was burnished to a ruddy sheen. The towel was thin and small, he could barely close it around his waist, and there was no robe. He dried himself as best he could and came out into the room, naked.

Natalie sat with her laptop open in her lap. As he appeared, she read aloud, " 'During Operation Accountability, Lieutenant Amitai Shasho, serving as platoon commander in the Golani Infantry Brigade, took part in fighting against Hezbollah terrorists outside the Lebanese village of Yater. While out on an ambush, Lieutenant Amitai Shasho's platoon came under mortar and rocket attack, and casualties were sustained. Working under heavy enemy fire, Lieutenant Amitai Shasho organized the evacuation of the platoon, and dragged two wounded soldiers to safety, one of whom survived. During this evacuation, Lieutenant Amitai Shasho sustained serious injuries to his leg and shoulder. With his actions, Lieutenant Amitai Shasho demonstrated resourcefulness, courage, presence of mind, brotherhood of arms, and exemplary dedication to his mission. For this act, he was awarded the Medal of Courage.' "

"It's not true," he said.

"Really? It didn't happen?"

"It happened. But . . ." His voice trailed off.

"But what?"

He shrugged. "They give you the medal to make you proud. To convince you that it was worth it."

"And it wasn't?"

He stood, naked, in the middle of the room, and shivered.

"Come here," she said, patting the bed beside her.

He sat down on the edge.

"Tell me what happened. What's an ambush?"

"Just, you know. Lying in the dirt. Waiting for terrorists. Or the people they call terrorists. If it's you who's in the foreign country, and the people you're waiting for arguably have more of a right to be there than you do, who's the terrorist?"

She would not let herself be distracted by questions of whether Israel was justified in its invasion of Lebanon. Instead she said, "You were attacked."

"Yes, we came under fire."

It had begun as it always had. They marched to the ambush site, set up their missile launchers and thermal cameras, added bullet feeds to their machine guns, and unrolled the mattresses on which they would lie for the hours of their shift, staring into the night, mining the slop in their treat bags for Gummi bears and soggy wafer cookies, things that could be eaten silently so as not to give away their location. Then the dull thunk of missiles being launched, earthshaking explosions. Mortars and rockets.

"And you saved your men?"

"I ordered a retreat."

He knew if they stayed they would all be killed, so he led his men through Katyusha fire, blinded by flashes of light so bright they blanched his vision for days. Dust and dirt flew at his face, sealed shut his eyes.

"And you had to carry two of them?"

"I didn't carry them."

"But that's what it says."

"I helped them walk. It wasn't a big deal."

Like inchworms, they'd crept. Or like lovers, he and Lior belly to belly, his leg thrown across Miki's hips. He'd grab Lior's vest with both hands, heave him forward a few inches, then reach back with his right arm, and haul Miki up. Miki's right arm hung useless, but he could scramble with his legs. Lior's legs, however, were left behind in the hollow created by the mortar blast. They humped along, six inches at a time, for minutes or hours, for Amitai's whole life.

"One of them died," she said.

"Yes."

The blood pumped from Lior's stumps despite the tourniquets Amitai had tied, and by the time they reached the medics Amitai's uniform was soaked black from the waist down.

Two medics hovered over Miki, binding his arm and loading him up on a stretcher. Two more crouched next to Lior and then left him alone while they probed Amitai's body looking for wounds.

"Are you injured?" one of the medics asked.

"Lior's injured. His legs were blown off, in case you didn't notice."

The medic took a pair of scissors and sliced open the leg of Amitai's pants, exposing his torn-up thigh, white fat and red flesh and very little brown skin. The medic slammed a pressure bandage across the wound, then did the same to the hole in Amitai's shoulder. Amitai winced at the pain he was only now aware of. He looked away, to where Lior lay, blood no longer oozing from the tourniquet-tied stumps.

"I'm trying to understand," Natalie said. "Why does this make you so angry? Because one of your men died?"

"Yes."

"But you did everything you could. I mean, obviously. Or they wouldn't have given you a medal."

He'd forced the medics to take him to the rest of his men, who were collapsed in a pile, hanging on to one another while this one vomited, that one wept. He'd counted them over and over, like a mother duck with her ducklings, rubbing his hand over their heads and down their limbs, making sure they were whole, consoling himself with having at least saved them.

And then his commander, snarling through the radio. He'd been ordered to hold fast, hadn't he heard? Over the open transmitter, yes, he'd replied, but Hezbollah listened to their transmissions. Everyone knew that anything said over the open transmitter was bullshit. He lay there, on the stretcher, listening to his commander shout that he'd be court-martialed, that his command would be terminated, his soldiers turned over to another, braver officer who wouldn't retreat when ordered to hold fast, who would let all of them die, if that was the order given by the command.

Would the bond to his country, to the people whom he was supposed to consider his own, have ruptured if it weren't already frayed? Would he have felt so betrayed had he not grown up on Kibbutz Hakotzer, if he had not sought in the army what had been missing from his childhood, a community in which to belong, a sense of loyalty and identity?

Lying in the filth of the torn-up Lebanese hillside, he had felt it break with a palpable snap. Not his leg, but his heart.

"The medal doesn't mean anything," Amitai said. And indeed when he had been notified that he would not be court-martialed but celebrated, rewarded with a silhouette of swords and olive branches fashioned from dull gray nickel and attached to a red ribbon, he had felt nothing. He was in America by then and had not even bothered to return for the ceremony. His father had accepted it in his place.

"Well, it meant something to the man you saved."

"I don't want to talk about this anymore."

"Okay." Her voice trembled, and he was conscious only then that he had shouted.

"I'm sorry," he said. "This is just because of Tamid. I'm angry that Tamid told you the story, and I'm angry that he's here in Oradea. He's making things very difficult for me. He made me upset, but now I'm calm again. Let's stop talking about this." His voice began racing, and though he tried, he could not slow down. "We need to consider our next step with Varga. I'll approach him again tomorrow. Perhaps Tamid's presence will end up being to our benefit. Tamid will threaten Varga with a lawsuit, and then, when I renew my offer, I'll seem like a savior."

But she was not so easily distracted. "Help me understand why this makes you so upset. I want to understand."

How could he explain what it felt like to be so disconnected, so lost? He grabbed her in his arms and pressed his face into the hollow of her neck, and she held him, softly stroking his back. He thought for a moment that he might cry, but instead he tugged her underwear down her legs and pushed inside her. She did not resist or even seem surprised, and he wondered how badly it would screw up his life if he were to love this girl.

25

ALL AMITAI'S EXPERIENCE TOLD him that if Varga had the painting and wanted to sell it, the man would have phoned by now. But it was already five o'clock. He and Natalie had spent the day lying on the bed in their tomato-red hotel room in Oradea, the tomato-red bedspread crumpled beneath them, staring at Amitai's cell phone. It might have been a stone. It was the most inert object in the universe.

"He isn't going to call, is he?" she said at last.

For as long as Amitai had been in the business of Holocaust reclamation, his priority had been the minimization of risk. He would pursue objects of acknowledged value or of potential value soberly assessed, engage in negotiations in a way that might veer at times toward the uncomfortable but never became rancorous, and disengage at the first hint of disputation or squabbling. Moreover, he was willing, always, to walk away. The broker who had no personal stake in the outcome of the negotiation was the likeliest to be satisfied.

By every rule of his trade as he had always conducted it, therefore, assessing the situation with an eye jaundiced from experience, the wisest course was to pack up and return to Budapest. From every angle, as he considered the job, he saw only the possibility of failure if not disaster. Varga was an unpleasant man, and though Amitai had dealt with his type before, there was always the risk that he would carry out his threats to call the police. Worse, it was possible that the painting would turn out to be something much less than it appeared to be in the photograph or that, regardless of its merit, it would fail to catch the fancy of those collectors willing to pay hundreds of thousands or even millions of dollars for a Max Ernst, even if Komlós had been an unacknowledged influence on him.

But the greatest risk of all was that Amitai was so involved, so enmeshed, so personally committed to this search, that he hated the idea of walking away.

He wanted desperately to succeed. He feared that after all that had happened between them last night, if they left now and went back to

Budapest, Natalie would lose faith in him, and what was between them would be over. He desperately wanted to feed her illusory hope as he fed his own. But he could not.

"No," he said. "He isn't going to call."

"So what should we do?"

"Fold our tent," he said. "Go back to Budapest."

"Amitai, no! Not without knowing. We have to at least try to find out if Varga has the painting. We can't just—"

"Fail? Sure we can. This is the nature of my business. When I fail, nothing is gained or lost. It just stays as it was before. Anyway, it won't be a total failure. We'll go back to Budapest and find an Einhorn heir for you to return the necklace to. You can do what your grandfather asked. We can accomplish that at least."

"No," Natalie said. "We owe it to Nina Einhorn and to Vidor Komlós to at least try to get the painting back. Otherwise, they died for nothing."

"They did die for nothing."

"Yes. Of course you're right. But we can salvage something. For Komlós, at least. We can restore his reputation, the one Varga's grandfather stole from him."

Even though he wanted her to think he was a kind of magician who could find what was lost, restore what had been stolen, right what had been wronged—even though he wanted her to love him—he could not let this pass.

"Komlós's reputation is worth nothing to Komlós, Natalie. His name, his legacy, they don't even mean anything to Jill Gillette, his supposed relative. She had never heard of the man before I found her and told her there might be a little money to be made. That's what this is about, not finding lost paintings or salvaging stolen reputations. Money."

"I don't believe that. And I don't believe you believe it, either. You're not fooling me, Amitai. You say it's all about business, but I can see how much you care. You want to find it as much as I do. You want to right this wrong."

"You know this."

"Yes. And I know something else. You've fallen in love with me."

It caught him off guard, but he didn't show it. He was too skilled a negotiator for that.

"Just for the sake of argument," he said. "Say that all of this is true."

"All of it?"

"Just for the sake of argument. First of all, if Varga doesn't call, it's over. And he hasn't called. Second. Well, second, Tamid has probably already gotten to the man, and between his lack of finesse, his ignorance of the art market, and his ham-handed threats of litigation and the wrath of the Israeli government, I am sure that not only did he not acquire the painting for Yad Vashem, he just scared the shit out of Varga, who will now never admit to owning the painting. And third, and this is the likeliest: there is no painting. And that is why Varga hasn't called."

"Yeah," said Natalie. "But don't you want to know?"

The black Mercedes pulled up in front of the house on Strada Costache Negruzzi and idled. A moment later, the driver, wearing a black chauffeur's cap, got out and went around to open the door for his passenger. With a flourish, he helped her out of the car. She was a stunning redhead in a flowing black coat, a knit dress with a plunging neckline, and a pair of stiletto-heeled boots.

"This is so wrong," she said.

"It's fine," said the driver.

"I should be wearing a pair of sneakers and, like, an orange down vest."

"He doesn't know that."

"Are you sure?"

"We aren't selling the reality, we're selling the dream. The Romanian dream. For that, you look perfect."

She nodded, looking uncertain. It was her plan in outline and his in detail, and he gave it a 30, 35 percent chance of succeeding. He kept this estimate to himself, but she was no fool, and she was learning to read him, and though she had been gung ho all morning, now all at once she seemed to be experiencing doubt.

"Walk back and forth," he told her. "Don't look at me, look at the house."

She obeyed, clicking back and forth along the sidewalk in front of the house that Varga's grandfather had stolen from some Jews named Einhorn.

"Say what a nice house," he suggested.

"What a nice house."

"It might just do."

"It has that certain something we're looking for."

"Good. Now, remember," he said, speaking in an undertone, hardly moving his lips. "It's probably not just hanging there on the wall. It might be in a cupboard or in a cabinet. Maybe even in the attic. These houses don't always have basements, but if there is one, make sure he takes you down there, too. You have the flashlight?"

"I do."

"Your phone?"

"Yes."

"You checked to make sure the camera works?"

"Yes."

"Good. Now remember. It might get unpleasant. Varga is not a very nice man."

"He's an anti-Semitic pig," she said, bright and smiling, miming her rapture with the house. "But why should Natalie Kennedy care what he thinks about Jews?"

In her (fake) Chanel purse she carried a stack of business cards, express printed at a copy shop down the road from their hotel, that identified her by this name, the most glamorous American name they could think of.

Amitai got back in the car. He straightened his black tie and settled more snugly on his head the peaked cap he had bought, for fifty dollars, right off the head of a limo driver parked in front of the hotel. Then he watched as she tottered to the door in her high heels.

He rolled down the window. Varga was not likely to trouble an anonymous limo driver with a glance, and even if he did, Amitai was confident that the cap was sufficient disguise. People never bothered to pay attention to those who served them. Waiters and drivers were the most invisible people in the world.

"Hullo!" Natalie gushed as the door opened. "Are you the owner of this wonderful house?"

Though Amitai could see that it was Varga who'd opened the door, he could not hear the man's mumbled reply.

"Wonderful!" Natalie trilled. "My name is Natalie Kennedy. I work for Warner Brothers Pictures. In Hollywood."

The idea had been inspired by the movie posters in Varga's living room, and Amitai hoped now that he'd been right, that the man was indeed a fan of American films.

"I'm a location scout," Natalie said. "My job is to find places to shoot movies. We're making a movie here in Oradea, and I've been looking for ages for a house just like this one! Turn of the last century, intact, not broken into apartments. Honestly, I never thought I'd find it. Do you mind if I come in?"

Varga did not let her pass.

"Listen," Natalie said. She glanced around as if looking for eaves-dropping neighbors, then said, "I'm not supposed to tell you this, but it's a very high-budget film."

Varga said something, and she laughed, a delightful trill. "Why would you say that? Oradea is just the place! All that European mystique. Seriously, won't you let me come in? I won't take more than a few minutes of your time. And I promise it will be worth it." She rubbed her thumb and index finger together. "Warner Brothers pays top dollar for locations."

Varga spoke again, but Natalie held up her hand. "You know what? That's fine. I just noticed that house across the street." She pointed to a villa opposite. "It's a similar house. Not as nice, but it might do in a pinch. Sorry to have troubled you."

She offered Varga a glance at her perfect behind as she headed down the path to make her lucrative offer to his neighbors.

This time Amitai heard him as he called, "Please! Come back. Is wonderful house! Perfect house for movie!"

As Natalie swept by him through the door, Varga spoke again, but Amitai heard only her reply. "Yes, my great-uncle. But of course I never knew him. He was assassinated years before I was born."

Thirty-eight minutes and nineteen seconds after she gained entry to the house that had been stolen from the Einhorns, the door opened again, and Natalie raced out, the flaps of her black coat fluttering oddly behind her. She looked like a crow with a broken wing. She ticktocked awkwardly down the steps on her high heels, threw open the back door of the car, and tumbled inside.

"Drive!" she shouted.

Varga burst through the front door, moving much more quickly than Amitai would have thought possible for a man of his age and girth.

"Go!"

Amitai slammed the car into gear and took off down the narrow street with a melodramatic squeal of tires. Natalie shrugged out of her coat and climbed into the front passenger seat, buckling herself in with a determined air, as though she were expecting bumps and blind curves.

"Dude," she said, "I'm going to need you to go way, way faster than this."

26

IT WAS A FIFTEEN-MINUTE drive along a well-maintained road to the border. Amitai stuck to the speed limit, glancing again and again in his rearview mirror. It wasn't until they had flashed their passports at the lackadaisical border guards and crossed back into Hungary that he relaxed enough to ask Natalie what had happened.

"At first it went great," she said. "You were right. He's a huge movie buff. His place is covered in *Scarface* posters and, like, *American Gangster.* He was only too happy to let me inside."

"He didn't seem suspicious? Did Tamid get to him?"

"He wasn't suspicious. Not at first. He didn't mention Tamid. But I don't know, maybe he was just fucking with me."

She had told Varga that the movie she was scouting, to be directed by the Coen Brothers, was set in the late 1920s, at the end of the Jazz Age. At this, Varga—as much as, he was obliged to admit, he loved the Coen Brothers—had experienced his first stab of doubt. The Jazz Age, in Romania?

Natalie lowered her voice.

"Okay, Mr. Varga, look, this is just between you and me, all right? Can I trust you?"

Varga looked hurt. Could she trust him? What kind of question was that?

"Obviously, with a production like this . . . the plot is absolutely under wraps. Total lockdown. But if you promise to keep it to yourself . . . ?"

Varga nodded.

"The lead character . . . and we have a big star . . ."

"Is George Clooney?"

She looked astonished. "Oh, my God. Yes! How did you . . . ?"

Varga downplayed his burst of perspicuity.

"I feel like *you've* been scouting *me*. Anyway, he's an American jazz musician, a trombonist, right, who leaves San Francisco and ends up coming to Romania in search of love."

"Romanian women are very beautiful," Varga said, nodding.

"Exactly," she said. "It's a historical film, so I'm particularly interested in the older parts of your house. We'll be bringing in furniture, of course, appliances and artwork, things from that period. But I, well, I'd love to see if you have anything, already here in the house, that we might be able to use. We pay very generous rental fees."

Impressed with her credentials, with her expensive clothes, with the black Mercedes parked in front of the house, Varga had been unctuous and accommodating as he showed her into the living room cluttered with ugly furniture. She diligently photographed the room and its contents, from every angle.

There were no paintings of any kind hanging in the living room, nor in the dining room, which was their next stop. But in the library, a landscape hung over the fireplace. Pretending interest in the bric-a-brac displayed on the cracked marble mantel, she aimed her camera at the painting.

Now she showed Amitai the image, and he risked a quick glance.

She said, "I thought maybe the Einhorns were art collectors. That it might be worth something. Or maybe they bought other work from Komlós."

"If that's a Komlós," he said, "then I have made a terrible miscalculation. He's not an artist at all."

"What? Why?"

"This painting is from a kit. Paint by numbers."

"No shit!" she said, hunching over the small screen.

"You don't see the lines? There's even an empty space."

She zoomed in on the picture, squinted, and laughed. "Number twenty-six. Looks like it was supposed to be green. Oh well. Anyway, I took pictures the whole time, right? I kept telling him it was just what we were looking for, a real authentic Romanian house of the period. Perfect for our show. I called it a 'show,' see, that's what movie people say, not 'movie' or 'film.' Then I asked if there was a view from the top floor."

As he led her upstairs, she prattled on and on. "I kept saying 'verisimilitude.' I could tell he had no idea what it meant."

Varga took her up to the attic, where, he said, his family stored their old and broken things, many of which might be brought down to furnish the house. For an additional fee, of course.

"Of course," she said.

The attic extended the whole length of the house. Though dusty and unused, it was brightly lit by a long row of harsh fluorescent lights that flickered above their heads. She took photograph after photograph of the broken-down dressers hulking against the attic walls, of chairs with torn cane seats, of steamer trunks, one labeled with a sticker from the port of Haifa, Palestine. At the sight of that sticker—clear evidence, she was sure, of the Einhorn family—her heart began beating with such force that she worried for a moment that the sound might be audible amid the silent whirl of dust in the attic.

"This is fantastic!" she gushed, hoping her effusiveness would be sufficient explanation for her flushed face. "The art director will be over the moon."

"'Over the moon'?"

"Happy! Very happy."

After that they went back downstairs. She hovered for a moment in the front hall, insisting, "You must keep in very close touch with me. My phone number and my e-mail address are on my card."

She said to Amitai, "And then, since we seemed to be pretty much out of rooms, I told him I needed to pee."

There was a narrow, whitewashed five-panel door. She opened it, and before Varga could object, closed it smartly behind her.

The painting was hanging on the wall opposite the toilet.

Amitai couldn't help it. He gasped.

"I know!" she said. "In the bathroom! When I saw it, I jumped like a foot in the air. I swear, I must have peed all over the place. I had to buy some time, so I made a couple of, like, straining noises. Then I got really close to it. It's in the cheapest wooden frame. Clearly Varga has no idea what it might be worth. I stared into the eye of the peacock. You know, it's not just a black dot like it seems in the picture or like a peacock actually has. It's hazel. Like a woman's eye. It looks more like the eye of a peacock feather than the eye of an actual peacock."

And, hanging in the painting as it hung on Natalie, in the shadowland between her breasts, was Frau E.'s locket. It was depicted in painstaking, hyperreal detail, each jewel and filigree rendered in paint so thick the locket cast a real shadow across the canvas.

"Show me," Amitai said.

"What?" Natalie said, suddenly anxious.

"The photograph! You took one, didn't you?" He groaned. "Please, tell me you remembered to take a picture of the one thing we're looking for."

"Can I just please finish the story?"

"I can't believe—"

"Just please let me finish."

She was enjoying this, he thought. He was going crazy, and she was enjoying telling the story. "Fine. Then what did you do?"

She leaned over the seat of the car, reached into the puddle of black wool that was her oversize coat, and pulled out the painting itself, in its plain wooden frame.

"I just put it behind my back, tied the belt of my coat, and ran."

27

THEY LEFT THE CAR with the valet of the Hotel Gellért, and Amitai carried the painting bundled in his arms in Natalie's coat like a sleeping baby, a stolen child no one else must see. He laid the bundle on the bed in their room, tenderly, as if not to disturb the slumber of what lay wrapped inside. He pointed to an overstuffed armchair in the corner by the television.

"Sit," he said.

Natalie sat. Now that she was done playing girl adventurer—now that she could see how badly he was taking this—her giddiness had vanished, and her manner had become watchful. She was waiting, he knew, for him to get angry, to scold her, lose his temper, explode. But he knew how women went about such things. He was not going to give her the opportunity to turn the tables, become the aggrieved party. Make no mistake, he was the aggrieved party in this affair. He was the one to whose world, with all its hairsprings and escapements of profit and morality carefully tuned, this woman had taken the hammer of her foolish idealism, her childish sense of justice, her lack of self-control.

He carefully untied the arms of the coat, unwrapped the painting. It was facedown, and he kept it that way, moving it onto the mattress. He hung Natalie's coat up in the closet, removed and hung up his own. He began pacing back and forth across the floor, not looking at her, not looking at the thing on the bed. He began silently to review the procedure that would be involved in returning the painting. If he did it himself, he would face prosecution. He needed an intermediary. Could he enlist Elek? Would Elek be willing to make the journey, to take the risk? Or would Elek refuse, given what he had revealed about his belief in the right of nations to their artistic patrimony?

No, Amitai would have to do it himself. He would say that a woman had tried to sell it to him, that he'd confiscated it and was now returning it to Varga. Would Varga believe him? If he did, perhaps he'd be grateful enough at that point to consider a sale. Or, Amitai thought angrily, Varga would call the police. What would life be like for an Israeli in a

Romanian prison? And even if he avoided incarceration, the success of his business depended wholly on his reputation among antique dealers, museum administrators, and low-level government officials. Were this theft to become public knowledge, he'd be ruined in Romania, in Hungary, and who knew where else. And if Tamid found out? The man would blackmail him. He would threaten that unless Amitai gave him the painting to turn over to Yad Vashem or to the Israel Museum, he would report him to the Romanian police or to Interpol or to whatever agency currently had jurisdiction over stolen Jewish property. Tamid would be thrilled to be granted the opportunity to ruin Amitai's career and his life. Amitai imagined for a moment the phone call to his uncle. Jacob's fury, his own humiliation.

He stopped pacing, stood staring at the painting lying facedown on the bed, and laughed out loud.

"Amitai?" Natalie said, astonished. This was not, it seemed, the reaction she was expecting. "Why are you laughing?"

"Why am I laughing? I always laugh when I see a good magic trick. And this, Natalie, this was an amazing trick you pulled off."

She looked up at him, her expression willing and worried at the same time, wanting to see the mood lightened, to be let in on the joke, fearing that it would not turn out to be very funny at all.

"Did I?"

"You did. You turned Vidor Komlós into Bruno Schulz."

He watched her face, prepared, if she looked blank or clueless, to strike her forever from the book of his heart, walk out of the room, leave her to deal with the mess she had made alone. When he saw that she understood what he was talking about, he didn't know if he felt relieved or disappointed.

"Okay," she said, sounding determined to match his hostile and aggressive calm, if that was how he wanted to play it. "First of all, I didn't, like, chisel it off a wall. It was hanging on a hook. So what I did is not irreversible. If you want to, we can just get in the car, drive back to Oradea, and return it."

She sat expectant, hands on her knees, making a show of it. All he needed to do was say the word. That was when he realized the extent of the damage she had done to his Swiss-movement life. The moment passed, irretrievably.

"Second," she said, "say I did turn Vidor Komlós into Bruno Schulz, how is that a bad thing? Schulz has got to be one of the most famous

Jewish artists of the last century. And I don't see how what they did was so wrong."

"Are you serious?" he said. "Those *baheimot* from Yad Vashem, those art-thug friends of Dror Tamid? They go in there with crowbars and pickaxes, they tear the fucking murals right off the walls. There was significant damage."

"The murals had been there in that apartment for decades, derelict, rotting inside a kitchen cupboard."

"They'd been found. They were being excavated."

"That's not how it happened."

"Oh, really. And you know how it happened?"

"Yes, I do. This German filmmaker, of all people, got obsessed with Schulz and the nursery murals. He goes looking for them, they're supposedly long lost, but they're right there, in the cupboard of this miserable apartment, where they'd always been, because it turns out they weren't lost, it's just that no one had bothered to look for them. Not the Poles who made such a big deal out of Schulz being this great Polish genius and damn sure not the Ukrainians. They didn't look, because they didn't care. They only cared when we dared to take them."

"We?"

"Okay, you. Israel. Yad Vashem. Whatever."

"Not me. I am always careful to act within the law."

"Whose law? The laws of the people who stole the property in the first place? Do you know what happened after the Schulz murals were taken? After everybody freaked out about those horrible Israelis, how dare they, destroying the sacred property of Poland and Ukraine? The parts of the murals that Yad Vashem left behind were vandalized. But I guess you're saying, what, you're saying it was their right to do that, because by law the murals were their property."

"Thank you, Natalie, you just proved my point."

She looked puzzled, going back over what she had said, looking for the flaw.

"The Poles and the Ukrainians never cared about Schulz's murals until Yad Vashem took them. True. Absolutely correct. And, in just the very same way, the Hungarians and Romanians never cared about Vidor Komlós. I'll go further: they never even heard of Vidor Komlós. But you can be damn sure they're going to care now. Now that we've stolen the painting? Vidor Komlós will become a cause célèbre! You have guaranteed that. You have just fucking guaranteed that!"

The echo of his outcry rang against the surfaces of the hotel room, the pipes in the walls. Then silence.

Slowly, she rose from her chair. She walked silently to the bed. She lifted the painting, turned it over, and laid it faceup.

It was one of the most beautiful things he had ever seen, and one of the most terrible. The frank eroticism of the woman's nude body, sensual and ripe. Her skin, alabaster pale in places, and then blushed a tender pink. The dense, brilliant color of the feathers on the peacock head, a dozen different iridescent blues, their intricate texture. The peacock's demonic, piercing eye, not black but green, even hazel. The peacock's head with its woman's eye virtually burst from the canvas. The painting was at once opulent and unsettling, lush yet stark, sensual yet deeply disturbing, and Amitai was conscious suddenly of a painful, erotic longing. He ached to fall into the arms of this woman. He knew that in those arms a man who had always felt homeless could feel finally at home. He understood why Varga had kept it in the bathroom of all places. If it belonged to him he, too, would hang it in a private, intimate place, where he was the only one allowed to look at it.

Natalie stripped off her boots. She wriggled out of her dress, pulled her hair out of its tight bun, and lay down on the bed next to the painting. He sat down beside her and put his hand on her soft, warm belly, granting her absolution with his touch.

"No way am I giving it back to that motherfucker," he said.

"Right?"

"You're right. You did the right thing."

"So what are we going to do with it?"

"We will bring it home."

"How?"

The better question was, What home? Whose? Where would he take this painting he wanted more than he'd ever wanted anything in his life? Anything except, perhaps, the woman lying beside it.

"I'll figure it out," he said.

28

THE NEXT MORNING AMITAI received an e-mail from Mrs. Vázsonyi at the Jewish library. She was sorry, she wrote, to inform him that her research had turned up no surviving members of Ignác Einhorn's family, though it appeared that there was a connection, albeit distant, to the family of Baron Móric Einhorn. The noble branch had survived the war but had not fared well under communism. There were rumors that some number of them might have escaped via Austria to America, where they were said to have shed the title and changed the name. Of Nina Einhorn's family, named Schillinger, there was even worse news. Only one, a brother, had lived through the war. His wife and children had been killed by the Arrow Cross, and he had never remarried. He had died a bachelor in the early 1960s. There was, it seemed, no Einhorn or Schillinger on whom Natalie could foist the five-gram locket that dangled so heavily from her neck.

Mrs. Vázsonyi also wrote that she had taken the liberty of searching for heirs of the other young woman in the photograph, the dwarf, Gizella Weisz. Here, she wrote, she had been more fortunate. In May of 1944, all seven Weisz siblings had been deported from the Dragomireşti ghetto to Auschwitz, caught up in the same genocidal wave that had sent Ignác and Nina Einhorn and their family to their deaths.

"I wonder if Nina and Gizella saw each other," Amitai said. "At Auschwitz, I mean. If they ever met again."

Natalie raised an eyebrow, surprised, he guessed, that he would express such a romantic, even optimistic, idea. He supposed that he was a little surprised himself.

"The Nazis deported half a million Hungarian Jews to Auschwitz in fifty-six days," Natalie said. "The trains ran daily, and most people were taken from the ramp straight to the crematorium. Unless by some miracle they were on the same train, they wouldn't have been alive in the camp at the same time."

He had known this, of course. The image of two friends reunited however briefly for a final farewell had been in the nature of an offering, a gesture meant to cheer her in the wake of Mrs. Vázsonyi's news about the Einhorns.

"Still," he said, unwilling for some reason to relinquish the point. Perhaps the gesture was really meant to cheer himself. "You're talking about what was typical. What happened to Gizella wasn't typical."

The Weisz family, it turned out, had been saved from immediate extermination at Auschwitz by Dr. Mengele himself. Consumed by a bitter rivalry with another German expert on dwarfism, and in the thrall of a bizarre sentimental attachment to the German folktale of Snow White and the Seven Dwarfs, Mengele had taken on the seven Weiszes as experimental subjects, under his direct protection, and thus they had lived to be liberated by bemused soldiers of the Soviet army. After the war, Mrs. Vázsonyi wrote, the seven Weisz siblings had all immigrated to Israel.

"Gizella died in 1981," Natalie read aloud from the e-mail. "She was eighty-eight years old."

"A long and interesting life," Amitai said. "A tragic life."

"I wish my grandfather had just opened the damn locket and found the photograph thirty years ago. I feel like such a failure. It was the last thing he asked of me. Honestly, it was the only thing he ever asked of me."

"But before 1989, he wouldn't have been able to come to Hungary and would never have been able to discover who Gizella was or where she went."

"That's true, I suppose."

"And if he had not sent you on this particular errand, you would not have met this particular fool." She melted against him, and he drew her close. Then he turned her to face the painting. "I know it feels fruitless, like you failed. But if you hadn't decided to start your search, then you never would have led me to this incredible work, this masterpiece. And then who would have stolen it?"

He kissed her, but she pulled away from him. She was still not ready or willing to be consoled.

"Look," Amitai said, deciding to give it—to give them—one more chance. "Mrs. Vázsonyi writes that Gizella's brothers both had children. So there are descendants. Not descendants of Nina's, true, but blood relatives of Gizella. If you wanted, you could give the necklace to Gizella's nephews or nieces. Or if they aren't alive anymore, then to their children. They probably still live in Israel. So how about this: I will take you to Israel, and we will find one of them and give her the necklace. How does that sound?"

"Really?" she said, brightening, then narrowing her eyes as if doubting him, his state of mind or sanity, knowing the way he felt about the place, the home that he had lost. "I don't know. How does that sound to you?"

"It sounds like I must be very serious about you."

"And?"

"And that worries me."

"Yes," she said, smiling. "It worries me, too."

29

THOUGH NONE OF THE Lilliput sisters had themselves had children—in those days it was believed that a woman of their size could not survive a pregnancy or delivery—the brothers were fertile and prolific, and it had been a simple matter for a man used to tracking down the second cousins, once removed, of people who had vanished without a trace into pits in the Carpathian forest to find Dalia Gur, the living grandniece of Gizella Weisz.

"Every Jewish dwarf who comes to Israel calls me up and expects me to serve them coffee and cake," said Dalia Gur, over the phone. "Enough already."

But Amitai had promised that he and Natalie wanted nothing from her, not even cake. On the contrary, he told her, their visit concerned the return of an item of some value, one with a connection to her aunt Gizella.

And so they found themselves sitting at Dalia Gur's kitchen table in Kfar Yakov, outside the port city of Haifa. It was a small moshav, a village of stuccoed houses with red-tile roofs, manicured gardens, and playgrounds, and reminded Amitai of Kibbutz Hakotzer, which, like Kfar Yakov, had once been a thriving communal agricultural settlement. Kfar Yakov was now a struggling bedroom community, its fields empty of crops, its barns shuttered, its fruit trees unpruned, its houses full not with farmers but commuters barely surviving in an economy so precarious that an increase in the price of cottage cheese caused them to take to the streets in protest. Dalia exemplified this transition. Her husband, she told them, was born on the moshav and had inherited his father's cattle farm. The business had flourished for a brief and exciting period during the European mad-cow scare but afterward had floundered, a victim of EU subsidies and a problematic agricultural economy. The room they sat in was small and shabby, the plastic shutters snapped shut against the afternoon sun. It smelled faintly of grilled onions. Dalia Gur was in her early thirties, a woman who might have been pretty were it not for her furrowed brow and anxious, pursed lips. Her husband, she told them, eked out a living as a personal trainer at a local health club, and she at an Internet start-up, remotely managing a team of customer-support staff based in Bangalore.

"Who knows how long we can make this work," she said. "Soon if we want to make a living we might have to move to India." She turned to Natalie and switched to English. "So, you are, what? A graduate student? You came across something of my aunt's in your research?"

"Not exactly," Natalie said. "My grandfather served in the American military in Salzburg after the war."

And then, with help from Amitai, Natalie told Dalia the pitiful tale of the Hungarian Gold Train, which had left a broken country carrying the looted treasure of a murdered people, headed for nowhere in particular, only to be looted all over again when it arrived.

"Was it really a train full of gold?" Dalia said.

"Not so much gold," Amitai said, "as property. Furniture, dishes, furs. And some jewelry. Watches. Necklaces."

"*Nu*," Dalia said. "Show me."

Natalie wasn't wearing the locket. This morning she had wrapped it in tissue and placed it in her purse. She took it out and handed it to Dalia.

Dalia held it up to the light and studied it. Amitai looked at it as well, wondering about the intention of the craftsman Lajos Kozma who had made it, of the person who had bought it. How had it ended up around Nina Einhorn's neck? Had Nina bought it for herself? Had Gizella bought it for her? Had someone else made the purchase? Had Nina been the first to wear it, or had someone passed it on to her? Each person who'd touched the locket—the craftsman, the unknown purchaser, the woman or women who had worn it—had imagined for it a destiny. But none could have imagined that the locket's destiny would turn out to be bringing him and Natalie together. He smiled, amused at the romantic turns he seemed unable to prevent himself from taking.

Natalie raised a questioning eyebrow. He took her hand and squeezed it gently.

Dalia said, "It's pretty. Old-fashioned."

Natalie reached over and sprang the invisible catch. The locket opened, revealing the tiny photograph within.

Dalia bent over and peered at it, pinched the bridge of her nose, looked again.

"Is it Gizella? But she's so young! So beautiful." She cupped the locket in her palms, like a drop of precious water on a burning plain, staring at the photograph. "We have only a few photographs from this time, you know? Most were lost in the war. Oh, my God. My God." She wiped tears from her eyes. "I wish my grandfather was alive to see this photograph. I wish Gizella was alive! Or Gitl, the youngest sister. Any one of them."

"I'm so sorry," Natalie said.

Dalia said, "Wait, I will show you more pictures. There is one where Gizella looks just a little older than this."

A hallway connected the kitchen to the living room, and from the wall of this hallway, where it hung surrounded by dozens of others, Dalia removed a photograph. It was the five Weisz sisters, posed in two rows, the three in front on diminutive stools, the two in the rear on regular chairs.

"Okay, so this"—Dalia pointed to one of the sisters in the back—"she is Bluma, the eldest. And next to her is Frieda. On the bottom is Judit, in the middle Gitl, and next to her, see? Gizella!"

It was unmistakably the same woman. The five sisters were dressed in identical light-colored gowns. Judit wore a choker of pearls, Bluma's hands and arms were decorated with rings and bracelets, and Frieda and Gitl wore necklaces of dark beads. Gizella, alone among them, wore no jewelry, and she alone had short hair, bobbed to her chin.

"This other woman in your picture," Dalia said. "Who is she?"

"A friend of Gizella's. It's her locket, we think."

Across Dalia's face passed the look of a woman mentally crumpling a lottery ticket and tossing it aside. "So not my aunt's. That's too bad."

Amitai asked, "Did Gizella talk about any special friends from her youth? This young woman, her name was Nina Einhorn. Nina Schillinger, before she married."

"I don't remember Gizella mentioning any special friend. But she was a very social person, you know? She went with a lot of clubs. Socialist club, bridge club, singing club. Always with the clubs." She peered again at the photograph in the locket. "What is written here? On the posters?"

Natalie said, "They're standing in front of the main hall of a big international women's suffrage congress that was taking place in Budapest. Gizella was the private secretary of a woman named Rózsa Schwimmer, a famous Hungarian suffragette and feminist, one of the organizers of the congress."

Dalia smiled. "Yes! Yes, I remember my grandfather told me a story about this. Gizella moved by herself to Budapest. You understand, this was a big scandal. For a young woman, a dwarf, to leave home like this? Shocking, you know? But when she was young, Gizella was a feminist, very independent. In Budapest she got in some trouble, maybe a man, I don't know, and she came back in disgrace."

Amitai and Natalie exchanged a glance. He nodded, and Natalie told Dalia what they had discovered about the events at the opera house, the banner and the pamphlets, and even about the tabloid report of Gizella using her sexual perversions to distract the guard.

At this, Dalia laughed. "You know what?" she said. "Maybe you won't believe me, you don't want to hear it, but those little old ladies? They were very sexy! You know, like . . ." She wiggled her shoulders and batted her eyelashes. "Ay, Gitl, I'm telling you. Always with the boy-friends. And Gizella, too. Men loved her. She married three times. At least three, maybe four. Regular-size men, you know? Not dwarfs. She outlived every one of them."

And then Dalia's expression hardened. She handed the necklace back to Natalie. "Okay, so, now what?"

"Excuse me?"

"Yes, fine, it's Gizella in the picture, but you say the necklace belonged to the other girl, Nina. So what do you want from me?"

The chain trailed over Natalie's wrist, the locket swinging. Amitai waited for her answer, but she said nothing.

"Is it valuable?" Dalia asked.

Natalie did not answer, so he did. "It depends. The gemstones are real, but they're semiprecious. The piece might be interesting to a collector of suffragette memorabilia because of the colors, which are the colors of the movement, and because of the photograph."

Dalia switched to Hebrew. "Look, I don't want to be pushy, but like I told you, my husband lost the family business, and I have no guarantee that I'm not going to lose my job tomorrow to some Indian in Bangalore. We have three kids. We could use the money. Are you one hundred per-cent certain it wasn't Gizella's?"

He answered her in English, "Ninety-five percent certain. Maybe ninety-eight."

Still in Hebrew, Dalia said, "So just because I'm curious, how much is it worth?"

He continued to speak English. "I doubt we could get more than a couple thousand for it. Maximum."

"Dollars or shekels?"

"Dollars."

"Well," Dalia said. "That's not nothing."

Natalie said, "You can have it."

Dalia was caught off guard. "You will give it to me?"

"Yes."

"For me to keep? For myself?"

"You can do what you want with it."

"Whatever I want? Even . . . sell it?"

Natalie held the necklace in her hand for a moment longer, then she thrust it at Dalia. "Here. It's yours. Sell it, keep it, I don't care. I promised my grandfather I would give it to someone who had a more rightful claim to it than he did. What you do with it is none of my business."

Amitai tried to read Natalie's expression, but all he could see was a show of encouragement, maybe even a touch of enthusiasm. Was this how she wanted it? To have the piece sold the way every piece of property he'd ever searched for had been sold? For an arbitrary price, devoid of pain and history, just the sum and product of the weight, condition, and market value of its constituent gems and gold?

Dalia took the necklace from Natalie, and for a moment he thought she might put it on, let the weight and the story of it, of Lajos Kozma and Nina Schillinger Einhorn and Gizella the dwarf and Jack Wiseman and his granddaughter Natalie, hang beautifully from her throat. But instead she laid it with a click on the table in front of her and did not look at it again.

"Can you help me get it appraised?" she said.

30

NATALIE HAD CROSSED THE WORLD as an act of contrition for a theft that had its origin in the Holocaust. Now that she had atoned for the meaningless crime that had nonetheless weighed so heavily on her grandfather, she wanted to visit Yad Vashem. She told Amitai he needn't join her, and at first he considered depositing her in a taxi and spending the day visiting his parents or, better yet, alone in the hotel, staring at the painting. He had not gone to the memorial and museum since he was a boy, and then only because occasional pilgrimages to the site were required of all Israeli schoolchildren. But he suddenly knew that though he would visit his parents before leaving Israel, he wanted Natalie with him, so he could introduce her to them. He found himself unaccountably willing to join her at Yad Vashem, to see what she would see, having come so far.

As they made their way through the crowds from the parking lot filled with tour buses to the entrance of the museum, he began to regret his decision, awash in a sudden preposterous anxiety that they might run into Dror Tamid. As if the man spent his days patrolling the museum, looking for art brokers to excoriate. And, well, what if he did spend his days that way and caught up to Amitai? What was Amitai afraid of? The painting was secure in the hotel safe, Elek having assisted Amitai in procuring almost legitimate exit permits for it. After the conversation with Tamid about the Herzog paintings, Amitai had wondered if Elek would decline his request for help, but his friend had said that while it was true that he had come to believe that the works of Hungarian artists should remain in Hungary, as the alternative in this particular case was not a museum gallery but a wall in the stinking toilet of a Romanian anti-Semite, he felt no qualms about engineering the painting's export.

Nothing in Yad Vashem was as Amitai remembered it from his childhood. The museum had been vastly expanded and improved. Before it had been stark and beautiful in its way, but nothing like this. They wandered along the prism walkway from gallery to gallery, past the multimedia displays, the cases of artifacts, the photographs enlarged to cover an entire wall, the meticulously restored carts and spinning wheels, suitcases and mangled pieces of industrial equipment. He assumed they would spend a few hours at the museum, but it was late afternoon before they finished moving slowly through the galleries and entered the Hall of Names.

He stood in the circular hall, beneath the huge rotunda full of photographs. They rose up above his head, an immense dome of wedding pictures and identification pictures, formal studio photographs and candid snapshots. Sepia, and black and white, as recent as 1945, and decades older. He craned his neck and stared up, faces upon faces upon faces, higher and higher until they blurred and he could no longer make out their features, until he felt that he was staring up into the sky itself, a heaven of faces, infinite and gray. He closed his eyes, and behind his eyelids the faces swung in great slow arcs like constellations making their way across a year of nights. He had not eaten all day, which might have explained his light-headedness, but not the profound sense of loss and sorrow that he felt. He had spent his working life immersed in the Holocaust but never allowed himself to draw any nearer to it than the countless objects, the paintings and silver plate and sculpture and jewelry, that it had cut loose from their owners and set adrift. Before this moment he had thought of the victims only in terms of the things they owned, in terms of what could be claimed and what must be accounted forever lost.

When he opened his eyes, Natalie was gone, and he searched for her, circling the room with a mounting panic, a foolish dread. He found her sitting at a video kiosk. He rushed over, stood behind her, and put his hands on her shoulders. She leaned back against his belly. He buried his face in her hair, her glorious hair, and inhaled its smell of verbena and balsam.

"Look," she said. "Did you know about this? The Pages of Testimony?"

"It's a biographical database. A record of every person who was killed. I've used it a few times, to figure out if an heir is still alive. At the beginning it was just rows and rows of black binders. Then it was on microfilm. Now it's all digitized. Sometimes there's just a name. Sometimes you find everything. Date of birth, job. Where they lived. How they died. It depends on the memory of the person who filled out the form." He realized what she must be contemplating, staring at the screen with her finger poised to touch it, held half an inch away. "Do you want to look for Nina?"

"I've been trying to work up the nerve."

"What are you afraid to find?"

"I don't know."

"It's incomplete. Only two and a half million names. Are you afraid you'll find nothing?"

In good Jewish style, she responded with a question. "Did you ever search for Vidor Komlós's name?"

"Years ago, when I first started looking. It always lists the name of the person who originally filled out the form. I thought if there was a page for Komlós, perhaps it might have been filled out by a relative who knew what had become of the painting. But there was nothing."

Gently he shifted her aside and took her place at the keyboard. He brought up the search screen and put in the surname "Einhorn," first name "Nina." For place he typed "Hungary." He hit enter, feeling Natalie stiffen beside him. A name appeared on the screen. Nina Einhorn, of Budapest.

"Is it her, do you think?" Natalie asked. "It's Budapest, not Nagyvárad."

He clicked on it. Nina Einhorn. Maiden name: Schillinger. Date of birth: December 7, 1893. Approx. age at death: 51. Place of birth: Budapest, Hungary. First name of victim's father: Marcus. First name of victim's mother: Irma. First name of victim's spouse: Ignác. Permanent residence: Unknown. Victim's profession: Unknown. Place and activities during the war: Unknown. Circumstances of death: Unknown. Place of death: Unknown. Date of death: Unknown.

There was a separate section of the form for information about the submitter, a declaration in which the signatory swore that the information was correct to the best of his or her knowledge. The person to so affirm in the case of Nina Einhorn was Gizella Weisz. Under the line for relationship she had written "Friend."

Natalie pressed her fingers to the signature, which was in roman cursive, though the form itself had been filled out in Hebrew. "Gizella didn't know anything about Nina, not even that she'd moved to Nagyvárad. They must have lost touch after Gizella was arrested, after Ignác saved her and she was sent away."

Amitai scrolled back to the top of the screen. There was a photograph scanned and appended to the entry, the image, by now so familiar to them, of Nina as a proud young suffragette in a white dress, with the banner of the congress rippling behind her. Someone, perhaps Gizella herself, had cropped the second young woman out of the photograph. All there was to see of Gizella was a bit of white sleeve at the corner of the frame.

They read and reread the Page of Testimony for Nina Schillinger Einhorn, though it conveyed so very little information.

Natalie said, "Can anyone fill out a form? Or do you have to be a survivor?"

"Anyone with information, I think."

"Why didn't you ever fill one out for Komlós?"

It had never even occurred to him. "I don't know. It seemed presumptuous, I guess. Who am I to bear witness to his life?"

"Who better?"

There was in all likelihood no one now living, he thought, who had known Vidor Komlós. There was no family, beyond the single distant relative whom Amitai had unearthed, a person who had never even heard of Komlós, let alone met him. There were no surviving friends. Natalie was right. Komlós had no one better to remember him than the son of Syrian Jews, an art thief, heartbroken and, after a long day, dizzy with hunger.

They filled out the Page of Testimony together, using what they knew of Vidor Komlós, which was not, after all, so much less than Gizella Weisz had known about Nina Einhorn. They filled in Komlós's name, his parents' names, his date of birth, the address of his family home, his profession, and the approximate date of his death.

Out in the parking lot, as Amitai unlocked the door of the car for Natalie, she said, "I started the whole thing because my grandfather felt that he had wronged someone, and to honor him, I had to honor that feeling. I accepted his idea that I could fix something for him if I found the woman whose necklace he had taken, or if I found someone related to her, and gave the necklace back. I imagined the scales balancing again." She turned back to look at the museum. "But of course it hasn't been about any of that, has it? My grandfather is dead; he'll never know what I did with the necklace, or that I did anything at all. This obsession has just been a useful container for my grief for my grandfather. And I guess even my grief for my marriage."

"You've known that all along?"

"Yes, I suppose so. But I think what I didn't understand until now is that all my life, my experience of the Holocaust has been the very same thing: a useful container for feelings. Here was this colossal, unprecedented tragedy that, by virtue of my religion, I was free to adopt as my own. Because of the Holocaust, I was permitted—no, I was entitled—to feel all the pain that my blessed and comfortable life had spared me. But it was never my tragedy. Collectively, as a Jew, yes. But personally? No."

Amitai shook his head, almost smiling, because here he was, feeling for the first time that the tragedy of European Jewry *did* belong to him. Before today, his lack of personal connection to the Holocaust had made it a distant history, no more relevant to him than any other. But Natalie, the locket, the painting, the Hall of Names, taking responsibility for Komlós in the Pages of Testimony, these had brought him to the realization that, merely by virtue of being a Jew, even a Jew from another place and time, it was his history, too. Not personally, but collectively. It belonged to him, as he belonged to all those Jews rising up into the infinite ceiling in the Hall of Names. He and Natalie were in the same place, but they had come from different directions.

31

AMITAI AND NATALIE STOOD in a gracious gallery encircled by marble archways in the Museum of Fine Arts in Budapest, Hungary, holding glasses of champagne, and listened to the long series of moderately dull speeches by the museum's directors, its trustees, and various governmental officials. Elek stood with them, having, despite his protestations to the contrary, been widely credited in the Budapest newspapers with engineering the return of Vidor Komlós's *Portrait of Frau E.* to its native land. He was in fact due today to receive a medal from the mayor himself. A medal, Elek assured Amitai, that he would just as soon sell in his shop as pin to his breast.

The crowd was small; no more than two or three dozen Hungarian art lovers had chosen to celebrate the discovery and presentation of the lone extant painting, as far as anyone knew, by a great artist who had always been too unknown even to be forgotten. But this state of affairs would soon change, Amitai thought. Before bringing the painting back from Israel to Hungary, Amitai and Natalie had stopped in Paris and shown it to a few major art critics and museum curators, including Werner Spies, the world's foremost expert on the work of Max Ernst. Spies had provided the critical link between Ernst and Komlós, recalling a conversation he had had with Dorothea Tanning, Ernst's wife. She had not known Komlós, of course. She had met her husband in New York. But she remembered when Ernst first heard of Komlós's death. It was Chagall who told him. He'd heard it from a Hungarian immigrant he'd met at a party. Dorothea told Spies that Ernst was very upset, that he'd told her that though they'd only met once or twice when Komlós visited Paris, they had had an intense friendship, the source of which was their mutual fascination with birds. There were so many artists who died during the war. Max Jacob, Ernst Kirchner, Otto Freundlich. Max Ernst himself was interned. But when he heard about Komlós, Dorothea said, it made him especially sad.

"Did she tell you how Ernst met Komlós?" Amitai had asked Spies.

"I think perhaps through Klee or Kandinsky? Someone at the Bauhaus."

"Moholy-Nagy?"

"It could have been."

Thus, with Spies's expert assistance, Amitai established Komlós's presence in the web of important artists of the twentieth century, and though his threads were few, he was convinced that once Komlós became known he would be revered.

When Amitai had called to inform his great-uncle first of how he'd acquired the painting and then of his decision not to offer it for sale but to donate it to the Hungarian museum, Uncle Jacob had been furious. He had threatened Amitai with everything up to and including not simply termination of employment but of his relationship to the New York branch of the Shasho family and to the Syrian-American Jewish community as a whole.

"You cross me like this, Nephew, and no Shasho will speak to you ever again," Jacob Shasho had said.

Amitai might have been more troubled by this prospect were he not already guaranteed to lose both his job and his family in America by virtue of an item that he had in his pocket at this very moment. He had taken delivery of it early this morning while Natalie thought he was busy soaking on the men's side of the Gellért Baths. Elek had sent him dozens of images of diamond rings in the style of Hungarian art nouveau, from among which he had chosen a large round stone set in a platinum filigree. Elek had replaced the small blue sapphires in the circle surrounding the diamond with alternating amethysts and peridots.

"You know, sapphire or amethyst, I charge you the same," Elek had said, his business acumen not at all dulled by his gratitude for Amitai's decision to return the Komlós to Hungary.

"I wouldn't expect anything else," Amitai had replied.

The moment he put the ring on Natalie's finger, his family in New York would be lost to him. The red hair she had inherited from her grandmother had its origins, some generations back, in a tiny village along the River Barrow in County Kilkenny and the edict decreed that once Amitai married this granddaughter of a convert, no Syrian-American Jew could see him again. Though he cared little about his uncle's, Amitai had been concerned about his parents' reaction, and when he had brought Natalie to meet them in Israel, he had taken his father aside to ask not permission, but rather his blessing, no matter that the woman Amitai intended to marry was not, by the standards of the Shasho family patriarch, a Jew.

His father had voiced no objection, and Amitai had left it at that, though he would, over the years, sometimes wonder what his parents' answer would have been had they not been put as children in the care of Youth Aliyah and sent to a kibbutz in Israel but had instead ended up in Brooklyn like so many of their cousins.

By now Elek had enjoyed more than a few glasses of champagne, and he was uncharacteristically giddy as he raised his glass. "Another toast," Elek said. "To Amitai Shasho, for standing up to the formidable Dror Tamid and insisting that the painting be returned to Hungary."

Tamid had done his furious, spitting best to convince Amitai, with threats and vilification, with pleading and guilt-trippery, that the painting of Komlós belonged, by right, to Israel, and in Israel. "Komlós was a Jew, tortured by Nazis and murdered by Hungarians," Tamid had said. "Only in Israel can his work be seen in the proper moral context."

Amitai had been tempted to retort by asking Tamid who would put Israel in its proper moral context, but in fact he had found himself unable to completely dismiss Tamid. After all, everything the man said was true. If Hungary had viewed Komlós as a true citizen, equal to any other, then he would not have ended his life in the misery of the Jewish labor brigades. But had Komlós been a Gentile, or had the anti-Semitism of Hungary and its German ally not prevailed, Komlós might have been drafted into the Hungarian army and died on the Russian front. He might have met any number of other fates no better than the death that had found him. In the end, Amitai opted to attempt the impossible. Though it was a presumption of terrible magnitude, he had allowed himself to imagine what Komlós would have wanted.

And that, Amitai decided, was what every artist wants: for his work to be recognized as important and influential, as historically relevant. To that end, Elek had convinced the Museum of Fine Arts in Budapest to loan the painting both to the Centre Georges Pompidou in Paris and to the Neue Galerie in New York, for exhibits on the influences of the surrealists.

But in choosing a permanent home for the painting, Amitai felt less confident. There was no record of what Komlós felt about his native land, whether he considered himself a Hungarian or, as an artist, a citizen of the world. In the end, this donation, inspired in no small part by the defense of his friend Elek for Hungary's right to maintain control of its artistic patrimony, had been the clearest way Amitai could find to honor Komlós. The presence of his painting in Hungary, and the international excitement that Amitai hoped would result as its story was told and the painting admired, would serve as a reminder that this great Hungarian artist, this elemental part of Hungary's cultural legacy, was a Jew.

To that end, he had made it a condition of the donation that the museum include in the painting's description card specific reference both to Komlós's religion and to his death in the Jewish Labor Service. Elek had expressed to Amitai the hope that this notation would inspire the museum to revise the description of the Herzog El Grecos to include a similarly honest discussion of their provenance. About this possibility, Amitai was less optimistic than his friend.

When Elek moved off, veering tipsily to the left, Natalie took Amitai's arm and kissed his cheek.

"I think this was the right thing to do," she said.

"You 'think'?" He laughed. "Given how much it cost to silence Attila Varga, I would hope for a little more certainty." Amitai had all but emptied his bank account, the savings of a decade and a half poured into the pocket of the Romanian, to keep him from going to the press or the police with his story of the two lying and thieving Jews. It had been worth the expense, however, when the international newspapers, following up on Tamid's denunciation, had sought out Varga for comment and received a tale of a careful custodian, a fair offer by an honest broker, and a painting returned to its rightful place.

Natalie said, "If you need me to be certain, I can do that for you. I'm certain that you found the right home for the painting."

"Home," he said.

"Yes."

Such a small word, with such a complex web of meanings. She was right. The painting was finally at home. And so, he thought, was he.

"I have something to ask you," he said, reaching into his pocket.

Three

BUDAPEST

1913

· 32 ·

IN THE SPRING OF 1913, nearly a decade ago, I was asked by a colleague to undertake the analysis of his niece, a young lady of nineteen years, whom he described as suffering from neurasthenia complicated by chronically recurrent dyspepsia of a hysterical origin. My acquaintanceship with my referring colleague, a prominent Pest physician specializing in disorders of the kidney and urethra, was of long standing and fair intimacy. He was a fellow member of the board of governors of the Magyar Israelite Medical Association and also a fellow alumnus of the Medical Faculty of the University of Vienna. My final year at that august institution was Herr Dr. S.'s first, and we both lodged at the Pension Wettendorfer, which had the distinction of being one of the few pensions serving Jewish medical students to be furnished with an indoor commode. I was less well acquainted with Herr Dr. S.'s brother, though we traveled in similar social circles. Prior to assuming her treatment, I had on a few occasions the privilege of meeting the charming young Nina S. She had impressed me as a psychically normal girl, though perhaps inclined by virtue of her high intelligence to neurotic excitability when in stimulating company. The S. family is of fine reputation, possessing among its members a number of wealthy financiers, attorneys, and at least one court councillor. It was thus with great interest, even pleasure, that I anticipated Nina S.'s arrival in my surgery on the morning of May 5, 1913.

I wish I could say that Miss S. greeted our appointment with similar optimism and good cheer. On the contrary, when she entered the room, she was irritable, even angry. Her dress, of the reform style, uncorseted and loose flowing, was of winter wool, gray and gloomy in color, matching her demeanor. The day itself was fine, a harbinger of what I hoped would be an especially pleasant spring, and I could not help but notice that her attire stood in marked contrast to the sprightly floral muslins that my own daughters wore that day. Though Miss S. denied being warm, I nonetheless opened a window to give her the benefit of the pleasant lilac-scented breeze.

Miss S. refused to take her place on the analysand's couch, despite the cheerful nosegay of the season's last violets that my wife had thoughtfully placed on the small table by the head. Instead she perched stiffly on a chair, her mouth drawn into a thin line, quite a feat considering the generosity of her plump lower lip.

"How can I help you, my dear?" I said, my tone far more avuncular than forensic. Over the previous few years, as I had progressed in my own analysis with the brilliant Sándor Ferenczi and learned from him the utility of empathic reciprocity in the analyst/analysand relationship, I had begun to treat my patients with the love and affection they often lacked and craved. Though I know the S.'s to be devoted, even over-indulgent, parents of their three children, I was confident that Miss S., like all my patients, would respond better to affection than to formality. However, my concern aggravated rather than consoled her, and she bristled.

"I am afraid, Dr. Zobel," she said, "that you have been misled by my father and my uncle. I am not, in fact, in need of your assistance, at least not medical."

"Ah!" I said. "But you are in need of another kind of assistance?"

"The only thing I need is for you to convince my father that I am not in the early stages of dementia praecox."

"Surely your father has no fear of such a drastic diagnosis. Your uncle certainly expressed nothing of the kind to me."

Miss S. was fair, with yellow hair and a porcelain complexion uncommon in people of our race. Her delicate skin showed her every mood, and her cheeks and throat now blushed pink. "Do you know what inspired my father to insist on this appointment?" she asked.

"Your uncle raised the possibility of neurasthenia."

"Do I seem neurasthenic to you?"

She was hardly enervated; she radiated energy. This alone did not, however, disprove her uncle's diagnosis. Fatigue, though a primary symptom of the disorder, is not always present. Depression and anxiety can be and often are expressed as precisely the kind of agitation and irritability that Miss S. was now exhibiting.

In a soothing voice, I said, "Your uncle also told me that you suffer from a pain in your stomach."

"He told you that this pain was dyspeptic and recurrent?"

"You are well versed in the terminology, I see." I was not surprised at Nina's facility. Familiarity with medical jargon is characteristic of a certain kind of hypochondriacal patient.

"I should hope so," Miss S. said. "I am preparing to enter medical college next year."

"Are you? I was not aware."

"Yes, I am, despite the fact that neither my father nor my uncle approves of women physicians."

Since the ministerial statute of 1895 allowed for women to enter the Faculty of Medicine here in Budapest, there had been a great influx of female students, though I myself had not yet been forced to confront them in my neurology and psychiatry lectures. Though I did not confess as much to my patient, I am obliged to admit to having possessed an ambivalence about the presence of young lady students in my chosen profession. There are areas, such as the fields of hygiene, pediatrics, and even obstetrics, that are in many ways suited to the female mind and sensibility. Women are naturally predisposed to care for the family, children, and the means of reproduction, and there are certain classes of women who can perform these functions competently and perhaps even more sensitively than men. However, I had concerns about exposing young ladies of class and discernment both to the rigors and to the harsh physical realities of modern medicine. Many of the common and necessary parts of a student physician's training would be offensive and disturbing to such young ladies. I think I can be forgiven for rebelling against the image of girls like Miss S. or my own daughters, girls from conservative and proper Jewish homes, examining the pustulating papules of a patient suffering from secondary-stage syphilis.

I could not help but sympathize with Mr. S.'s antipathy to his daughter's choice of profession and was relieved that my own daughters had shown no such inclinations. In fact, on that very morning, my wife and I had determined to accept on behalf of our eldest daughter, Erzsébet, the marriage suggested by an elderly relative who made her living facilitating such arrangements. The young man in question was himself a student of medicine, and while considering Miss S.'s ambitions, I for a moment entertained the ludicrous notion of Erzsébet meeting her intended for the first time not in her mother's parlor but in the autopsy theater, their hands mutually immersed in the viscera of a diseased corpse.

I determined, however, not to alienate my young patient by allowing her to see my doubts about the suitability of her ambitions. I said, "Do you, as a fledgling physician, agree with your uncle's diagnosis of your symptoms?"

"No. The pain, while recurrent, is not dyspeptic. Nor do I suffer from abdominal ulcers. I suffer from"—here she hesitated and flushed but continued—"I suffer from nothing more than severe menstrual cramping." I could see that she was doubly embarrassed, both by the topic and by her own shame in discussing it, and this affirmed my feelings about elegant and cultured women and the medical profession. A young girl's pretty flush when referring to such matters is understandable, even desirable, but a doctor can feel no such compunctions.

Miss S. rushed on, "It's only that my father does not understand that most women experience these symptoms. It's not a disease. It's normal."

Maintaining a matter-of-fact tone of voice in order to assure her that I found our conversation to be utterly decorous—an analyst, after all, must speak without indignation or revulsion on all topics, even the most bizarre of sexual perversions, and certainly something as commonplace as menstruation—I said, "Some cramping is normal, I agree. However, it is not uncommon for intense pain during the menstrual period to be hysterical in nature, not physical, and thus resolvable with treatment and analysis." I refrained at this moment from addressing the most likely source of her pain, excessive masturbation and a consequent shame response. There would be time, once she grew trusting of me, to lead her toward this logical conclusion. I continued, "How intense is your pain?"

For a moment Miss S. did not reply, but then, grudgingly, she said, "Very."

"Wouldn't you like it to be less so?"

"Of course."

"Well, then perhaps I can help you. Here is what I suggest. Let us meet a few times to explore this pain of yours, to consider if it might have a genesis in psychic trauma rather than physical. If we are successful in ameliorating it, then that will be wonderful. If not, then what will we have lost but a few hours of time, time spent in one another's surely not-unpleasant company?"

She frowned and said, "I won't be hypnotized."

"Why not?"

"I don't wish to be."

"Well, then I shall not hypnotize you. Though I must say, by precluding hypnosis you do remove one of the analyst's most artful tools. Perhaps you'll change your mind."

"I won't."

"There are many other means to our mutual end of relieving your pain. Conversation, exploration, massage."

"Massage?"

"Dr. Sigmund Freud has had marvelous results with gentle massage in the treatment of hysteria. This is something we might explore together. Again, only if you are willing."

She was silent for a few moments, weighing, I imagined, the unpleasantness of her monthly pain against the indignity of ceding to her father's insistence on treatment.

Finally, she said, "Dr. Zobel, there is one thing I ask of you."

"What is that, my dear?"

"I ask only that if you determine that there is no psychical remedy for my symptoms, but that they are purely physical and normal, in short, if you find me to be sane, you tell this to my father."

"Of course. It is my obligation as your physician to inform your father of my diagnosis. I would do nothing else."

"Good."

"Earlier you mentioned that you believe your father to fear that you suffer from dementia praecox. Why, do you think, does he anticipate that diagnosis?"

"My father is a great reader."

"Is he? He has this trait in common with his brother, then. Your uncle and I have often shared books with one another."

"Recently he received a book by someone named Alexander Pilcz."

"Ah, yes. Pilcz. He is a member of the department of psychiatry at the University of Vienna, where your uncle and I were students."

"Do you know this man?"

"I am familiar with his work."

A number of years before, Pilcz had published a study of comparative-race psychiatry that was at the time considered among the seminal works in the field. I myself have not found his various charts and graphs of the predisposition of different races to certain psychiatric ailments to be useful, though perhaps this is due to my discomfort, as a member of the Israelite race, with his conclusions. It is, after all, hardly pleasant to be told that by virtue of one's race one is much more likely to be insane and feebleminded. In 1906, when Pilcz's work was first published, I drafted a letter to the *Journal of the Vienna Medical Faculty*, questioning the doctor's conclusions about Jewish predisposition to psychoses of the hereditary-degenerative type and especially to youthful imbecility. Upon consultation with my wife, however, I thought better of the letter (which did, as she said, sound more heated than analytic). The fields of psychiatry and psychoanalysis are far too rife with discord and disagreement, and I have found over the years that it is best to do what one can to avoid feuding with one's colleagues. This is, dare I say, especially important for a physician of the Israelite race, as our Gentile colleagues are sometimes too ready to accuse us of unseemly competitiveness. At any rate, nowadays, the benign anti-Semitism in the work of Pilcz seems positively quaint, and were I to busy myself with writing letters of opposition to everyone who besmirched the reputation of my religion, I would have no time to eat or sleep, let alone work.

Miss S. said, "Pilcz's book has convinced Papa that I, like so many Jewish women, am doomed to fall ill with dementia praecox and spend my life wound up in restraining sheets in an insane asylum, screaming obscenities and tearing out my eyelashes."

I laughed at the hyperbole of her image, and she graced me with a small smile. I was delighted to see Miss S. adopting my own playful attitude. Despite herself, the young lady was enjoying our conversation. Though modesty usually prevents me from saying so, I would be remiss in not alerting the reader to my facility with this kind of patient. Young women flourish under my care because I am comfortable with them. Having daughters of my own, I have a natural affinity for the young of the gentler sex, and they for me.

"Would you like to know what evidence he has for this?" she continued.

"I would."

She ticked them off on her fingers. "Number one, that I insist on studying medicine, a sure sign of pending insanity, don't you think? Number two, and this is an even greater offense in his mind, that I refuse to consider marrying the boy he and my mother chose for me when I was still in swaddling clothes."

I interrupted. "You are betrothed?"

"No, I am certainly not betrothed. It is only that Mama and one of her cousins have been scheming since we were babies for their children to marry, and Papa is, if anything, even more eager for the alliance."

"Do I know this young man?"

"Probably. It's Ignác E."

"The son of Baron Móric E.?"

"No. The son of Jenő and Berta E. of Nagyvárad. A lesser cousin of the baron's. Though they are wealthy enough, as my mother never tires of telling me. Shall I continue presenting my father's evidence for my dementia, or has my refusal of the proposal of a member of the illustrious E. family, no matter how minor a branch from how minor a distant city, convinced you that my father is right?"

I could sympathize with her father's frustration at his daughter's refusal to acquiesce to the match. The object of my Erzsébet's pending betrothal, while a fine young man from a family in good standing in the community, was nowhere near as illustrious as Nina's potential husband, yet were Erzsébet to take against him, I would be most annoyed. Still, dementia praecox? Hardly.

"I will reserve judgment on the suitability of the young E.," I told her. "Pray continue."

"The third evidence of my supposed insanity is that I refuse to lace my corsets so tightly that my eyes bug out from my head, like other girls my age. The fourth is that I spend my own allowance to subscribe to the journal *Women and Society*. The fifth, that I not only attended a lecture by Mrs. Rózsa Schwimmer but dared to suggest to my father that he might consider joining the Men's League for Women's Suffrage . . ."

At this I could not restrain a bellow of laughter. The idea of the pontifical fogy Marcus S., vice president of the Israelite Congregation of Pest, a man ever attired in sober black, never plaid, morning coats, who'd sooner wear a boot on his head than replace his top hat with a stylish bowler, petitioning the king to give the women of Austria and Hungary the vote was, perhaps, the most amusing idea I'd heard in months.

"And finally," Miss S. said, acknowledging my laughter with a raised eyebrow, "number six, that I have befriended Gizella Weisz, who is not merely a feminist and disciple of Mrs. Rózsa Schwimmer but also a dwarf."

"A dwarf?"

"Yes, a dwarf. And what of it? Half of my father's own friends are certified imbeciles, so why should he view my friendship with a dwarf as a sure sign of insanity?"

"You're being a bit harsh on your parents' society, are you not? Though not a friend, I consider your father a fond acquaintance. Perhaps I am an imbecile, too?"

"Perhaps you are, Dr. Zobel. I'm afraid I don't know you well enough to say yet."

The clock in the hall chimed. "And I'm afraid our time together is up," I said. "But we shall continue this discussion tomorrow, yes? Shall we say ten o'clock?"

She sprang to her feet. "All right. Yes. We can meet again. But I have an appointment with my tutor to prepare for my *matura* in the morning, so it must be in the afternoon."

How well I remembered the strain I underwent during my own final examinations from gymnasium. No fewer than three young boys in my class attempted suicide in the days immediately prior. Given that she was in the midst of this arduous preparation, Miss S. struck me as remarkably composed. And though I knew neurosis to be an expert masquerader, still for a moment I could not help but think that the girl, though probably neurasthenic, was as sane as I.

"Of course," I said. "I will have to adjust my calendar, but I shall send word first thing in the morning." Though my afternoon clients, women of leisure, would not object overmuch to being shuffled around, I would refrain from telling them that it was for the sake of a busy young girl studying for her final exams. That they might not have tolerated so willingly.

Miss S. extended her hand, and I kissed it.

"Thank you, Herr Dr. Zobel," she said. "This was not as miserable an experience as I had expected it would be."

"My dear, Nina . . ." I waited for a moment to gauge whether she would take insult at the familiar use of her given name. As she appeared unoffended, I continued, "If we accomplish nothing more than alleviating such unpleasant expectations, then I will consider our time together to be well spent."

· 33 ·

NINA ARRIVED AT OUR second session dressed for an outing. In contrast to the dull gown she'd worn the day before, today she looked beautiful, had even adopted the tight lacing that she had claimed to find so objectionable. I am the son of a dry-goods merchant and the grandson of a simple tailor—a not-uncommon heritage for a Jewish physician of comfortable means in those halcyon days of Israelite assimilation into Magyar society—and so I know women's clothing well, and this gown of Nina's cost at least five hundred kronen. Her trim figure was shown off to great advantage by the white accordion crêpe de chine of her blouse waist, and there was an amusing bit of suspended spangle ornamentation hanging from the girdle of gilt soutache and black braid that cinched her waist in the wedding-ring style. I could not help but think of my own darlings Erzsébet and Lili, desperately strapping themselves into their corsets, lacing the wretched things so tightly I feared permanent constriction of their bowels, and achieving nothing close to even twice Nina's tiny waist. Nor was this the only reason that I hoped that Erzsébet and Lili had not caught sight of my young patient as she passed through the apartment to my consulting room. My daughters had for weeks now been engaged in a no-holds-barred millinery campaign on behalf of a poke bonnet decorated with Numidi feathers, and I, their cruel and vicious opponent in this battle, had refused to accede to anything beyond vulture aigrettes. Nina's hat, an adorable and daringly small tam-o'-shanter of sky-blue taffeta silk, was trimmed with an ostentatious quantity of Numidi plumes. Were my daughters to see it, I feared they'd be fortified in their energies for months of warfare.

Sadly, Nina's mood failed to match her gay attire. She was, if anything, more gloomy and dark tempered than she had been at the beginning of our interview the day before, and I feared all the good work I'd done ingratiating myself had been for naught.

"Something troubles you," I said, once she settled herself in the chair, eschewing again the analysand's couch. "Do you regret your decision to continue our conversation?"

"No," she said. She opened her reticule, a tiny silk thing festooned with azure beading, and removed from it a silver case, from which, to my astonishment, she took out a cigarillo. She screwed the cigarillo into an ivory holder and placed it between her lovely lips. Leaning forward, she asked, "Have you a match?"

"Nina!" I said. "Surely you don't smoke." She was not, of course, the first lady I'd seen smoking, though I doubted that any who took up the habit deserved the honorific.

Abashed, she returned the cigarette to its case. "Many women smoke."

"Many? Indeed?"

"Some."

"Is this a new fad in your feminist circles?"

"It's hardly new. And anyway, Doctor. It's not like I'm in public, on the street or in a coffeehouse. No one can see me."

"And do you frequent coffeehouses, Nina?" My doubts about her father were fast disappearing. What yesterday appeared to be overreaction to a young woman's normal small rebellions seemed suddenly to be a reasonable assessment of her state of mind. Smoking! In coffeehouses!

"I certainly don't usually frequent the Café Lloyd, though I was there today, forcing down a disgusting *dobos* torte." Disdain for the Lloyd dripped from her lips like chocolate buttercream from between the layers of the dessert.

"You are not fond of that coffeehouse?"

"It's just so predictable. A lawyer at the Lloyd. It's about as original as a sculptor at the Japan."

"Where would you have preferred to have gone?"

She hesitated, then laughed. At herself, it turned out. "The Japan Coffee House. With the artists and writers. Or the New York!"

"But you went instead to the Lloyd. With whom?"

"This afternoon I was in the company of Mr. Ignác E. Chaperoned by my mother, of course, because she would hardly have let me eat cake alone with a man. Who knows what might happen?"

"I thought Mr. E. lived in Nagyvárad?"

"His parents are originally from that city. But they have lived in Budapest for some time. Probably to take advantage of the family connection to the baron."

"That doesn't seem to be very generous a presumption. Surely there are other reasons to remain in the capital."

"I suppose," she said, crossing and recrossing her pretty ankles in their patent strapped shoes. Her heel was higher than any I would have allowed my daughters.

"Would you like to lie down on the couch?" I asked. "It's very comfortable. My own dear wife embroidered the pillow slip, and the Turkish rug is very soft."

"No," Nina said, though she sounded a bit less sure than the last time she'd refused my offer.

"So you met Mr. E. for cake," I said. "Did you enjoy yourself?"

"Hardly."

"Then why did you go?"

"Because my father said that if I didn't, he would not allow me to take my exams."

For the purposes of this case history, I will do my best to recount Nina's assignation with the young E. as she told it to me and ask the reader to forgive me any small embellishments. These are based on what I know of the people involved, of the location of the rendezvous, and of the history of the families. Any indulgences I permit myself are designed only to enhance the literary merit of this case history, which, to be useful, must provide more than a mechanical transcription of my patient's utterances. I realize that there are analysts who would take issue with these statements, who would insist that the sole point of a case history is to note the analysand's own words as a stenographer might, but I am of the school that views truth as the goal of our communal project, and though it seems counterintuitive, truth sometimes demands license in the presentation of fact.

The invitation to join Mr. Ignác E. for coffee and cakes at the Café Lloyd was delivered not to Miss Nina S. but rather to her mother, with the understanding that the younger woman would be present. This was not the first assignation suggested by the young man, but it was the first to which Nina had acquiesced, and that only because her father had demanded it as a condition of her sitting both her *matura* and the medical school entrance examinations for which she had been preparing for upward of six months, indeed for all the years of her enrollment in Veres Pálné's esteemed Girls' Gymnasium of the Hungarian Women Training Association.

Nina had spent many hours over the years in the stultifying (her word, not mine) company of the young Mr. E., but only at family parties, dinners, and balls, the purposes of which were not exclusively the social interaction of the two young people. At a ball, Nina could escape her suitor. Even at a dinner, she could turn her head and address the gentleman on her left without being considered too terribly rude. But with their knees all but touching beneath the small marble circle of a café table, the edges of their saucers snug alongside each other, and the crumbs of hazelnut cake from the fork of one drifting onto the plate of the other, Nina had no choice but to converse directly with the young man whom she had come to consider not her suitor but her nemesis.

The unfortunate boy viewed their rendezvous as an opportunity for lovemaking, something he made clear by presenting her with a delicate nosegay of violets, not, I imagine, unlike the one that I had asked my wife to prepare for the little table alongside my office couch. Violets, it seems, are the chosen springtime flower both of makers of love and of physicians of the psyche. To Nina's mother Ignác gave a gaudy quantity of red tulips and yellow daffodils.

"I kiss your hand," the young man said, lowering his lips to Nina's narrow kid-covered fingers.

"It's good to see you, Cousin," she said. "How are my aunt and uncle?"

"Oh, Nina," her mother said. "Our families are hardly as closely related as that. Berta is my second cousin, not your aunt, and that makes Ignác nothing more than, what, your third cousin? Your second cousin once removed? Barely related at all." Mrs. S. settled herself in her seat, removed her needlework from her large reticule, and began poking the needle through the fabric. "Now, children," she said, "you mustn't distract me. I'm working on a particularly intricate bit, and this is meant to be a Holy Evening gift for your father. Talk quietly amongst yourselves, and when the waiter comes, order me a cup of coffee with plenty of cream and a *zserbó*."

"We're not at the Café Gerbaud, Mama. They won't have *zserbó*," Nina said.

"They have something similar," Ignác said, waving over the waiter. He placed Mrs. S.'s order and then turned to Nina. "For you, Nina? I can recommend the *dobos* torte. I remember that it's your favorite."

"No, thank you," Nina said. "I'll just have a coffee. No cream."

"Don't be silly, Nina," her mother said without lifting her head from her needlework. "You love *dobos* torte."

"I'm not hungry."

"You girls and your fashions." She leaned toward Ignác conspiratorially. "Perhaps you can explain it to me, dear Ignác. Why are girls today so obsessed with their figures? They object to eating sugar, have you ever heard such a thing? Nina won't even join her father and me in the evening anymore for sweet liqueur and cakes. Ridiculous, isn't it?"

"Mama, I thought your needlework was unusually demanding?"

The waiter cleared his throat, and Nina snapped her menu closed. "Fine. *Dobos* torte."

"The same for me," Ignác said.

Once the waiter was gone, and Mrs. S. had returned to the needlework that needed, it seemed, far less of her attention than she insisted, Ignác presented Nina with a package tied up in crisp paper and a bit of string.

"You didn't need to bring me a gift."

"But I know how fond you are of poetry, and this is the very latest thing, according to the clerk at Kellner's."

Nina opened the paper to reveal a fat book bound in dark leather. "*The Inferno?*" she said.

"Dante!" Ignác said, pleased that she'd recognized it and obviously quite happy with his choice.

"You've given me a copy of Dante's *Inferno?*"

"Translated by Mihály Babits. He's very good."

"Have you read much Babits?" Nina asked, all innocence. "You've enjoyed his poems and stories in *Nyugat,* perhaps?"

"Er, yes."

"Hmm." Nina glanced around the handsome room. "And do they take *Nyugat* here, at the Café Lloyd?"

Most of the men crowded around the tables in the dark-paneled room had a newspaper or periodical spread out before them, and dozens more were draped over the wooden newspaper racks, like towels hanging in a bathhouse. The majority of these were daily papers ranging from conservative to radically conservative, though Nina spied the distinctive blue-and-yellow cover of the *Budapesti Szemle,* the oldest and most respectable literary journal. Some men even appeared to be daringly immersed in the day's *A Hét.* The urbane and cosmopolitan *Nyugat,* with its eponymous westward-looking literary focus, was, however, nowhere to be seen on the tables of the economic and legal titans of Budapest as they indulged their sweet tooths and caffeine addictions in the crowded room of the Café Lloyd.

"Is there other poetry you prefer?" Ignác asked.

Nina reached into her bag and pulled out a slim volume. "Have you read any Charlotte Perkins Gilman?"

"I haven't had the pleasure."

"She's American," Nina said. "This is the first of her books of poetry to be translated into Hungarian."

He accepted the proffered volume doubtfully.

"Her best book is a novel called *The Yellow Wall-Paper*. Do you read English?"

"Not well."

"Well, I imagine it's been translated into German." Nina knew this for a fact, because, despite the implication, she read very poorly in English and had herself been forced to explore Gilman's terrifying world in translation.

"Perhaps I'll pick it up," Ignác said.

"You really ought to. It's all about a woman driven mad by the restrictions imposed on her by her husband."

At this moment in her narrative, Nina turned to me and said, "And you, Dr. Zobel? Have you read Gilman's book?"

"*The Yellow Wall-Paper*? I cannot say I've had the pleasure."

"Well, you ought to. It might afford you insight into what happens to a woman when she is forced into an unasked-for 'rest cure' instead of being allowed to pursue her passion for work."

The rest of Nina and Ignác's assignation, I fear, proceeded with no improvement. By the end Nina had worked herself up into the state in which she had walked into my consulting room, though she acknowledged that it was likely that Mr. E. noticed little of her agitation. Indeed he suggested that Nina and her mother join him and his own mother at the light opera on Saturday evening, to see *Perfect Woman,* featuring the preeminent vaudevillians Fedák Zsuzsa and Király Ernő. Before Nina could insist on her lack of interest in either the tango or operas about the tango, her mother had agreed.

Now, perched on the edge of her chair in my consulting room, Nina peeled off her kid gloves and tossed them aside. She placed her hands on either side of her waist and, groaning softly, pressed at her corset. I recognized the motion from my own wife and daughters, who often waited barely a second after the doors closed behind company before poking and prodding at the bones of their corsets to try to alleviate the pain caused by the garments.

"Please, Nina," I said. "Do lie down. You'll be so much more comfortable."

"Oh, all right!" she said, as though I had been doing nothing for the past half hour but importuning her to put her feet up.

She stretched out on the couch, crossed her feet at the ankle, and, reaching around behind her neck, even unbuttoned the top few buttons of her shirtwaist.

"Better?" I asked.

"Yes," she admitted grudgingly.

"Tell me, my dear. What is it about Ignác E. that troubles you so? Does he remind you of someone or something?"

"He reminds me only of his tiresome self."

"I wonder if there is not someone or something deeper in the recesses of your mind, some experience or person poor Mr. E. reminds you of. Are you adamant in your refusal to consider hypnosis?"

"Yes."

"In that case, perhaps we can attempt an alternative analytic technique. I will say a word, and you simply say the first thing that comes into your mind. Are you ready?"

In lieu of reply, she sighed.

"Yes," I said.

"Fine, yes. We can try it."

"No. I mean that was the word. 'Yes.'"

"'Yes'?"

"Yes. I mean, rather, is your response 'yes' to the word 'yes'?"

"No. My response to the word 'yes' is 'no.'"

"All right then. The next word is 'no.'"

"Yes."

"Happy."

"Sad."

"Mother."

"Father."

"Father."

"Angry." She hesitated. "Oh dear."

"Don't be concerned. It's a simple exercise. There is no wrong answer. We'll continue. Bourse."

"Father." She seemed relieved at the benign nature of this response.

"Love."

"Ridiculous."

"Is that your response?"

"Yes."

"We'll continue. Marriage."

"Bill of sale."

"Nina, the point is not to be shocking or to try to convince me of any-thing. It's simply to say the first thing that comes to mind."

"That is the first thing that comes to mind. How could it be otherwise? I just spent the afternoon with a purchaser who all but lifted my lip to examine the state of my teeth. I am being sold like a broodmare, Herr Dr. Zobel. Auctioned off to the highest bidder."

"Ignác E. is not so very wealthy as all that, is he?"

"All right then. I am being sold but not even to the highest bidder. I am discounted goods, though of course my father doesn't think so, given how much he complains about the size of my dowry. How absurd is that, Dr. Zobel? My father insists that I marry and at the same time complains that my dowry will bankrupt him."

"Why do you think your father is so eager for you to marry Mr. E.?"

"Because Ignác's father is a principal in a banking concern of similar size to my father's, and my father believes that if they join forces they will rival the larger firms. My father cannot afford to buy the E. firm, but conveniently, he and Jenő E. not only have wives who are cousins, but they have opposite-sex children of marriageable age."

"Perhaps the motives you attribute to your father are unduly venal. Perhaps he simply feels that given how much the two families share in common, given the closeness of your ties, the marriage is likely to be a success."

I knew, even as I said this, that I was being disingenuous in not acknowl-edging the accuracy of Nina's assessment of her father's motives. Of course the man must consider the financial implications of his selection of a husband for his daughter. Not to do so would be irresponsible.

Nina said, "I have been generous with my father. His true motivations are even more venal than I've said. Although he would never admit it, what my father wants more than anything is to have a family connection to the Baron Móric E."

"Surely your father knows that the baron is now a good Christian Magyar and associates little with the Jewish members of his family."

"Never underestimate my father, Dr. Zobel. For all you know he means Ignác and me to convert for the sake of resuming relations with the noble branch. He has already talked of changing our name."

The S. surname, like many of those of our people, gives away its religion in its first Galician syllable. My own name, Germanic in origin, though we too hail from Galicia, does the same. Even in those most egalitarian of days, before the Great War, when the discriminations of our current less-fortunate times were nearly unimaginable, there were professions in our great Magyar nation in which it was difficult to progress with a name like Zobel or S., and were I not a member of a profession that boasted such a large percentage (well over forty!) of Israelite practitioners, perhaps even I might have succumbed to the temptation to change my name.

If we members of the Mosaic tribe hope to be regarded as completely equal, we must not differ in any detail from the other subjects of the Crown of Saint Stephen. Details like dress and language can seem trivial, but they can serve to isolate us from our surrounding communities. Witness, for example, the lot of the Jews of Galicia from whom many of us are descended. Though none of us can deny that anti-Semitism exists here in Hungary, especially in the wake of the Jewish purges and the recently passed *numerus clausus* restricting Jewish enrollment in universities to 5 percent, still it is a far cry from the pogroms experienced by our ancestors and even currently by our cousins in eastern Europe. This difference exists because most of us have altered our attire, our conversation, indeed many aspects of our way of life, in order to fit into this society that has welcomed us so well. Hungarian liberals and anti-Semites alike might routinely complain that Budapest is too Jewish, that the press and the bourse are under our control, that Hungarian literature is being "Judaicized." Still, even in the current climate we are secure here in Hungary, not least because of our assimilation.

To Nina I said, "Many Jewish families have of late changed their names. Not all of those have done so as a prelude to conversion. And come to that, many fine and upstanding Jews have found it suits their lives and ambitions to convert." My own sister Sarolta had recently been baptized into the Catholic Church at the insistence of her children, though their reasons for abandoning the faith of our fathers was problematic at best. My niece and nephews are as nasty a bunch of social climbers as you'll ever meet.

Nina said, "Dr. Zobel, are you a reader of *Women and Society*?"

"The feminist periodical? I have perused it on occasion. The elder of my sisters is a subscriber. You would like Jolán, Nina. She is a professional woman. A teacher of mathematics. I think you'd find her interesting."

Unlike my younger sister Sarolta, who married before her eighteenth birthday, Jolán never attracted the attentions of any man, or at least not one whom she could tolerate the idea of marrying. "It's different for a man," she would say when I would remonstrate with her on what I considered at the time to be an excessive selectivity. "If you choose unwisely, at worst you'll have to spend an hour or two of every day gazing across the dinner table at your bad decision. A woman who makes the same mistake spends the rest of her life scrubbing the stains from the underdrawers of someone she despises."

"Good Lord, Jolán!" our mother had cried. "Your mouth. Your terrible, terrible mouth!"

"Not to mention the fact that it's hardly you who'll be scrubbing anyone's underdrawers," I said. "You'll surely employ a washerwoman."

"I am speaking figuratively," Jolán said. "I will neither literally nor figuratively scrub the underdrawers of someone whom I do not love."

As blessed as she is with intellect and wit, Jolán possesses features as severe as her tongue and was not, in the end, obliged to reject the advances of many suitors, let alone ascertain the state of their undergarments. Instead, she pursued to the extent possible a career as a mathematician, though as a woman her opportunities were limited. When no Hungarian faculty would enroll her, she went to Germany to study at the Mathematical Institute of Erlangen with a female mathematician named Emmy Noether. Eventually, frustrated in her desire to complete her doctorate by the Institute's limitations on female students, Jolán returned to Budapest and became a lecturer in mathematics at a women's teachers' seminary.

"I'd like to meet your sister," Nina said. "Other than my professors at the gymnasium, I don't know many women professionals. Only the ones I've met through outings of the Feminist Association."

"I shall arrange it, then. Perhaps we can revivify your fondness for *dobos* torte with more agreeable company."

"Perhaps, though I fear the pastry is lost to me forever. But I ask you about the magazine because in a recent issue they published an article about marriage. The author was unnamed—she said only that she was a feminist woman. She wrote about the hypocrisy of using the word 'love' to describe contemporary marriage. She pointed out that marriage isn't about love. It is an economic transaction. The bride's family chooses a groom of suitable financial status and then pays him to take their daughter."

As a father about to embark on the negotiation of his daughter's marriage, so crass a description of the process made me uncomfortable. Thankfully, I was practiced in the analyst's art of neutrality of demeanor and Nina did not notice my discomposure.

"Do you know, Dr. Zobel, what my dowry is to be?"

"How could I?"

"It's probably like your own daughter's."

"Doubtless much more." A mere physician cannot, of course, provide what a lion of the bourse can.

"One hundred thousand kronen. My husband will claim one hundred thousand kronen, and then he will be expected to provide me with a three-thousand-kronen monthly allowance."

I was aghast at the figure, an order of magnitude greater than what I had determined to offer Erzsébet's suitor. Did I need to reevaluate? I wondered. Was I being naïve and unduly parsimonious? Would the figure I had decided on be enough?

Nina continued, "And then, of course, there is my trousseau."

The word in her mouth was a profanity.

"Do you know that in addition to my linens and clothing I come complete with the furnishings of a four-room flat? Every cupboard, every washbowl chest, every bedstead and upholstered settee."

Good God, I thought. If I was to protect the contents of my bank account, I must hope that this magnanimity was unique to Nina's family and not a reflection of the expectations of the young men of the community as a whole.

"Every aspect of my dowry and my trousseau is considered part of a transaction, Dr. Zobel. If I die without a live born child within six years, my family will reclaim the amount in full. If I die after six years but before nine, again without children, they will receive two-thirds. And so on."

"Dear Nina, nowadays dowry is much less formal and prescribed than it once was. It is more a way for the bride's family to assist the young couple in maintaining and furnishing their home than a strict accounting."

"The author of the article said that it is a farce to consider this kind of transaction anything but economic. True marriage can only happen between two economically independent people. The ideal marriage is free of pecuniary interests and is about nothing but pure love."

"This ideal you describe sounds very wonderful in the abstract, but how is a woman to be financially independent? Surely that is nothing more than a fantasy."

"When I have my medical diploma I will be able to earn my own independent living. And then I will be able to choose to marry a man whom I love. If I marry, it will be based on love. Not money. Love!"

By now Nina's face was as red as the beets in my mother's—may her memory be for a blessing—Sunday borscht. Sweat poured from her brow and she was breathless.

It was time to calm her agitated nerves. "Let us return to our free association," I said. "The next word is 'banana.' "

" 'Banana'?"

"Yes."

" 'Banana'?"

"Yes, Nina. 'Banana.' "

"Yellow."

"Train."

"Travel."

"Suitcase."

"Travel."

"Monocle."

"Dr. Zobel and his wandering eye." She clasped her hand over her mouth. "Oh dear, Dr. Zobel. I'm so sorry."

"It's nothing, my dear. You are engaging in the process just as it was meant to be practiced."

We proceeded with free association, and though it helped to ease Nina's nervous excitement, I cannot say that either of us garnered any new insights from the process. The intuitive leaps that can sometimes lead to new and deeper understanding on the part of both the analyst and analysand were missing from this session. I determined at that point that if I were to make progress with this young patient, I would need to turn to other methods, including dream analysis. As she was gathering her things and preparing to leave my consulting room, I asked her to keep a small notebook by the side of her bed to jot down her dreams.

"You must write them down immediately, before you rise from your bed. Otherwise, they will be lost to memory."

Nina seemed eager to explore this analytic form, and we closed our interview with both of us very much looking forward to what we might learn together at the next one.

· 34 ·

OVER THE NEXT MONTH, Nina and I continued our analysis, much of it consumed with discussions of a persistent dream. In the dream, which occurred nearly every night for three weeks, Nina rushed through the Budapest East Railway Station, arriving at her platform only to find that the train had departed without her. Though she initially could not remember where the train was going, when pressed she thought perhaps Vienna. Together we discussed the possibility that the dream of missing the train signified her anxiety about missing an important opportunity in her life. Medical school, she insisted, and reminded me that both her uncle and I had attended medical school in Vienna. I told her that in dream analysis the most obvious interpretation is not necessarily the correct one, and sometimes it is even the opposite of the obvious that is true. It's well known that train travel, especially through tunnels, symbolizes sexual intercourse. It was my view that the missing of the train by Nina's dream self expressed her fear of missing out not on a profession but on a normal sexual life, on marriage and children. She resisted this interpretation, though we discussed it for many days. She even came to one appointment clutching a copy of Dr. Sigmund Freud's *Interpretation of Dreams,* a book with which I am, of course, intimately familiar, as I have worked for many years on a translation of the seminal volume into Hungarian. I undertook this task at the urging and under the leadership of Dr. Sándor Ferenczi himself, in celebration of the formation of the Hungarian Psychoanalytic Society. Though work on the translation has gone more slowly than I or my mentor had anticipated, I expect to be finished sometime in the not-too-distant future.

Nina showed me a passage she had underlined. "Dr. Freud writes that departing on a journey is one of the best authenticated symbols of death," she said. "So missing the train might simply be my mind soothing me by reassuring me that I won't die."

"While I agree that dreams of missed trains might in some instances be consolation for the fear of death, I am not confident that such is the case for your dream. Do you think very much about death, Nina?"

"No. Hardly at all. Does any nineteen-year-old who isn't sick or in the army think of death?"

"Some do. There are even some children who fear death."

"Of course I fear death, who wouldn't? But I don't worry about death. There's a difference."

"Indeed," I said, wondering, not for the first time, if there was anything wrong with my young patient beyond a difficult relationship with her father.

I was reassured about the purpose of our treatment days later, however, when her menses arrived, and she experienced even more painful cramping than usual. I was able to alleviate her agony to a small extent with light abdominal massage and with warm compresses, concurrent with the suggestion that the pains were psychogenic. The moderate success of this therapy increased my confidence that the root of the pains lay in contiguous trauma, and in that session and later ones I encouraged Nina to sift through her memories in search of the instigating moment.

She recalled her first menstrual period in great detail, and though initially I had hopes of locating the trauma in that first experience, it seemed to have passed relatively easily. Her mother had prepared her for it with admirable straightforwardness and tact, and Nina remembered little if any anxiety connected with the anticipation of the experience and no fear with the arrival of the blood. On the contrary, she remembered eagerly anticipating her "womanhood." The only element of surprise was at the intensity of the pain. Her mother had told her to expect cramping and had instructed the maid to refresh her hot-water bottle frequently through the first few nights of her period, but apparently the severity of Nina's pain took them all by surprise. Though our first discussions failed to yield an insight and thus a complete alleviation of her symptoms, I remained confident that with further analysis we would arrive together at the trauma at the root of her ovarian neuralgia.

In the month of June, nearly a week passed without us meeting, a lag I prefer to avoid. It is the very intensity of the doctor-patient relationship that lends analysis its particular utility. But unfortunately Nina gave me no choice in the matter. From the fifteenth through the twenty-first, the International Woman Suffrage Congress met in Budapest, and Nina was utterly consumed with the congress's goings-on. Her friend Miss Gizella Weisz, the diminutive secretary to Rózsa Schwimmer, had arranged for her to be made a page at the congress. Nina took her tasks very seriously and absented herself from my care for the full duration.

I would not have seen her at all during this time, except that I found myself curious about the congress. Mere members of the public were not invited to observe the congressional meetings, and none of the ancillary lectures interested me overmuch, but I did go down one afternoon to the congress headquarters simply to take in the sight of the world's largest gathering of suffragists and feminists. I was hardly alone in my curiosity. It seemed the entire city had assembled in the square, even the mayor himself was there, glad-handing suffragists and their opponents alike. I was surprised and gratified by the diversity of women attendees. There were many examples of my sister's type, women of the bourgeoisie whose moderate prosperity allowed them the liberty and position from which to agitate for rights their poorer sisters hadn't the time nor inclination to demand. But there were also groups of working women, seamstresses and factory workers, even agricultural workers, the very women who I had imagined would have been both ignorant of and too busy for such assemblies. There were even peasant women from the Hungarian countryside and from other parts of Europe's hinterlands attired in brightly colored, handwoven, and embroidered traditional garb.

I had nearly given up hope of finding my young patient amidst the hordes of reveling feminists, when I noticed a group of young ladies dressed in white gowns, their chests festooned with purple sashes. Each girl held in her hands a nine-foot pole, at the top of which fluttered banners with the names of different languages. Clutching the sign DEUTSCH, with the seriousness of a general's standard-bearer, was my Nina. She stood proud and tall, her pretty face wreathed in smiles. As I made my way through the crowd, I saw a stout elderly woman approach her. Nina bent over, nodding vigorously, and then scanned the crowd. Her eyes lit on one of the Boy Scouts who had been recruited to act as guides for the congress members. She motioned him over and transferred the old woman to his care. Her role, she explained when I reached her side, was to provide help to any German-speaking delegates who might need assistance or directions.

I said, "I imagine that so many women speak the language that you are run off your feet."

She laughed. "Not at all. I mean, yes, yes, I am working very hard. But it's wonderful. You'd never believe who I've met, Dr. Zobel!"

She proceeded to enumerate a long list of Teutonic ladies, none of whom I'd ever heard of but all of whom were "very important" to the cause of universal suffrage. In the previous forty-eight hours, all the greatest female minds of the German-speaking world had apparently asked Nina's help in finding the toilet.

"And the lectures, Herr Doctor!" She moaned, near rhapsodic. "I have learned more in the past days than in all my life until now."

"Indeed?"

"Yes. Did you know that one of the first female physicians was a woman named Agnodike in ancient Greece? She practiced gynecology and obstetrics in Athens, at a time when it was forbidden for women to practice medicine at all."

"I had not heard of her."

"It's true! Oh, one moment!"

"*Wie kann ich Ihnen helfen?*" she said, turning in response to a small hand laid on her arm. But it was not in fact a lady in need of *Hilfe*. Her interrogator was none other than Miss Gizella Weisz, the tiny creature who had arranged for Nina's employment at the congress. Nina bent to kiss her friend's cheek and then, clutching her hand, turned to me.

"Dr. Zobel, let me introduce Miss Gizella Weisz, my friend. And more important, private secretary to Mrs. Schwimmer herself!"

"Ah, that great lady," I said, my tone teasing. It is not that I didn't admire Mrs. Schwimmer. She was held in general high regard in those days before her devotion to the cause of radical pacifism became widely known, before she was forced to leave Hungary for Vienna and ultimately, as I understand it, the United States. I teased Nina and her diminutive friend because their admiration of Mrs. Schwimmer reminded me of my sister's. So devoted as to be nearly hagiographic.

"Mrs. Schwimmer is indeed a very great lady," Miss Weisz reproached me.

"Yes, of course she is. Forgive me. I meant no disrespect."

"What are you doing here, Dr. Zobel?" Nina interrupted. I flattered myself that she desired to distract her two intimates from the possibility of altercation.

"I came to see what it was all about," I said.

"And what do you think?" said Miss Weisz, still stern.

In a voice as serious as the small woman obviously believed the occasion demanded, I said, "It's wonderful. Inspiring. So many gathered to further one exceptional cause."

"And you are a supporter of woman suffrage?" she said.

"There are women of my acquaintance who are far better suited to cast a ballot than many of the men who are currently at liberty to impose their ignorance on the nation." I was indulging in a moment of self-admiration for my adroit nonresponse before I noticed that neither Miss Weisz nor Nina had been fooled.

At that moment, a gentleman in a long duster coat approached. He was carrying a camera, the legs of its tripod clearing a swath in the crowd before him. "A photograph, sir?" he asked. "Of you and your"—he hesitated a moment—"your daughter? And the midget?"

I roused myself to my full, admittedly unimpressive, height and said, "Sir, this 'midget,' as you call her, is none other than the private secretary of Mrs. Rózsa Schwimmer."

He gratified me with a look of surprise and mollified me with a tip of his hat. "Very sorry, sir. And ladies. Might I offer you a photograph at a discounted rate?"

The girls protested, but I could tell that despite the manners of the photographer they were eager to immortalize their participation in the glorious event. The photographer urged Nina to remove her sash in order to look "harmonious" with her friend, so she handed me the sash and her sign to hold. They posed, Gizella on an overturned apple box the photographer's assistant provided for the purpose. Though they tried to maintain expressions suited to the seriousness of the occasion, their joy could not be suppressed. Their smiles were wide, their eyes bright, and their faces aglow.

I gave the photographer a portion of the cost up front, took his card, and made arrangements to pick up the pictures at the end of the month. The girls were then whisked away by Nina's fellow pages. Apparently their services were needed at the far end of the square, where the morning meeting of the executive session of the congress was coming to a close.

35

WHEN SHE RETURNED TO my consulting room on Monday, June 23, Nina was exhilarated. She recounted to me in great detail the rest of the goings-on at the congress, most particularly the opening speech by Mrs. Carrie Chapman Catt, the American president of the International Woman Suffrage Alliance. Had Nina told me of her reaction to this speech when we met that day at the square, I would have encouraged her to refrain from further participation in the congress. Roused to a neurotic frenzy by the exhortations of the American woman that all women of education, refinement, and achievement should take to the streets not to beg for but to demand their right to vote, Nina and Gizella, clutching copies of their feminist newspaper, rushed through the streets of the city, ignoring the solicitous concern of the Boy Scout guides. They needed no one to walk them home, the girls insisted. They did not need a hansom cab or directions to the trolley car or the electric subway that ran beneath Andrássy Avenue. In fact, they would not go home at all.

Their scheme, harebrained and thoughtless, the product of overheated imaginations and overstimulated nervous systems, was to storm the opulent New York Café, to stride manfully between the gilded pilasters and demand to be seated on their own, without chaperones. As rebellious as she was, I am confident that Nina would not have alone made such a spectacle of herself. It was Miss Weisz who encouraged her, who claimed that she had often taken coffee with Mrs. Schwimmer unescorted by a man and that there was no more reason for two young women to need a chaperone than for two young men.

I can only imagine the scene of the girls sweeping into the coffee-house: Nina a bridal vision in white lawn and lace, Gizella similarly clad, but looking by virtue of her size more like an infant at her christening than a bride. Ignoring the disapproving sniffs of the older male denizens of the café, the two girls sat themselves at a table in the very center of the room.

Nina sat stiffly, her shoulders back, her chin raised. She busied herself gazing at the opulent drapery, the clock above the doorway, the friezes on the walls, anything to avoid catching the eye of someone she might know or, worse, someone who might report her presence to her parents. Nina and Gizella were by no means the only women in the café. There were tables along the galleries of the New York that were habitually occupied by "actresses" and other young women of a type who seek employment of a kind that would have shocked my determinedly sophisticated patient had she but known of its existence. What Nina and Gizella did horrified me. Even in cosmopolitan Budapest, even among the enlightened bourgeoisie, even as unmarried young women and girls gained hitherto unimagined freedoms of education and association, it was unheard of for a girl of good family to be out in so public a place with only another young lady for company.

Within a few moments of their arrival, a young man approached their table. He wore a crumpled and shabby jacket and had an ink stain on his cardboard collar, as if to advertise his status as a writer, one of the young talents for whom the headwaiter kept a ready supply of "dogs' tongues," long sheaves of paper on which they could jot their caffeine- and alcohol-fueled thoughts.

"Miss Weisz!" he said. "How delightful to see you." He reached for her small hand, bent over it with a flourish. "I kiss your hand."

"Good evening, Endre," Gizella said. Gizella Weisz, though of typical achondroplastic somatotype—oversize head with prominent forehead, normal-sized trunk, shortened limbs, broad hands in trident configuration, with short metacarpals and phalanges—was quite beautiful. Or, rather, she managed despite her deformity to project a certain magnetism. She wore her luxurious dark hair coiled high on her head. She outlined her thickly lashed eyes with kohl and rouged her lips, a dramatic style that would have been cause for consternation in a young lady of average stature. But for all her feminist and radical ideals, her face paint, her reform dress, and her cigarettes in their silver case, Miss Weisz was, like Nina, a properly brought-up young Jewish woman, of good, if not wealthy, family. Later on, I was to learn that she hailed from a village in northern Transylvania, her father, though also a dwarf, a rabbinic scholar of some renown. She should have known better.

The young man asked Gizella, "Won't you introduce me to your lovely friend?"

"I absolutely will not. You're a menace and the last person she should know," Gizella said.

"Please do come to join us at our table." He pointed to one of the alcoves along the wall of the café, where a few tables had been pushed together and a group of resolutely literary types sat smoking cigarettes and gossiping. As if in response to the young women's gaze, one of them leaped to his feet, took up a scrap of newsprint from the heap of journals and books littering the table, and began to recite a poem at full volume.

"Shall we?" Gizella asked Nina. "They're a very entertaining claque, though I can't promise they won't ravish us. Endre is a complete cad."

The young man flung his hand over his heart and shouted, "I will defend your honor to the death!"

"Foolish boy," Gizella said.

"No, look!" He pointed to a white line pleating the dark hair of his left eyebrow. "A dueling scar! Honor is everything to me."

"Last week you told me that poetry was everything to you. Which is it?"

"Both!" he said. "Honor and poetry. Come!" He swept Gizella's chair back and lifted her lightly to her feet. Nina stood up on her own but took his proffered arm and allowed him to escort her to the alcove, where the crowd of young men happily made room for them.

For the rest of the evening and late into the night Nina and Gizella were entertained by the young men. Endre in particular attached himself to Nina, sitting close to her and at one point leaping up onto his chair to recite a section of János Arany's poem "Dante."

At this point in Nina's account of the events of the evening, I interjected, "'Dante'? A strange coincidence, no?"

A pretty flush stained Nina's cheeks. "How do you mean?" she asked.

"That this young man should recite Arany's 'Dante' only a month or so after another young man gave you a copy of *The Inferno*."

Nina bit her lip. I waited. Finally she said, "It wasn't a coincidence."

"No?" I asked, hiding from her how thrilled I was that she trusted me with what was obviously a significant and even embarrassing confidence.

"I told Endre—er, Mr. Bauer—about Mr. E.'s gift."

"Why did you tell Mr. Bauer about a gift you received from another young man?"

She shrugged. "I thought he would find it amusing."

"'Amusing'?"

She fumbled with her reticule, pulling out a silver compact, snapping it open and shut a few times before blurting, "It was such an absurd present! Dante's *Inferno*! Of all things."

"You don't care for Dante?"

"I haven't read him. I'm not interested in him. I'm interested in contemporary poets!"

"Like Arany?" János Arany, as we both well knew, died more than thirty years ago.

"Like Charlotte Perkins Gilman. Like Anna Akhmatova!"

"Did you enjoy the young Mr. Bauer's recitation of Arany's 'Dante'?"

"It was amusing."

"How so?"

"He did it very dramatically. Sarcastically, I suppose."

"Your young Endre does not approve of Arany?"

"Endre is not mine, and I don't know what he approves of or doesn't approve of. It was a game. Nothing more. He recited his own poetry as well."

"And was that to your liking?"

She again opened her compact and snapped it closed. "Yes. Yes, it was. Certainly more than Dante's *Inferno*."

Nina and Gizella remained at the café until after 1:00 a.m., at which point their young suitors attempted to walk them home. The girls wisely resisted, however, consenting only to allow the young men to hail them a cab.

"Weren't your parents very concerned about you? Surely it's not usual for you to be out so late."

" 'Concerned'?" she said. "Perhaps. My father was certainly angry."

I did not need Nina to tell me this. I had, by coincidence, seen her father on Saturday morning, at the Dohány Street Synagogue. I do not regularly attend services—I'm afraid I am one of those three-holiday Jews our Israelite leaders spend so much time bemoaning—but every year on my father's *Yahrzeit*, I escort my mother and sisters to synagogue so that we might all say Kaddish for the man to whom religion was so much more important than it is to any of us. Even my sister Sarolta joined us on this occasion, though the poor woman was forced to hide her face beneath a heavy veil to keep from being recognized and having her crime reported back to her priest or, worse, to her unpleasantly striving children.

My mother and sisters went up to the lower of the two women's galleries, and I attempted to take an inconspicuous seat about three-quarters of the way back in the palatial nave, more basilica than shul. Unfortunately, an usher took my arm and propelled me forward. On an ordinary

Saturday morning in June, even this, the largest synagogue in Europe, home of a great and wealthy Jewish community, could not muster more than a meager congregation. Not even a rumored forty-four kilograms of twenty-four-karat gilding could persuade the unobservant to sit beneath those soaring arches.

I closed my eyes while I waited for the organ and choir to signal the beginning of the service, but was immediately interrupted by an angry whisper.

"Dr. Zobel! Imré!"

I peeled back a reluctant eyelid to find Nina's father standing before me, cloaked in a capacious tallith and an air of righteous indignation. I began to struggle inelegantly to my feet—a man of my girth is not well accommodated by a wooden pew, no matter how spacious and beautifully carved—but Mr. S. put a restraining hand on my shoulder. Instead, he sat down next to me and bent his head to mine. As he pressed his mouth close to my ear, I repressed a shudder. The generous lips that were on the daughter so sumptuous were on the father fleshy and glutinous.

"You call this progress, Dr. Zobel?" he whispered furiously. "My brother promised that your talking cure would end my daughter's rebellions, and instead she is worse even than before."

"Has something happened, Mr. S.?"

"'Has something happened?'" His mimicry of my tone and accent was cruel. That I grew up speaking Yiddish is something I refuse to be ashamed of. My family is of Galicianer origin, but none can question our loyalty to our Magyar home. I am a patriotic Hungarian, whatever traces might remain in my accent.

"Yes, something has happened," Mr. S. whispered, spraying saliva into my poor ear. "All this week she has been gallivanting around the city. Instead of being home, asleep, as she should be, she has been seen in the company of artists and radicals! Radicals, Dr. Zobel!"

I tried as best I could to remind my patient's father that I had assumed the responsibility of treating his daughter's ailments, physical and psychical, and while I might as a father of daughters agree that Nina's behavior was unacceptable, as a physician I had been forthright from the beginning in informing him that psychoanalysis was not designed as a cure for youthful rebellion.

"This is far more than youthful rebellion," Mr. S. insisted. "Nina has become irrational. Erratic. She has been behaving like a . . ." He shuddered. It is only women of ill repute who frequent coffeehouses without chaperones. What had poor Nina done to her reputation?

The outraged father continued, "My brother assures me that her behavior is a sign of deep psychical distress. Dementia praecox, Dr. Zobel! That's what we're dealing with."

I resisted the urge to offer Mr. S. a wager that his brother, a urologist, had less experience with my organ of expertise than I with his, and instead promised that I would discuss the matter with Nina.

"We have made great progress in our dream analysis," I told Mr. S., perhaps less than candidly, as I was quite frustrated by Nina's refusal to see her dream of missing the train in its true light. "I am confident that as her treatment progresses you will see more and more tangible results."

"Marriage, Dr. Zobel," he said as he lumbered to his feet. "That is the goal. The result of your treatment must be that Nina abandons her neurotic ambitions and accepts her role as a modest Jewish wife and mother."

Should I have been more firm with Mr. S.? While it is indeed true that ambitions out of proportion to ability are often a sign of neurotic grandiosity, I had yet to see any indication that Nina fit that description. On the contrary. The girl earned top marks at her gymnasium. She was diligently and by all accounts successfully preparing for her *matura* and her medical school admissions examinations. Even her uncle, who disapproved of her desire to study medicine, admitted that her tutors felt her to be eminently qualified. Indeed it was he who described her to me as possessing a "rare and admirable intelligence."

It was understandable that her father would prefer that she lead a more conventional life. I, too, would object to my daughters pursuing any career, especially one so demanding. I would certainly have been as horrified as he had my daughter been out at night unaccompanied. The question remained, however, whether a girl's rebellion and eagerness to thwart her parents' desires were in and of themselves evidence of neurosis. I was as yet unable to affirm either way. True, most young women have little difficulty in acceding to the knowledge and experience of their elders and betters. And yet, with each passing day of my acquaintanceship with this particular young woman, I had become more impressed by her intellectual acumen, by her wit, by her verve. Far from being outsize, her ambitions struck me as entirely realistic, not evidence of neurosis but a genuine and well-considered assessment of potential.

Nonetheless, neurotic or not, staying out until all hours with young men of vague repute was hardly acceptable, and I admonished Nina strongly to resist such temptations in the future. "If for no other reason," I told her, "than that it is bad for your health. You need your rest to continue our work together."

Nina snapped her compact a final time, tucked it into her reticule, and said, "You bring up a good point."

"I do?"

"I have grown fond of you, Dr. Zobel. Very fond. You're a kind man, and I've enjoyed our time together. But I am no closer to understanding the point of our work together than I was a month ago."

You will forgive my immodesty at saying that my services as a physician are highly sought after in Budapest and beyond. Never before had I felt myself to be in the position of forcing treatment on both patient and patient's family. This goes a small way to explain the impatience with which I responded, "Must we do this again, Nina?"

At my vehemence, her confidence seemed to waver, and she bit her lip.

I continued, "Do you have no desire to recover from the crippling menstrual cramps that have had such a deleterious effect on your life?"

"I do. I just . . ."

"What?"

"I'm just not sure the talking cure can help."

"Are you a doctor?"

"You know I'm not."

"Am I a doctor?"

She gave a small moue of impatience.

"Am I?" I insisted.

"Of course."

"Well then, whose confidence is relevant? That of the trained, experienced physician or that of the young girl?"

Though I waited, she didn't answer.

More gently, I said, "Nina, my dear. What kind of a physician will you make if you persist in resisting medical advice?"

After a moment she sighed and said, "A poor one, I suppose."

I am ever so slightly ashamed to admit that I was relieved to have bested her in this conversation. "Exactly. A poor one. Now, let us return to a topic immediately useful to resolving your hysterical pain." I pulled out my notebook and leafed through the pages. "We've addressed the issue of your experience of the menstrual period itself, and I think we both can agree that we did not there discover the site of the initiating trauma."

I waited for her to agree. When she didn't speak, I said, "Correct?"

"Correct," she said.

I resolutely ignored her grudging tone. "I would like to explore further an issue that my colleague Dr. Sándor Ferenczi has found to be present quite frequently in cases such as yours."

"Cases such as mine?"

"Cases of hysteria." I hesitated for a moment and then continued as I'd planned. "Nina, I must insist now that you take your place on my examination couch. It is crucial for the next phase of our work."

I had only in the previous year adopted Freud's use of the analytic couch. Before that my patients sat in a chair on the other side of my desk or, if I needed to use massage, lay on the examination table. Those patients too ill to leave their beds at home or in the sanatorium I sat next to, in a chair pulled up to the bedside, often holding their hands in my own. But the year before I began treating Nina S., I was invited to hear Freud lecture before the Vienna Psychoanalytic Association (to which my application for membership was pending) and became convinced by the good doctor's argument in favor of the couch. Since following his example, I found that being liberated from eye contact with the analyst inspires greater confidences on the part of the analysand, especially when discussing issues of a sexual nature. Young women naturally avert their eyes when embarrassed and ashamed. Lying on a couch, with the analyst out of sight in a chair behind, they can indulge the illusion that they are alone, which allows them to more freely discuss their sexual experiences.

Nina finally acquiesced to my insistence that she lie down. After the excitement of flouting her father's authority and of spending the evening in the company of strange young men, I believed, correctly it turned out, that she might be due for a breakthrough, so before taking my seat behind her, I went out and instructed my nurse to release the remaining patients in my waiting room. As I returned to my office, I heard my nurse encouraging my disappointed patients to return after lunch for afternoon office hours.

"Now, Nina," I said, sitting down behind her. "We are going to discuss something difficult, and even terrifying. I want to assure you that I would not put you through this if I didn't think it might expose the traumatic source of your pain."

She inhaled tremulously, her bosom quivering beneath the silk of her shirtwaist.

"Relax," I said, laying a hand on her forehead and smoothing her hair. "Breathe. In through the nose, out through the mouth."

She took a few breaths, and I matched my inhalations and exhalations to hers.

"Nina, I'd like to talk now about sexual matters."

Like all my young female patients, she had a visceral reaction to the word. Her skin fairly trembled beneath my hand. I cupped her cheek with my palm, calming her. A note, here, about technique. Like my mentor, Dr. Ferenczi, I believe heartily in the importance of expressions of affection between analyst and analysand. I have learned from him to think of the traumatized as children in dire need of a parent's fond embrace. It is for this reason that I often embrace or stroke my patients. I believe it to be conducive to treatment and cure.

"Nina, are you familiar with the work of my esteemed colleague Dr. Sándor Ferenczi?"

"I know who he is. My uncle tried to convince him to treat me before coming to you."

This surprised me. I had assumed that it was by virtue of our long acquaintance that Dr. S. had beseeched me to undertake the care of his niece. Had I known that I was his second choice, I might not have made such a concerted effort to adjust my calendar to accommodate an old friend. But then I would have been robbed of the opportunity of getting to know such a lovely and lively young woman.

I put aside my wounded vanity and said, "Dr. Ferenczi and I often consult on one another's cases."

"Have you consulted on mine?"

"We reserve our consultations for our most dire patients."

"I'm glad to hear that my case is not dire."

With a gentle pressure of my hand on her forehead I brought her attention back to the matter at hand. "Dr. Ferenczi and I have had cause to discuss at great length a theory about one of the primary causal factors in the development of psychopathology. It is his opinion, and one that I am inclined to share, that hysterical symptoms are often caused by the trauma of sexual seduction in childhood."

"Sexual seduction?"

"Dr. Ferenczi has found that many patients, particularly those suffering from narcissistic, borderline, and psychotic conditions, experienced sexual seduction at the hands of a parent or parent figure."

"Have you found this to be the case with your patients?"

"Perhaps less frequently than Dr. Ferenczi, but then he is quite often the psychoanalyst of last resort. His cases are thus more complex. But even in my own practice I have discovered a disturbing number of cases of the seduction of girls by their fathers."

Her reaction surprised me. Rather than break down in tears, as other patients have done when confronted with this terrifying truth, Nina began to laugh.

"Are you asking me if my father seduced me? My father? Really, Dr. Zobel?"

"I assure you, Nina, that it is far from uncommon. I cannot tell you how many young ladies have confessed the very thing that you find laughably unimaginable."

"Confess? Why should they confess? They committed no crime. Surely if any confessing was necessary, then it was on the part of their fathers."

"A bad choice of word. Nina, I wonder if your attempt to distract me from my question doesn't indicate a fear of the answer."

"My father never seduced me, Dr. Zobel. I should think he was far too busy seducing his various mistresses to think about me in that way."

"Your father has mistresses?"

"Of course. Don't you all? My mother says that a mistress is as necessary to a man of our class as a decent pipe stand or frock coat."

"You and your mother have discussed your father's indiscretions?"

"We don't make a habit of it. But there was a small scandal a few years ago when my father took up with my younger sisters' governess. You might have heard about it."

I had not, and this surprised me. My own wife, secure in the attentions of a husband who found her as sexually compelling at age forty-nine as he did when she was but nineteen, was fond of sharing such gossip with me. I was surprised that this morsel had not caught her attention.

"Did you perhaps catch your father and the governess in flagrante? The witnessing of such a scene might be just the traumatic source we have been looking for."

"No. I found out at school. Miss Lanier, the governess, was a distant relation of one of my classmates, and it was to this family that she retired once her condition became unmistakable. Greta, my classmate, and I were competing at the time for first place in arithmetic, and there was no love lost between us. She told the entire class about my father and Miss Lanier. I still bested her, though, at that week's mental-arithmetic competition. Small comfort, I suppose. At any rate, all of this happened long after my crippling menstrual cramps began."

"Her condition? Was there a baby?" I'm afraid there was no therapeutic reason for this question. I just knew that when I told my wife the story she'd expect to hear what happened in the end.

"Miss Lanier lost the baby. As to whether my father still sees her, that I can't tell you. He has others, though. Or at least I assume he does. Perhaps that's why he's so horrified at the thought of my going to the New York Café. That might be where he meets his paramours."

"There certainly are young women of that sort at the New York," I said. "Though I imagine that he's less concerned with you meeting a young lady like that than with you being taken for one."

Nina laughed. "Are you so very scandalized by me, Dr. Zobel? Do you worry that people might think I am of easy virtue?"

"I worry that you seem inclined to take your virtue for granted. Once lost it is unrecoverable."

"Now you sound like Mama."

"Again you've distracted me from the issue at hand! What are you afraid of discussing, Nina? Why run from this conversation? If not your father, then was there another who seduced you when you were a child, your uncle perhaps?"

"My uncle! Good Lord. What a horrible thought. No, Dr. Zobel. No one has seduced me. I am still pure."

I had no choice but to smile at the archness of her tone. But still I pressed her. "You are very sure that you have had no childhood sexual experience? None at all?"

She cast her eyes down at her hands.

"Nina? Did you have a sexual experience as a child? With a caretaker, perhaps? Or a sibling?"

"No. Or, rather, there was one thing that happened, but I didn't know the man."

Victory! At last! It took all my will to compel my voice to maintain its dispassionate tone. "Indeed? Tell me more about this."

"There's nothing to tell. It was at a picnic. I was perhaps six or seven years old. I was paddling in a stream with some other little girls. I remember our mothers had warned us not to get our dresses wet, so we had stripped down to our petticoats and drawers. I believe one of my older cousins was meant to be watching us, but she'd gone off somewhere. I looked up and I saw the father of one of the other girls standing on the bank, just a few yards from us. He had unbuttoned his trousers and was holding his . . . his thing in his hand." For all her forthrightness, for all her frank interest in the scientific and the medical, Nina S. was still a young, innocent, and cosseted girl unable to bring herself to speak the terrifying word.

"You saw his penis?"

"I don't think I knew what it was. Only that it was strange. He was strange. Now of course I know. But I'm not sure what I knew then."

"What happened?"

"I shouted for Mama. By the time she got there he was gone. I told her what happened, and she got very angry."

"Did she confront him?"

"I don't think she believed me. At any rate she berated me for having gotten undressed, packed me up right away, and took me home. I remember being particularly outraged because we missed the fireworks. I think it was the king's birthday, perhaps? Anyway, there were to be fireworks that night, as soon as the sun set, and because Mama was so angry, she didn't let us stay for them."

As traumas go, this one was hardly as dramatic as I'd hoped. I would have thought that a girl like Nina would have required more in the way of incident to inspire a lifetime of such terrible pains and cramping. However, I knew at that moment that we had discovered the source of her hysterical ovarian neuralgia.

I explained to Nina that as we had now identified the traumatic source of her pain, it would dissipate if not disappear. Some of my learned colleagues will perhaps dispute this notion as overoptimistic, but all will grant me that the power of suggestion is a necessary tool of the analyst. It was important to me that Nina understand that we were well on our way to a cure.

36

I CONFRONTED MY NEXT SESSION with Nina in a state of discomposure not easily overcome. My normally pleasant midday meal had been
disturbed by an unusual family altercation. The afternoon previous, my
wife had taken both Erzsébet and Lili to call on the mother of the young
man whom the matchmaker had presented to us for consideration. The
appointment was intended as an opportunity for the lady to meet Erzsébet, to take the girl's temperature, so to speak, as a potential daughter-
in-law. And to take, I imagine, the temperature of my wife, though the
two ladies had long known each other, fellow members of the Israelite
Women's Organization of Pest. The young man himself was not supposed to be there, busy as he was with his medical studies. However,
the day's lectures had been canceled as a result of a demonstration by a
nationalist students' organization—a foreshadowing, we now know, of
the ugly protests that would eventually culminate in the imposition of
limitations on the numbers of Jewish students allowed to matriculate at
Hungarian universities—and the young man was not only home when
my wife and daughters called but spent the hour in the parlor with them.
Under different circumstances, this might have been an ideal opportunity for the two young people to converse under their mothers' watchful
eyes. However, the unanticipated encounter proved to be a disaster, and
my normally sweet-tempered daughter spent the next day's luncheon
haranguing her mother and me with her objections to András Nordau's
suit. After much wailing and knotting of damp handkerchiefs (on Erzsébet's part, not mine), I was made to understand that her objections
amounted to a globule of white saliva that attached to the young man's
upper lip, connecting periodically in a string to his lower.

"So he'll wipe his mouth," I told my hysterical child.

My sense fell on deaf ears, and nothing was accomplished beyond
Erzsébet rushing away from the table, leaving behind an untouched
plate, which, as one who abhors waste of any kind, I had no choice but
to finish myself.

I was thus not merely distressed but also mildly dyspeptic when Nina arrived in my consulting room, and though I had intended to spend our session going over her memories of the traumatic incident at the picnic, I was unprepared to withstand the assault of yet another young girl with an agenda of her own. When she entered the consulting room I could not help, despite my unusual state of mental and physical discombobulation, but to smile at her attire. She wore a coarse khaki coverall with pantaloons rather than a skirt, tight at the ankles, revealing a full two inches of pale stocking above the top of her low-heeled boot. The coverall was paired with a middy blouse with a wide navy-blue silk tie. On her head was perched a small straw boater, also trimmed in navy blue.

Indicating her dress, she said, "I'm afraid I didn't have time to change."

"Did you spend the early part of the day working the barges on the Danube?"

"Very funny. The Feminist Association held a boating excursion this morning."

"Hence the nautical attire."

"Do you like it?"

"I've never seen anything quite like it before."

"They're called overalls. They're quite popular in America, especially among women laborers. They're very comfortable."

"They look very comfortable. How, might I ask, did you come to adopt the fashions of the American proletariat?"

"I bought the pattern at the bazaar at the Suffrage Congress exhibition hall and had our seamstress make a pair for me and a pair for Gizella. Mama nearly had an apoplectic stroke when she saw me wearing them. But I think they're marvelous."

"And Gizella? Does she look as marvelous in hers?"

"Gizella won't wear them. She's very particular about her clothing, and she said they'd make her look like a little boy. But all the younger women at this morning's outing wanted a pair."

"Did you enjoy your excursion?"

"Very much. We boated along the river for a while, and then we had lunch and heard a lecture beneath the oaks on Margaret Island."

"A lecture?"

"It was quite fascinating. All about reforming the social and legal status of domestic servants. Did you know, Dr. Zobel, that our maids are utterly defenseless against the advances of their male employers? You would not believe the stories Mrs. Grossman told."

"Indeed? Who is this Mrs. Grossman?"

"Janka Grossman. She has written on the subject of the rights of domestic servants for *Women and Society*. I'm sure you know that the young boys of Pest are encouraged to use their maidservants for . . . for sex." The disgust with which she said the word did not, I fear, bode well for Nina's future husband.

"Shocking!" I said, recalling with fondness my own dear Marta, the young kitchen servant whose attentions both culinary and sexual formed such an important part of my early life.

Nina said, "And when the maids fall pregnant, they're simply sent back to their villages to fend for themselves."

A wise and experienced girl, Marta used to rise from our nest beneath the warm eiderdown of her narrow cot in a corner of the pantry and clean herself inside and out with a solution of sodium bicarbonate and warm water. She remains to this day in the employ of my mother. The wasp-waisted, capacious-bosomed Marta of my youthful nights has long since turned into a squat and big-bellied old woman, her mouth devoid of all but a single tooth, her vast quantities of luxurious blond hair reduced to a gray braid no thicker around than my pinkie. But still the merry eyes remain, and she is as fond as ever of this overgrown boy to whom the years have hardly been more gentle.

"You found this lecture very interesting," I said. "Exciting, even?"

"Inspiring. Infuriating."

"'Infuriating.'" I considered this. "In one of our last appointments you told me about your father's sexual indiscretions. Did the lecture remind you of this? Did he or does he have liaisons with the family servants in addition to the governess? Have you witnessed such an encounter?"

"You seem so sure that my fury must be a result of my 'witnessing' something. Can't I just be disgusted at this kind of outrage without having to witness it personally?"

"Perhaps. Though it is often the case that reactions this visceral are indications of latent trauma."

"You and your traumas, Doctor!"

"Haven't we discovered together the sexual trauma at the root of your menstrual pain?"

"I don't know. It depends what you mean by 'discover.' There was no lost or submerged memory that you helped me to recall. I've never forgotten that man at the stream. It was ugly and unpleasant, but no matter how I try I can't think of it as so dramatic that it is sufficient to explain a lifetime of painful cramping."

"Our unconscious minds are difficult to understand. They function very differently from our waking selves. I once had a patient who was unable to tolerate the taste of dairy products, merely because years before she witnessed a cat lapping milk from a bowl, an incident that caused her no more than minor disgust at the time. Once she recalled the incident, the symptom disappeared, and she was again able to enjoy her coffee with cream."

"Well, it remains to be seen whether or not my symptoms disappear."

"When do you expect your menstrual period?"

"In a couple of weeks."

"I have high hopes."

"You're a very optimistic man, Doctor."

"Perhaps I am. Can I encourage you to indulge my optimism for a while?"

"Why not?"

"Consider again the question of your father's relationship with the servants. Are you sure there wasn't an incident, perhaps one long forgotten, that caused this morning's lecture to be particularly interesting to you?"

Nina frowned. "Well," she said after a few moments' consideration. "I suppose it reminded me of a story I heard a few years ago. One of the reasons I became determined to study medicine."

I leaned forward in my chair, hoping that we might again be reaching a point of breakthrough. "Indeed?"

"Yes. It's nothing I witnessed myself, or, rather, the incident itself is one I only heard about secondhand. What I witnessed was the distress it caused."

"Go on!" It is at times so difficult to maintain a proper physician's pose of disinterested equilibrium.

"It was not long after I began my studies at the gymnasium. I woke up one morning late for my morning classes, because our maid, Etel, didn't wake me. I scrambled into my clothes and rushed into the kitchen. I was very worried about being late, and I shouted at Etel for having forgotten me. I found her sitting with Riza, the cook, and they were both crying. They didn't want to tell me what happened, but I forced them to. I was a very willful child, and they were used to doing as I said."

"I can imagine."

She arched one of her well-formed eyebrows but continued, "A girl they knew, the maid of one of our neighbors, had died. Riza said the girl had been forced to go to an 'Angel Maker,' but then in the end it was she who became the angel. She was a nice girl, from the same village as Etel. Etel and Riza were both beside themselves. The police arrested the midwife who performed the procedure, and later on I found out that she was given a year in prison for the crime. A year for killing a young girl. But you know what was worse?"

"What could be worse than that sad tale?"

"The seducer was the eldest son of the poor girl's employer, a young man I've known for years and years, ever since his family moved into one of the upper-level apartments of our building. He was forced to pay a one-hundred-kronen fine to the court. Nothing more. He served not a single day in jail."

"Terrible," I said. I was surprised that the young man had faced any punishment at all. His seduction of the young maid must have been unusually blatant for his identity even to have been discovered. "Though I'm not sure I understand how this inspired you to consider a career in medicine."

"It was an outrage, Dr. Zobel!" Nina said, her voice rising. "I defy you to find a woman on earth who would not be outraged by such a thing."

"I will grant you that. But why medicine, Nina? Why not law, in order to prosecute such miscreants?"

"Surely you know the answer to that question."

"I assure you I don't."

"Because women are not permitted to study law in Budapest. The faculty will not admit women, and my father would sooner bury me alive than send me to Zurich or Vienna to read law. Anyway, my mind is inclined more to the scientific and to the practical. I want to roll up my sleeves and help women like that poor little maid."

"You would become an abortionist?" I asked, aghast.

"Why not?"

I sat in stunned silence.

"Calm yourself, Doctor. That's not my ambition. What I want is to be a physician to whom women will come with all their various problems and pains, because I believe—no, I know—that women feel more comfortable sharing such intimacies with other women. I will be a good doctor not in spite of my sex, Dr. Zobel, but because of it."

Though it was hardly in my interest, I couldn't help but wonder if this might not be true. All medical men are aware of the struggles inherent in treating women, particularly older women whose modesty often precludes even the most general of examinations. How many times have I heard my gynecologist colleagues complain of the frustrations of trying to treat a woman who refuses to shuck her skirts, even in the presence of the most dispassionate of physicians? Some have even sought my assistance in figuring out ways to convince their patients that their doctor finds no sexual satisfaction in scrabbling about in ancient and malodorous vaginas.

But what about my own specialty? While there are even now, a full decade on from those months I shared with Nina S., only a small number of female practitioners of the art and science of psychoanalysis, might the argument not be made that a woman would feel more comfortable confiding her deepest secrets in a doctor of her own sex? I fear the answer to this question, and search for comfort in the hope that the crucial element of transference might be complicated by the fact of a female analyst. The gifted psychoanalyst becomes both a paternal figure and a love object. Without this transference, treatment is impossible. A maternal relationship is not at all similar and brings with it far more unpleasant attributes and possibilities.

37

IT HAS BECOME FASHIONABLE of late for some psychoanalysts to argue in favor of the maintenance of a distance between analyst and analysand outside the consulting room. I have even heard some suggest that an analyst should whenever possible refrain from analyzing his friends and intimates. As a follower of the great Sándor Ferenczi, I reject this. Intimacy with and love for our patients are the keys to effective treatment, and social consort is efficacious in creating that bond, not destructive of it.

Furthermore, I also reject maintenance of distance as quite simply impracticable. The Jewish populace of Budapest, as assimilated as it is, has still in many ways the flavor of a small community or even a large extended family. Yes, we are one million Jews in Hungary, but sometimes it feels as if we all know one another, as if we are all cousins three, four, or five times removed. Certainly this is true in my own medical profession, where nearly half of the physicians are my coreligionists, two-thirds of those in private practice like me.

The unique circumstances of Jewish Budapest (or Jew-dapest, as the mayor of Vienna snidely, though perhaps accurately, dubbed this magnificent city) make it impossible for an analyst to avoid having a social relationship with his patients. It was inevitable that my family and Nina's would come across one another while out in company, especially when one considers that she was in my care at the instigation of her uncle, my acquaintance of many years. So it was that on the following Saturday, my dear wife, our two daughters, and I took our midday meal at the home of Dr. S., Nina's uncle. Joining us were my sister Jolán, who was in the practice of dining with us on Saturdays; Nina; her parents and siblings; and the E.'s, Jenő, Berta, and Ignác, the young man to whom Nina's parents wished her to be betrothed. Far from being concerned with a breach of (I believe pointless and, in fact, destructive) psychoanalytic distance, I was eager to have the chance to observe Nina outside the consulting room. I wanted to study her interactions with her parents and siblings. I also wanted to see how she behaved toward the young man whose advances she found so loathsome.

Frankly, I was also relieved to take my wife and daughters out into company, where the topic of conversation would not involve Erzsébet's own troubled marital prospects. My daughter had continued to express her objections to the match her mother and I had made for her, inventing one excuse after another. We were not for a few more days to discover that the real problem was that she had settled her affections on another young man.

Although we were the first to arrive—my wife's devotion to the cause of punctuality makes her something of an anomaly among our Magyar compatriots—we did not have long to wait for our fellow guests. Dr. S.'s apartment is, like my own and like most who share our profession and station in life, on the *étage noble,* and Nina's family's progress up the single gracious flight of steps was boisterous, her younger siblings making no effort to temper their exuberance. Their mother berated them at top volume, shouting that they would disturb the neighbors and earn their uncle's wrath. Mr. S. emitted no sound from his lips, but the force of his shoes on the marble steps set the solid old building atremble. Only Nina managed a dignified restraint. Nina and her friend, the adorable Miss Weisz.

Those of our acquaintance who have described Mrs. S. as a shrew do a disservice not only to a fine and handsome woman, whose agitation and irritability are more neurotic than malignant, but to women of our faith more generally. One day I will write a monograph on the topic of the virulent anti-Semitism at the heart of the representation of contemporary Jewish women of the bourgeoisie as devoted to pomp and luxury, devoid of honor and deference to their husbands, quick witted but only in the service of their own interests. How much of this condemnation will we recognize if we switch the word "woman" for "Jew"? How many times have those who despised the Israelite race referred to us as shallow, venal, vain, feminine, weak, sexually predatory? All adjectives tossed in opprobrium also at the fairer sex. For the purposes of this case study of Nina S., however, I will acknowledge that her mother is a woman with a selfish, even narcissistic, personality, who nonetheless adores her children and is willing to oppose even her husband in support of their interests. Hence her simultaneous desire for Nina both to realize her dream of attending medical school and her worry that such an ambition would make her daughter "emancipated" and thus unable to achieve a marital match that would reflect well on her parents.

I grant to her detractors that Mrs. S. might be a wearying dinner companion to a person unable to muster sufficient interest in the topics of conversation most fascinating to her, notably, the history, tribulations, victories, and ambitions of the various members of the S. family. Luckily enough, I was most eager to converse with her on these topics, particularly on the subject of Nina. Like her daughter, Mrs. S. possesses a charming conversational vivacity, and it was with great detail and color that she recounted the tale of how it was that Gizella Weisz had come to join them at dinner that evening.

The family had been dressing for their outing when the maid announced Miss Weisz's arrival. (I took this opportunity to compliment Mrs. S. on her gown, an elegant ensemble of broadcloth and chiffon, of a color my dear departed father used to refer to as "wisteria," as distinct from the less-vibrant "lavender" or the darker and richer "aubergine." She was most gracious in accepting this compliment, though we both understood it to be no more than her due.)

"We're expected at your uncle's in less than an hour," Mrs. S. called to Nina as the girl put the finishing touches on her hair. "You must make your apologies to your friend and send her on her way."

"I've invited Gizella to join us," Nina said.

"Excuse me?"

"I've asked her along for dinner."

"You can't invite a friend to your uncle's house. Really, have you lost all sense of decorum?"

"I telephoned Aunt Sophie, and she said Gizella is welcome. She said she was eager to meet her, in fact."

Mrs. S. bustled into her daughter's room, her dress still unbuttoned and two rolls of firm flesh spilling from her tight-laced corset. "First of all, you know you're not to use the telephone without asking permission. And second, if your aunt expressed any eagerness to meet your friend, it's only because Sophie has always liked the circus. Shame on you for turning a family dinner into a freak show."

"And I'm the one with no sense of decorum?" Nina muttered under her breath.

"I heard that."

"I don't care. Aunt Sophie isn't interested in Gizella because she's a dwarf; she's interested in her because she works for Rózsa Schwimmer. Mrs. Schwimmer spoke at a meeting of the steering committee of the Israelite Women's Organization of Pest last month, and Aunt Sophie was very impressed. She's even taken a subscription to *Women and Society* in order to read Mrs. Schwimmer's articles."

"Ridiculous!" Mrs. S. said, turning her back to Nina and indicating with a peremptory shrug of her shoulders that the girl attend to her mother's buttons. "Sophie is no radical."

Nina began doing up the long line of tiny bone buttons. "Mrs. Schwimmer writes many things that are hardly radical at all. I'm sure even you might find yourself agreeing with much of what she says."

"Preposterous."

"For example, you believe that girls should be educated, don't you?"

"You know I do."

"So does Mrs. Schwimmer. And you despise the fashion for large hats."

"There is nothing as foolish as a woman sailing through the streets with a dirigible attached to her head, forcing anyone who passes to duck into traffic to keep from being decapitated."

"Mrs. Schwimmer published an editorial against bizarrely large hats in last month's paper, saying the only reason women wear them is to make other women envious."

"They wear them because they're fools who wouldn't recognize fashion if the entire city of Paris were to drop on their dirigible-clad heads."

"There," Nina said, straightening out her mother's chiffon collar. "You're buttoned up. And now I must go greet my friend. Be nice, Mother."

Mr. S. was even more startled by Gizella's presence than was his wife, but he limited himself to a scowl and to stalking down Andrássy Avenue ahead of his family, forcing them to trot to keep up. The brothers S. lived in nearly identical buildings a few blocks apart on the boulevard. I have had the privilege only of being welcomed into the public rooms of these apartments—the parlors, dining and morning rooms, and to Dr. S.'s study—but they are sufficiently similar to my own that I know what remains behind closed doors. Like my own apartment, each of theirs includes the kitchen, the bathroom, at least two and perhaps three bedrooms for the family, and rooms on the very top floor, where the servants from all the building's apartments live together cozily and at sufficient distance from their employers.

It was less than a decade previous that my wife and I had acquired an apartment like those of the S. brothers, complete with heavy oak furni-

ture, clocks and other ornaments, the ubiquitous oil portraits of ancestors actual or assumed, each room decorated in a different style, the
parlor Empire, the dining room Biedermeier, the morning room modern, the better to show off my dear wife's sophisticated grasp of fashion
and decor. Before we graduated to this relative opulence, we lived in
the same building where we now reside, but one floor up, in a smaller,
less-gracious apartment, with ceilings that, though high, failed entirely
to soar. And before that we were in a building on a less-desirable street,
though still in the Lipótváros district, where my poor wife had to climb
no fewer than three flights of stairs, even when she was heavy with our
Erzsébet and Lili and burdened with packages. How many times did I
come across her resting against the railing on her way up to the third
story, never once complaining but always eyeing with undisguised longing the more commodious lodgings on the lower floors?

Dr. S. was a collector of art of the Jugendstil movement and had, in
pride of place above the intricately carved mantel in his formal parlor,
one particularly striking painting. A satyr or goblin, covered in orange-
and-black-striped fur, holding in his arms a pale tree fairy with hair of
rose petals. A garment of leaves barely covered her naked body. Where
the fairy's arms embraced the goblin's, they turned to long white tree
branches. His butterfly wings artfully concealed the cleft between her
legs. The painting was erotic, not merely because of the prominent pink
nipples of the fine-featured fairy, but because of the contrast of her delicacy with his fur-clad brutality. My daughters were mesmerized by it,
though not so much as Nina, who, though she had surely seen it hundreds of times, could not at first seem to break away her gaze.

As a psychoanalyst I am comfortable with the unconscious erotic life
of girls, especially hysterical girls. To be compelled in a small way by the
erotic is normal; to be in its thrall is evidence of gynephilic disturbance,
a kind of masculine jealousy and even bisexuality caused, as we know,
by the deleterious effects of masturbation. Watching Nina's fascination
with the painting, I determined that we would, at our next meeting, no
longer refrain from discussing this delicate issue.

I greeted Nina with a kiss on her hand. When I bent to the task of
reaching her friend Gizella's plump infant's fingers with my lips, my
back creaked, and both girls smiled.

"Alas, I am old for such gallantry," I said.

"You, Dr. Zobel?" Gizella said, batting her heavily lashed eyes. "I
refuse to believe you're a day over forty."

"A day, a decade. What's the difference?" I said. "A man is only as old as the women who assent to his company."

"Well, then it's settled," Gizella said. "You're twenty-one. Like me."

"Not nineteen, like our charming Nina?" I said.

"Now you're trying to make me jealous," she said. "I was under the impression that Nina was merely your patient, and it was my company that made you cross the room."

Gizella charmingly fingered a large pendant that hung from a heavy gold chain around her neck. A delightful example of Jugendstil enamel work and gold filigree, the pendant was decorated with a stylized peacock in vivid purple and green, with white accents and multihued gemstones.

"What a beautiful necklace you have," I said.

"My employer, Mrs. Schwimmer, presented it to me on the occasion of my birthday." She slid her fingernail into an invisible seam and the pendant sprung open. "Isn't it ingenious?" she said. "It's a locket, but you wouldn't know unless you were told." She held the locket out so I could examine the tiny photographs inside. "This is my father."

With the help of the magnifying glasses I keep tucked in my waist-coat pocket, I could see that Miss Weisz's father gave the impression of strength and fortitude, though first one had to overcome the initial shock of seeing a rabbi in full Galicianer regalia—long curled sidelocks, heavy beard, fur hat, black frock coat—in miniature. He stood on a chair, but this prop only made him seem even more diminutive.

"Very striking," I said.

"My father was a most handsome man."

It was true, beneath the beard he was handsome, with a Roman nose, wide, sensual lips like his daughter's, and her same black eyes. His face was attractive, though his hunched and misshapen body, of course, was not.

"He most certainly was," I said.

"For a dwarf," she said.

"A very handsome man," I said firmly.

Mrs. S. seemed excessively annoyed by my mild flirtation with her daughter's friend, and came to hover over us until I belatedly offered her the section of sofa next to her daughter where I sat. Gizella perched on a small upholstered stool that Sophie S. had graciously made available for her.

The doctor's wife joined us now, bearing a silver tray on which were arrayed small squares of flatbread spread with smoked salmon mousse and decorated with sprigs of chives. The ladies demurred, but I helped myself to an hors d'oeuvre.

"Mm," I said to Sophie. "Delicious."

"I have the most wonderful new cook," she said. "She's a village girl, but her last job was at the French embassy. She was only a kitchen maid, but the chef was from Paris, and he taught her well."

"You're always so lucky with your servants, Sophie," Mrs. S. said. "I've had Riza forever, and still anything beyond a simple *paprikás* completely defeats her. You should have seen the catastrophe she made of last night's fried goose liver."

"It was fine, Mama," Nina said.

"It was black! And as dry as the skin on an old crone's feet."

"Sister-in-law!" Sophie said. "How you talk! Dr. Zobel will think we are a family of farmers!"

"Perhaps farm animals," Nina said.

"My father-in-law wasn't a farmer," Mrs. S. said, determined both to ignore the joke and to defend her family's bourgeois credentials. "He was a wheat merchant."

Nina said, "Grandfather taught me how to drive a plow when I was a little girl."

"That was for show, darling," Sophie said. "Do you remember, Irma, our father-in-law's team of carriage horses? Those beautiful black Hanoverians and his grand barouche? How many times as young brides did we make him drive us up and down the Corso, so we could show off our splendid hats?"

The arrival of the E.'s interrupted the sisters-in-law's reverie.

Mr. Jenő E. was a man of substantial girth, more substantial, I daresay, even than my own. His bald pate was decorated with a sprinkling of pinkish brown moles. His voice was loud, and he was a friendly, if not particularly intelligent, man. Of his wife, Berta, it was difficult to garner any impression at all, so languid was she. Her hand was limp in my own, and she mustered no more than a faint moue in lieu of a greeting.

Ignác E. gave the impression of being a fine, healthy young man, tall like his father, with the broad shoulders and protruding chest of an athlete. The boy was a gifted swimmer, a member of the Hungarian Olympic team, who placed fourth in the four-hundred-meter freestyle in London in 1908, painfully close to earning a medal. He was quite nearly as busy in his position as treasurer of the Hungarian Athletic Club as he was in his job as one of the only Jewish lawyers in the Royal Prosecutor's Office of Budapest. Ignác described to me his latest acquisition, something he called a Jantzen elastic swimsuit, which he felt confident would increase his speed in competition.

I fear I do not share the obsession with athletics that consumes so many of my fellow Hungarian Israelites, for whom love of sport is second only to love of nation. I often wonder if this urge to display physical prowess, to compete and above all to win, might not be a symptom of a lingering sense of inferiority. After all, no small number of the strapping young Jewish men who fill the myriad fencing clubs, swimming associations, rugby societies, and water-polo teams are descended from bent-backed Galicianers, who concerned themselves with the development of their brains and their bankbooks rather than of their physiques. Still, it is men like Ignác E. who are the norm in our community, not I, and it speaks well of him that he achieved so much in his chosen sport.

I wondered if this athleticism was something Nina and young Ignác might have in common. After all, though I was not aware of her being currently engaged in any organized sporting activity, Nina once told me that as a girl she'd won prizes in archery. Also, she possessed a pretty female version of the broad shoulders and nipped waist that made Ignác such a striking young man.

My musings about their common interests were interrupted by a vigorous argument between the two. Though it was difficult at first to determine the precise genesis of the discord, soon I realized that the young man must have cast aspersions on the set to which Miss Weisz had recently introduced Nina.

"Radicals and layabouts?" Nina said, her voice shrill with outrage.

Ignác said, "They agitate against the government! They make no secret that they wish to see the king deposed."

"They must make some secret of it," Miss Weisz said calmly. "Otherwise they'd be dining on bread and water in the Budapest prison, not coffee with cream in the New York Café."

"Nina doesn't really know these people," Mrs. S. interjected. "And she never frequents the New York. Certainly not unescorted."

The young people gazed at her, momentarily flummoxed at her blatant untruth.

"But I've already told him I was there, Mama," Nina said.

"Once! You went there once. And only because she took you." Mrs. S. glared at Gizella.

Ignác said, "I don't know why your radical friends haven't ended up

in prison, Miss Weisz, given that my office prosecutes radicals and insti-
gators every day. If they aren't being prosecuted I can only imagine that
it's a result of their sloth. They're all talk, no action. I went to gymnasium with men like these, and I can tell you that if any one of them does
a single decent day's work in a year, I'll eat my hat."

"Shall I bring you a knife and fork?" Nina said. "Perhaps you'll want
some salt and a pepper pot to make it go down easier. Because I can tell
you with utmost confidence that they work."

"Scribbling sonnets and submitting them for publication in their
friends' two-pfennig periodicals is not work. And that's all they're good
for, these New York Café fops. Poetry and anarchism."

"An ideal existence!" I said with, I fear, forced joviality. "As long as
it's accompanied by a plate of *kiflie* and a nice strong espresso."

Nina, too angry even to acknowledge my joke, said, "You ridicule
these men, Ignác, men who spend their days trying to create something
beautiful, and yet what do you do all day? What do you create?"

"I create a just society."

"You prosecute the destitute and inoculate the wealthy. You protect
the titans of finance at the expense of the poor. How you can live with
yourself I have no idea."

"Nina!" Mrs. S. said. "Apologize to Ignác immediately."

"Apologize for what? For telling the truth?"

"For being rude!"

Ignác bowed stiffly from the waist. "I require no apology. Indeed it is I
who owe Miss S. an apology. I was not aware that she was so closely asso-
ciated with the New York Café set. Had I known they were her intimates
I would not have criticized them."

"They are not my intimates!" Nina said furiously. "But I do know
them well enough to know that they aren't dilettantes. Right, Gizella?"

"Some are dilettantes perhaps," Miss Weisz surprised us all by saying. "Though there are others who work as hard, I expect, as you do,
Mr. E. My good friend Endre Bauer not only writes poetry but he's also
an office clerk. And he tutors Latin and Greek in the evenings. Endre is
poor and supports his mother and at least three sisters with his wages. I
think the man lives on coffee and air."

Ignác, shamed perhaps to contemplate the difference between the
hours of his employment and those of a poet who earned his bread copy-
ing documents and tutoring the sons of the wealthy, said, "I apologize
again for my comments."

"Oh for goodness' sake," Nina said. "Stop apologizing. We know you don't mean it."

"Nina!" Mrs. S. snapped.

Never has the dinner bell been greeted with more relief.

The evening's discomfort, however, was not yet at an end. As we approached the dining table, Sophie S. hovered over us, trying to distribute five men and one boy amongst eight women in a way that would permit neither siblings nor husbands and wives to sit side by side. I have always detested this insistence at dinner parties on separating the spouses. My work schedule is so onerous, my leisure time so limited, that what I miss most of all is proximity to my wife, whom on most days I see only briefly, for a few minutes at breakfast, and when I have no engagements for the midday meal. Though we continue, despite our advanced age and the disapproval of our housemaid, to share a bed, it is only rarely that my wife is sufficiently immersed in a novel or bit of needlework to be awake when I return from my coffeehouse in the evenings. All of which is to say that normally I would have preferred being seated next to her. However, my perch between Mrs. S. and Miss Weisz allowed me to experience at close range the bombast that resulted from the girls' failure to raise their glasses when Dr. S., as is his custom, toasted the king.

"To his imperial and royal apostolic majesty, Franz Josef I, emperor of Austria, king of Hungary!" Dr. S. said, raising his glass.

Busy as I was raising my own glass, I did not notice that neither Miss Weisz nor Nina had lifted theirs until Nina's uncle drew the company's attention to it.

"Do you not like the wine?" Dr. S. said, scowling. "Shall I pour you something sweeter? A honeyed Pálinka, perhaps?"

"No thank you, Uncle. The wine is fine," Nina said.

"Then why don't you drink?"

Miss Weisz took a small sip, but Nina did not.

"I prefer not to," she said.

"But you just said the wine is fine."

"The wine is fine. It is the toast that I object to."

"You object to what? To the king? You object to the king of Hungary? Is that what you're saying?"

"I object to any ruler who disenfranchises half his constituents."

At the far end of the table, my sister, whom I know to share Nina's beliefs, raised her glass to her lips, the better to hide her smile. Others were not so amused.

"Nina!" her father bellowed, causing the women around the table to jump and Ignác to wince.

"I'm sorry, Papa, but as a woman . . ."

"You are not a woman. You are a foolish, hysterical girl, who knows nothing. Do you hear me? Nothing!"

Those unfamiliar with the feelings of his Jewish subjects toward the king might be surprised at the willingness of a father to so chastise his daughter in company, most especially in the company of the family to whom he hopes to be united in matrimony. But for us Hungarian Israelites and our brethren in Austria, Franz Josef was more than a king. We Jews had seen kings come and kings go, and things had remained much the same. Before Franz Josef, we existed in a state of unease, waiting for the inevitable pogroms and expulsions, the rise of the fanatical and the murderous, from Antiochus Epiphanes' desecration of the Second Temple to the Teutonic Crusaders' massacre of the Jews of the Rhineland, to Torquemada's Spanish Inquisition, to the miseries perpetrated by our own Leopold the First. But even a young and foolish girl like Nina, a girl enamored of the egalitarian and socialist nonsense spouted by coffeehouse radicals, knew what King Franz Josef had done for her people. She knew that it was he who bestowed on us our equal rights, informing the majority by edict that he would tolerate no discrimination by virtue of religion. It is because of his tolerance and protection that we flourished in Austria and in Hungary. It was because of him that we could hear the phrase "Jew-dapest" and respond not with fear but with amusement and pride. And it is only because he is no longer with us that the rulers of this nation have felt at liberty to enact such loathsome statutes as the *numerus clausus,* which make life so much less secure and pleasant for the Jews of Hungary. Loyalty, patriotism, and love of country and king inspired Mr. S.'s fury at his daughter and, I fear, it was foolishness that allowed her to take her haughty leave from the table.

"Excuse me," Miss Weisz said, leaping down from the cushions placed upon her chair so quickly that I had not the time even to assist her. She followed her friend from the room. We listened in silence as the door to the apartment closed firmly behind them.

Ignác E. rested his forehead in his hand, sighing far too wearily for a man of his young age.

"Oh dear," his mother murmured.

"And what have you to say?" Mr. S. snarled at me.

"I?"

He stopped his tongue, no doubt not eager to destroy what remained of his daughter's reputation by referring to her status as my patient.

Nonetheless, I spoke. "I fear that Miss S. and her friend may still be under the sway of the excitement of the International Woman Suffrage Congress. There were so many political speeches, so many radical women storming hither and thither. Young girls are terribly impressionable, and I imagine that such scenes are being enacted throughout the dining rooms of Buda and Pest. But I assure you ladies and gentlemen, these fits of political excitement will pass. Soon enough our young ladies will find another, more suitable outlet for their energies."

My own daughters gazed demurely down at their plates, though I could not help but wonder if I'd not caught a glimpse of something in Erzsébet's eye. I hoped fervently that my patient's disobedience had not communicated itself to my daughter, who, whatever her current objections, was going to end up married to András Nordau, if her mother had to hog-tie her and drag her to the chuppah.

My sister Jolán said, "I attended some of the events of the congress, and I can attest to the general air of excitement. And as a teacher of girls, I can also attest to their impressionability."

"You know what I find works wonders in distracting a young girl when she's in a mood like this?" my dear wife said. "A hat. Yes, a hat is just the thing, isn't it, girls? To take your mind off foolish things."

I winced, sure that my wife would now suffer rebuke from the furious Mr. S., but before he had time to speak, Lili lifted her eyes and said, "Mama, you read my mind. I was just thinking that if I had a hat with Numidi feathers I wouldn't have any room at all in my head for anything else. Certainly not for politics."

Oh, my sweet girl, defusing the tension so elegantly!

"I think it's time for a toast," I said, raising my glass.

The S. brothers looked astonished, but politeness demanded they respond by lifting theirs.

"To the milliners of Budapest!" I said. "Long may they prosper!"

"To the milliners!" the guests around the table replied. And then the cook arrived with the soup.

· 38 ·

I ASSUMED THAT IN the wake of the unpleasantness at the dinner party Nina and I would have much about which to speak. Certainly I was eager to discover what her reaction was to her father's rage, whether, for example, it had elicited any physical symptoms or sensations.

Nina's outburst had inspired discord in my own home, and not of the sort that could be resolved by the indulgent purchase of a new hat, no matter how ostentatious. Late that evening, Erzsébet had knocked on our bedroom door. In her white cotton nightdress and plaits she looked much as she had as a little girl, and I grew misty recalling how she would nestle her soft head against my shoulder, her hair fragrant of lavender soap, and listen to me as I read her a good-night story. Now, however, my daughter's cheerful round face was unusually grave, and she begged our permission to speak. We granted it, of course, and she confessed that the source of her objection to András Nordau was not the dampness of his lips, nor his large feet (something about which she'd recently begun to complain), but something far more serious.

"What is it?" my wife asked, her frustration with our normally compliant daughter obvious in her tone.

With tears in her eyes Erzsébet explained that András was a fine young man, very nice. Even attractive. The problem was that she was in love with someone else.

"In love? Don't be ridiculous," my wife said.

"With whom?" I asked, seeking to maintain equilibrium despite my astonishment.

The young man in question was someone we knew well, the son of a distant cousin of mine who lived by coincidence in our very building. My relative owned a publishing house, and though not wealthy was a respectable man. Despite being something of a freethinker, he was moderate in disposition and in politics, and by every indication his son had followed in his footsteps both professionally and temperamentally. The young man was, in short, a perfectly acceptable match for Erzsébet, but for the fact that we had already decided on another. And, more impor-

tant, but for the fact that his mother was a Protestant. No. I am not being
fair to the woman in question. My relative's wife had converted to Juda-
ism in order to marry her husband, and was by all accounts a dutiful Jewish wife. However, though by inclination and background I am firmly of
the Neologue tradition of faith, my dear wife comes from an Orthodox
family, and though she herself has rejected those constraints and, on the
rare occasions when she attends synagogue, is far more comfortable in
our congregation than in the one in which she was raised, the thought of
her daughter marrying someone her parents would not have even considered Jewish was impossible to contemplate.

Suffice it to say that the result of Erzsébet's confession was more tears,
and my wife's demand that our daughter never lay eyes on the young
man in question ever again. I wisely kept to myself the observation that
given that we lived in the same building, that was a feat not even my
accomplished spouse could engineer.

Though I would not have confided my own family troubles in Nina, I
was not even permitted to inquire into the ramifications of her outburst
in her own home. She arrived for her appointment on time, but she did
not sit down. She stood in the middle of my consulting room, forcing
me to keep to my feet as well. She held her fine kid gloves in her hands,
twisting them with a ferocity that caused me to wince.

"I cannot stay, Dr. Zobel," she said.

"Have you another commitment?" I picked up my leather appointment book and leafed through it. "Shall we reschedule for later in the
day, or simply resume tomorrow at our usual time?"

"No, sir."

"Dear girl. There can be no formality between us. Clearly you have
something to say. Speak up."

"I can't see you anymore."

"Has your father forbidden it?"

"No. Though I imagine that if I'd seen him he might have done. My
father is a man who likes to apportion blame, and I'm sure he'll levy
some on you."

"You haven't seen him since our dinner? That was two days ago."

"I haven't been home."

I was astonished and horrified at the thought of a young girl, the age
of my own daughters, absent from her home for so long. "Nina! Where
are you staying? With whom? This is very grave news. Very grave
indeed."

"Don't be concerned, Doctor. I am safe and well. I'm staying with Miss Weisz. She rents a room from a relative in Király Street."

I grimaced at the thought of this lovely and gracious young lady living on a street populated by laborers and tradesmen of the lowest kind. "Do your parents know where you are?"

"No, and I hope you won't tell them. I have had no choice but to cut ties with my parents."

"Nina! Sit. Please. You are in need of counsel, surely you realize that. A girl of your age cannot simply 'cut ties' with her parents. I am confident that nothing you have done is irrevocable. There is still time for you to go home." I fervently hoped that this was true.

"I will not go home, Dr. Zobel."

"Are you afraid, dear girl? You mustn't be. Your father was deeply angry, true, but by now his rage will have calmed. I will go with you to ensure your safety."

"You miss my meaning, sir. I am not afraid to go home. I simply won't. Things have progressed beyond that now."

Chill dread crept up my spine. What had she done? "Is there someone else staying with you? A man? Dear God, Nina, have you moved in with that young radical, what was his name? Endre?"

"What must you think of me, Dr. Zobel, to ask such a question? I told you, I am staying with my friend."

"Then what are the 'things' you speak about? What has 'progressed'?"

Nina extended her hand to me. "Thank you, Dr. Zobel, for your company and counsel over these past few months. I can't say that you've cured me of my menstrual cramps, but I have found our sessions interesting nonetheless. I shall remember them and you with fondness."

"What in heaven's name are you about, girl, with these valedictory speeches? What are you planning?"

But she left without another word.

I did not know what to do. As a father, I felt strongly that the appropriate action was to go to Nina's parents and inform them of her whereabouts. At the time I had no idea of the extent of her peril; I worried only that she and Miss Weisz were planning to run away, to Vienna perhaps, or even to Paris. Were I merely a family friend I would have considered it my duty to rush to her father. But I was also Nina's physician, and as her physician I owed her a certain duty of confidentiality. I wasted precious minutes wondering about the extent of this duty. Were I to have discovered during an examination, for example, that Nina suffered from a fatal disease, I would immediately have told her parents, even if I deemed it unwise to tell the patient herself. Did this rise to that level? Was her peril sufficient to justify becoming an informant? Surely her parents knew her well enough to look for her first at the home of Miss Weisz. A moment's thought would be sufficient to reach the conclusion that that was where she was likely to be. I tried to reassure myself that they knew of her whereabouts and had chosen, for the moment, at least, to allow her to remain there unmolested.

But what if they had been turned away by Miss Weisz? What if the dwarf had convinced them that Nina was not with her? I could only imagine my own wife's reaction under such circumstances. She would be beside herself with anxiety and fear.

So why was I hesitating? I determined to look unflinchingly at my motivations. Was it the patient herself who inspired my inclination to confidence? Did I seek to protect her from her father's wrath for her sake, or for my own? Did I fear her anger if she found out that it was I who informed them? Had I stopped being an observer and wise counselor and become something else in my own heart, if not in hers? Had I lost control of my countertransference, succumbed to my emotions? Did I desire that beautiful young girl?

No! No! Nina was my patient, a hysteric who was incapable of making wise decisions. The voice within me that argued in favor of her stability, her sanity, her right to do and go where she wished, was nothing more than an expression of my failure as a psychoanalyst, my refusal to recognize and wrestle with my countertransference. I had no choice but to go to her father.

And so I rushed to the S. apartment on Andrássy Avenue, where I left a note for Mr. S. with the maid, informing him of Nina's whereabouts. My responsibility carried out, and my conscience assuaged, I went back to work, though I fear I did not bring my best attention to the rest of my patients. It was difficult to ignore the foolish sensation that I had committed an unforgivable betrayal.

39

WHEN I NEXT SAW Nina S., she came to me in a storm of tears, her life in tatters and her future likely destroyed. Though my own agitation and anxiety during that period cloud my memory of the events, I will do my best to re-create them as she recounted them to me, and also as I read about them in the newspapers. Since that terrible week, I have had opportunities to discuss what transpired with a few of the players, including Gizella Weisz, whom I had the pleasure (and relief) of encountering a number of years later, at Bad Gastein in Austria, where I had repaired to take the waters and where she and the other members of her talented family of singers had been engaged to perform. More immediately to the events I describe, I spoke at length with Ignác E., who sought me out to beg my discretion in the matter. Though it is routine practice to change the names and identifying features of patients in published case studies, in this case because of the infamy of the incident and the particular characteristics of the actors (an anarchist dwarf!) mere anonymity might not have sufficiently protected the identity of Nina and her family. It was out of respect for his wishes that I refrained from publication until now, more than a decade after the events transpired, when the changes in our government are such that no harm can come to any of the participants, even if someone should trouble to discover who they were.

The reader will forgive me, yet again, for describing the incidents as though I were myself present. My temerity is understandable, I think, because of the intimate knowledge I possess, both of the events and of the psyche and character of the major player herself.

My supposition that my message to Mr. S. would result in Nina's immediate return to the bosom of her family was incorrect. On the contrary, I fear my betrayal of her confidence resulted only in forcing her into the arms of the people who would be her undoing. Though I believe the events of July 1913 must have been in the planning stages for some time before Nina made her escape, I have often over the years wondered if I unwittingly set in motion Nina's catastrophe. Had I remained silent, might she have chosen in the end not to involve herself in such radical and foolhardy action?

I cannot know. All I do know for certain is that when Mr. S. went to Miss Weisz's lodgings to demand his daughter's immediate return, he was not permitted to enter. He might have forced his way in, but for the menacing brawn of the concierge's son. Mr. S. went immediately to the police and returned not an hour later, this time accompanied by two armed constables, but by then the two girls had fled the premises, leaving behind no clue to the location of their next refuge. It is possible that even they did not know where they would be going after quitting the establishment.

Mr. S. sought the arrest of both the concierge and her son, on grounds of interference with a father's legitimate authority over his daughter, but the constables found convincing the woman's pleas. How was she to know that Mr. S. was in fact the girl's father, and not an angry suitor posing as such? Or worse! After all, the man was unfamiliar to her, and as the girl had given her name as Maria Horváth, they did not share a surname. Moreover, the landlady told the constables, they looked nothing alike. Mr. S. was a swarthy man, obviously of the Hebrew persuasion. It had seemed impossible to her that the pretty blond Maria was a Jew.

"'White slaver,' that's what I thought," the woman said. "And why wouldn't I? After all, that's what so many of their kind get up to, isn't it? I'll not be blamed for trying to protect a good Hungarian girl from the likes of him." She stuck a derogatory thumb in Mr. S.'s direction.

To Mr. S.'s fury, the constables nodded sagely, blowing air through their brush mustaches. "She's got a point, sir," one said.

The other chimed in, "She was only trying to protect your daughter. You like as owe her thanks, if you think about it."

"Thanks?" Mr. S. fumed. "Thanks? To the woman who kept my daughter from me, who has sent her on to who knows where?"

"Now I won't take that for a minute," the lady said. "I didn't send her no place. She went on her own, her and sweet little Gizella." To the constables she said, "The darling little one I'll miss for sure. Wee thing, no bigger than a baby, with the most astonishing head of hair. Nearly down to her knees! She used to let me comb walnut oil into it, just like I do to my own. She'd sit on a little stool and I'd smooth the oil through her hair and she'd tell me stories of her family, all of them itty-bitty dwarfs like herself. Oh I will miss her. I surely will." She glared at Mr. S. She would neither forget nor forgive that it was because of him that she'd lost her sweet little Gizella.

Mr. S. reported the egregious behavior of the constables to an acquaintance in the office of the mayor, but no action was taken against them, either because the man's position was not as glorious as he had led his friend to believe, or because the constables' superiors felt as their underlings had, that the actions of the concierge and her son, while unfortunate and ultimately mistaken, were understandable. After all, she'd spoken no more than the truth. The conspicuous role of Jewish brothel keepers and procurers in prostitution in central and eastern Europe in the late nineteenth century has long been a source for much anti-Semitic rhetoric.

Thus, Mr. S. did not find his daughter. He could never have imagined that she and Gizella would take refuge in the disreputable Tabán on the southern slopes of Castle Hill in Buda, in the apartment Endre Bauer shared with three friends, men who were, like him, former members of the Galileo Circle, who had come to believe that that organization's liberal mindedness and social radicalism were too cerebral and thus ineffectual, and that the time had come for radical political action.

I have it on the authority of both Nina and Gizella that their friendships with the young men who sheltered them remained platonic. Both women were adamant on the subject, and I have no reason to disbelieve them, particularly because in the years since, I have come to the conviction that Nina's libido, prematurely awakened by the trauma she experienced at the stream and (though she and I never had opportunity to explore this, and I am thus making an educated guess) by excessive masturbation in early childhood, leaned toward the homosexual. Homosexuality is one of the essential traits of the obsessive-compulsive constitution, and though her only obsessive-compulsive symptom was her devotion to her academic studies, it was likely that she was at the time under the sway of a transient lesbianism that protected her from sexual involvement with the young men, and incidentally from developing a fully realized transference with me. Nina herself would have objected to this conclusion, insisting that her affections for Gizella were only ever sororial, but my readers no doubt are aware that homosexual inclinations are most often unconscious.

Endre and one of his compatriots, a Ruthenian from Northeast Hungary by the name of Miloš, vacated for the girls the small bedroom they shared, and set up their own pallets in the parlor in which the residents of the apartment took their recreation and their meals. One can only imagine Nina's reaction to these bachelor accommodations. She was, after all, a product of the Jewish bourgeoisie, and thus used to the ministrations of maids and laundresses. Girls like Nina slept on pressed linens scented with lavender water, beneath soft eiderdowns and on pillows of the finest goose down. The dirt-stiffened and yellowed sheets and the rough woolen blankets would have felt miserably harsh on her fine milk skin. And yet she overcame her disgust, even embraced these deprivations as evidence of her liberation from the tyranny of her father's rules and expectations, from his insistence on seeing her ambitions not as proof of a rigorous and able intellect but as the delusions of a neurotic.

Nina and Gizella hid in the apartment for a fortnight, never leaving even for a breath of air. In a cautious move, the young radicals switched their allegiance from the New York to the Japan Coffee House. This move, protested by Endre but insisted upon by the more cynical and thus wiser Miloš, saved them from discovery. The threatening but decidedly unimaginative detectives hired by Mr. S. spent nearly every evening in the New York Café, drinking coffee and eating pastries, and waiting patiently for Nina to appear. Periodically they would interrogate the patrons about the whereabouts of "a pretty blond girl and a dark-haired dwarf," and who knows what information one of Endre and Miloš's fellows might have inadvertently let slip under the influence of the glasses of Pálinka they regularly imbibed.

Fortunately, the dull-witted detectives never bothered to trouble the denizens of the Japan Coffee House, despite its fame as the favored gathering spot of various radicals, even including those women of Budapest's feminist movement who were not afraid to be seen in such a place without the chaperoning company of a male relative.

The plan was perfected at the Japan Coffee House and brought back to the apartment where the girls were by then growing tired of their own company and eager for a change of circumstance and an alleviation of the boredom that is an inherent result of being confined to cramped quarters in a time of great stress. The plan was complex, and required the participation of more than half a dozen individuals, including, among others, an employee of the Budapest Opera House, an ancient prostitute, a lady's seamstress who was Miloš's occasional mistress, the chauffeur of a wealthy merchant, and a middle-aged circus acrobat who had once worked the boards with an uncle of Gizella's. It was Nina, with her scholar's fine penmanship, who hand-lettered the banner with the simple slogan, "Votes for All! We Demand Universal Suffrage!"

On the day of the action, Nina and Gizella donned sumptuous evening dress, Gizella's her own, Nina's Parisian finery borrowed by Miloš's seamstress from the wardrobe of a Viennese noblewoman so wealthy and spoiled by her Hungarian husband that it would have taken a fleet of accountants six months to catalogue the contents of her closet. Even were Nina to bump into the baroness at the opera, the great lady was not likely to recognize her own gown. Accompanying them as their putative chaperone was the elderly whore, whose costly widow's weeds the seamstress had purloined from yet another client.

An hour before the curtain was to rise, Nina, Gizella, and the costumed prostitute set off, escorted by Gulya the acrobat, who looked only slightly uncomfortable in his guise as bourgeois father and second chaperone. Endre and Miloš had left precisely thirty minutes before, as they were to travel by tram, but a hansom cab was waiting for the others. That neighborhood of dark and dismal tenements had not often seen the services of a hansom, and the driver's resentment at having to navigate the narrow rutted street was only partially assuaged by the novelty of helping two attractive young ladies, one a perfect miniature, up into his cab.

The four arrived at the Opera House and joined the crowd streaming up the steps to the triple-doored entrance, between the seated statues of Franz Liszt and Ferenc Erkel that adorn either end of the magnificent Neo-Renaissance façade. I imagine that the girls' anxiety and excitement were such that neither bothered to notice the glorious lobby, with its soaring double staircase, columns of gray marble, and rich red arches. But of course Nina at least had been there many times before.

Gizella's appearance caused its usual stir, with elegant ladies spying and whispering from behind their fans, and gentlemen not bothering to hide their ogling. But her expensive gown and the propriety of her two chaperones reassured the crowd that the dwarf's presence at the opera, if curious, was not unacceptable, and though she was noticed, she was not accosted.

Gizella was far too short to see over the crush of people, and Gulya's accent too provincial (and the prostitute's utterly inappropriate), so to Nina had been assigned the task of finding the correct ticket taker. Her instructions were to locate a man with ginger hair and a mustache sharpened into aggressive points. Upon presenting her tickets she was to say, "My aunt bought us these tickets, and I do hope the seats are good."

All went according to plan. The ticket taker nodded gruffly, took from Nina the cheap tickets and instead of tearing off the stub and directing her up to seats high in the gallery, returned to her four tickets of thick, creamy card stock, with a box number embossed in gold.

"Enjoy the performance, mademoiselle," he said.

She thanked him, and the four conspirators swept up the grand staircase to their newly assigned box.

Though the boxes benefited from the Opera House's elaborate air-conditioning, a state-of-the-art ventilation system with fans blowing across blocks of ice beneath the floorboards, sending cool air up through grates beneath every seat, Nina's excitement made the atmosphere seem to her thick and stuffy, and she wished she had thought to bring a fan. Her palms were damp with sweat, and she longed to peel off her long satin gloves. She fanned herself with her program and gazed out over the crowd. At one point she believed she recognized a former classmate in one of the seats below, and immediately sank back, hiding as best she could in the gloom of the velvet-upholstered box.

After a few moments, as agreed, Gulya repaired to the smoking lounge, where he met up with Endre and Miloš. The fog created by the smoke of hundreds of cigars and cigarettes in the lounge was said to be so absolute that lovers could meet there for trysts without fear of discovery. Nina hoped that rumor would not in this case disappoint, because the plan called for Endre, Miloš, and Gulya to wait in the lounge, hiding from view in the smoke.

The first strains of the opera *Erzsébet Báthory* filled the house. It was perhaps appropriate, given the circumstances, that the opera on that evening was Sándor Szeghő's variation on the vampire myth, a cataclysmic failure that opened to dreadful reviews, and closed immediately thereafter, only partially a result of the ruckus caused by Nina and her co-conspirators.

Nina's parents, like most of their set, regularly attended the opera, and from the time she was a small girl, she frequently joined them. My own daughters, though not musical, found the costumes and scenery exciting enough to sustain their interest at least until the interval. But for Nina, it was the music that enraptured. She had, as was expected of a girl of her class, studied the piano from childhood, and like many individuals with great scientific and mathematical gifts, she was similarly adept at music. She alone in her family possessed such skill. At one point Nina's piano instructor suggested to her parents that she might be a prodigy, but though she played exceptionally well, and even composed, it was always science that compelled her closest attention, and once she became a serious student, she allowed her musical education to take second place in her efforts.

Uniquely on this evening, Nina could not listen to the music. She was flush with excitement, and to her surprise only very slightly afraid. When the strains of the first aria hung tremulously in the air, she and Gizella, without looking at one another, rose to their feet. Abandoning the prostitute, whose services were now complete, they slipped out of the box in a rustle of silk petticoats, their long trains whispering over the carpets that muffled the gentle creaking of the well-polished wooden floorboards.

The girls walked swiftly down the hallway toward the Red Parlor and the royal box behind it. But for the occasional evenings when the Dual Monarch or a member of his family was in residence, the royal box sat empty, guarded only by a single officer of the Hapsburg household guard, armed with a decorative sword that had never once been drawn. As the girls strode purposefully down the passage toward him, the guard raised his hand in warning. "Entry is forbidden!" he called out in German. At that moment, Gizella collapsed with a cry of distress.

The guard, a gallant old gentleman, in his last posting before retirement, would soon enough regret the combination of chivalry and curiosity that caused him to leave his post and come to the aid of the lovely little dwarf. When his attention was thoroughly engaged by the prettily moaning Gizella, who had hitched up her skirts to show him a miniature ankle in supposed agony, Nina called out the planned words:

"Oh my dear little friend! Please help her!"

Gizella chose this moment to gyrate in the guard's arms, revealing her entire black-stockinged leg, and even giving a hint of the dark cleft at the top of her thigh. The guard thus distracted, Endre, Miloš, and Gulya appeared and slipped unnoticed into the Red Parlor and then through the set of double doors into the royal box.

"Please help her!" Nina repeated to the guard. "Carry her down to the lobby and ring for a doctor!"

The guard glanced warily at the empty hallway. "I can't leave my post."

"Please!" Nina said.

"It's not permitted. I'll stay with her while you go find an usher."

At this Gizella cried out loudly, overcome by nonexistent pain.

"She'll disturb the audience!" Nina said. "Never mind. I'll take her myself."

Nina was a strong girl, fully capable of lifting the child-sized Gizella, but she made a great show of strain as she hoisted the tiny woman a few inches off the ground, and promptly dropped her. Gizella wailed loudly and the guard paled.

"Stop!" he said. "For God's sake, you'll hurt her!" Effortlessly, he picked Gizella up in his arms. "You stay here and watch the door. I will send someone up in a moment. No one ever tries to pass, but if they do, just bar the way."

I am confident that I know Nina well enough to presume her moment of regret, as the gallantry of the kindly guard whose career she was about to ruin proved to her that just as an omelet requires the breaking of eggs, so too does revolution demand the destruction of innocents.

As soon as the poor man had disappeared down the passage, Nina ducked into the box, where she found her fellow conspirators busily at work. The curtain was drawn, blocking the box from the view of the audience below. The acrobat Gulya had removed his gloves, shoes, and stockings and had shinnied up one of the columns flanking the curtain. He clung there, his toes digging into the grooves in the moldings.

Nina lifted up her skirt. She and Gizella had folded and rolled the banner into a flexible tube of fabric that they had pinned to the bottom of Nina's corset. She removed it now, and handed it to Endre. Endre stared at the bulges of soft naked flesh at the top of her stockings, and only then did she comprehend that she was standing before a man, her skirt hitched high above her waist, her chemise and undergarments exposed. Blushing furiously, she dropped her skirts.

Endre recovered his composure, and tossed the banner up to Gulya, who stretched out his arm to catch it. For a perilous moment it looked like the acrobat might fall, but he dug in his toes and maintained his perch. He removed from his pocket a hammer, its iron head covered in noise-dampening felt, and spat a nail from his lips into his hand. Holding on only with his thighs and toes, he silently hammered one corner of the banner into place. Once it was secure he was about to let go when Miloš whispered furiously, "Goddamn it, you buffoon! You've done it backward."

Nina craned her neck and saw that Gulya had indeed affixed the corner of the banner so that the painted text was visible to them, inside the box. Had Miloš not noticed, when they opened the curtains the audience would have seen nothing but a blank canvas.

Gulya tore the banner loose, flipped it around, and hammered it in again.

"Hurry!" Nina called. "We have no time."

Gulya slid down the column, gripping the free end of the banner in his teeth. Miloš bent over at the base of the other column, his hands pressed to his knees. Gulya loped four steps and, using Miloš's back as a springboard, vaulted up the other column. He shinnied to the top and hammered in the other side.

As he slid to the ground, the banner slowly unfurled. Once it had reached the ground, Miloš and Gulya took up position on opposite sides.

"Ready?" Miloš asked.

Endre pulled a sheaf of pamphlets from beneath his frock coat. Nina had not been made aware of the plan to release any pamphlet, nor had she been consulted on its message. The banner's plea—"Votes for All! We Demand Universal Suffrage!"—was simple. The pamphlet called for something else entirely. It demanded an end to the parasitic Hapsburg monarchy, denounced the Diet of Hungary as a tool of repression, and called for a revolution by workers of all nationalities against a system that allowed for the privileges of a few based upon the slavery of all. It enjoined that society be established on a new basis, where all property would be held in common and where each, producing according to his abilities and his strength, could consume according to his needs.

As Miloš and Gulya flung the curtains open, revealing the banner painted in Nina's educated script, Endre threw the pamphlets off the balcony.

For a moment there was no reaction. Then, one by one, the audience noticed the white pieces of paper falling like snow from the royal box. They lifted their heads and saw the banner. They strained to make out the text in the dark.

The singers, blinded by the stage lights, kept on warbling their doomed phrases.

"Where is he!" Endre cried furiously. And as if in response, the house lights blinked on, revealing the conspirators' demands for universal suffrage.

At that moment the doors of the box burst open and the guard, accompanied by two ushers, burst through.

"Run!" Miloš shouted.

Nina hitched her skirts up and ran, dodging around the thick arm of one of the ushers. The guard and ushers were intent on capturing her male companions and did not bother to give her chase. She tore down the passage to the private royal staircase and flung herself down the marble steps, just ahead of the guards who soon swarmed it. The ginger-haired man had done his job, extinguishing the lights in the lobby as he lit the ones in the house, and so Nina was able, as planned, to disappear into the crush of audience members as they poured out of the hall into the dark. She hurried out the door, now one of many astonished operagoers whose evening of lady vampires and bad music had been interrupted by the action of radicals.

A man standing next to her balled up one of the pamphlets and threw it to the ground. She picked it up and, keeping herself hidden in the crowd, hurried onto Dalszínház Road, and then turned into Lázár Road, where she found the merchant's chauffeur waiting as planned. She flung open the door and collapsed into the rear seat.

"Where are the others?" the chauffeur asked.

"I don't know," she said. "Gizella isn't here?"

Gizella had been supposed to take advantage of the hullabaloo to duck away. If all had gone well, she would have been the first to arrive at the getaway vehicle. Terribly anxious for her friend, Nina began to cry. The plan was for the car to wait no more than ten minutes after the first alarm bells and police sirens, no matter if the conspirators arrived or not, and though she tried to argue with the driver, he had served nearly a decade in a hussar regiment and knew that above all a soldier must stick to the plan. And so they left, Nina and the chauffeur the only members of what would come to be called the Opera Conspirators to avoid capture.

It was only as they were driving away that she read the inflammatory pamphlet. "My God," she said aloud as the car careened through the streets of Budapest. "What have we done?"

40

THOUGH I WOULD LIKE to think that it was the atmosphere of trust and caring that I had created during my consultations with Nina that led her to my home that evening, honesty compels me to admit the possibility that she came to me simply because she had nowhere else to turn. Afraid that if the police had arrested Gizella, Endre, Miloš, Gulya, and perhaps even the prostitute, it would not be long before they determined their identities and discovered their address, she did not go back to the apartment in the Tabán. This decision proved critical in saving her, as within an hour the police were indeed at the door to the apartment and promptly arrested everyone inside, including not only the two other official residents, neither of whom was directly involved in the action, but also the cousin of one, a young man recently arrived from a distant town, who chose that inauspicious evening to drop off a bundle of his cousin's laundered shirts and a mended suit jacket. Had the poor young man been even slightly more derelict in his promise to his aunt, he would have avoided spending sixty miserable and pain-wracked days in the Budapest prison, would have kept his full set of teeth for at least a few more years, and might even have embarked on the brilliant career as a painter that he had imagined when he left for the big city. As it was, he returned home bereft of both his front teeth and his dignity, and from then on labored not as an artist, but as a factotum in his uncle's flour mill.

Nina considered going home, but she feared that once Gizella's involvement was publicized, her own would not long be kept secret, and she refused to bring the wrath of the police down onto her family. And so it was to me that she came, and it was only by extreme good fortune that she found me at home alone. In those days of my middle age, it was my custom after dining with my family to return to work, but rarely to my consulting rooms in the front of the apartment. Usually I spent an hour or two visiting those of my patients too infirm to come to me. On the rare evening I did not spend trundling about Pest from sickbed to sickbed, I repaired to my coffeehouse, where I read medical journals or made notes for the case studies I had lately begun to assemble for publication. That evening, unusually, my wife and daughters were visiting with a neighbor, the chambermaid and cook had been given the evening off to attend a vaudeville performance, and I was home alone.

When the porter's bell rang, I ignored it, only realizing at the second bong that I had in fact dismissed my help. Grumbling at the intrusion, I answered the intercom that had recently been installed to save our ancient porter and concierge the trouble of climbing the stairs to announce visitors.

"A Miss S. to see you, sir," the porter said, his voice muffled through the mouthpiece. I of course instructed him to send Nina up, and rushed to open the door for her. I had not seen her since she left my consulting room two weeks before, and my attempts to reach her parents had been fruitless. I was thus beside myself with worry.

"My girl, my girl!" I said, embracing her. I held her close to my chest, my hands splayed over the delicate silk of her gown. She trembled in my embrace and I whispered in her ear, "My dear, sweet girl."

A tendril of her hair caught in my lips and I breathed in her gardenia scent, and a barely noticeable trace of sour sweat.

Nina's knees buckled. I wrapped a supportive arm around her waist and led her to the analysand's couch. I laid her on the Turkish carpet draped over the couch and spread a blanket over her. Then, my knees creaking and crackling with the unaccustomed effort, I knelt down beside the couch and smoothed her hair away from her flushed and perspiring face. I pressed my lips to her forehead in an avuncular kiss.

"My darling," I said. "What has happened to you? Tell your dear Imré what's wrong." (I am sure that no one familiar with the school of loving and supportive mutual analysis created and practiced by my dear friend and colleague Sándor Ferenczi would have found anything unprofessional in my words or attitude.)

Nina said, "Please, Dr. Zobel. I need your help."

"You have it. Tell me, dearest. Whatever has happened? Is it a man? Have you been . . . defiled?"

She waved my question away. "Nothing like that. But I can't tell you anything. I beg you not to ask. Just, please, I need someplace to stay. Until tomorrow, or for a few days perhaps. Just until I figure out where to go."

Like most women, Nina did not weep prettily, but with a great rush of tears and mucus, her face mottled red and white. Though my profession has exposed me to a copious amount of tears from both sexes, I have always found it hard to resist those of a young lady, and thus I immediately agreed both to shelter her and to hide her whereabouts. At that moment I thought only that she had been in the company of a man who had treated her ill. That her problems were criminal and political rather than romantic did not occur to me.

Where to put her became my immediate problem. My wife, a mother herself, would not tolerate the idea of keeping such a secret from Mrs. S. I could hear her voice in my mind as clearly as if she'd spoken the words aloud. "How would you feel if someone hid Erzsébet or Lili from us?" My thoughts riffled through my family and acquaintances, trying to come up with someone of impeccable discretion, to whom I could trust the responsibility of the care of a girl in Nina's distraught condition. I settled, inevitably, on my sister Jolán.

Upon her return from Germany, Jolán had decided to move out of our mother's house. At the time I was furious, rejecting her explanation that soon enough Mama's age and health would require more filial devotion, and that she wanted to "experience solitude" while she still had the chance. "You'll have time enough for solitude when Mama dies!" I had insisted, but to no avail. My implacable sister ignored my vehement opposition and calmly removed herself to a suite of shabby but genteel furnished rooms within walking distance of the school where she taught. How grateful was I now for her intransigence!

Jolán was not on the telephone—she resisted any technology that permitted our mother to harass her any more than was necessary—and so Nina and I had no choice but to arrive at her home unannounced. She greeted us at the door wrapped in a Japanese kimono, her hair in a long braid over her shoulder. Worn down this way it was suddenly possible to see how much of it had silvered. Far more, though it is perhaps vain to say so, than my own, though I am nearly four years older. As I write this a decade after the events transpired, Jolán is gone, lost to cancer of the breast, and what sparse hair I have left is white as snow. But at the time I recall noting how old she looked, and worrying that she might not be strong enough to handle the responsibility I laid at her door.

"What in heaven's name are you up to, Imré, traipsing around the city in the middle of the night?" she asked.

"It's my fault," Nina said from behind me, where she'd been concealed in the gloom of the hall.

"Let us in, quickly," I said. Jolán's apartment was on the fourth story, the floor directly below the one reserved, even in these simple buildings, for the servants, and I feared that someone might peer out and see my young fugitive. At the time I had no inkling that Nina had done something that might result in her being sought by the police. I knew only that I had undertaken to protect her, and I was concerned that she might by some unfortunate coincidence be recognized. The gossip network of servants is notorious.

In the end it was Jolán in whom Nina confided, and then only once I had been peremptorily dismissed and sent on my way home, where I spent an unpleasant night tossing and turning and vowing that my stubborn sister was going to be put on the telephone, whether she liked it or not.

The next day I had a full calendar of patients, and not wishing to spark my wife's curiosity, I was forced to stay in my consulting room for the entire early part of the morning. I should mention at this point that concealing my actions from my dear wife caused me no small consternation. Over the decades of our marriage, Mrs. Zobel has been more than a helpmeet and a lover, she has been a friend in the true nature of the word, a person in whom one can confide, a person whose counsel one can trust. It pained me to deceive her, but I knew my wife well. As devoted a wife as she is, she is even more devoted a mother, and her thoughts would have been with Mrs. S. She would not have been able to refrain from letting that unfortunate woman know that her daughter was safe.

It is my custom when my schedule permits to take a short break at 10 a.m. to enjoy a cup of coffee and a quiet half hour with the morning's newspapers. I debated forgoing the ritual and rushing across town to my sister's apartment, but I had patients due to arrive after the morning break and discretion demanded that I keep to my schedule. I arrived at the Szabadság Coffeehouse, pulled a few newspapers from the rack as I walked in the door, and signaled to the waiter to bring me a coffee.

"*Mit Schlag, Herr Doktor?*" the Viennese waiter asked.

"Why not?" I asked. I only occasionally indulged myself, but even before I opened the papers I felt it a likely morning for the comfort of cream in my coffee.

On the cover of each of the papers I normally read in the morning—

Pest Diary, Hungarian Nation, and, my tabloid indulgence, the *Sun*—were screamingly large headlines. ATTACK ON THE OPERA HOUSE, THE PRIDE OF BUDAPEST! read the *Pest Diary.* ANARCHISTS INVADE THE KING'S BOX! read the *Hungarian Nation.* The *Sun,* typically, took it a step further: BOLSHEVIK GIRL-DWARF AND CONSPIRATORS WREAK HAVOC ON OPERA!

Oh, Nina, I thought. What have you done? What on earth have you done?

41

IT WAS JOLÁN WHO determined the course of action that saved both Nina and Gizella from prosecution and incarceration but resulted, to their mutual heartbreak but to Nina's family's relief, in their permanent breech. Nina had not waited for the morning papers to arrive. As soon as I was gone, she confided in my sister what she had done, explaining, as Jolán later told me, that the message had gone awry.

"It was supposed to be about universal suffrage. About the rights of all people to vote, regardless of class or sex. But my . . ." She hesitated.

"Your accomplices?" Jolán said drily.

"My friends printed pamphlets calling for revolution by the worker against the empire. Their motives are pure," she hastened to add. "There's terrible injustice in the world. So much poverty! But revolution? I had not thought of myself as a revolutionary!"

"Granting women the right to vote for the first time is not revolutionary?"

"Oh, it is . . . it's just . . . I fear they might be misunderstood as calling for a violent overthrow of the government."

"And you fear violent revolutionaries, anarchists, and Bolsheviks will be punished more severely than suffragists."

"Exactly."

Though other countries were notoriously cruel in their treatment of women seeking the right to vote, the Hapsburg Empire, whatever the flaws perceived by Nina's radical friends, had never tortured or even imprisoned women demonstrating on behalf of suffrage. In England, British suffragists were incarcerated and, when they went on hunger strikes to protest the brutality of the treatment they endured, were force-fed with great violence, using nasal tubes far larger than necessary for the procedure. In Budapest and Vienna, however, suffragists demonstrated virtually unmolested. The mayor, as I said, even attended the Suffrage Congress. Of course, neither the Diet nor the king had any intention of granting women the vote, but still, violent reprisal was not part of the Austro-Hungarian response. One could argue, I suppose, that our

Magyar feminists were of a more timid stripe than their hunger-striking brethren abroad, but I think Rózsa Schwimmer and her sisters would take issue with that characterization. No, Franz Josef and his government had been open-minded and generous with the suffragists, but this was most assuredly not the case with the Bolsheviks and anarchists who made no secret of their desire for his usurpation. And how could it be otherwise, given that the king had lost his beloved queen to an anarchist's treacherous knife?

It was nearly dawn by now, and Nina and Jolán were both exhausted. "I shall have to turn myself in to the authorities," Nina said. "There's no other choice. I can't put my comrades in the position of hiding my identity."

"Nonsense," Jolán said. "What good will that do? Another neck for the noose."

Nina flinched, but stiffened her spine. "If that's the case, I cannot let them die alone."

"Let's leave off with the Sarah Bernhardt performance, shall we?" Jolán said. "I was speaking metaphorically. I have no idea if your accomplices are facing execution. No one was hurt in the action, correct?"

"Of course not! We would never have caused anyone harm."

"Then surely they will be facing only long prison sentences. Though, frankly, I'm not sure I myself wouldn't prefer death to a decade of hard labor. At any rate, we must think sensibly."

"All right then," Nina said, now annoyed. "How's this for sensible? If I fail to turn myself in, and my friends are forced to give my name, surely things will go worse for me. Surely the court will give me some credit for my honesty if I voluntarily appear."

"Perhaps," my sister said. "But I don't know that, and neither do you. What we need, my dear, is the assistance of an attorney. And I know just the one."

There were many people in Budapest and even as far abroad as Germany and England who read about the arrest of Gizella Weisz, suffragist, assistant to Rózsa Schwimmer, and dwarf. Delegates to the International Woman Suffrage Congress remembered Gizella, for who wouldn't? Her stature and her beauty made her memorable. There might even have been those who recalled her bosom friend, the two of them as often as not dressed in matching white gowns, eagerly crowding the back of the hall when their duties permitted, to hear the speakers and witness the debates. I imagine that over morning coffee and tea, ladies of the suffrage movement throughout Europe exclaimed over their morning newspapers and telephoned one another to ask urgent questions and share suppositions. Surely a few of the ladies of the German delegation, in whose service Nina had been a page, even remembered or thought they remembered the name of Gizella's close friend. "Lili?" they likely asked one another. "Nina?" The great Rózsa Schwimmer certainly knew the name of her secretary's friend. And then there were those of Nina's acquaintance who had met the dwarf in her company. Her extended family, friends from the community of Budapest feminists and suffragists, a few girl-friends from gymnasium, a number of the women with whom she studied for her *matura* and her medical school admissions examinations. And, of course, the E.'s, who had dined with Gizella, and who had witnessed Nina's final rupture from her parents. All of these people undoubtedly knew or worried that Nina S. might be involved in her closest friend's imbroglio, and none, not a single one, reported her to the agents of the Hapsburg police.

But though none of the dozens of people who knew or suspected that Nina might be implicated took their suspicions to the authorities, neither did they keep them to themselves. There are few who can resist the allure of gossip, few who are able to comply with our religious tradition to avoid *lashon horah*, speaking ill of others. There were rumors and whispers, many though not all hushed by the time Nina made her way down the aisle at the Dohány Street Synagogue to the chuppah made from the tallith of her husband's great-grandfather.

When I read about the terrible exploits at the Opera House, I rushed from my coffeehouse to my sister's apartment, my journey crossing, it turned out, with that of the telegram she had sent begging that I come at once. Once there I found myself in complete agreement with the women's plan, though I expect that even if I had had doubts they would not have tolerated them.

From the apartment I hastened to the Royal Prosecutor's Office of Budapest. I waited in the ornate antechambers for no more than a moment before I was ushered inside by a clerk.

Ignác E. leaped to his feet when I entered the room, shooed the clerk out, and shut the door.

"My God, Doctor," he said. "What has she done?"

Ignác's tie was askew, and through the flaps of his unbuttoned jacket I could see circles of damp staining the underarms of his shirt. This privileged young man had never known a moment's deprivation in his life, had by virtue of fine family connections and a more than passable intellect made it to heights in his profession unusual for a man of his youth and, more important, his race. Previous to this, his most serious discomposure had been a result of failing to earn a medal in his Olympic swim race. His consternation was a credit to him and to the intensity of his affection for Nina, despite both her actions and the disdain with which she regularly treated him.

"She is involved, isn't she?" he said.

"Yes," I said, "I fear so. But please believe me, Ignác, Nina is not a radical."

"I wish I could believe you, but look." He passed me a copy of the newspaper *Hungarian Nation,* in which was reproduced an image of the pamphlet that had fluttered down from the royal box. "These are the words of Bolsheviks and anarchists."

"Nina had no knowledge of the pamphlet. Yes, she committed a crime, but she believed her protest to be on behalf only of suffrage. The young men kept the pamphlet a secret from her and from Miss Weisz."

An expression of relief passed over Ignác's face, but only for a moment before he said, "And her Ruthenian accomplice? A known revolutionary!"

"I'm sure Nina knew nothing of this."

"Is the man her . . . her lover?"

"No! Absolutely not. Neither is the other man, Endre Bauer. He is merely a friend."

At that word, Ignác sputtered in disgust. "You see, Dr. Zobel, I was under the foolish impression that I was her friend."

"You are, sir, you are. It is because of that friendship that she has asked me to come to you."

"She asked you to come?" he said, hopefully. No matter what Nina felt about this young man, his affection for her was true.

"Yes. She is desperate for your help."

"Ah. Of course. It is legal counsel she seeks."

"Yes, legal counsel. But also your friendship. She is all but alone, Ignác. She needs a friend."

At war in Ignác's heart were dueling impulses, one to punish the girl who had rejected his advances, the other to save the woman he admired and knew he could one day love.

"Do you promise, Dr. Zobel, to be honest with me?"

"I do."

"Then tell me. Her virtue. Has it been compromised? Is she chaste?"

"Need you ask?"

"Yes, I am afraid I must."

So I told him what I hoped was true.

Ignác E. determined that our first step must be to speak to Miss Weisz, and luckily my profession offered him an excuse that he would not otherwise have been able to counterfeit. Ignác apprised his superiors of the petition by Miss Weisz's personal physician to visit her and ascertain her physical condition. He requested permission to accompany the physician, in order to ensure no rules were violated. These requests were considered, reinforced by an additional petition from a senior prosecutor, an acquaintance of Mrs. Rózsa Schwimmer, and eventually granted.

The necessary documents complete with official wax seals and signatures having been swiftly obtained, we repaired together to the Central Police Holding Facility, where we found Miss Weisz imprisoned in a small, malodorous cell, its damp stone walls furred with mold and inscribed with the desperate scribbles of previous occupants. She sat perched on the edge of a torn straw mattress, her feet swinging in the air above the filthy floor. The place was less a modern penal facility than a medieval dungeon, and even Ignác, though familiar as a prosecutor with the types of accommodation afforded by the realm to its delinquents, was disgusted by the treatment meted out to Miss Weisz.

She had at least been allowed to remain dressed in her own clothes, although likely only because no alternative existed in her size.

Though the dear girl's spine was stiffened by pride, her relief at seeing us was palpable. Her eyes welled with tears, which she blinked quickly away. I performed a quick but thorough physical examination. Though no bones were broken, her wrists and ankles had been badly cut and bruised by the iron chains that the gendarme had used to restrain her. Her ribs too were bruised and she flinched beneath my probing fingers. At my insistence she spat into the linen handkerchief I held beneath her chin. Her sputum was tinged red. Her gums, I saw when I importuned her to open her mouth, were bloody, a few of the teeth loose.

"Did someone strike you?" I asked.

"I fell," she said.

"Pushed?"

She shrugged. "The others?" she asked.

"Your accomplices have all been arrested and are being held here as well," Ignác said.

Her olive skin paled to a sickly yellow. "I feared it was their screams I was hearing all through the night."

"The men are being treated as well as can be expected," Ignác said, laying meaningful stress on the word "men."

"And?" she said, her clear voice reverberating like a bell in the stone shell of the room. I was not surprised years later to find out that Miss Weisz was a gifted singer who, with training and in a world devoid of bias against the deformed, might have been an accomplished mezzo-soprano.

"And that is all," Ignác said.

Miss Weisz glanced at me, imploringly. She feared prying ears too much to say Nina's name, but I knew she was knotted with concern for her friend.

"All is well, dear little Miss Weisz," I said.

"Well?" she repeated.

"Yes. Well."

"Safe?"

"For the time being," Ignác said. "But everything depends on you. Cooperate with the authorities, tell them all you know about the men with whom you conspired"—again that all but unnoticeable emphasis on the word "men"—"and all will continue to be well."

"I will not tell anything to anyone," she said.

"Of course not," I said. "Of course not. You'll say only what must be said, about these men who so shamefully took advantage of your innocence, who used you to further an agenda you did not support."

"I will say nothing. Nothing about anyone."

Ignác glared at her. He was standing on the other side of the cell, as far from her as the constricting walls would allow. "You'll say what you're told to say, if you value your life."

"I value freedom, Mr. E. Honor and freedom and dignity and justice. But life alone? What is there to value in that?"

I said, "Miss Weisz, dear girl. Please don't be so silly. Look around you. Is this where you want to finish your days? Here in this horrible cell or in another like it?" A black beetle scampered across my shoe and I flung it off and crushed it beneath my sole. "Amidst the vermin?"

"The rats come out only after the sun sets," she said.

"Is imbecility one of your afflictions?" Ignác asked.

I shook my head at him, and laid a calming hand on Gizella's small one. "Mr. E. is justifiably concerned. About your future. Yours and . . . others'."

"Mr. E. can rest assured that I will speak of nothing and no one, no matter what he and his fellow prosecutors demand."

The door to the cell creaked open, and the jailer's face peered in. "Will you be needing more time, sir?" he asked Ignác.

"No," the prosecutor said, and swept out of the cell.

I gave Miss Weisz a last squeeze of her hand and stood to follow him out.

"Dr. Zobel," she said.

"Yes, my dear?"

"Can I ask . . . If you would . . ."

"What?"

She blushed furiously and raised a trembling hand to her face. Only now did her tears fall. "I need bandages. Supplies. It's . . ." She motioned to her skirt, which was stained and damp.

"Your menses."

"Yes," she said, crying now in earnest. "I have asked to see the matron, but . . ."

"Worry not. I'll have a basket sent to you immediately. Are you in pain?"

"No."

"That at least is a relief," I said, again turning to the door.

"Doctor! Wait," she said. She reached into her bodice and extracted something she had secreted there. She held it out to me, and with some trepidation I took it. It was the peacock pendant she had worn on the night of the ill-fated dinner.

"Can you give this to my friend for me? Please."

I nodded and closed my hands around the locket. "Do you know what they say about peacock feathers?" I asked her.

"That they bring ill fortune. Mrs. Schwimmer always said that was superstitious nonsense. She said that if one is seeking to change the world, one must always embrace what others fear."

"I will give your friend the gift." But I did not. Not right away. Because whatever Mrs. Schwimmer said or did not say about fortune and superstition, it seemed to me that both Miss Weisz and my darling Nina could benefit from a little good luck.

"To be female is no picnic," I said to Ignác when we were safely ensconced in the rear seat of his British Rolls-Royce automobile.

He laughed sourly. "That particular female's troubles are of her own devising. They have nothing to do with her sex."

I glanced meaningfully at the back of his chauffeur's bristled neck.

"Speak freely," Ignác said. "My father imported James from London along with this car. The man speaks passable German and French, but not a word of Hungarian."

"I trust that Miss Weisz won't turn on her friends."

"Everyone turns eventually, Dr. Zobel. There are very few strong enough to resist interrogation. In my years of legal practice I've never met one."

"But, respectfully, sir, you are young. You have not been practicing for very long. Perhaps Miss Weisz will surprise you."

"This is a large conspiracy with many players, most of whom are now in custody. The rest will surely follow. Someone will speak. There is only one way to save Nina."

I felt a profound relief. I had feared that there would be no solution at all to protect my darling girl. "And what is that?"

"She must speak first."

42

THAT AFTERNOON A CONFERENCE was held in the apartment of my sister. Never had those modest rooms hosted such illustrious company. In addition to Ignác, there was his father Jenő E., Nina's own father, her uncle, and a cousin of the family, the famed solicitor Zoltán Thuz, who boasted good relations with the Budapest police and who had the greater advantage of being a convert to Catholicism whose confessor was none other than Archbishop János Csernoch of Esztergom. In addition, though he would never himself attend such a gathering, the Baron Móric E. had sent his personal secretary. And of course there was I.

The topic of our consultation and concern might as well have been absent, so little was her opinion sought. As the room filled, Nina sat in a ladderback chair, her eyes cast down at her lap where her fingers knotted and unknotted. She had brushed her hair back and tied it in a severe bun at the nape of her neck, and borrowed from my sister a drab shirtwaist and skirt, which hung on her like a sack. Only her feet betrayed her. Jolán has tiny feet, a characteristic of all Zobels, female and male, and so Nina wore the high-heeled slippers of scarlet satin that matched the stolen evening gown. Her only other choice would have been to go barefoot.

Mr. S. did not greet his daughter when he entered the room. Even for me he had only the barest of civilities. The other gentlemen were more generous, but only Ignác came to Nina. He extracted one of her hands and raised it to his lips. He then bent to her ear and whispered something. When I later asked him what he said, he told me, "Just that all would be well, and that she could trust me to care for her, now and always."

Nina, when asked the same question, told me that his actual words were, "It will take time, my darling, but someday I know I will forgive you."

The negotiations were complex, and involved esoteric matters of law, questions of criminal culpability and evidence, and a heated debate about the average dowry of a girl of comparable class. In the end, the dowry that was agreed upon was ten times what otherwise would have been Nina's portion. It was so large that her father would be compelled to appeal to his family and his bank for loans. When even this was insufficient, he would have no choice but to sell the family's summer cottage in the Carpathian Mountains. The lawyers were confident that with Nina's agreement to give secret testimony against her accomplices, and with the substantial influence they together wielded, they would not only be able to secure her freedom, but also to keep secret her identity.

"And what if they return at some point, those men?" her father asked. "If they try to blackmail her?"

Mr. S.'s cousin, the famed solicitor, dismissed the possibility. "You can rest assured, sir. We will not be hearing from any of them ever again."

"And Miss Weisz?"

At the sound of the soft, tremulous voice, the men in the room turned to Nina, astonished.

"Miss Weisz?" she said, more strongly now. "She must go free, too."

"Be still!" Mr. S. thundered.

Nina lifted her eyes, defiant. "I won't agree unless you promise that Miss Weisz will also go free."

"My dear girl," said Zoltán Thuz, "your friend is in the hands of the authorities. She was arrested at the scene of the crime. It would be a much more complex endeavor to secure her release."

"But not impossible," Ignác said softly.

"No," Thuz replied. "Not impossible. Just damned difficult."

"Nina, if I give you my word that we will do our best to save her, will you agree to the terms?" Ignác said.

"How can I trust you?" she said, speaking only to him.

Jenő E. sputtered. "You, who have proved yourself absolutely untrustworthy, question the honor of my son?"

Ignác said, "I can give you no more than my word. But my word is good. Surely even you will allow me this."

Nina gazed into his eyes for a long moment. Then she nodded. "Yes. I will agree. But please, Ignác, please save my friend."

· **43** ·

NINA CAME TO VISIT me once more, a few months after her wedding, to which I had not been invited. This exclusion had not surprised me—though I knew myself to have been instrumental in her salvation, I did not expect her family to acknowledge this, for to do so would compel them to admit that she had needed saving. My wife had been hurt to find no invitation in the post, but soon enough she was busy planning a wedding of her own. Erzsébet made as lovely a bride as a father could dream of, and her young groom was both bashful and dashing, a combination designed to delight any girl, and any girl's mother, as well. My dear wife had initially resisted my decision about Erzsébet's marriage, but once she realized that my resolve was firm, she came around. A successful publishing house provides a fine employment on which to support a family, and though those in my profession know more than most that love is no guarantee of marital success, neither does it impede that possibility. At any rate, Simon Goldziher has made us grandparents three times over, and Erzsébet seems very satisfied with her match. For a brief while we even nurtured the hope that Lili would take Erzsébet's place in the affections of thrown-over András, but he ended up marrying a lady from Debrecen. In the end we were spared tragedy. András served as a physician in the Great War, and died during the Siege of Przemyśl. Lili settled adequately, though less happily than her sister, with the heir to a moderate dry-goods fortune.

When Nina came to visit me in my consulting room that final time, she told me that she and her new husband had spent a restful three months at Bad Gastein, the very spa at which I would, years later, encounter Gizella Weisz.

"And I see that you are expecting," I said.

She startled. "How did you know? It's very early yet. I have not even told my mother."

I pointed to her bosom. "A swelling of the breasts is often the first indicator of pregnancy, even before a missed menses."

She put her hand to her chest, which did indeed swell delightfully beneath the sheer organza of her blouse.

I asked, "And your marriage? Is it happy?"

Ignoring my question, she turned to my bookshelves and slid her finger along the spines of the volumes.

"*Anatomy: Descriptive and Surgical,*" she said, taking the book from its place. She leafed for a moment through its pages, staring as if entranced at the complex and graphic illustrations.

"I used to own this book," she said. "Though my English is not really good enough to understand it well."

"You own it no more?"

"My father took my medical texts. He gave them to a deserving but poor young student at the medical college, along with a scholarship to complete his studies."

"Ah."

"So you see, Dr. Zobel, because of me there will be another physician in the world. A male one. But still, I can find comfort in that."

"Yes," I said. I came and stood next to her. Her full skirt brushed the wool of my slacks. I burned at that moment with the injustice of what had been lost. I knew Nina would be a fine mother, a good wife, but she would have made an outstanding physician. An unusual talent, a brilliant mind. I found and still do find myself furious at the squandering of her gifts, not only for her sake, but for the myriad patients she will never cure, the discoveries she will never make, the lives she will never save. How many people will die, have died, because of the wasted talents of intelligent and gifted women, forced into domestic drudgery, corseted by paternal demands, strangled by denial of opportunity? Too many to count. Too many to contemplate. Too many.

I pulled my handkerchief from my pocket and made a great show of blowing my nose, to disguise my tears behind a sudden allergic fit. "The autumn winds," I muttered. "They bring dust from the plains. It disagrees with my sinuses." I gave a last, honking blow and returned the soaked bit of fabric to its customary pocket. "And Miss Weisz?" I asked. "Have you heard anything of her?"

True to his word, Ignác had managed to secure Gizella's release, though on grounds that I had no doubt the girl herself found humiliating. She was like a child, the young attorney had argued to his superiors at the prosecutor's office. Short in stature and limited in mind, she had been easily swayed by the malevolence of radical men. This argument was not dissimilar to the one made on Nina's behalf, though in that case influence and gratuity had a greater impact on the outcome of her situation than in Gizella's. Nina was not only never prosecuted, but her name was kept out of the press. Gizella had no one able to pay for her release and so was forced to rely on the court's mercy. Acceding to Ignác's description of her as all but an idiot, infirm in both body and mind, was the humiliating price she had to pay for freedom.

"I saw her before she left Budapest," Nina said.

A condition of Gizella's release was that she abandon Budapest and return to her family in Transylvania. When she heard that her friend was to be banished, Nina went to the train station in secret, something she accomplished with great difficulty as she was no longer allowed to go out in public unaccompanied. On the morning of Gizella's departure, Nina repaired to her room, claiming to be suffering from a recurrence of her crippling menstrual pain.

"Are you sure?" her mother had said. "Surely it's not time yet."

"Yes, I'm sure," Nina had said. "Perhaps the worry of the past weeks has brought it on early."

"Have you enough bandages?"

"Yes. I just want to lie in a dark room, alone."

"I'll send the chambermaid up with a hot-water bottle."

For the hot-water bottle Nina exchanged a pile of cloths that she had soaked in blood from a small incision she made on the inside of her thigh. She then slipped out her window which gave onto the landing, and ducked into the servants' stairway. Luck was with her, and no one was on the landing, in the stairway, or on the street immediately below, and she hurried away, unnoticed beneath a large hat and veil.

When she reached the train station, she had very little time left if she was to avoid discovery. Soon the maid would return to take away another pile of soiled linen and refresh her water bottle.

Nina saw Gizella through the window of the second-class women's carriage. The dwarf sat on the hard wooden seat, her back stiff and straight. Her head was bare and to Nina's astonishment she saw that her friend's gorgeous hair, the endless locks that had been her pride, was shorn, cropped like a boy's, or like a prisoner's. Gizella gazed unseeing out of the carriage window. Nina stopped on the platform beneath. The glass was dingy, and when Nina tapped on it, it left gray smudges on the soft white kidskin of her gloves.

Gizella jumped, but immediately returned her expression to blankness. With only the slightest movement she inclined her head toward the interior of the carriage. Nina backed away from the window to give herself a better view, and saw a man in a policeman's uniform positioned outside the interior carriage door. To her surprise she felt no fear, only determination.

"Open the window," she mouthed.

Gizella gave a brief, nearly invisible but nonetheless firm shake of her head.

"Please."

Gizella glanced at the guard. She hesitated a moment as if deciding, and then pulled up the sash.

Nina heard the officers—there were two of them, it appeared—call out.

"It's so warm," Gizella called back to them. "Just for a moment, for air."

Nina waited, concerned that one of the police officers would come to the window, but so ingrained was the prohibition against entering the women's carriage that they only snarled at Gizella to keep it open no farther than a few inches.

This was enough, however, for the two girls to converse.

"Are you all right?" Nina said. "Did they hurt you?"

"No."

"Your hair."

Gizella shrugged. "Have you word of the others? No one will tell me anything. They've even forbidden me the newspaper."

"Hard labor."

"All of them?"

"Yes."

"Even Tanya?"

"Yes." The poor seamstress who had stolen only for her lover's sake had nonetheless been sentenced to seven years' incarceration, an injustice that would torment Nina in her freedom. Through Jolán, Nina would send the woman packages, though few reached her. Nina was determined to help her upon her release, but never had the opportunity to carry out this wish. Tanya died five years into her sentence, when the Spanish flu tore through the prison camp where she was employed sewing uniforms for the soldiers fighting the final war of the Austro-Hungarian Empire.

Endre and Miloš's innocent roommates would be released after nearly a year in the purgatory of pretrial detention, and Endre, Miloš, and Gulya would be liberated from prison with great fanfare in 1919, when Béla Kun and his dictatorship of the Proletariat took power over Hungary. Endre Bauer became a functionary in the Political Investigating Authority, where he made it his business to terrorize Ignác E. Had the regime lasted any longer than a few short weeks, he might have succeeded in engineering Ignác's arrest, and perhaps even Nina's. In the end it was he at the wrong end of the hangman's noose. The White Terror that ended the transient Hungarian socialist utopia and saved Ignác proved a disaster for most of the Jews, inspiring as it did the *numerus clausus* and God only knows what else to come. Of the other conspirators less is known. Miloš left for Ruthenia and thereafter disappeared from view. Gulya returned to the circus, where I understand he remains to this day, the patriarch of a family of gifted acrobats.

"Poor Tanya," Gizella said.

"Yes," Nina said. "At least the old woman is safe." And indeed the prostitute who'd acted as chaperone was never captured. Sometimes when I pass crowds of such ladies in which one strikes me as particularly elderly, I wonder if it is not she.

Gizella said, "They tell me it's Ignác E. I have to thank for my release. And for yours, I presume?"

"Yes."

"Will you marry him?"

"Yes."

"Don't."

"I have no choice."

"You always have a choice. Run, Nina. Go somewhere, study medicine. Be a doctor. It's all you've ever wanted."

"There's nowhere to go."

"Go to America!"

"I can't." But for a moment Nina indulged a fantasy of a new life in a new world. A small practice in an anonymous city. A settlement house, like the ones she'd read about in the feminist newspaper, where she could treat poor immigrant women and even perhaps inspire some to follow her into the field. And then she allowed the dream to dissolve, like powdered aspirin in a glass of water, leaving behind only a bitter residue.

Gizella said, "Did you promise to marry him in return for my release?"

"Not just yours. Mine too."

"A bad bargain."

"No."

"One prison for another."

"A gilded cage is hardly a prison." As she said them, Nina knew that the words were at once true and false. The petty tediums of a Budapest matron, even those of a Transylvanian performing dwarf, could not be fairly compared with the torments of hard labor. And yet chains, no matter how delicate and finely wrought, still chafe.

With a great clanking and a rush of steam and smoke, the train lurched to life. Nina stripped off her glove, stood on her toes, and pressed her bare hand to the glass. It was gritty beneath her palm, and cold. Gizella glanced fearfully at her jailers, and then did the same. They remained this way, connected by a pane of glass warming ever so slightly beneath their touch, until the train began its slow, lurching motion out of the station.

"I haven't seen her since," Nina told me. "Nor heard from her. I don't know if she writes and my father takes the letters. I telephoned Mrs. Schwimmer, but even that lady has had no word."

"I have something for you," I said.

I went to my desk, took the key from its hiding place, and opened the locked drawer to which none, not even my wife, has access. From the drawer, I removed a small package wrapped in oiled paper and tied tightly with string. With my paper knife I sliced open the string, opened the paper, and revealed a pouch sewn from rich, heavy velvet. Inside that lay an enameled pendant on which was painted a brilliant peacock decorated with gemstones in purple, green, and white.

"Gizella's locket!" Nina said, rushing to my side.

She smelled of citrus and verbena, sharp and tangy, fresh and clean.

"Open it," I said, pouring the locket and its chain into her hand.

She slid her fingernail along the side of the pendant and activated the hidden spring. The secret locket popped open.

"What is this?" she said, peering closely at the photograph. "It's not the same photograph!"

I handed her my magnifying glass, and she gazed for a long moment at the tiny picture of two young ladies, one small, one tall. One dark, one fair, in matching white gowns, behind them billowing the banners of the International Woman Suffrage Congress.

"Gizella entrusted me with the locket, but I had no opportunity to give it to you until now. I feared to send it to your home."

"My father would have destroyed it. And the photograph?"

"Don't you remember? The photographer who took your picture that afternoon when I came to the congress? I took his card and found him. He printed a photograph for me small enough to fit in the locket."

I had also paid for a larger image, one that resided in my locked drawer, but which I would eventually slip between the pages of *Gray's Anatomy,* where I would come upon it whenever I was troubled by a tricky diagnosis and required a reminder of the basics of my medical education, or whenever I wanted to see Nina's face. Years later, after encountering Gizella at Bad Gastein, I had the photograph copied at not insubstantial expense, and sent to her, care of the manager of the Lilliput Guild. I was disappointed that she never wrote to thank me, but perhaps the photograph never reached her.

"Will you wear it now?" I asked.

"Yes," Nina said. "And always." She handed me the locket and I moved behind her and draped it around her fragrant neck, where it nestled in her powdered décolletage.

As my thick fingers struggled with the clasp, I allowed myself to breathe in her scent, to feel her soft hair against my cheek. When it finally caught, I did not move, but instead remained close to her, feeling the length of her body against my own. I dreamed for a moment of slipping my hands around her waist, of cupping her breasts in my palms, of pressing my lips against her soft, white neck.

My esteemed colleagues, readers of this case history, do not think I fail to appreciate your response to the paragraph above. I can hear the clucking tongues and feel the condemnatory glances as you dismiss my heartfelt words as failed countertransference. You think I have fallen into the dark hole of the unconscious that lies in wait for every psychoanalyst. You reprove me for projecting my own traumatic history on my patient. You insist that Nina is nothing more than an object for my distorted perceptions of previous relationships. You revile me with that most awful word: "inappropriate." Even those of you who are disciples of my esteemed, my beloved, Sándor Ferenczi tar me with this brush. You might celebrate my "emotional reactivity." You might praise me for creating a corrective emotional context awash in empathy in which my patient can be nurtured, even cured. But you would never recognize my feelings for Nina for what they are. You call it countertransference. But it is not.

It is another thing. Unrequited. Never to be acted upon.

Love.

Epilogue

NEW YORK

1948

THOUGH THE ROOM WAS only half full, and the rows of crushed-velvet chairs closest to the podium nearly empty of occupants, Jack slipped into a chair in the back. Worried that he would feel self-conscious wearing his academic tweeds to the showroom of a prestigious auction house, he had chosen to dress, this morning, in a fashionable three-button suit with a notched lapel, worn with a boldly striped tie in a Windsor knot. Now he felt overdressed. The scene was not the frantic hive of natty gold dealers and dandyish antiques merchants that he had imagined. On the contrary. The auction was poorly attended, and the shabby dealers and buyers seated on the chairs looked bored rather than thrilled by the contents of the catalogue.

If Jack's train had not suffered an interruption of service yesterday between 7:12 a.m. and 7:57 a.m., if he had not forgotten his book on the kitchen counter when he'd rinsed out his coffee cup, then he would not have been compelled to read the *New York Times* with unusual thoroughness, from front to back, and would thus in all likelihood never have seen the advertisement in the Arts section announcing to the public that the Parke-Bernet Galleries would be holding an auction of gems, watches, silverware, china, and stamps. The items to be sold were, according to the ad, in a formulation that struck Jack as curious if not weaselly, "war victim assets," and proceeds would go to the Intergovernmental Committee on Refugees.

Even though he had not been able to determine that the property to be sold had in fact come from the doomed wagons of the Hungarian Gold Train, he was so eager to attend the auction that he had considered canceling his morning class. Most of the students taking Ancient Greek I in summer school had failed it the previous year, and he knew they'd be relieved to have a day's break from second-declension omicron-stem nouns. He was too conscientious, however, to indulge either their indolence or his own anxiety. He waited until after class, though he skipped his usual hours in his carrel in Butler Library, where he was at work on his graduate thesis.

He had missed the beginning of the auction and thus any announcement that might have been made about the source of the property to be sold. By the second lot, however, he was sure he was in the right place. Where else but the Gold Train would the Intergovernmental Committee on Refugees have acquired this much Hungarian Herend porcelain? Though a few large pieces were auctioned individually, the rest was sold in bulk, hundreds of vases, figurines, bowls, pitchers, and sets of service at a time. The items went quickly, and the auctioneer did not seem displeased with the bidding. There was less interest, however, in lots 16 to 28: a dozen lots of watches, also sold in bulk. When the auctioneer brought his gavel down, confirming the sale of thousands of men's gold watches for a meager two dollars apiece, Jack was so astonished that he nearly missed the crying of the next lot, number 29, "Enameled Jewelry."

As the bidding crept along, he slipped his hand into his pocket, as if to reassure himself that the pendant was still there. More than two years before, the morning he left Salzburg for Hamburg, where he was to board the first of three ships that would eventually deposit him in Hoboken, New Jersey, he had gone to the warehouse to hand over the keys to his replacement, a young property-control officer who would be present the following year when another young American, this one a lawyer working for the Intergovernmental Committee on Refugees as a reparations officer, arrived with a team of four appraisers and an expert in jewelry to catalog and inventory the contents of the train. Over the course of ten days, these men would work their way swiftly through the warehouse, appraising the property in bulk rather than individually, a technique agreed upon after a representative from Gimbels department store had toured the warehouse and announced that it would take his complete staff, working full-time, not weeks or months but years to examine, itemize, and appraise even just the individual pieces of silver, let alone the rest of the train's contents.

On Jack's last day in Salzburg, the fate of the contents of what people had only recently taken to calling the Hungarian Gold Train was yet to be decided. To Jack of course it had long since become clear that the property would never end up in the hands of the heirs of its former owners. As he watched the daily trainloads of Jewish refugees streaming into Salzburg, he believed that eventually the United States would take the easiest and most financially sensible route and hand over the property to the Jewish Agency to be sold, with the proceeds used to care for the

DPs and to facilitate their resettlement as far as possible from the pale of American responsibility. As far away as Palestine, for example.

And the truth was that by then Jack was not sure that this was not after all the best solution to the problem of the Hungarian Gold Train. The task of identifying individual owners of each piece of property was monumental. Moreover, hundreds of thousands of Hungary's Jews were dead and, of those who survived, thousands were leaving their homes and their country, escaping the Soviets as they should have escaped their own countrymen a decade before. Perhaps selling the contents of the train to benefit the DPs was the only solution that approximated justice. The argument made by the Hungarian Jewish remnant that the property should be given to them to sell, the money to be used toward rebuilding their community, was appealing, but only if one ignored the malign and burgeoning Soviet influence in Hungary. Was anyone so naïve as to believe that anything turned over to the Hungarians would eventually reach Jewish hands? Moreover, wasn't the Jewish Agency's solution the one that Ilona herself had supported, in that last grim conversation before she disappeared forever from his life?

Jack would recall these considerations when, years later, he would read in the *New York Times* about the defection from Hungary of senior officials of the Finance Ministry, who subsequently provided information about the ultimate disposition of the most valuable of the Gold Train assets, the jewels and gold stolen by Árpád Toldi and confiscated by the French. Nearly two thousand kilograms of gold and precious gems had been promptly turned over by France to the Hungarian government, which had determined, with equal promptness, that there was no way to positively identify ownership of the gold and jewelry and thus no reason to assume it had belonged to Jews. The Jewish community of Budapest, which had petitioned the French government so long and so vociferously for the property's return, recovered not a gram of gold, not a single diamond.

On that spring morning in Salzburg in 1946, while he had waited for his replacement to show up, Jack had walked the aisles of the warehouse one last time, eventually reaching the stuffy corner where he had stored the most valuable items, the gold watches and jewelry, the small quantity of gems. He noticed the case of watches from Nagyvárad and took it down from where he'd hidden it months before. He opened the case and traced his fingers across the address stamped on the brittle pink silk. He wondered if he would ever again have cause to read the name

"Nagyvárad." And why would he? The city had vanished even more surely than the woman he loved. It was Oradea now, a Romanian town. Hungarian Nagyvárad and the Jews who inhabited it were gone.

He was about to close the case and return it to the stack, when he noticed the black velvet pouch that contained the purple, green, and white enameled peacock pendant, that harbinger of ill fortune. He unwrapped the pendant and held it, feeling it once again grow warm in his hand, as it had the first time he'd touched it so long ago, when he'd been a different man, with a different idea of what bad luck meant. Without allowing himself to think about what he was doing, he wrapped the pendant in its velvet and placed it in his pocket. Then he walked back up the aisle, laid his keys on the makeshift desk he'd built for himself at the front of the warehouse, scribbled a note for the man who would take over his fruitless job, and bugged out.

Jack had quickly grown ashamed of the lapse of character and judgment that had allowed him to steal the pendant, and had he not left Salzburg that very day, he might have rushed back to the warehouse and returned it to where it belonged. Now, two years and a lifetime later, he listened as the auctioneer settled on a price for the lot of thousands of pieces of enameled jewelry from the Hungarian Gold Train. One dollar and fifty cents per piece.

One dollar and fifty cents.

In the next day's newspaper, Jack would read that the auction had netted not the hundreds of millions of dollars estimated beforehand but less than two million dollars, enough to feed and house the displaced Jews of Europe for approximately one week. His plan had been to turn the necklace over to the auction house so that it could be sold and the proceeds used for the benefit of the survivors of the camps, the displaced persons, children and men and women like Ilona. But in the end what he had stolen turned out to be all but worthless. One dollar and fifty cents. Enough to feed, what? A single person for a single day?

In the end the real wealth of the Hungarian Jewish community had not been packed in crates and boxes and loaded onto that train. What is the value to a daughter of a single pair of Sabbath candlesticks passed down from her mother and grandmother before her, generation behind generation, for a hundred, even a thousand, years? Beyond price, beyond measure. And what of ten thousand pairs of similar candlesticks, when all the grandmothers, mothers, and daughters are dead? No more than the smelted weight of the silver. The wealth of the Jews of Hungary, of all of Europe, was to be found not in the laden boxcars of the Gold Train but in the grandmothers and mothers and daughters themselves, in the doctors and lawyers, the grain dealers and psychiatrists, the writers and artists who had created a culture of sophistication, of intellectual and artistic achievement. And that wealth, everything of real value, was all but extinguished.

Jack left the auction house, the pendant still in his pocket. Later that night he would put it in his handkerchief drawer, where it would remain for years, like a bookmark between ironed white pages. Over the decades of his life, he would on occasion open up the small velvet parcel. In the years immediately after the war, holding the pendant would trigger a trace of longing, a remnant of regret. But eventually even that grew faint, its meaning lost in time and the accumulation of other memories and other loves. And then one day—the last day—he would pass the pendant and its complicated legacy of memory and forgetting on to his granddaughter Natalie, in the hope that in her hands it would become an agent of redemption that would allow her to move beyond the myopia of grief, that it would help her transform longing into purpose.

But on that early summer's day in 1948, standing in his handsome suit on the corner of East Fifty-Seventh Street, Jack took the pendant from his pocket and held it up so that the gems at the tips of the peacock feathers glinted in the sun. His treasure amounted to little more than fool's gold, worthless in his pocket. And yet he felt curiously untroubled by this depreciation. He had stolen the necklace because, though it had never belonged to anyone she knew, though she herself had rejected it, it reminded him of Ilona. But the thing that glittered now in the New York City sun was not a souvenir of the woman he loved and whom he would never see again. It was nothing more than a talisman of the irrevocable fracture of their relationship and of the incalculable loss of her entire world. A more impulsive man might have flung the pendant into the briny filth of the East River. Jack returned it to his pocket and walked home.

Acknowledgments

WERE IT NOT FOR the invitation of the lovely and generous Eleni Tsakopoulos Kounalakis to visit her in Budapest, this book would not exist. She provided invaluable assistance, both inspirational and editorial. She's a marvelously loyal friend.

Others in Hungary eased my way, including Judit Acsady and the indomitable Lena Csóti, without whose research assistance I would have been lost. Thanks, too, to Judith Friedrich, John Cillag, Marsha L. Rozenblit, and András Gerő. I could not have written this novel without the guidance of Ronald Zweig, whose book *The Gold Train* is a phenomenal piece of research. I'm grateful, too, to Gábor Kádár, author along with Zoltán Vági of another helpful volume, *Self-Financing Genocide: The Gold Train, the Becher Case and the Wealth of Hungarian Jews,* and to his generous wife, Christine Schmidt. Anna Kluth provided research assistance in Salzburg. Chris Doyle, Matthew Ritchie, Gwenessa Lam, and Diana Shpungin did their very best to correct my egregious ignorance about art. Dean Schillinger helped with medical facts. Julie Orringer and Andrew Sean Greer gave thorough reads at critical times. Michael Sheahan, with the guidance of Chris Doyle and the help of Tristan Salman, built me the world's most beautiful studio, where I wrote much of this book. The wonderful editor Lisa Highton gave final and invaluable advice.

I am truly lucky to be in the hands of two of the most generous and supportive women in the publishing business, Mary Evans and Jenny Jackson. Thanks, too, to Rachel Vogel and Sarah Lutyens for their unceasing efforts on the book's (and my) behalf, to Lydia Buechler and all the terrific people at Knopf, and to Kaela Noel and Jennifer Kurdyla.

I am blessed with the unflinching support and love of my mother, Ricki Waldman, and with her meticulous copy editor's eye.

Two weeks at the MacDowell Colony is worth six months of creativity and productivity in real life, and I am stunned that such a place exists and lets me visit.

The home-front help of Rachel Lemus, Brandy Muñiz, and Xiomara Batin made my work possible.

Without the unstinting support, calm intelligence, and unending good cheer of Amy Cray, I wouldn't be able to tie my own shoes, let alone write a novel.

Sophie Chabon, Zeke Chabon, Rosie Chabon, and Abe Chabon tolerated long absences and foul tempers with grace that should not be expected of children, and had Sophie not accompanied me to Dachau, and buoyed me along with her inexhaustible curiosity and wellspring of empathy, I would not have had the courage even to go.

Finally, my husband, Michael Chabon, makes every day, every thought, every word, finer than I have any right to deserve them to be.

A Note About the Author

AYELET WALDMAN is the author of the novels *Red Hook Road, Love and Other Impossible Pursuits,* and *Daughter's Keeper,* as well as of the essay collection *Bad Mother: A Chronicle of Maternal Crimes, Minor Calamities, and Occasional Moments of Grace,* and the *Mommy-Track Mystery* series. She lives in Berkeley, California, with her husband and four children.

A Note on the Type

The type used in this book was designed by Pierre Simon Fournier *le jeune*. In 1764 and 1766 he published his *Manuel typographique*, a treatise on the history of French types and printing, and on what many consider his most important contribution to typography—the measurement of type by the point system.

Printed and bound by Berryville Graphics, Berryville, Virginia

Designed by M. Kristen Bearse